David Wishart studied Classics at Edinburgh University. He then taught Latin and Greek in school for four years and after this retrained as a teacher of EFL. He lived and worked abroad for eleven years, working in Kuwait, Greece and Saudi Arabia, and now lives with his family in Scotland.

Praise for David Wishart:

'As ever, Wishart takes true historical events and blends them into a concoction so pacy that you hardly notice all those facts and interesting details of Roman life being slipped in there . . . Salve! To this latest from the top toga-wearing 'tec of Roman Times!' *Highland News Group*

'It is evident that Wishart is a fine scholar and perfectly at home in the period.' *Sunday Times*

DAVID WISHART

White Murder

NEW ENGLISH LIBRARY
Hodder & Stoughton

First published in Great Britain in 2002 by Hodder & Stoughton
First published in paperback in 2002 by Hodder & Stoughton
A division of Hodder Headline

A New English Library paperback

4 6 8 10 9 7 5 3

A CIP catalogue record for this title is available
from the British Library

ISBN 0 340 77128 3

Typeset in Plantin Light by Palimpsest Book Production Limited,
Polmont, Stirlingshire
Printed and bound in Great Britain by
Clays Ltd, St Ives plc

Hodder & Stoughton
A division of Hodder Headline
338 Euston Road
London NW1 3BH

For Liz Strachan, who wanted to see
more of Bathyllus

DRAMATIS PERSONAE

(Only names of main characters are given)

CORVINUS'S FAMILY, HOUSEHOLD AND NEIGHBOURS

Perilla: Corvinus's wife

Bathyllus: the major-domo

Alexis: the gardener
Lysias: the coachman
Meton: the chef

Petillius: the next-door neighbour
Tyndaris: Petillius's housekeeper

THE FACTIONS

Whites

Pegasus: the dead driver
Cammius, Lucius: the faction master
Cario: his son
Hesper: master of stables
Typhon: a placard man
Uranius: current principal driver

Greens

Natalis, Titus Minicius: the faction master

Blues

Acceptus, Gaius Sextilius: the faction master

Reds

Pudens, Gaius Rufrius: the faction master
Felicula: his wife
Laomedon: the principal driver

OTHER CHARACTERS (ROME)

Cascellius, Quintus: vegetable-seller and Greens supporter
Charax: a freelance builder; one of Renatius's customers
Delicatus, Titus: deputy in the Eighth District Watch
Eutacticus: head of a betting cartel
'Laughing George': Eutacticus's muscle
Lippillus, Decimus: commander of the Public Pond Watch
Renatius: the owner of the wineshop where Pegasus is
    murdered
Serapia: a seller of medicinal supplies
Valgius, Titus: Eighth District Watch commander
Vitellius, Lucius: one of the current consuls

OSTIA AND SICILY

Agron: Illyrian friend of Corvinus's, resident in Ostia
Florus, Quintus: a horse-breeder
Histrio: a livery-stable owner
Leon: mate of the *Phorcys*
Maximus: captain of the *Phorcys*
Sopilys: a stevedore; former employee of the Greens

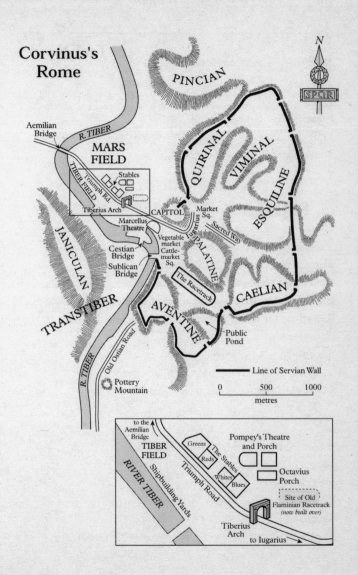

Corvinus's Rome

N
SPQR

Aemilian Bridge
R. TIBER
MARS FIELD
PINCIAN
QUIRINAL
VIMINAL
ESQUILINE
Stables
Triumph Rd.
TIBER FIELD
Tiberius Arch
CAPITOL
Market Sq.
Marcellus Theatre
Sacred Way
Cestian Bridge
Vegetable market
Cattle-market Sq.
PALATINE
Sublican Bridge
JANICULAN
The Racetrack
CAELIAN
TRANSTIBER
AVENTINE
Public Pond
Old Ostian Road
R. TIBER
Pottery Mountain

—— Line of Servian Wall

0   500   1000
              metres

---

to the Aemilian Bridge
TIBER FIELD
Pompey's Theatre and Porch
Greens
The Stables
Reds
Octavius Porch
Triumph Road
Whites
Blues
Site of Old Flaminian Racetrack *(now built over)*
Shipbuilding Yards
RIVER TIBER
Tiberius Arch
to Iugarius

I

There're worse places to hole up in when the poetry klatsch takes over the living-room and your wife throws you out for the duration than Renatius's wineshop on Iugarius. The wine's good for a start, a cheap, no-nonsense, swigging Umbrian that he brings in direct from the family farm near Spoletium but which could've walked all the way to Rome by itself. Then there's the seedy, spit-and-sawdust ambience and matching clientele, which is a definite plus for the area. With Market Square and the Senate House just up the road, Iugarius wineshops – and there're several, all with classy modern-style frescoes and Gallic beechwood furniture – are packed in the late afternoon with jolly, back-slapping broad-stripers and pushy young business execs. If you haven't experienced the joy of these guys yourself, then believe me: the last thing you want when you're relaxing over a jug is a loud-voiced pack of the world's élite at the next table swigging overpriced Falernian, calling the consuls by their first names and swapping hilarious anecdotes about leaky aqueducts and building tenders. Renatius's punters are tunics, which means most of the buggers have chins, speak through their mouths and would stand comparison with an intellectually chal-lenged parrot.

So. There I was, killing time in Renatius's wineshop until Perilla's poetry pals had finished juggling their anapaests or whatever the hell they do at their literary meetings and it was safe to go home. I was halfway down the jug with a plate of sheep's cheese on the side and getting pleasantly stewed when the mystery man turned up.

You don't see royalty much in Rome, not in Renatius's, anyway, but if he'd been a prince of the blood from one of the eastern client-kingdoms slumming it incognito he couldn't've created a bigger stir; which was interesting because like I say Renatius's is definitely tunic country and these guys don't impress easy. Yet the moment he walked in the door you could've heard an olive bounce, and Renatius himself moved so fast to show him to a table that he blurred. That was weird, too: you'd expect it in an upmarket cookshop, but any wineshop I've ever been in you find your own table, and if there isn't one free then tough. Added to which the last time I'd seen Renatius move that fast was when a stray dog wandered in and cocked its leg against the counter, and as far as I could see there was no difference between this guy and the other half-dozen punters currently soaking up the booze.

I poured myself another slug of Spoletian and inspected him over the top of my cup. It was none of my business, sure, but I couldn't help wondering what kind of semi-divine being we'd got here. Scratch the prince of the blood theory. Whoever he was, the guy was no easterner, let alone royal (I'd've guessed southern Italian, and if he rated more than a plain mantle I'd eat my boots); Renatius wouldn't stir himself for any common-or-garden noble, home-grown or imported; and I'd bet a gold piece to a meatball that none of his clientele would recognise a visiting scion of the Commagene royal house if it leaned over and bit them. So where did that leave us?

Early thirties, lad-about-town type: sharp haircut, good quality tunic and enough flashy personal jewellery to fit out an Aventine cat-house. He was no Market Square patsy, though, that was sure; there were muscles under that tunic, the arm that lifted the wine jug had tendons you could use for catapult cable, and I'd hate to face those hard, cold eyes across the table in a needle dice game. All that plus the fact that the whole room bar me obviously knew him and was treating him like one of the Sacred Shields of Mars while he acted like he expected nothing less could only mean one thing. Or one of two things, rather. Our mystery pal was either a top swordsman or a ditto driver; either of which qualifications, as far as the punters in Renatius's were concerned, put him less than one step down from Jupiter himself.

Personally, I'd go for the second option. Gladiators tend to be tall, even the lighter netmen: netman or not, quick on your feet or not, you don't last long on the sand if you're a short-arse with stubby legs and no reach; not when you're matched against two hundred pounds of mean beefsteak armed to the teeth and anxious to check out the colour of your liver. This guy was a runt. A steel and whiplash runt, sure, but if he clocked in at any more than five-two and ninety-eight pounds then I was a blue-rinsed Briton. Which, of course, was perfect for the cars because the less there is of the driver the more chance the team has of romping home clear of the competition.

Me, I don't follow the Colours. Yeah, I can keep my end up in a barbershop conversation, and Perilla and I go to the races now and again at the bigger festivals, but I'm no fan. Fans're something else, and every tunic is a fan born. Renatius's clientele mightn't be in the league of the weirdos who paint every room in their house green or blue and sniff the favourite's droppings before the race to check that it's in prime running condition, but the tunic who doesn't know his way around the teams well enough to play spot the hero when he walks into the local wineshop just doesn't exist. So I sat back and watched developments.

Not that there were any at first. Renatius's kid son Lucius brought the man his jug and a plate of olives, setting them down like they were honey cakes on a shrine, and Mystery Boy was left to his own majestic thoughts while everyone else went into huddles and muttered away quietly. Every so often the guy glanced towards the door like he was expecting someone, but if so his pal wasn't showing.

Ten, fifteen minutes in, he stood up suddenly and beckoned to Lucius. Conversation in the room switched off like it would in the local temple if the cult statue decided to stretch its legs in the middle of the ceremony, but Mystery Boy didn't seem to notice. Probably he was used to it and it didn't bother him any more, one way or the other.

The kid went over like he was walking on eggs. He had to swallow twice before he got his voice to work.

'Yes, sir?' he said.

'Where's the privy?'

I could see the blush spread over the kid's face from freckle to freckle: obviously in Lucius's personal world demigods didn't ask questions to do with normal human functions. Besides, Renatius's is pretty basic; the guy might just as well have asked for directions to the bath suite. I grinned and sipped my wine.

'Uh . . . I'm sorry, sir.' Swallow. 'We, uh, we haven't got one.'

'You haven't got one.' Mystery Boy didn't smile, but one of the regulars, a little wizened monkey of a guy called Charax with plaster stains down his tunic, sniggered into his wine cup. 'So where do your customers piss?'

'Uh . . .' Lucius was beginning to look desperate. 'In the alley, sir. Round the side. There's a wall at the end. You can't miss it.'

Charax choked on his wine. Mystery Boy ignored him. He nodded to Lucius and went out, closing the wineshop door behind him.

The place erupted like a schoolroom when the master pops out for a breath of sanity.

'You can't miss it, right, Lucius?' Charax said when he'd finished coughing his lungs out. 'Not on less than two jugs, anyway.'

'Nice one, lad.' That was Renatius.

If the kid had been blushing before, now you could've used his ears to signal ships. Understandable: he'd just had his chance to impress the great man with his witty repartee and he'd blown it all over the shop. Being ten is tough.

'Hey, Lucius,' I said. 'Who is the celebrity, by the way?'

Lucius's jaw dropped. There were a couple more laughs, at me this time. 'But that's *Pegasus*, sir!' he said.

Tone like he was speaking to an idiot, which in the race-mad kid's eyes I suppose I was. Yeah, well, I'd got that one right, at any rate. The guy was a driver; or not just a driver but one of *the* drivers, currently. Even I knew Pegasus: half the plaster statuettes on sale outside the Circus had his name on them. Not that that would've been any help with the face, mind, because they all came out of the same mould, whoever they were supposed to be, and the names were written on later; but the name itself, that was a different thing altogether. 'The Greens' lead?'

'Not any more, sir. He's driving for the Whites now. Or at least he will be when the new season starts.'

'Is that right?' I sat back while the kid mopped the table. Now that was something you didn't hear of every day, a Green high-flyer transferring to the Whites. Blues I could've understood, because as far as professional street cred's concerned the Blues and the Greens are pretty well on a par. Whites and Reds are definitely the poor relations. Sure, transfers among the factions go on all the time, and it's common enough for a second-rater on the Blue or Green team to make the switch to White or Red just so's his name comes higher on the programme, but for one of their top-notch drivers to do the same is like a Praetorian moving to the Watch. Worse, the guy hadn't just moved down a peg, he'd changed camps as well: on the track the Whites run point for the Blues just as the Reds do for the Greens. Still, I was no racing buff. No doubt it made sense somewhere along the line. I went back to my wine and cheese.

I wasn't the only silent drinker now. For the next ten minutes the whole room held its communal breath and kept one eye on the door, waiting for the guy to reappear. He didn't. Finally Charax cleared his throat. 'Maybe he's missed the wall at that,' he said.

His mates chuckled. Renatius was rinsing cups at the sink. He didn't turn round. 'Come off it, Charax,' he grunted. 'Joke's over.'

'You want me to check on him, Dad?' Lucius was hopping with excitement. 'Just to see if he's all right?'

Renatius shrugged and reached for a towel. Lucius dashed off. We waited.

The kid hadn't been gone two minutes when he was back. He didn't come in, though.

'Uh . . . Dad?' He was chalk white. The hairs rose at the nape of my neck.

'Yeah?' Renatius said over his shoulder. 'Close that door, boy, there's a draught.'

'Dad, I, uh, think he's dead.'

It took a moment to register. Then Renatius dropped the towel and was through the door in five seconds flat; and the rest of the wineshop, including me, were about two seconds behind him.

Dead was right.

The guy was slumped face-forward against the end wall of the alleyway. On the back of his tunic, just level with the heart, was a broad red stain.

There was one of these horrible pauses while we all tried to persuade ourselves that we weren't seeing what we were seeing. Renatius shook his head.

'Oh, shit,' he murmured. 'Oh, holy Jupiter.'

The other punters crowding the narrow alley said nothing. Even Charax had shut up.

Bugger. Well, someone had to make a move. 'Renatius, get everyone back inside, okay?' I said. 'Then you stand guard at the mouth of the alley to make sure no one comes barging in. Oh, and send Lucius to the local Watch station.'

'Waste of time, consul,' Charax murmured without taking his eyes off the body. 'The commander's Titus Valgius. The guy's a total prat.'

I ignored him. 'Just do it, Renatius.'

The big man nodded. He was looking grey. 'Come on, lads,' he said. 'Show's over.'

No one moved; ogle, ogle, ogle. I sighed. Hell: I'd seen this before, and I hated it. Give the great Roman public a corpse or an accident to stare at and they'll stand there all day. There was only one answer: expensive, sure, but it'd save a lot of hassle in the long run. And where Renatius's regulars were concerned it'd work every time. 'Fine,' I said. 'Drinks

are on me. At the counter, for the next five minutes only.'

'You're a gent, Corvinus.' Charax beamed. 'Pos-
sessed of true leadership qualities.'

Oh, Jupiter! 'Just fuck off, Charax, okay?'

'Certainly, sir. Fucking off at once, sir.' He did, and
the other ghouls followed him.

Which just left me and the corpse.

2

Okay; so what had we got? I couldn't in all conscience touch anything, not with Valgius on the way, but if Charax was right in his assessment of the Eighth District Watch commander's professional capabilities then maybe it wasn't such a good idea to rely on them. Besides, any clues or ideas I came up with I could pass on to my Watch boss pal Decimus Lippillus over at Public Pond and let him do the tactful thing.

First things first. I knelt down and examined the corpse. Purse all present and correct, buckled to the tunic belt, the drawstrings fastened tight. Not a simple stab-and-grab, then. That had been a possibility, sure, but only an outside one: Iugarius isn't the Aventine or the Subura, and although the Market Square district has its share of cutpurses and sneak-thieves you don't get all that many knifemen, at least during the daylight hours. I sniffed: there was a strong smell of urine. Sure, the wall had probably been used for pissing against for generations and that would account for most of it, but I could see that the dead man's tunic was soaked below the belt. Added to which, from the way he was lying I'd guess that when he'd been stabbed he'd been facing forward no more than a foot from the wall.

In other words, the murderer had got him in mid-flow. I stood up and looked behind me. The alleyway was a dead-end, but it was shaped like a Greek gamma or a Latin L turned bottom over top, with the wall at the tip of the shorter bar. That meant two things: first, that he would've been hidden from the road, and second that even if he had turned to see who was coming up behind him, which given the alley's purpose he probably wouldn't've bothered to do, he'd only have had a moment or two after the guy rounded the corner to react. And if he was halfway through a piss with his hands otherwise occupied his reactions would've been pretty slow.

Okay; so far so good. What did it all add up to?

The actual course of events was straightforward enough: Pegasus comes out of the wineshop and turns into the alley; whereupon the killer – call him X – gives him time to unlimber then follows him and drives in the knife while his back is turned. We could do better than that, though. First of all, the intact purse, the kink in the alleyway and the short time span involved all taken together meant that an unplanned killing wasn't likely; and for the last two to fit properly X had to have been keeping a stake-out on the wineshop door. Which meant that he'd either followed the Mystery Boy to Renatius's in the first place or he knew he'd be in there at that particular time. In either case the poor bastard had been targeted, maybe even set up.

Okay; so who could X have been? For a start, he was pretty cool-headed. Late afternoon, Iugarius may not be heaving but it's still one of the busiest streets in

the city. Our pal X had walked into a dead-end alley
in broad daylight, killed a man and then walked back
out again with a fair percentage of Rome's honest
citizens hurrying past not twenty yards from the scene
of crime. And a two-way business it had to be, because
unless he was a seven-foot-tall athletic ape shinning
over the wall at the far end wasn't an option. Sure,
if X didn't know the topography he might not have
realised the alleyway *was* a dead-end, but that just
made the killing even more risky: it takes real guts
to follow a guy with a drawn knife in your hand when
any moment you might meet some innocent punter
coming the other way.

The other thing about X was that for reasons already
given he must've known his victim. The fact that
Pegasus was a public figure blurred the issue here,
sure, because it meant it wasn't necessarily mutual;
like I said, the racing game attracts some real weirdos
among the fans, and it wasn't beyond the bounds of
possibility that he'd been stalked by one of these
nuts who breathe, eat and sleep the factions and was
nursing some kind of grudge. On the other hand, he'd
been expecting someone, that I'd bet on, because in
the time he'd been sitting in the wineshop his eyes
had never been far from the door. And if the killing
had been a set-up then the other guy was a prime
candidate for X.

I took a last look round. Yeah, well; there wasn't any
more I could do here, and I didn't particularly want to
be caught crouching over the body when Rome's finest
eventually showed up. Some of these Watch guys have

very limited imaginations. I walked back to the head of the alley where Renatius was fending off the ghouls. There were quite a few of these by now – Jupiter knows how these bastards click on to the existence of even an invisible corpse, but they do; instinct, maybe – and they were craning their necks like so many silent vultures.

'Everything okay, pal?' I said.

Renatius was looking a better colour. Happy, even: he'd had time to think, a murder in your side alley does wonders for business, and although he was a nice enough guy he still had a living to make. 'Sure,' he said. 'More or less. Lucius has gone for the Watch and Charax is looking after the store.'

'*Charax?*' Oh, hell. 'Uh . . . you think that's wise?'

'No. But then again I'm not paying for all the wine these bastards get through while we're stuck out here and Lucius is up at the Square talking to Valgius.'

Ouch. I hadn't thought about that aspect of things at the time. With Charax filling the jugs I'd bet this business was already costing me an arm and a leg. Still, it was too late to worry now, the damage had been done. I glanced across the street.

Yeah; I'd remembered right. Facing the wineshop door was the entrance to a tenement screened by scaffolding and building materials. Perfect cover for someone who wanted to keep an eye on the comings and goings of Renatius's customers, especially since I couldn't see any workmen. Which come to think of it was odd, with so much daylight left.

Unless . . .

I groaned. Oh, bugger! Thank you, Jupiter! Thank you so bloody much! I'd bet; I would just bet . . . !

'Uh . . .' I pointed. 'That wouldn't be where Charax and his pals are working at present, would it?'

Renatius followed my pointing finger. 'Yeah, it would, as a matter of fact. Although I wouldn't use the word "working" myself.'

Never a truer word was spoken: I wouldn't either, on reflection. In fact, I doubted that, unexpectedly rich though it was, Charax's vocabulary included any terms in the category 'work'. Whoever had given these three deadbeats the job of doing the place up needed his head examined.

'Uh-huh,' I said.

'It belongs to old Atellius over on Tuscan Street.' Renatius was still grinning. 'The Buildings Officer threatened to have it condemned unless he fixed it up and Charax made him an offer the cheapskate sod couldn't refuse. Sure, he and his mates're just plastering over the cracks but a greased palm or two'll do the rest. Me – well, let's just say I wouldn't spend any more than five minutes in there even with my hardest hat on.'

Yeah; that made sense. Still, one got you ten that our friendly neighbourhood knifeman had done just that, and stayed a lot longer than Renatius's five minutes. Cool was right: he couldn't have known that Charax and his pals were the most unconscientious builders in the history of domestic architecture, and with their local wineshop open and serving just across the road the chances of them coming back this side of tomorrow's breakfast were about equal to seeing the college of priests do a choreographed striptease on Mars Field. No doubt, though, he'd've had a story ready. I was beginning to have a real respect for X.

The vultures, give or take the odd try-on, were being pretty well-behaved, which was all the more under-standable because there were two or three respectable mantles among them pretending they were just hang-ing around passing the time of day. Most of the pack had been content just to stand and gawp at the brickwork. Now, suddenly, they parted and three big guys with a couple of slaves in tow carrying a rolled-up stretcher pushed their way through.

The Watch had arrived.

Not Valgius himself, though: these guys were def-initely tunics, and not too friendly tunics at that. I introduced myself and got a concerted glare like I'd just proposed a four-way orgy.

'So where's the corpse?' the biggest guy, definitely the leader, growled. Yeah, right; so much for the amenities. I gave him my best smile and stepped aside.

Wordlessly, Renatius jerked a thumb over his shoulder in the direction of the wineshop's vertical privy. The guy grunted, made a sign to the stretcher-bearers and headed off for what was left of Pegasus, accompanied by his mates.

'Cheerful bugger, isn't he?' I said.

'That's Titus Delicatus.' Renatius didn't smile. 'You're lucky. This must be one of his good days.'

'Yeah?' Mind you, it was no concern of mine. Now

the professionals had arrived I could head on back to
Perilla and a – hopefully – poet-free house with the
easy conscience of a citizen who's done his duty to the
Senate and people of Rome. After I'd paid through the
nose for the wine that Charax and his pals had sunk in
my absence, of course. Speaking of which . . . 'Uh, I
think we can go in now,' I said. 'Quickly.'

We left the future supervision of the vultures to the
Eighth District Wonders and joined the party inside.
Which was more or less what it was. Evidently Charax
had taken the opportunity to round up a few of his
local cronies, because there were more customers than
there had been, and the Spoletian was flowing free. In
both senses of the word.

Charax was behind the bar. 'No problem, consul,'
he said cheerfully. 'I've kept count. I make it five jugs,
plus the cheese and olives. Oh, and I grilled Annius
here a sausage.'

A small squat guy with ears that stuck out like the
handles of an amphora grinned at me and raised the
sausage in question in salute. Bastard. I pulled out
my purse and tipped most of the contents on to the
counter. Then I poured myself a large one from my
own interrupted jug and sank it at a gulp.

Young Lucius was dithering on the sidelines. I called
him over.

'You didn't see Valgius himself, then?' I asked
him.

'Oh, yes, sir.' The kid was looking a lot brighter now.
Obviously he was beginning to enjoy the situation.
'Only he was too busy. He sent Delicatus instead.'

I frowned. Odd. Me, I'd've thought a well-known figure like Pegasus would've merited the boss's personal attention. 'You told him who the dead man was?'

'Yes, sir.'

'And?'

Lucius shuffled his feet. 'He – uh – he just laughed and said, "Is it really?"'

Jupiter on wheels! This was a Watch commander? 'He said *what*?'

The boy was blushing again. '"Is it really?", Valerius Corvinus.' A conscientious kid, Lucius, and for all his literalness no bad mimic: I could hear the total lack of interest in the guy's voice even at second hand. 'Then he said, "Well, well!" Sort of dry, like, you know?'

'Didn't he ask . . . ?' I stopped. The door had opened and the Three Graces came in. These guys were fast workers. Too fast, to my mind.

Maybe Renatius thought the same, because he frowned and said, 'You boys finished already?'

'Sure. Nothing to keep us.' Delicatus helped himself to a piece of cheese from the counter. 'Knifed and robbed. No hassle. We'll put in the usual report.'

My stomach went cold. 'Hang on, sunshine,' I said. 'What's this "robbed" business? The guy's purse was still on his belt. I saw it myself.'

Delicatus stopped chewing. His eyes shifted on to me and stayed there. Then he said over his shoulder; 'Hey, Sextus? Publius?'

'Yeah?'

'Either of you lads see a purse?' The other two

Watchmen shook their heads. His eyes hadn't left my face. 'There you are, sir,' he said. 'No purse. You must've been mistaken.' His jaws started working again and he swallowed and turned back to Renatius. 'We'll do our best to find the killer, sure, but it happens all the time. Like I say, no hassle. Leave it with us.' He nodded to the company and moved towards the door. 'Enjoy your day.'

Holy Jupiter, I didn't believe this! Some of the guys in the Watch may hardly be more than jailbait themselves, but they aren't stupid; and filching a corpse's purse, especially when they're not first on the scene, comes within the definition of sheer lunacy. Cashiering's the best they can expect, with a ripped back courtesy of the public executioner thrown in for free, and the game just isn't worth the candle.

'Wait just a moment, pal,' I said.

He stopped and turned slowly. 'Yeah?'

I glanced at Renatius. 'Renatius. You saw the purse, didn't you?'

He hesitated, then shook his head. 'No. Can't say I did. Sorry, Corvinus.'

At least he had the grace to look sheepish when he said it. Sure, he could have been flannelling, but that wasn't how Renatius worked: he was straight-down-the-line honest, he'd no axe to grind, and I could tell from the vibes that he didn't like Delicatus at all. Besides, there was no reason why it shouldn't be the simple truth; the dead man had been slumped over facing the wall, Renatius and the others had been standing behind me, and I hadn't seen the purse myself until I knelt down to look for it. Still, I wasn't giving this one up; no way, never. 'Look, friend,' I said to Delicatus, holding on to my temper. 'Take it from me. The guy's purse is there. Or it was.'

He gave a shrug that set my teeth on edge. 'Then it'll still be there now, sir,' he said. 'You want to check, maybe?' He grinned. 'Just to set your mind at rest and keep the record straight?'

I pushed past him and through the door. The two public slaves were waiting outside surrounded by the pack of respectful vultures. They'd set the stretcher with the body on the pavement and they watched impassively as I pulled the covering blanket away.

The guy's belt was empty.

I went back in, my brain churning.

'Happy now?' Delicatus asked. One of his supporting cast sniggered, then turned the snigger into a cough.

I didn't bother to answer. We all four knew it was gone, and we all knew where. It couldn't've dropped off, because it was tied on; which only left one other explanation for its absence. If I'd had the nerve and the muscle to frisk these honest public servants I'd've found it inside one of the bastards' tunics.

Angry as I was, I forced myself to think. What the hell was going on here? Watchmen just didn't do things like that. If Lippillus had caught one of his lads looting a murder victim he'd've strung the bastard up by the balls until he dropped off. Literally. Whistled while he did it, too.

Unless they'd had definite instructions . . .

I remembered what Lucius had said about Commander Valgius's reaction when he'd told him who the victim was, and the thing suddenly made sense. At least, some kind of sense.

'Which faction do you support, sunshine?' I said. 'Not Green, by any chance?'

Delicatus's face froze, while his two mates suddenly got interested in their feet. Bull's-eye! 'What's that got to do with anything?' he said.

'Just a question. And your boss wouldn't happen to be a big Greens' supporter too, would he?'

Silence; but something in the bastard's eyes shifted.

'Because I was thinking,' I went on. 'Pegasus drives for the Whites now, right? Drove. Whatever. One of the opposition teams.' Jupiter, this was sick; but it shows you just how seriously some of these nuts take their racing. 'He'd gone over to the other side. Under these circumstances someone who was a big Greens' fan himself might not be too sorry to see his name taken off the race card. And in that case he mightn't exactly be all that desperate to go into the whys and wherefores of the guy's death, either.' I paused. 'Any of that strike a chord with you at all, pal?'

'Listen to me . . . sir.' Delicatus was staring at me like he'd cheerfully make two trips with the stretcher. 'Because I'll say this only once. The man was knifed for his purse. We'll look into the matter but like I said it happens all the time. Commander Valgius'll agree, I can tell you that now.'

'I'm sure he will. All the same—'

'What's more, so would Sertorius Macro.' He let the name hang. 'If you wanted to take it that high.'

The room went very quiet, and beside me I heard Renatius draw in air between his teeth. Delicatus had just done the equivalent of throwing the title deeds to a Baian villa on top of a pot of pennies. I was being called, and everyone knew it, including me.

We weren't dealing peanuts here. Macro was the Commander of Praetorians, and although he didn't figure in the direct Watch line of command he was the emperor's representative in Rome. For which read Prince Gaius's, because that twisted amoral bastard held the real power these days. And Gaius was so fanatical about the Greens that when he was in Rome he held banquets at the stables and invited the horses.

Oh, shit.

'Macro won't back Valgius,' I said. 'Not in a million years, not over something as small as this. If your boss wants to bury the case out of spite he's on his own.'

'You want to bet on that?' He wasn't even pretending to be polite now.

I stared back, my fists bunched. No. That was the problem: I wouldn't bet on it, and he knew I wouldn't, not with the prospect of a straight slugging match with an imperial in view. However convinced I was. Our current crown prince – and so his rep – would be far more likely to buy the bastard who'd zeroed Pegasus a drink than peg him out for the crows.

One thing was sure, though. Delicatus may have won the battle but he hadn't won the war. I didn't give up that easy, especially not after a clumsy threat like that. If Watch Commander Valgius wanted a clear case of murder shoved down a hole and forgotten about then Macro or not he could go and whistle through his ears.

Not that I was stupid enough to say as much to Valgius's grinning pet gorillas here. I left them to Renatius and went home.

3

There was no sign of Bathyllus in the entry lobby when I got back, which was strange because whatever time I rolled in our bald-headed hernia-suffering major-domo would be waiting for me with the obligatory jug and wine cup. Sure, his prognosticative faculties went on the blink occasionally – even Bathyllus was human, if only just – but it didn't happen often, and there was always a reason. Usually a nasty one, like the last time when the fuller's pick-up man had fallen over a bucket outside the servants' latrine and left his nice holystoned kitchen corridor awash with five gallons of mature cleaning fluid. I stripped off my mantle and yelled for him.

He came at a run, or what passes with Bathyllus for a run, did a quick double-take and slowed down.

'I'm sorry, sir,' he said. 'I didn't hear you come in.'

'No problem, sunshine,' I said, and handed him the mantle. 'Everything okay?'

'Pardon, sir?'

Oops; this could be bad: Bathyllus can be deaf sometimes, but his deafness is selective and that's the time to worry. However, on this occasion it seemed that the question had simply gone past him. He looked – 'distracted' was the word, and Bathyllus never gets distracted. 'I only asked if everything was okay, little guy. No fire in the hypocaust, no skivvies running amuck with carving knives?'

'Certainly not, sir. Everything is fine.'

'You sickening for something, then?'

'*No*, sir!' He folded the mantle. 'Did you have a pleasant afternoon?'

I winced. 'Don't ask, pal. Just don't ask. The poets gone?'

'Yes, sir. An hour ago. Dinner will be served shortly. Meton has been getting a little anxious.'

Uh-oh; that was a fresh worry. I recognised an expurgated version when I heard one. Our touchy-as-hell chef was obviously nursing a delicate sauce and I'd been within a cat's whisker of becoming persona non grata; which where Meton's concerned is not something you want to be unless you happen to like fish paste with your dessert. 'Fine, fine. The mistress around?'

'In the atrium, sir. I'll bring you your wine straight away.'

'You do that, Bathyllus.' I went through. Perilla was sitting by the pool with a tablet and stylus. Maybe it was something about my face, but she took one look and set them down beside her chair.

'Marcus?' she said. 'What's wrong?'

I gave her the usual welcome-home kiss, stretched out on the couch, and told her about the body in the alley.

'Oh, Marcus! Not again!'

Jupiter! From the lady's tone you'd think I'd iced the guy myself! 'Look, it's not my fault, okay?' I said. 'I was minding my own business. He just went out for a piss and never came back.'

She sniffed and retrieved the wax tablet. 'Corvinus, I trust you to spend a quiet hour or two in a wineshop while I have an all-too-rare cultural afternoon and you go and trip over a corpse. That is *not* minding your own business.'

'I didn't trip over it. I just tagged along with the crowd.'

'Do you expect me to believe that? Honestly!'

I had my mouth open to answer, but at that moment Bathyllus oozed in and plonked down the tray with its jug and brimming wine cup. 'Your wine, sir,' he said. I took a swig of the Setinian. After Renatius's Spoletian it was like having your tonsils massaged with velvet. 'Also, dinner is served. Red mullet stewed with aniseed and a bean and chicken quiche with cumin.'

I sighed; when the little guy said 'shortly' he meant 'shortly'; I'd been lucky right enough. Still, I was grateful for the interruption; the climate in the atrium had turned distinctly cool.

We trooped next door with no let-up in the frost.

'So how was your day?' I asked finally, while the minions wheeled in the boiled eggs and raw vegetables.

'Don't change the subject,' Perilla said. Snapped.

Uh-oh. I shelled an egg and dipped it in fish sauce. Finally Perilla put down her celery stick.

'All right,' she said. 'Who was he, and what exactly happened?'

'Fifty-two.'

'I beg your pardon?'

'I was counting, lady. You made fifty-two before you cracked. That's a record.'

'Corvinus, I will kill you.'

I grinned and chewed: nothing annoys Perilla more than knowing she's been sussed. 'Yeah. Right. The guy's name was Pegasus. He—'

Her eyes widened. '*The* Pegasus? The charioteer?'

'Uh-huh.' I gave her the rest, including the details of my little brush with Delicatus and his cronies; at which point the lady's mouth set in a line you could've used to slice marble.

'Marcus, I really don't think you should get involved in this,' she said. 'It's Watch business.'

'I told you. The Watch aren't interested. Or at least that bastard Valgius isn't.'

'Turn it over to Decimus Lippillus, then.'

But I'd thought about that on the way back. 'I can't do that. First because Lippillus is Public Pond and it would offend the guy's professional ethics to poach, second because I don't like the smell of the case already and that smart midget'd likely end up with his backside in a sling.'

'My point exactly.' Perilla shelled an egg of her own. 'Marcus, dear, listen to me. You cannot afford to tangle with Sertorius Macro. Let alone Prince Gaius.'

Oops; mistake. I backtracked. 'Macro isn't involved, lady. That was just Delicatus shooting his mouth off.

And the prince is on Capri whooping it up with the Wart.'

'Do you have your fingers crossed or am I just imagining it?'

I uncrossed them. 'Look, Perilla, forget conspiracy theories, okay? Pegasus had jumped the fence. One gets you ten all we've got here's a simple case of racegoer's fever. The new season's coming up and Valgius and his ultra-Green gorillas were just too happy to hear that the guy had hung up his tunic to make any waves. End of story, right?'

'So why do you have to interfere?'

Jupiter's balls! 'Because it was murder; not just a killing, but murder. If I don't interfere then no one else will. Also I don't like having my arm twisted. And cut the hypocritical crap. You're just as curious as I am.'

'Hmm.' She dipped the egg in sauce. I'd got her; sure I had. 'All right. So what's the theory so far? I assume you have one.'

I shrugged. 'The gods know. I'd say the murderer had arranged to meet the guy at Renatius's, only instead of turning up he'd squirrelled himself away in the empty house across the street, watched for Pegasus to come out again then followed and stabbed him. That's as far as I go.'

'Pegasus was waiting for someone?'

'Sure. Or that was the impression I got. He was keeping an eye on the door, anyway.'

'How?'

'How do you mean, "How", lady?'

'Did he look relaxed or anxious?'

'Oh. Yeah. Right.' Good question, and one I hadn't thought of. Relaxed would mean he was easy in his mind about whoever he was meeting, anxious the opposite. I cast my mind back. 'Relaxed. Not obviously anxious, anyway.'

'Very well. Now why? I mean, why kill him in the first place?'

I took a swig of Setinian. 'Could be several reasons. Professional or personal. Like I said, the guy had shifted teams recently, Green to White. That wouldn't be popular in certain quarters.'

Perilla's hand paused over a stuffed olive. 'Green to White? Isn't that unusual?'

'Yeah. That's what I thought. It happens, sure, but—'

'But not with drivers of that calibre.'

'Right. It's somewhere to start, anyway.' I frowned. 'Hey, lady. I didn't know you were a racing buff.'

'I'm not an absolute idiot, either, Corvinus.'

Ouch. 'Uh . . . yeah. Yeah. Right.' I crunched on a carrot stick.

'He can't be all that old, and he's been doing very well lately. Or am I wrong?'

'He's been doing okay.' Like I said before, I'm no racing nut and I couldn't've gone into details, but you can't have your chin scraped in a Market Square barber's without the guy with the razor giving you his unsolicited views ad nauseam on how the factions are shaping. Most of the time I just close my ears and nod when nodding doesn't risk a slit windpipe, but I distinctly remembered that the guy had had more than his fair share of wins in the last two sets of games.

'So why did he change, then?' Perilla said.

I sipped the wine. Yeah; that was something I'd wondered about myself when young Lucius had mentioned it, only now having an answer was more important. Or it might be. Green to Blue or vice versa, sure, like I said, no problem; but there are only two reasons, normally, for a lead driver with the top teams to move down a level. One is simply age, when his reactions slow and – skilled driver or not – he loses his edge over the up-and-coming youngsters; the other, which has the same effect, is that his nerve goes because of a bad spill or something similar. Even so, the guy tends to stick with the original team, if only out of pride, or – sometimes – he moves across to an equivalent level in the second-string Colour: Blue to White or Green to Red. I could be wrong on either, of course – reading some kind of illness for age in the first – but I didn't think so, not with the recent wins he had notched up.

Which left the rarer, third reason . . .

'Sir?'

'Hmm?' I came back to myself: Bathyllus, with the mullet and the quiche. 'Yeah, okay, Bathyllus, serve away.'

I topped up my cup from the jug on the table. Well, at least we had a logical starting point. The Green and White stables – in fact, the stables of all four factions – were in Mars Field, a stone's throw from the Tiber. I could go there tomorrow, have a word with Pegasus's current and former bosses.

They might, too – at least the White boss might – be able to shed a bit of light on what his top man had been doing at Renatius's. No reason why he shouldn't go there, of course, but the factions, like most other closed groups in the city, are a gregarious bunch. They have their own favourite wineshops, and when they're off-base the drivers tend to stick to them. Besides, although the Whites – like the Reds – are a second-string team their stables're self-contained units, with eating and drinking facilities on site. That was another problem that needed solving.

I looked up. Perilla was watching me with a small smile on her lips.

'What's tickling you?' I said.

'Nothing, Marcus.' She started in on her mullet. 'Nothing at all.'

Sometimes I wonder about that lady. I held up my plate for Bathyllus to fill. He slid the mullet off the serving dish. It missed and landed on the table.

The little guy looked mortified. He scooped the fish up on to the plate with the spatula. 'I'm terribly sorry, sir, that was clumsy of me,' he said. 'I'll get a cloth at once.'

I watched his retreating back. One thing our major-domo wasn't was clumsy; it went with 'distracted'. And a lot of his sarky snap was missing, too. Odd; more than odd. 'Hey, Perilla,' I said. 'What's biting Bathyllus?'

'I don't know, dear. He's been distant all day. I did ask, but he only sniffed at me.'

Yeah; been there, had the experience. Jupiter! Staff!

It wasn't anything we'd done, at least, I was sure of that: even the little guy's huffs don't allow him to compromise where his job's concerned. The same went for the opening of fresh hostilities in his ongoing battle with the anarchist Meton. Whatever was going on under that hairless pate it was something very much out of the usual.

Well, I wasn't going to push. Bathyllus isn't exactly the type you can take into a quiet corner and have a heart-to-heart master-and-slave chat with. If it was important we'd find out eventually. I ate my mullet.

Something out of the usual was right; but then at that stage I couldn't even have guessed at the answer. That came out later.

Even then I didn't believe it.

4

Well, we'd got spring, finally. The weather over the past few days had been a hangover from winter, but this was real March stuff, bright and blustery, and the city looked like someone had just taken it to the cleaners to have the grime washed out. Even the crowds were different. Most of the time your average city-centre punter is a prime contender for the All-comers' Unfriendly Bastard title and you need to move sideways fast if you don't want to be mown down by yard-wide old biddies en route from the vegetable market; but that morning even the chunky bullet-heads who do the portering in the Velabrum seemed willing to give an inch or two. There weren't any pigs flying over the Capitol, either.

I turned up Triumph Road and headed for Mars Field. The stables are all in a line on the stretch between Pompey's Theatre and the river: adjacent-paired Blue/White and Green/Red, with the Blues and Greens being the biggies, self-sufficient units more like a country farm than something you'd normally find inside the city boundaries. Or rather something between a farm and a military base, because racing's a big business in Rome, horse-nobbling's endemic and security procedures are tighter than a gnat's sphincter. Mean, too: try sneaking in past the gate guards and you're likely to leave in a hurry with a few bust ribs and a deficit in the teeth department. Get caught with serious cash or a suspect substance under your tunic and you don't come out at all.

The Whites' stable was second in the row after the Blues, just beyond Tiberius Arch. The guy outside the big double gates looked like he'd been put together from the same material they'd used to build the wall, and whatever effect the spring weather had had on the rest of the population it obviously hadn't stretched his length. I got a scowl like I'd turned up clinking with enough bottles of whacky medicine to put the entire string of nags on their backs with their hooves in the air.

'Yeah?' he said.

'The boss around?'

'Who wants him?'

I gave him my name. 'I'm looking into the death of one of your drivers. Pegasus.'

If I'd thought that might ease matters I was wrong, because all it got me was a long stare. Not a particularly friendly one either.

'You with the Watch?' he said finally.

This was the tricky part. 'No. But I was in the wineshop when it happened. And when the Watch turned up. I thought maybe your boss might like a second opinion.'

'Is that so, now?' Cement-Features didn't bat an

eyelid. The stare raked me from crown to toes before he gave a grudging nod. 'Okay. Wait here.'

Not that I'd any option, because when he disappeared inside he closed the gate behind him and I heard the clunk of a bar thudding into place. I stepped back and looked around.

Military base was right: the wall must've been ten feet high, with broken pottery shards spiking the top. It stretched all the way back to a junction with the Blues wall a hundred yards down the road, and it was smooth-faced with concrete: no foot- or handholds. You might've got over with grappling-hooks and a rope, sure, but that'd be what it took, nothing less. And I'd bet sides and rear were the same.

The gate opened and Cement-Features came back out, looking almost friendly. 'Okay,' he said. 'The boss says he'll see you. You follow me close, right?'

'Right.' I went through the hallowed portal and he shut it behind me, pulling the heavy bar down into its sockets. 'Uh . . . what's the boss's name, by the way?'

That got me another stare; not a hostile one this time, just an unbelieving one like young Lucius's when I'd asked who Pegasus was. Fair enough; every racegoer out of leading-strings, whichever team he supports, knows the names of the four faction masters. 'Cammius,' he said. 'Lucius Cammius.'

I was looking round me with interest because this was the first time I'd been inside a faction stable. It was a complete world in itself. Over to the right, beyond a fenced exercise yard, were the stables proper: long and low like a series of army barrack blocks with tiled roofs and half-doors every two or three yards. Some of the doors had an equine head sticking out above the bottom flap, but most had piles of dirty straw outside and what looked like a small army of guys beavering away with pitchforks loading the stuff on to carts. There was a hell of a lot of it. Disposal must've presented quite a logistical problem, and I was just lucky the breeze was blowing in the right direction.

'How many horses have you got here, friend?' I asked.

I was only making conversation, but obviously that information came into the classified category. Cement-Features gave me a suspicious look and no answer.

We went through what turned out to be the workshop area: smithies, tackle shops and so on, all busy, all well manned; like I say, the factions operate as self-contained units, like an army camp. I breathed in. The whole place smelled of horses and leather, and it *buzzed*; there isn't a better word, because the feeling was like being inside a giant beehive, with the qualification that there were no drones around, just workers. Single-minded workers at that. The fans aren't the only obsessives. The racing world's all about obsession, and when you're inside it the rest of the city might just as well not exist.

Past the workshops the buildings moved upmarket. Cement-Features led me to a stone-built block that could've done duty for a permanent army headquarters and through the main door.

Upmarket was right. We were in an entrance hall that wouldn't've disgraced a proper town house, and the decoration had that same obsessive feel to it: a frieze, running all the way round the walls, of horses with their drivers standing next to them, the guys all in white tunics with whips and round racing helmets. Both the horses and the drivers had names written underneath, like this was some kind of roll of honour. Maybe it was, at that, but I wasn't risking any more questions.

C-F knocked at the biggest door, waited for an answer, then opened up and stood aside.

I'd expected the usual formal lounge; what I got was a businesslike office with a big desk and stacks of book cupboards with most of their pigeonholes filled. I'd also expected one guy, but there were two: one behind the desk, the other in a visitor's chair to one side. The decor was more horses, including a beaut of a bronze on a pedestal in the centre that looked like it might be a Greek original.

'Valerius Corvinus?' The guy behind the desk stood up and held out his hand. 'Lucius Cammius.' We shook: the hand was hard and dry, and it gave mine a quick, sharp squeeze that fitted the character of the room. He'd be in his mid-sixties: medium height but chunky, strong face and short grey hair like a wire brush, eyes like chips of gravel. Narrow stripe on his mantle, but an accent that was pure provincial Spanish: if he was purple-striper grade then he'd clawed his way up and bought his way in. Not that I had any quarrel with that: a large slice of the hereditary variety were overbred slobs. 'The gate man says you've come about Pegasus.'

'Yeah, that's right,' I said.

'Pull up a chair.' Cammius sat down. I glanced behind me and found a no-nonsense, wood and leather folding stool. I pulled it over and sat on it. 'This is Gaius Acceptus. He heads the Blues.'

The second guy nodded. He was a good ten years younger than Cammius and definitely a step up the social ladder: chiselled patrician features, well barbered, wearing his smart narrow-stripe mantle like it was a natural extension of his character. The sort of man you'd expect to find fronting a top-notch team, or any other successful business, and being totally in control. Knowing it, too. 'Pleased to meet you,' he said. The voice fitted the appearance: top-drawer, bland, quietly confident.

'Now, Corvinus.' Cammius rested his hands on the desk. 'I'm told that you're not Watch. Nor are you from the city judge's office, and that doesn't leave much. What's your involvement and what's your angle?'

Straight to the point, no messing. Well, that matched the rest. I cleared my throat. 'I was in the wineshop at the time of the murder and I saw the body. The Watch seem to think the motive was simple robbery. It wasn't.'

Things went very quiet. Acceptus flashed me a sharp look, but Cammius's expression didn't change. He leaned back in his chair. 'You sound pretty sure of that,' he said.

'I am.'

His eyes held mine. I felt that I was being turned inside out, assessed. Finally he grunted and said; 'All right. Care to tell me why?'

'Like I say, I saw the body myself, before the Watchmen arrived. The man's purse was still on his belt and it hadn't been touched.'

'Watch Commander Valgius says different.' I noticed the grammar slip. Also that Acceptus's straight-bridged nose twitched and he pursed his lips. 'I'll ask you again because it's important. You say you're sure. How sure, exactly?'

Problems with grammar or not, the guy was no hayseed: the grey eyes were level, and very, very smart. 'One hundred per cent,' I said. 'The purse was there, then it wasn't.'

Acceptus laid his fingertips together and touched the praying hands to his lips. Cammius grunted again.

'You're accusing the Watchmen of stealing it,' he said. Statement, not question.

I had to go careful here. Carefully. Whatever. 'I was with the corpse when the guys turned up. When they'd finished the purse had gone.'

'Then your short answer's yes.'

I shook my head. 'No. I'm saying the purse was removed. And that it had to have been removed by the Watchmen. That's a different thing from claiming theft.'

'Maybe it is. But what other reason could there be?'

I was beginning to feel uncomfortable. The interview

was turning into an interrogation with me at the blunt end, and although the Blues' boss had moved his chair back slightly and crossed his legs as though he were staying outside of things he was still taking a keen interest. 'Delicatus and his pals are Greens' supporters. So is Valgius. The dead man used to drive for the Greens before he switched.'

Cammius held up a hand. 'Hang on there a moment. Let's get this straight. You mean the Watch – or the Eighth District branch of it – are claiming that Pegasus was killed by an ordinary thief so they can drop the case? Or at least supply an uncomplicated motive for the killing?'

'Yeah.' Smart was right. 'More or less.'

'That isn't likely. Watchmen don't do that kind of thing. Especially Watch commanders.'

I shrugged. 'You're in the business, sir, I'm not. I'm only going by what happened.'

'Actually, the fellow has a point, Lucius,' Acceptus said. 'I know Titus Valgius of old and he's a stinker. Now it's none of my concern and I wouldn't dream of advising you, but I wouldn't trust him more than half. And Pegasus was a damn good driver, streets ahead of your other lads. Given luck he could even have won you a race or two come the new season. Corvinus here is right: Valgius wouldn't be sorry to see the back of him.'

I could almost hear Cammius's teeth grate at the plummy vowels and the drawling tone, but his answer was quietly spoken. 'Oh, judging by last season's results I think we'll do well enough against the Greens,

Gaius, even without Pegasus. Better than your lads've been doing lately, certainly. And luck won't come into it.' Acceptus's smile disappeared like it had been washed off with a sponge. Cammius turned back to me. 'As to your theory, Corvinus, I'm afraid whatever Gaius says I still don't believe the City Watch would falsify evidence.'

Fair enough; but if I wanted to take the case any further I needed to go selectively deaf at this point. 'The other thing that intrigued me,' I said, 'was that the guy was obviously expecting someone to join him. I was wondering if maybe you could suggest who that could have been.'

That hit home, with both of them. Acceptus gave me a sharp look and the Whites' boss went very still. 'Really?' he said.

'Yeah. He was sitting opposite the door and keeping his eye on it like he expected someone to walk through it any minute. I can't be certain this time but from the way he was acting I'd lay good money.'

'And the person didn't appear subsequently?'

'Uh-uh. At least if he did he didn't announce himself.'

Cammius's fingers tapped the desk several times, then stopped abruptly. He turned to Acceptus. 'Gaius, Valerius Corvinus and I have to talk this over. You'll excuse me and we can finish our business later.'

Acceptus didn't move. 'Perhaps as head of the senior faction,' he said, 'it would be better if I stayed.'

'No.' Cammius didn't snap, but the note of finality in his voice was obvious. 'Pegasus was a Whites' driver and this is a Whites' matter. It won't take long, and I must insist.'

I could almost hear the air crackle. The Blues' faction master got to his feet. Slowly. He wasn't happy, I could see that; or maybe 'fit to be tied' describes it better. 'Very well,' he said. 'I'll be free later in the day. Perhaps you'd be kind enough to drop over then. When you have a spare moment, naturally.' You could've used the tone to keep fish fresh in August.

'Surely I will.' Cammius stood up as well.

'I'll see you anon, then.'

Huffy as hell. We waited for the door to close, or rather slam. When it did Cammius turned back to me. He was frowning. 'You're a racing man, Corvinus?'

'Uh-uh. Not me. Two or three times a year, max.'

'That's a pity. I wouldn't've had to apologise because you'd've understood. Gaius Acceptus thinks the traditional partnership gives him a licence to run the Whites as well as the Blues, especially since he's been in the business for longer than I have. Sometimes it's good to remind him that we're independent heads of separate teams.' He almost smiled. 'Wine?'

I'd thought he'd never ask. This sounded promising. 'Yeah. Yeah, that'd be great.'

There was a tray with jug and cups beside the door. He picked up the jug – it was solid silver, and it looked heavy – poured for us both, handed me mine and sat down again. I drank: not bad stuff, not bad at all. Only thing was, I couldn't place it.

He must've noticed my expression. 'It's Spanish,'

he said. 'Not from one of the big new commercial estates, though. It comes from a vineyard planted by the Carthaginians three hundred years back. Original vines, or so the maker claims. He's an old business acquaintance of mine, and his family've been farming the land for generations. They say Hannibal's father would drink nothing else.'

Well, I hadn't heard that old Barca had been much of a wine buff, but if so I couldn't fault his judgment. It was liquid velvet, not in the imperial Caecuban bracket but still as good as the best Setinian. 'Who's his city dealer?' I asked.

Cammius chuckled; with Acceptus gone he was thawing fast. 'No one; he doesn't export. And because the yield's low he only sells to friends. Selected friends, at that. My share's no more than ten jars a year and friend or not he makes me pay through the nose, but it's worth it.'

'You're from that part of the world yourself?' I was being polite; like I say, you could've used the guy's accent to grate cheese.

'New Carthage. I was a merchant there for thirty-five years before I retired. Ran a fleet of ten ships at the finish.'

Yeah, right; that made sense. It didn't just explain the wine, it explained the jug as well. Plus the pricey bronze. Retired merchant-shipowners can be seriously rich people. Mind you, to own a faction he'd have to be rolling. 'So when did you take over the Whites?' I asked.

'Five years ago, when my wife died and I moved to

Rome. The last gentleman' – he said the word like it tasted sour – 'to manage them had eaten and whored his way through what should have paid the bills and made them a team to be proud of in themselves. Which, Corvinus, is my intention, despite what plans Gaius Acceptus may have to the contrary. When the mastership came up for auction I jumped at it. If it had cost twice the money I'd still have paid. Running a faction is the most satisfying job in the world.' He smiled. 'Especially for a Spaniard, because the Spaniard who has no love for or interest in horses is a corpse.' He caught himself, the smile vanished and he made the sign against the evil eye: Spaniard was right. '*Absit omen*. My apologies, and also for allowing my tongue to run away from me in other ways. So. Back to business. Tell me more about this theory of yours.'

I told him; the whole thing, including the idea I'd had about the murderer hiding in the building across the way.

'Pegasus, now. You're sure he was waiting for someone? Absolutely sure?'

'Yeah.' Interesting; I'd noticed that was the aspect of the affair he'd latched on to before. As, indeed, had Acceptus. 'You, uh, think that's important, sir?'

'Oh, yes. It's important. Much more perhaps than you realise, not being a racing man yourself.'

'Yeah? And how would that be?'

'Pegasus had his habits. One of them was, he might've gone drinking outside now and again but he had his favourite shops and he stuck to them. When the Watch told me he'd been found in an alley off Iugarius I wondered if they'd got the right man. Now you tell me he was meeting someone. In the racing business, Corvinus, these two things – a strange wineshop and a meeting – don't add up well. Certainly not to something I intend to ignore.'

'You mean he had a scam going?'

'Let's just say I'd be interested to know who the other man was. Very interested.'

'The guy's dead. If there was a scam, that's dead too.'

'Maybe so, maybe not. Every faction has its secrets. If one gets out then the faction master has to know before he can take the appropriate steps. But he judges. Only him, no one else, because that's what being faction master means. No one else has the right. You understand me?'

The grey eyes had gone diamond-hard. Cammius might be a nice enough old guy, but there was steel there, not far beneath the surface. And I'd guess that where his faction was concerned he didn't take any prisoners. 'Sure,' I said. 'Okay. So we both want to find the murderer. You give me a free rein and I'll do my best to nail the bastard. Do we have a bargain?'

He hesitated, then held out his hand. I took it. 'We have a bargain,' he said firmly.

'Fine.' We shook. 'So. Tell me about Pegasus. From the beginning.'

Cammius turned his wine cup between his fingers. 'He joined us almost exactly four months ago. The end of November, just after the Plebbies.'

'The Plebbies?'

'I'm sorry. I've taken to using my faction's own slang. The Plebeian Games.'

'Uh-huh. And he came over from the Greens, right?'

'He did.'

I hesitated: in the light of the recent spat with Acceptus this next bit was going to be tricky. 'Uh . . . forgive the question, but you happen to know his reasons?'

I half expected to be given my head in my hands like the Blues' faction master, but Cammius didn't bat an eyelid. 'No,' he said. 'And I'll admit I didn't think of asking. Gaius is right about that, at least. We were lucky to have him, very lucky. Pegasus may have had his faults but he was a top-notch driver, a real first-rater, and that's the thing in this business. More than the horses, even.'

'Yeah? And why's that, exactly?' I hadn't missed that 'faults', but you learn to go with the flow, and the guy was talking. I could pick up on the details later.

He grunted with amusement. 'You really aren't a racing man, are you, Corvinus? A race isn't just won by the fastest team, that's only half of it. It's also about timing and position, and as such you can't afford to make mistakes with either. Give your team their heads too soon and you lose, too late and you lose. Box yourself in, give the man behind space to get through, take just one turn too sharp or too wide and you lose. Losing's simple, no matter how good your horses are. Pegasus didn't lose easily. He read the field as if he carried the book in his head. He was a natural, something we didn't have and we needed badly. It's a tragedy that he died. Especially when he did.'

'He was that important?'

Cammius set down the wine cup. The amusement had gone like it had never been, and only the steel was left. That and a slow, deep anger. 'Five years it's taken me to build up this faction,' he said. 'A lot of time, a lot of money, more sheer bloody sweat than you can possibly imagine, Corvinus, even if I don't regret it.' I said nothing. 'Next season was going to be the first Whites' year for decades. We'd got the horse and now we had the man. A few good wins to use as bait and we could've held our own with the Greens and Blues pulling in the cream of the up-and-coming drivers; and drivers is what we need. Yes, Pegasus was that important.'

I sipped my wine. 'Which horse would that be, now?'

He looked fazed for an instant, and I remembered young Lucius. Same expression. 'Polydoxus,' he said. Then, when I didn't react, his mouth twisted. 'You really don't keep up with the racing news, do you?'

'Uh-uh.' The name rang a faint tonsorial bell, sure, but no more. I had enough difficulties holding the names of the drivers in my head without worrying about the horses. 'You'll have to tell me, I'm afraid.'

He took a sip of wine. 'We bought him as a five-year-old early last season from a Spanish breeder, ran him a couple of times in the minor heats to break him in then moved him up to the top of the card. He drew second with the Blues at the Floralians, beat them into third at the Apollinares, then won his races in Caesar's Victory and the Romans. Acceptus and the Greens' boss Natalis were spitting blood.' Oh, yeah; it was coming back now. Last September, the time of the Roman Games, Market Square had been full of it: the Whites' wonder horse who'd wiped the smiles off the bookies' faces and put every Green and Blue fan in the city into mourning. 'He's fast now, and he'll be faster yet. More than that, he takes the rest of his team with him, and that's something better than gold in a horse. With a top-notch driver behind him he'd've been unbeatable.'

I'd got his drift now. Tragedy was right. 'And four months ago you hooked Pegasus.'

'Correct. Come the Megalenses in under a month's time, we'd've wiped the floor with both the Greens and the Blues in any race he ran. As it is, without him we'll have no more than a fair edge. Oh, there might be another young driver along in a year or two who can match Polydoxus, and if I'm lucky I'll get his name on a contract before Natalis or Acceptus do. The problem is, when he gets enough experience he'll move on up the ladder and I'll be back where I started.' Cammius reached for the jug and filled both our cups. The steel was still there, but it was dulled. 'Pegasus broke the pattern, Corvinus. I'm not getting any younger, and I'd've liked to sweep the boards before I go. See the Whites established as a proper faction and rub Gaius Acceptus's patrician nose in the dirt. You understand that?'

He was levelling; far more than I'd ever thought he would, maybe even more than he'd had any intention of doing himself, and just that fact alone impressed me. 'Yeah,' I said. 'Yeah. I understand.'

'I thought that maybe this season it might just happen.' He drank and shrugged. 'With Pegasus dead it seems I'll have to wait a bit longer.'

Which reminded me. 'You mentioned a while back that the guy had his faults,' I said. 'What would these be, now?'

Cammius hesitated, on his guard again. 'Nothing very serious,' he said. 'He threw his weight around, and it got the lads' backs up a bit. But then any lead driver worth his salt is arrogant, Corvinus. It goes with the job.'

'Uh-huh.' Yeah, that made sense. These buggers are celebrities, mega-stars who draw prime wages, lift the cream from the prize money and get their names on the cheapo statuettes the hawkers tout outside the Circus on race days. Not to mention being wined and dined by the aristocracy and pulling the occasional senator's wife. Still, your average lead driver didn't often get himself murdered. I had the distinct feeling that Cammius was holding back here. 'Just how much would "a bit" be?'

I hadn't stressed the question, but the guy was no fool. His eyes held mine as he set his wine cup down carefully on the desk. 'Not enough to kill for,' he said evenly. 'Not even close.'

'You can't be that certain, surely.'

'I am.' He frowned. 'Listen, Corvinus. You don't know the racing world. My lads are a team. Professionals. They have their jealousies and their dislikes, but they don't take them outside the gates. And they don't go beyond words, or maybe a scuffle at worst. Nothing that would damage the faction in any way. Ever.' The eyes hardened. 'You won't find your killer among my Whites. I'll tell you that now.'

I shrugged. Yeah, well, fair enough, there was no point in pushing things. He was entitled to his opinion, and maybe it was an informed one. Still, that was something I'd like to make my own mind up about. Certainly if Pegasus had been the arrogant type as far as a tendency to unpopularity went he'd be starting pretty high on the scale. As an ex-Green lead driver he'd be a very big fish in a very small pool. He'd know it, and they'd know it and hate him for it. Plus it wouldn't've been all that long ago when he'd been Public Enemy Number One. 'You, uh, think I could talk to some of these lads of yours?' I said. 'Maybe form a few conclusions of my own?'

I got that level, assessing stare again. Well, I'd been half expecting it this time: like I say, visitors aren't encouraged around the faction stables, unless they're five-star bona fide fans who can be milked for hefty contributions to Colour funds, like my old pal Prince Gaius.

Finally, he nodded. 'Very well. On two conditions, though. One, nothing you see or hear gets passed on, under any circumstances. Two, you don't go near the horses. I'm sorry, Corvinus, but we have our rules and we don't break them. If it's any consolation, I'd insist on the same strictures for any outsider.'

Well, it was the best deal I was going to get. The only deal, in fact. 'Agreed,' I said.

'Then I'll arrange it.' He stood up. 'You'd like to do it now?'

'Sure. Why not?'

'I'd best come with you, then. The lads get nervous unless they can match a face to a name and otherwise you might have a little trouble.'

I winced. Security was one thing, sure, but this went through paranoia and out the other side. The closest I could come to it was my time on Capri hobnobbing with the Wart himself. And even there they let you go to the latrine on your own.

That was racing for you, though. I had an idea I'd better get used to it.

5

We went out into the compound. The day had changed, as March days often do: the sun had gone behind a bank of clouds, and it looked like rain. Bugger; it'd be a long walk back to the Caelian, and I still had the Greens boss to see. That I wasn't looking forward to: one brush with the racing world was enough for a morning.

There was a middle-aged guy in a beige tunic over by one of these little altars horsey types are so fond of, to Consus or Mercury or the Twin Gods or such. Cammius raised his hand and beckoned, and he came over at a run.

'Corvinus, this is Hesper, our master of stables,' Cammius said. 'Hesper, Valerius Corvinus is looking into the Pegasus business for us. He's to be allowed to talk to anyone he likes so long as they're not working with the horses and on condition he confines himself to his remit. Clear?'

A master of stables is the equivalent of a private house's major-domo, or a legion's centurion; in other words, where your ordinary skivvy or squaddie's concerned the real boss of the place on an everyday level. Usually, like his equivalent, he's come up through the ranks, and I'd bet that applied to this guy. He was a swarthy, pint-sized southern Italian – it's a funny thing, but most people connected with the cars are small, not only the drivers – with a blurred slave brand on his arm: some ex-slaves try to burn them off with a poultice of vinegar and pigeon dung, but it never works. He gave me a scowl like I'd broken parole already.

'Clear, boss,' he said.

'You're responsible for him, and for making sure he leaves when he's finished.' He turned back to me. 'I have things to do, Corvinus, but I expect you to keep in touch.'

'Sure. No problem. Thanks for your help.' Well, that gave me the entrée, anyway. We shook, and he left.

Hesper stood looking at me for a while, sucking on a tooth; not that he had all that many to choose from; he probably gave them turn about. Finally when he'd had all the entertainment he could take he said: 'Okay, sir. Where do you want to start?'

Not exactly enthusiastic in tone, but I recognised the type: he had his orders, and although his personal inclinations might prompt him to tell me to piss off he was willing to shelve them for the present. Until I put a foot wrong, of course. At which point he'd have my guts for leggings.

'Where would you suggest, friend?' Like I say, a master of stables is the shop-floor expert. My policy's always been, if you've got yourself an expert the last thing you do is try to tell him his business. That way you save yourself a lot of time and grief. You save making an enemy, too.

Hesper shrugged, but most of the antagonism went out of his expression. Right decision. 'There's Typhon,' he said. 'He was the only one with any time for the Great Man, but then Typhon'd socialise with a brick if it kept him in booze.'

Uh-huh. Definitely not flavour of the month, our Pegasus. Mind you, that was only what I'd expected. 'Who's Typhon? One of the drivers?'

'Shit, no.' I got a grin that was mostly space; a bit like a temple front, but not as regular. Or as clean. 'He's a placard man.'

Right. Every faction has placard men. These're the guys who walk in front of the horses in the big parade before the races proper, carrying boards giving the names of the horses and drivers and how many wins they've had. 'Fine by me,' I said. 'Where do I find him?'

A touch of the stiffness crept back. 'You don't,' he said. 'We find him together.'

Whoopee, joy in the morning. With the boss's right-hand man breathing down my neck I'd bet anyone I talked to would keep a tight rein on his mouth, which is always a handicap. Still, the guy had his orders. 'Fair enough,' I said. 'Let's go.'

We headed off towards the back of the compound; as far, I noticed, from the stables block as it was possible to get. There were still plenty of buildings, but most of them were lean-to sheds: definitely the racing world's equivalent of the sticks. Through some of the open doors I saw the racing equivalent of attic-space lumber: old chariots without the wheels, shelves of paint-pots that'd probably been hardening to rock-like solidity since I put on my adult mantle and stacks of chipboard with the names of long-dead horses and long-gone drivers. Outside one of the sheds a weaselly little guy was sitting against the wall swigging from a travelling flask. When he saw us coming he quickly tucked it behind his back.

'Hey, Typhon.' Hesper beckoned. 'Leave that alone and come over here, you drunken bugger.'

Weasel-Face grinned, got up and ambled towards us. Drunk was an exaggeration, but he wasn't walking too straight, either.

'This is Valerius Corvinus. He wants to ask you a few questions.' Hesper stepped back and folded his arms: his way, obviously, of tactfully creating an area of private space.

Yeah, well, as interview conditions went it wasn't perfect, but it was all I was going to get. Not much of an introduction, either. I sighed.

'What about?' The eyes were shifty and bloodshot, but despite the guarded tone I had the impression that Typhon was no thicko.

I glanced at Hesper, but he'd obviously decided that he'd done all that his job required. 'You know Pegasus was murdered yesterday? The lead driver?'

'Sure. Stabbed for his purse in an alleyway.' He didn't seem too concerned.

'You were, uh, friendly with him?'

That got me a slow, calculating look. 'I wouldn't say

"friendly", chief. Not "friendly", exactly. I knew him, sure, but that's as far as it went.'

Jupiter! I'd struck a real equivocating type here. He'd've got on great with Charax. 'Fine, pal. We won't quarrel over words. You care to tell me about the guy?'

'He was okay.'

Uh-huh. The last of the big communicators. I'd have to spell this out. 'I understand he wasn't too popular with your colleagues. Let's start there, shall we?'

The guy's chest swelled with that 'colleagues' and he seemed to brighten. Maybe I was getting his measure after all: placard men come pretty low in the pecking order and anyone who feeds their self-esteem is off to a flying start. 'The lads weren't too taken with him, no,' he said. 'Threw his weight around from the start. Mind you, he had the right. He was just about the best car-man in the business, even Uranius admitted that.'

'Uranius?'

That got me the look I was beginning to get used to, the one that said: *This guy's a mentally defective cockroach.* Typhon's version didn't even make a pretence at disguise. 'Our first driver before Pegasus turned up. First driver again now he's dead.'

Uh-huh. I'd assumed there'd be somebody of that description – Pegasus must've taken someone's place, and whoever's it was wouldn't be a very happy chappie – but it was good to have a name. I glanced at Hesper, but he hadn't moved. 'He around at present?'

'Nah. He'll be out on Mars Field with the lead horses. He likes to exercise them himself.'

'I, uh, take it that this Uranius didn't like the guy.' I kept my voice neutral.

'Hated his guts,' Typhon said cheerfully. 'Not that he would've killed him because of that, if that's what you're thinking, chief. Uranius wouldn't hurt a fly, and Pegasus was team. Besides, the rest of the lads felt the same way, especially after the Plebbies.'

'Yeah? So what happened at the Plebbies?'

Typhon gave me a sycophantic grin. 'There wouldn't be a chance of a sub after all this, would there?' he said. 'Wear and tear on the memory and vocal cords, like?'

I glanced back at Hesper and raised an eyebrow. The guy had gone back to his scowling, although mostly it was directed at Typhon. I half expected him to put the brakes on the idea, maybe on Typhon as well, but he just shrugged.

'Suit yourself, Corvinus,' he said. 'It's your money.'

I took out my purse and extracted a silver piece, but I didn't hand it over: I'd met Typhon's type before, and the silver pieces ended up multiplying faster than rabbits.

'You're a prince, chief.' Typhon beamed.

'The Plebbies.'

'The Plebbies. Pegasus was driving for the Greens. He got one of our sprinklers in the final lap when he overtook our first car on the inside. Drove straight over him. He won, too, a length ahead of the Blues. That made it worse. It was an accident, sure, and the kid should've been watching out, but the lads wouldn't be in the mood to make allowances.'

'Uh-huh.' I wasn't too shocked, or even much surprised: accidents happen at every Games, especially to sprinklers, the guys whose job it is to run out as their Colour draws level and throw water over the horses to cool them down. Which is safe enough if the home team's in an outside position, on the same side of the track as the sprinkler, but any other permutation is risky as hell. Sprinklers are usually small men – smaller even than the usual racing types – or boys, and fast on their feet, but even so the long-term career prospects are pretty limited. 'He was killed?'

'Sure. The wheel got him. Backbone snapped like a rotten stick.'

'Uranius was driving the White car?'

'Yeah. He was running a blocker for the Blue ahead of him. To be fair, it wasn't Pegasus's fault. You have to take your chances where they're offered on the track, especially after the final turn, and Uranius was too far from the barrier.'

'The bastard had already chewed up Crito and Laomedon,' Hesper growled. 'Chance is one thing, dangerous driving's another. And Laomedon, for Consus's sake! He's a bloody Red! He was supposed to be on the same side!'

I looked at Hesper in surprise. His arms were still folded but he'd stopped sucking his tooth and his face was flushed. Yeah; here was someone else who hadn't carried a torch for the Whites' new lead. And it'd take a lot of dislike to make the equivalent of a legion's NCO forget himself enough to break the rules imposed by self-discipline, especially in front of one of the Other Ranks. 'I thought that was the idea of the circus, pal,' I said mildly. 'Put the opposition out of the race any way you can.'

'Not any way you can. That's what the stewards are for. Or it should be, rather. Pegasus drove dirty all the time, and the Greens've got these buggers in their pockets. Put on a show for the crowds, sure, but dirty tricks like swerving your wheel into another Colour's horses' legs don't make you many friends in the racing business. Especially when the other Colour's your own backstop.'

'Act your age, Hesper!' Typhon sneered. 'The Blue, sure, I'll give you the Blue. Crito's a decent lad, but Laomedon's no kiss-in-the-ring driver himself. And wrecking him didn't have nothing to do with the colour of his tunic.'

Too many names, but I needed to hang in here because they might be important later. 'Uh . . . Laomedon's a Red, right?' I said.

Both of the guys gave me the Look this time.

'Yeah,' Hesper said. 'Their lead driver.'

'Their First Spear, too.' Typhon snickered. 'Retired.'

There was something here I wasn't getting. And that crack about First Spear – the senior NCO in a legion – didn't make much sense either. Still, Hesper was grinning, so it had to be at least a passable joke. 'So what you're saying is there was some friction between

Pegasus and this Laomedon? He put him out of the
Plebbies because of a private grudge?'

'Private.' Typhon sniggered again. 'Good word. I
like *private*. *Private*'s good.'

I was patient. 'You care to elaborate, maybe, pal?'

He glanced down at the silver piece I was holding.
Yeah, well, the guy was good value, I'd give him that.
I took out a second coin.

'All right, chief.' Typhon was still grinning. 'This
piece of private friction was a redhead by the name
of Felicula. Laomedon was squiring the pants off her
until about five or six months ago when she dropped
him and picked up with Pegasus.'

Felicula. Not a high-class name, more Aventine than
Esquiline. Which was odd: like I say, these lead drivers
have the pick of the fast-track aristocratic debs and
spouses, and they tend to be choosy who they take up
with. It's a matter of kudos, too: once it gets around
that you're squiring (nice word!) the wife or daughter
of one of the city's top five hundred your reputation
takes a hike. To be wrangled over by two lead drivers
Felicula must be some lady.

'You got any biographical details for this paragon?'
I said.

Typhon didn't even blink at the polysyllables; smarter
than he looked was right. 'Sure. Her husband's Gaius
Rufrius Pudens.' The name came out slow and careful.
Probably out of respect for my intellectually chal-
lenged cockroach status. 'He's, uh, the boss of the
Reds, in case you didn't know.'

If Typhon hadn't blinked, I certainly did. Jupiter

alive! I didn't know Pudens, but even allowing for the usual feelings of a cuckolded husband I doubted if a faction boss would take kindly to an opposition driver squiring his wife. Laomedon was bad enough, but at least he'd be family, in a way. 'And you say the affair's been going on for five or six months?' I said.

'Give or take. It's common knowledge, inside the business anyway.' I noticed that Hesper had lost his frown: whatever the guy's personal feelings about the ex-first driver were, I supposed Pegasus's amorous exploits came under the appropriate heading of shafting the opposition. Probably, in the eyes of the faction, it was one of the few things he had to his credit.

'Okay,' I said. 'Point noted. Very much so. Now we're on the subject, you any idea who else might've had a grudge against the dead guy?'

Typhon and Hesper exchanged glances; I'd noticed that Hesper was loosening up, maybe because we'd moved to things outwith the faction.

'Tell him about the fixes,' he said.

The back of my neck prickled. This time I was ahead of them. Fixes are an old racing tradition indulged in by most disgruntled punters at one time or another, usually when they've lost their shirt five race days in a row and don't have a sixth to lose. Basically what the punter does is write something unpleasant re the driver of his choice – such as 'May the demon Arourobracos rip the bastard's innards out and piss on his grave' – on a thin sheet of lead, tippy-toe along to the faction stable under cover of darkness and nail it to the gate, then run like hell and wait for the curse to strike. Some lazy buggers, of course, drop it down the nearest well instead, but making sure the driver in question reads it does wonders for your chances.

'Pegasus had been getting fixes?' I said.

'Yeah,' Typhon said. 'Three of them, a month apart, nailed to the gatepost. All the same type. No words, just his name written backwards and a flying dagger.'

'A *what*?'

'A knife with wings.' His tone was casual, too casual, and the cocky tone was gone. I noticed, too, that he'd crossed his fingers for luck. Probably wise: some things you didn't talk about without taking precautions. 'You know witches can send them?'

Yeah, I knew. From report, anyway. Despite the lurid language, most fixes are just expressions of spleen, and about as effective, but this was hardcore stuff. The idea was, you chose your victim and you paid a bona fide witch to send a knife after them. An imaginary knife. Or it started out imaginary anyway, and got real right at the end, where realness mattered. All the poor bugger heard before it hit was the whistle.

Pegasus had died from a knife in the back, and there was no sign of the murder weapon. Maybe coincidence, sure, but coincidences happen, and this particular one put ice in my gut. You want to laugh, you laugh; you're in good company. Me, I don't make unsubstantiated judgments.

'You any idea who was responsible?' I asked.

Typhon looked at Hesper. The stables master

shrugged; too casual, like Typhon. 'No,' he said. His eyes shifted, and I could see his right hand moving in the sign. 'We, uh, found the last one yesterday morning.'

The day Pegasus was killed, in other words. I shivered as the goosebumps went into overdrive. Shit; that was all I needed, a demon murderer. If that was what had got the guy then I might as well give up now. Still, I had plenty to go on here even without the supernatural element. More than plenty: in fact, my brain was beginning to go into overload. 'You kept it?'

Hesper held my eyes. 'What do you think?'

I shivered again. No, maybe not. 'Fair enough,' I said, and handed over the silver pieces to Typhon. 'You've been very helpful. Thanks a lot, pal.'

Typhon grinned and slipped them under his belt. 'My pleasure. Any time. I'll drink your health.'

'You do that. Oh. One more thing. You have any idea what Pegasus could've been doing over on Iugarius?'

He shook his head. 'Sorry, chief. That's one I can't answer. He wasn't one for confidences, and me, I don't pry.'

Well, it had only been an outside chance at best. I turned to Hesper. 'I think I'll call it a day there. You want to take me to the gate?'

'Sure.' Wonder of wonders, I got a proper grin out of him, too. Maybe these racing guys were human after all. We set off back towards the entrance. 'Where are you bound next?'

After that business with the flying dagger I'd've liked to say 'the nearest wineshop' or maybe 'home', but the rain was holding off and it wasn't even midday yet. 'I thought I'd call in on the Greens. Get some sort of angle from them.'

The grin slipped. Uh-oh; mistake. Scratch the human. Yeah, well, I supposed it wasn't exactly the done thing in faction social circles at the end of a visit to say you were off to chat with the opposition. The next bit of the walk was pretty quiet.

Cement-Features was still on the door. I gave him a smile but his face didn't crack.

'Thanks for your time, pal,' I said to Hesper. 'I'll see you again.'

'No problem.' Hesper was frowning. I thought maybe it was the aftermath of the faux pas on the way over, but I was mistaken. 'Hey, Corvinus. When you're next door ask about a guy called Sopilys.'

I stopped and turned. 'Yeah? Why should I do that?'

'He used to be one of their grooms, six months back. I don't know what he's doing now, or what it was about, but he might be worth a word. He and Pegasus had a major punch-up outside the Black Cat.'

'The Black Cat?'

'It's a Green wineshop, just this side of the Sublician Bridge.'

Uh-huh; of course: the faction fans tended to have their own drinking holes, usually run by a landlord just as Colour-mad as they were. The Black Cat'd be one of these. 'Right,' I said. 'Thanks again, friend.'

'Don't mention it.' He hesitated. 'Pegasus was a bastard, sure, but he was our bastard. And he was a good driver. If you're after his killer then you've got my backing.'

Maybe I'd read Hesper wrong; well, it wouldn't be the first time. I set off for the Greens' stable.

6

I got my wish. Minicius Natalis, the Greens' boss, was out hobnobbing with the gentry and the guy on the gate – another slab-faced troll – wasn't about to let a strange narrow-striper across the sacred threshold without prior permission in triplicate. And I'd reckoned the Whites were bad. Yeah, well: I reckoned I'd done pretty good for a first day, and my tongue was hanging out for a chaser to Cammius's Spanish nectar. Besides, by pure but happy coincidence I'd got a wineshop figuring in the case, and the Sublician was almost on my way home. I could kill two birds with the one stone.

The rain was just starting as I went back down Triumph Road and turned right along the front of Marcellus Theatre. An itinerant pastry-seller covering up his tray pointed me in the direction of the Black Cat, halfway down an alley off the approach road to the bridge itself. It was raining in earnest now, and I was glad I'd brought my cloak.

The landlord was obviously one of the real, hundred-per cent, dyed-in-the-wool faction nuts. Green wineshop was right: the walls were green inside and out, the tables and benches were painted green, and there were about as many banners, pennants and statuettes around the place as one of the Circus hawkers could expect to shift in a good season. To cap it all off, the wall behind the counter had every Green win since Augustus was in rompers written up on it in table form, with plenty of room for additions. I didn't even bother to check out the lunch menu. Probably pea soup and spinach rissoles. And fortunately there wasn't a real eponymous cat on the premises, because it sure as hell wouldn't've stayed black for long.

Yeah, well. That's racing for you.

The only other customer was a tunic perched on a high stool at the counter. We gave each other a friendly nod.

'What'll it be, sir?' The landlord himself was a tall skinny guy like a long drink of water with an out-of-town accent. He was rubbing the counter with a blue rag.

I looked up at the wine board. On its own at the top, starred, was a pricey Falernian, but my rule is never touch the stuff you find in a city wineshop until you're sure of the place because nine times out of ten the nearest it's been to the municipality of Falerii is where it's sitting on the shelf. The other wines weren't all that special: the usual cheap-and-cheerfuls from Gaul and Campania that you find in any low-grade wineshop plus a bargain-basement Sicilian.

'Where're you from, pal?' I said to the owner.

He blinked. 'Uh . . . Adria.'

Not bad. Could be better, but not bad at all. 'You happen to have some Praetutian squirrelled away?'

The frown lifted: I ain't never met the wineshop owner yet who doesn't appreciate the customer that knows his own region, oenologically speaking. 'Maybe,' he said. 'Jug?'

'Make it a half. I need to stay reasonably sober.'

'You've got it. You want some cold Picenan sausage on the side?'

'Sure.' What that might be – wine's my bag, not sausage – I didn't know, but politics told me I should have it. 'Go ahead.'

I took off my cloak, shook it out and sat down on the stool next to the tunic – a solid, middle-aged father-of-five type who was nursing a wine cup and a plate of pickled cucumber – while he went to get the booze. Not a bad place, the Black Cat, if you made allowances for the furnishings. The floor was clean-scrubbed, the tables and the benches positively gleamed and someone, probably the proprietor's wife, had put a clay pot of narcissi on the counter. Yellow was safe.

'Nice weather for ducks,' the tunic said.

'Yeah.' I spread the cloak over another stool where it could drip. 'Hell on the rest of us, though.'

'You made a good choice with the wine. Pinnius gets it from his wife's cousin. It's good stuff.'

I turned towards him with pleasure. Shooting the breeze with other wineshop punters is something I enjoy, and he was obviously a talker. 'You a regular here, friend?'

He took a mouthful from his cup before he answered. 'Got a vegetable stall by the Temple of Hope. I buy from a wholesaler on the Island so I'm in here most days. It's on the way and you pick up the latest news on the team.'

'You follow the Greens, then?' Silly question in these surroundings, but the guy might simply be colour-blind, and the Reds didn't have many places of their own. Or maybe his choice of faction had something to do with his trade.

I needn't've worried, though; the guy was Green through and through. 'Always have,' he said placidly. 'Man and boy. Never miss a race if I can help. My eldest son's the same, desperate to be a driver. Mind you, kids that age – he's ten next birthday – they all go through that stage. I wanted it myself.'

The landlord came back with the half jug and the sausage; it had cumin and lovage in it and it could've been pork but I wasn't going to enquire more closely. I poured some of the wine into the cup and took a large swig. Good stuff, all right. Not up to the standard of the Latians but well worth drinking. 'The name's Marcus Corvinus, by the way,' I said.

'Quintus Cascellius.' We shook, gravely. 'Don't see many narrow-stripers round here.'

It was the usual polite request for reciprocal info, and I obliged. 'I'm looking into a knifing.'

'Yeah?' His face registered interest. 'You with the Watch?'

'Uh-uh. Purely private. The guy was a driver; you'll know him, he used to be with the Greens. Pegasus.'

'Sweet Mercury!' He'd picked up his wine cup. Now he set it down again. 'Pegasus is dead? *Pegasus?*'

He was staring at me like I was one of these messengers in a Greek play; him and the landlord both.

'Yeah. He was stabbed yesterday in an alley off Iugarius. You didn't know?'

The guy shook his head. 'I'm sorry to hear it. He may've gone over to the Whites but he was a fine driver. A joy to watch.'

'He come in here often?'

I'd made the question sound casual, but I could feel a shift in the atmosphere.

'When he was with the Team, sure,' the landlord Pinnius said, and I could just hear the capital letter: for Pinnius there could only be one Team. 'Not since he made the switch.'

His voice was guarded, and I noticed that Cascellius had suddenly become interested in his wine cup.

There was something screwy here. I took a bite of the sausage and chewed on it. That was okay, too, if you managed to rid yourself of the suspicion that the beast who'd contributed the meat part of it might've brayed rather than gone oink. 'Uh . . . I'm told he was involved in a brawl here about six months back. With another Green. A guy called Sopilys.'

Screwy was right: you could've carved your name on the silence with a chisel. Cascellius was still staring into his wine cup like it was a fortune-teller's scrying glass. Pinnius had gone back to polishing the counter. Finally he said, 'Yeah. That's right. Not inside, though.

On the pavement. And Sopilys was no Green. Not technically, anyhow.'

I let that last bit go for the moment. 'You care to tell me what happened?'

Pinnius shrugged. There was something aggressive about the movement, like he was within an ace of telling me to get lost. 'Not much to tell. Pegasus had been in here drinking. He left, ran into Sopilys. Next thing, they're punching hell out of each other. End of story.'

'He was on his own?'

'No. There were two or three other lads from the Team with him.'

'Uh-huh. And they broke it up, right?' They would: faction solidarity. Especially if the other guy was the aggressor and 'technically no Green'.

Pinnius hesitated. 'No. Not exactly.'

Things went very still. 'Just how not exactly is not exactly, friend?' I said carefully.

'It was a fair fight.' The guy didn't look happy. 'They let it go to a finish.'

Jupiter! It didn't make sense. Not any kind of sense. 'So who won?'

'Sopilys. He knocked Pegasus on his beam end and left him lying.'

'Was he hurt?'

'Two shiners, a bit of bruising. Nothing much. Like I said, they were only using their fists. The other lads took him home.'

'Okay. So what was the fight about?' Silence. 'You said Sopilys wasn't technically a Green. What's that supposed to mean?'

'He'd just been given the shove. He was one of the grooms.'

'Uh-huh.' I took a sip of the wine. 'Was there a connection between the sacking and the fight?'

But that was obviously one question too many. Pinnius laid the cloth down carefully. 'Look, friend,' he said. 'There's something you have to understand. The Green lads come in here to drink. If they want to talk racing with me or any of the other customers then they do it, but they don't volunteer information about what goes on inside the stables all that often and we don't ask, we don't speculate, and we sure as hell don't discuss it with strangers. That way everyone's happy. Okay?'

'So you don't know?'

'I don't know and I don't want to know. Whatever the reason for the fight was, it was private business and it was settled private. You want any more, you talk to Sopilys yourself.'

'I might just do that, friend,' I said. 'You happen to know where he might be at present?'

But I'd lost him; I'd lost both of them, because Cascellius wasn't looking too friendly now either. Pinnius shrugged; this time it was definitely aggressive. 'No idea,' he said. 'He's not anywhere around here, anyway, that I can say. I haven't seen him since.'

'What about Pegasus? He come in here much after the punch-up? Between then and leaving the Greens?'

Another shrug. He had picked up the cloth again. 'Can't recall one way or the other,' he muttered.

Hostile; definitely hostile, and tighter than a constipated oyster. I sighed. Bugger, there was *definitely* something screwy here, but I wasn't going to get any further by asking questions, that was certain, because the temperature was dropping by the minute. I finished my wine and sausage quicker than I'd otherwise have done, paid up and left.

Outside, it was throwing it down even harder: the rain was bouncing off the pavement and gurgling between the crossing-stones. Shit: under these conditions, walking's no fun, none at all. I broke my usual rule, took a chair from the rank in Vegetable-Sellers' Square and went straight home.

Perilla had just finished lunch when I got in. I changed into another tunic – even the short walk from the Black Cat to the chair rank had left my cloak sodden – and carried Bathyllus's welcome-home jug through to the dining-room. At least the Setinian had been all present and correct this time, although I couldn't say the same for Bathyllus. Whatever was eating the little guy, it was still chewing away, and he showed no signs of unburdening himself. Still, his eyes were bright enough, his nose was cold and moist and although he didn't have any coat to be glossy his bald pate was shining as usual, so I wasn't too worried.

'Hey, lady.' I kissed her and settled down on the couch. 'How has your day been?'

'Drier than yours, by the look of your hair. How are things going?'

'Not bad. But these factions are something else.

I'd bet there's more backstairs intrigue goes on than happens up on the Palatine.'

'So who did it?'

I glanced at her over my wine cup. She looked back demurely and I grinned. 'Cut it out, Perilla.' Still, it was time to sit back and work out just what exactly we'd got so far. 'You want to hear the story?'

'Do I have an option?'

I ignored that one: she didn't really mean it. 'Let's concentrate on motive, because that's all we really have to go on at present.' There was a plate of cold chickpeas with fennel on the table, practically untouched. I pulled it towards me and picked up a spoon. 'The guy wasn't liked, that's obvious, either by his Whites' team-mates or the Greens.'

'Start with the Whites.' Perilla settled more comfortably against the arm of the couch.

'Okay.' I took a mouthful of chickpeas and spoke round them. 'From their angle, Pegasus was an incomer from an opposition team. He put everybody's nose out of joint, he had a reputation for dangerous driving and just before he joined the faction he'd run down and killed one of their sprinklers.'

'Was it an accident?'

'Sure, as far as I can tell, but the kid's still dead. Those are the pluses, for what they're worth. On the minus side, I have Cammius's assurance that Pegasus practically carried the faction's future along with him single-handed, and to be fair that's a clincher. Everyone might've hated his guts, and probably did, but in this case simple hatred just isn't motive enough.'

Perilla frowned. 'That sounds a little sweeping, dear.'

I swallowed a mouthful of wine. 'Lady, you don't know these faction guys. I'd've said that too before this morning, but they're something else. I'm rapidly coming to the conclusion that where racing goes obsession just isn't the word. The faction comes first, middle and last.'

'Hmm.' Perilla helped herself to a stuffed olive. 'All right. Leave the Whites. What about the other factions? If Pegasus was as important as you say then it would be in the opposition's interest to get rid of him.'

'Yeah. Right.' I took another swallow. 'That's the line I'm working on. As I read it, they're all possibles, although the motives are mixed. Even the Blues.'

The lady's eyes widened. 'But Marcus,' she said, 'Whites and Blues are allies. Why should the Blues want him dead?'

'They're only allies from the outside. I've met the Blues' boss, and the guy was radiating jealousy so hard you could feel the heat. Whites are supposed to be second-stringers: they make the chances, but they don't win the races. Or they shouldn't. Pegasus was a first-rate driver, he played to win; the Blues are going through a bad patch and come the new season Whites looked set to cream them in any race the guy ran. Obsession again, but this time there's face involved. Getting beat by the Greens is one thing, but the Whites are another matter. Sure, I've no reason for fingering Acceptus, but if we're talking motive he's got just as much as any.' I spooned in another mouthful of chickpeas.

Perilla was quiet for a long time. 'Very well,' she said. 'You said all the factions. What about the Greens and Reds.'

I shifted on my couch. 'Take the Reds first. As far as racing goes, they've no real axe to grind. They're not in contention, they run point for the Greens. The motive there's personal. According to the guy I talked to at the stables Pegasus has been carrying on with the Red boss's wife and cutting out their lead driver.'

'Ah.'

'"Ah" is right, lady. Pure sex, the oldest motive in the world. Sure, the affair's been going on for five or six months, but the husband's usually the last to know in situations like that. I haven't come across him yet so I've nothing to go on, but I doubt he'd be too happy. Certainly it's worth chasing.'

'What about the driver?'

'Guy called Laomedon. He's a definite possibility. He has a reputation on the track, and Pegasus cut him up in the Plebeian Games. Reading between the lines, I'd guess the two of them had been needling each other since the lady made the switch.' I topped up my cup. 'Could be the needling turned into something more serious.'

'Five or six months on?'

I shrugged. 'Why not? Maybe he's the waiting type. Or he could just have seized his opportunity.'

Perilla sighed. 'Marcus, there are too many suspects.'

'Be grateful. It's better than having just a body and nowhere to point the finger.' I pushed the chickpeas away and reached for a dish of cold pork. 'Besides, I haven't finished yet. Not by a long chalk.'

'Oh, yes. The Greens.'

'They're the most interesting of the lot.' I bit into the sliced pork. It was one of Meton's favourite recipes: dry-marinated in salt, pepper and sage then cooked with a cumin sauce. 'First, they've got the best motive of all for wanting the guy in an urn. He was their top driver, he'd been with them for years and he knew the ins and outs of their stables, and I get the impression that that's important in the racing game. Every faction has its secrets, and a major transfer to the opposition could put them at risk.'

'Fair enough, as far as it goes,' Perilla said. 'Although as with your Laomedon I'd've expected them to make their move sooner. Second?'

'Second's the business with the missing purse. That was a cover-up if ever I saw one, and the only question is whether the Watch boss was acting off his own bat or if he'd had instructions.'

'There wouldn't have been time for that, surely. Valgius sent his men round straight away.'

'He could've known that the murder was going to happen in advance.'

'Oh, Corvinus! That is pure conspiracy theory!'

'Sure it is. All the same, it fits. By all accounts the bastard's about as straight as a viper's backbone. It would explain the murderer's choice of Renatius's, too. If Pegasus was decoyed there, which I think he was, then it'd be Valgius's lads who were called in.'

'If we're going to posit that degree of planning then why didn't the killer take the purse in the first place?'

'How should I know, lady? Maybe it was just a slip. And they couldn't've counted on an eagle-eyed sleuth like me being first to the body.'

'Hah!'

'Hah as much as you like. The cover-up still happened.'

Perilla ducked her head. 'All right. That was point two. Point three?'

I paused for another slice of the pork and helped it down with a mouthful of wine. 'Point three's a curious one. I'm not sure where or how it fits in yet, but one gets you ten it's important. Just before he joined the Whites Pegasus got mixed up in a fist-fight outside a wineshop, with an ex-employee. The lads who were with him stood back and let the fight happen. Pegasus was beaten up.'

'Marcus, I'm sorry but I don't see what relevance—'

'Jupiter, lady! Pegasus was the Greens' top driver! a) there's such a thing as faction solidarity, and b) where there are races at stake you don't let anyone damage your best asset. Yet Pegasus's mates sat on their hands while Sopilys took him apart. You don't think that maybe there's a slight inconsistency there?'

'Ah.' Perilla frowned. 'Yes, I suppose that is rather curious.'

'You bet your socks.'

'You don't know the reason for the quarrel?'

I shook my head. 'The guy in the wineshop either didn't know himself or he wasn't telling. Whatever it was, Pegasus was in a minority of one, and feelings were running pretty high.'

'High enough for Pegasus to move factions shortly afterwards, perhaps?'

'Yeah, that's what I was thinking.'

'So what could the reason have been? In theory?'

'Jupiter knows. Something to do with the racing side, certainly, because it seems that's the only thing these buggers take seriously. Maybe he was running some sort of scam, giving away faction secrets or selling races. That's my best bet, anyway. We'll just have to try and find out.'

The lady's brow was still furrowed. 'Marcus,' she said slowly, 'you say Pegasus was waiting for someone in Renatius's wineshop. If he was venal then perhaps he was playing the same game with the Whites.'

Yeah; that was a connection I'd been toying with. 'It's possible, sure,' I said. 'Cammius jumped to the same conclusion.'

'So if Cammius had found out then perhaps he set Pegasus up himself.'

I stared at her. 'Jupiter, Perilla, that doesn't make sense! Cammius is—'

'No, wait. If he were relying on Pegasus to win races and he found that his new driver was planning to cheat him then he would have a reason for killing him. Or am I wrong?'

No, she wasn't wrong; or not far wrong, anyway.

It was a theory, sure, one that hadn't occurred to me, and having met the guy I'd say where the faction was involved he might well be capable of murder, especially a well-planned one like this. However. 'Cammius wouldn't've needed to go to these lengths, Perilla. Besides, there are two major points against. One, Pegasus was the Whites' key to the future. He'd be no good to Cammius dead. Two, I swear Cammius knew nothing about a meeting. He could be a good actor, sure, but he felt genuine. And Pegasus's death had hit the guy hard. That he wasn't faking, no way, nohow, never.' I grinned. 'Besides, more suspects we don't need at this stage.'

Perilla sniffed. 'All right. Although that's hardly a reason in itself. Is that everyone?'

'Uh . . . not quite.'

'Oh, Corvinus!'

'Pegasus had been getting fixes.' I told her about the conversation at the Whites' stables with Typhon and Hesper, and the flying dagger tablets. She laughed.

'Marcus, you are *not* advancing a curse as a plausible cause of death!'

I flushed: me, like I say, I keep an open mind on witches, but Perilla isn't rational on the subject. 'Hang on, lady!' I said. 'We're talking motives here, remember? Whoever was responsible stipulated a death by knife. Pegasus was stabbed. Wriggle all you like, you can't just write that off as a coincidence.'

'I am not wriggling.'

'Sure you are. I'm not saying there wasn't a human hand involved' – I wouldn't totally discount the possibility, although I wasn't going to tell her that – 'but threat and result match. The fixes stay.'

'Marcus, dear, sometimes you amaze me.'

Well, I wasn't going to argue; besides, at that point Bathyllus came in to clear. Even so, the fixes came into the business somewhere along the line, of that I was convinced. Not that I was looking forward much to finding what the tie-in was.

Solid, three-dimensional murderers I can handle. Start messing around with magic and the gods alone know where it can lead.

I just hoped that I wouldn't be the next poor bugger to hear the whistle.

7

I hadn't thought, when I'd bearded the troll at the gate of the Greens' stables, to check whether the boss would be available next day, but I remedied that by sending a skivvy round to make an appointment. Also to check that I'd got the guy's name straight. It's always good to make absolutely certain who you're dealing with.

The Greens' faction master was a narrow-striper by the name of Titus Minicius Natalis. Given that, I'd expected – because the Greens are the toff team – someone along the streamed lines of Gaius Acceptus, but Natalis was a different type altogether: a pint-sized, bleary-eyed slob, running to fat, and with unshaven jowls you could've grated turnips on.

'Valerius Corvinus,' he said when the tame troll wheeled me into his office. 'To what do I owe the pleasure?'

Sarky; sarky as hell, and in a fake plummy accent that was obviously intended to needle me. That part I didn't mind – the man's personal hang-ups were his problem, not mine, and it was water off a duck's back – but you can take an instant dislike to some people, and for me Minicius Natalis came pretty high on the list. In fact, whoever dunnit as far as Pegasus's murder went I just prayed that Natalis was involved somewhere along the line just so I could see the bastard sweat. Unfortunately, things being as they are, he'd probably turn out to be as innocent as a babe in arms and the mainstay and delight of his ninety-year-old grandmother; but you can always hope.

'I'm looking into the death of one of your ex-drivers,' I said. 'Pegasus.'

If I was expecting surprise I didn't get it, not a flicker. Well, the knifing had to be old news now on the racing circuit. What I wasn't expecting was outright hostility.

'You with the Watch?' he said. The accent had shifted to pure backwoods Sicilian.

'No, but—'

'Then fuck off.' He glanced over my shoulder at the troll, who was still hovering. 'Escort Marcus Valerius Messalla Corvinus off the premises.'

Interesting. I wondered where he'd got my full name from; the skivvy would only have used the standard three, at most. However, the problem of Natalis's sources could wait; I had other worries at present. The air behind me shifted and I could feel stertorous breathing in my left ear-hole.

I didn't look round. 'Hang on a minute, pal. I only—'

'Pegasus is no concern of mine. Whoever knifed the bastard did me a favour. Now throw him out, Socrates.'

Socrates?

A big hand gripped the top edge of my mantle. I didn't think twice. Bending down, I brought my right fist round hard and punched the troll in the balls. He gave a whimper and let go the material. I straightened. 'Look, sunshine, I don't know what sort of scam Pegasus was into, but—'

Arms that could've belonged to a gorilla into body-building wrapped themselves round my chest and I felt myself being lifted.

'Wait!' Natalis snapped.

Me, I didn't have much option, not with my sandals a good inch off the floor; but then I wasn't the one he was talking to.

'Put him down.'

The soles of my sandals made contact and the arms unwrapped themselves. My ribs creaked back into position.

'That's better,' I said.

Natalis ignored me. 'Socrates, push off. And close the door behind you.' Thump thump thump slam. 'Right, Corvinus. I'll give you ten minutes. Have a seat.'

Seat, nothing: the visitor's chair I lowered myself on to could've doubled for an Asiatic client-king's throne. If I'd thought the Whites' place had a touch or two of luxury, this had it beat hands down and all the way to Baiae. That is, if you're into wall-to-wall gold leaf, crimson Cordoban leather and pink marble flooring. Also I was having difficulty seeing the swarthy midget's face above the huge model chariot and horses on his desk. If the real thing had had that much goldwork in the superstructure it'd've needed an elephant to pull it.

'Pegasus wasn't into any scam,' Natalis said. 'I just want to make that hundred-per-cent clear, okay?'

Yeah; and I'm the Wart's maternal grandmother in feathers and a tutu. And I really didn't like the bastard's manner. When in doubt, go for the jugular. 'Is that right, now?' I said. 'So why did he get into a fist-fight with Sopilys before he left the faction? And why did his mates leave him to have his lights punched out?'

Silence; Natalis didn't answer; he simply didn't answer. What I got was a hundred-candelabra stare from an absolutely expressionless face. 'Pegasus wasn't no slave,' he said at last. 'He was a free man. He wanted to walk, he walked.'

'All the way down from Green to White? And you obviously didn't understand the question, pal. What was he doing? Selling races? Doping horses?'

The guy's face turned a colour to match the upholstery. 'He did either of those things in my stable, *pal*,' he said slowly, 'and he isn't moving to the Whites, he's taking a trip downriver on his front.'

Ouch. Still, that was straight enough. 'So why did he go?'

'I told you. He wanted to walk, he walked.'

'With his mates pushing him.'

That got me the stare again. I had the impression that Natalis wasn't used to people answering back, and he didn't like it. 'He wasn't the most popular lead driver I've ever had, sure,' he said finally. 'But it was his decision, not mine. His contract finished with the season.'

He was lying, I'd've bet good money on that. Not that I'd be able to collect. 'So why did he want to walk? What was in it for him with the Whites?'

Natalis was still giving me the eyeball treatment, but he had himself well under control now. 'Maybe it had something to do with that screwball of a nag they've got,' he said. 'Maybe that Spanish trader down the road made him an offer he couldn't refuse. Maybe he had a death-wish. How the hell should I know? He wouldn't've come back here, that's certain. Never. Not even if the bastard had crawled all the way.'

'Speaking of death-wishes and nags' – I paused; was there a shift in the guy's expression? I couldn't be sure – 'you're sitting pretty now he's dead, aren't you? It must come as quite a relief that he won't be racing in a white tunic come the Megalenses.'

He leaned forwards until the gold charioteer's head was almost sticking up his left nostril. 'Listen, Corvinus. The day I have to worry about anything that White shopkeeper runs against me on the sand I'll give up racing and farm chickens. And I don't have to hedge my bets with a knife in anyone's back, either.'

'Not even if you've got Titus Valgius to bury the evidence?'

That fazed him. He blinked. 'Who the fuck's Titus Valgius?'

'The Eighth District Watch commander. He's one of your biggest fans. And he does a nice line in robbing corpses of their purses.'

Natalis shot to his feet like a rocketing pheasant.
I'd been right about pint-size: the little bastard's head
didn't come much further up above the desk. 'That's
it, Corvinus!' he said. 'You get the hell off my
property!'

I shrugged. Yeah, well, there wasn't a lot else I could
do; certainly we weren't about to forge the bonds of
a lasting friendship locked head to head like this. Not
that there was a snowball's chance in hell we ever
would do. 'Fine, pal,' I said. 'Suit yourself.'

I walked out with his glare burning my back. Maybe
it'd been a mistake to rattle the bastard's cage, but
I felt a lot better for it. Outside, Socrates the troll
was waiting, slightly crouched, to lead me back to
the gate.

So that was that; short and definitely not sweet. One
thing I was sure of, though. I wouldn't've taken Titus
Minicius Natalis's word on tomorrow's sunrise.

Okay; so I was persona very much non grata at the
Greens' stables. Be that as it may, I was still light on
information about Pegasus's career with the Greens.
So where could I go?

I was just cutting through Vegetable-Sellers' Square
when I remembered the punter in the Black Cat; what
was his name? Cosconius? Cascennius?

Cascellius. Quintus Cascellius. Right. And he had a
vegetable stall near the Temple of Hope; back a way,
near Marcellus Theatre. Good omen. Sure, it was an
outside chance, because we hadn't exactly parted on
the best of terms, but he'd struck me as a decent

type who'd at least had some sympathy for Pegasus. Certainly he was worth a visit.

I turned round and made for the Temple of Hope. It was on the very edge of Vegetable-Sellers' Square itself and, like the name suggests, vegetable stalls weren't all that thin on the ground in that quarter. I buttonholed an old biddy selling spring greens off a spread-out cloth and asked her for directions. Three stalls and an obligatory bunch of cow parsley later, I struck lucky. There was the man himself selling radishes to a tenement matron with a chest like the front of a grain barge.

'Hey, Cascellius,' I said. 'Remember me?'

I thought he might hand me a turnip and tell me where to put it, but he didn't bat an eyelid. 'The narrow-striper in the Black Cat,' he said. 'You still chasing knifemen?'

'Yeah. And it's Marcus Corvinus, if you've forgotten.'

'Nothing wrong with my memory, neighbour.' He put the copper coin the lady had given him for the radishes in his cash-box and gave me a long, slow, appraising look from under brows that would've done a bull credit. Come to think of it, 'bull' fitted him pretty well. I hadn't noticed it particularly the last time we'd met, but here on his own ground the guy radiated a solid placidity that was definitely taurine. 'What can I do for you?'

'Uh . . . you have time for a cup of wine? Not in the Cat.'

That got me the long unsmiling look again, and I

swear his lower jaw moved like he was chewing the idea over. 'Okay,' he said finally. 'You've got it. I make no promises, mind.'

'Great.'

He gave the cash-box to the woman selling dried herbs at the next stall. 'Look after the shop for me, Mammo,' he said. 'I won't be long.' The woman flashed him a couple of teeth like an odontically challenged beaver's. 'There's a wineshop in Plane Tree Yard, Corvinus. We can go there.'

He led me between the stalls and into a cul-de-sac where there were a few crude wooden benches round a stunted plane tree. We sat down at one of them.

'Nice place,' I said.

It was meant to be ironic – we had a line of dripping washing above our heads – but Cascellius nodded seriously. 'The landlord's from Verona. He serves the best Rhaetian in the city.'

I glanced at him. Yeah, well: you live and learn. And there ain't no reason why a fellow wine buff shouldn't sell radishes. The waiter was hovering. I ordered a jug of Rhaetian.

'Now,' he said when it came and we'd sunk the first quarter-cup.

'I need some information,' I said.

'So I gathered. To do with Pegasus, right?'

I hesitated. 'Along with other things, sure. But let's start with him, if you're willing.'

He shook his head slowly. 'It's not a question of willing, Corvinus. I can't help you. I'll tell you that now. That's can't, not won't, because I'm sorry the man's dead and I'd help if I could. I scarcely spoke to him, nor did anyone else, including his faction mates. He might've come into the Cat a lot but he wasn't a mixer.'

'He didn't have any close friends?'

'None that I know of. Not in the Cat, anyway.'

'Enemies?'

'He wasn't liked, even before the Sopilys business. But I never heard anyone actually bad-mouth him.'

Uh-huh. Well, not much mileage there. 'What can you tell me about Minicius Natalis?'

He frowned. 'Natalis?'

'The Greens' boss.'

'I know who Natalis is. What's your interest?'

'Nothing in particular. Just curious.'

'"Just curious", eh?' I got the long considering stare again. Then he shrugged. He might be slow, but the guy wasn't stupid: there was a brain under that curly topknot, and I'd bet he hadn't missed the implications of the follow-on question. 'Okay. I said I'd help and I will. He's worked his way up from nothing. The man's an ex-slave, from Leontini. Started out as plain Titus Minicius, drove for the Greens under the name of Olympius, bought his freedom and ended up as their leading driver.' Right; I'd forgotten that drivers tended to drop their own names and take fancy Greek ones when they joined the cars. 'He made his pile in prize money, but then he had a bad smash and broke his right arm. Shattered the bone. Some people say he lost his nerve after that. Anyway, he stayed with the Greens as master of stables and principal trainer. Ten or so years back when the previous boss died he made a deal with a consortium of purple-stripers to sub him and took over as faction master. That do you for starters?'

'He's good?'

'Of course he's good, he wouldn't be the boss otherwise. His backers got their investment returned twice over inside two years. He knows the business six ways from nothing, and he's hard, keeps the team on their toes. Rules his stable with an iron rod: one slip and you're out.'

Yeah; that was the impression I'd got of him. The guy was tough as nails. And the fact that his whole career had been with the Greens was interesting too.

'You mentioned a consortium of purple-stripers,' I said. 'Who would they be?'

'The top of the range. Imperial family, collaterals, Greens' supporters going way back before his time. Tiberius has never been much into racing, but the Julians were always Greens. Prince Gaius, of course, he's a prime supporter like his father and mother before him, and now he's got the emperor's favour he still chips in a fair amount.' Yeah; I knew that already. It was one of the things that was worrying me. 'Mind you, the Blues have their own gilt-edgers. The consul Vitellius, for example.'

Uh-huh. That I hadn't known. I didn't know Vitellius, either, but he had a reputation as a racing man. Not a very savoury one: a taker rather than a giver. If he was one of Rome's current top magistrates it was because he'd bought himself his seat in the chair. Mind you, that put him in good company. If 'good' isn't quite the right word.

'So how exactly are the Greens doing at the moment? Compared with their average, that is.'

Cascellius took a swallow of his wine. 'Okay. They had a few hiccups last year mid-season, mostly just bad luck, but they picked up later.'

'Hiccups?'

'They went down badly in Caesar's Victory and the Romans. Lead horse broke a trace in the first, the horses of the lead team were under par in the second. It happens. Nothing unusual.'

Maybe not, but the back of my neck prickled. 'Pegasus was driving in both?'

He glanced at me and frowned; like I say, Cascellius was no fool. 'Yeah. Yes, he was. But then he would be, wouldn't he? He was the lead.'

'Okay,' I said. 'Let's get back to Natalis. You say he's doing a good job.'

The suspicious look disappeared. 'Sure. He can afford to, with the money that's coming in, especially with Gaius on his side. He's brought the Greens on until the Blues can't compete: best drivers, best horses. He gets the cream from the prime studs in Africa and Sicily. Pays top prices so the Blues are shut out and have to go for second-best.'

'Uh-huh. What about Spanish horses?'

'They're good now, and they'll get better, but the Africans and Sicilians still have the edge. That's only my personal opinion, mind.'

I changed tack. 'How dangerous was Pegasus? To the other factions, I mean?'

'Lethal.' Cascellius sipped his wine. 'Oh, sure, he was only one driver with one team, but he was better than the Greens' second, and with that new horse of Cammius's he was unbeatable.'

'That'd be Polydoxus, right?'

'Right. The Greens aren't beaten easy. It'd come hard for them to go down in every race Pegasus ran in, even although they won the other six or seven on the day. That sort of thing builds up.'

'But if Pegasus didn't win every race? If he came in second to the Greens or the Blues on occasion, maybe because he fumbled a turn or let another guy through?'

'That would've made a difference, sure. It would've been the cumulative effect that would've done the damage. Not that I'd expect any different, myself. Pegasus was brilliant, but even the best drivers have their bad days, and no one can be hundred-per-cent certain of a winner. If they could then every bookie in Rome'd be out of business in a month.'

'Yeah.' My brain was buzzing. 'Right.' I topped up his cup. 'Okay. Now what about Sopilys?'

I'd thought the guy was relaxing, but that got me a guarded look. 'What about him?'

'He was one of the grooms, right?'

'Yeah.'

'And he was sacked. What for?'

Long silence. Finally, he shook his head. 'That I can't tell you, Corvinus. The Greens who come into the Cat are pretty close-mouthed, like Pinnius said. One day he was working at the stables, the next he wasn't. That's as far as I go.'

Bugger; if he didn't know for sure – and I wouldn't've put money on it – I'd bet he could make a good guess. However, the guy was being helpful and I didn't want to pressure him. 'You know where he is now?'

Cascellius was quiet for a long time. I thought it was reticence, but he was just thinking. 'He used to talk about a brother who was a loader down at Ostia. It's a long shot, but could be he's taken a job there.'

Long shot was right, but it was the only one I had, and Sopilys was one guy I had to talk to. 'Last question, friend, and then I'll let you get back to your vegetables.'

He shrugged. 'No problem, I'm in no hurry. Mammo's the wife's cousin. She'll handle both stalls, and we're never neither of us run off our feet. What's the question?'

'Not about the Greens or Pegasus. Or not directly. You happen to know where the Reds' boss lives? Rufrius Pudens? His house, not the Reds' stables?'

Again, I got the considering stare. Then he said carefully, 'You'd be wanting his wife, I'd assume. Felicula.'

Jupiter! I hadn't thought that angle would be public knowledge! But there again, maybe the Green team were only close-mouthed where racing and their own stables were concerned. It made me think about Pudens himself, though. If what his wife was up to

was that much in the public domain then the guy was
either totally blinkered or he couldn't care less. Either
way might be significant.

'Yeah,' I said, matching his tone. 'I might be, at
that.'

He cleared his throat. I'd put Cascellius down as
a family man with old-fashioned family values, and
I reckoned I hadn't been wrong. You could feel the
disapproval oozing out of him; also that he was doing
his best to hide it. A nice guy, Cascellius. Situations
like this, you usually got the leer or the tirade.

'He's on the Esquiline,' he said. 'Big house at the
top of Virbius.'

'Right. Thanks.' I hesitated. 'You, uh, know either
of them at all? Pudens or Felicula?'

'Not personally. I don't move in those sorts of
circles. I've seen them at the Games, sure, but remember I'm just a punter.'

'The lady goes too?'

'Never misses.'

Yeah, well, it was a stupid question, at that. If
Felicula had a thing about drivers – which from her
own track record I'd guess she did – then of course
she'd go. 'What's Pudens's background?'

'Plain-mantle. Where he's from I don't know.' Now
we'd moved back to racing Cascellius looked happier,
but the answer had a terseness about it that I didn't
understand. 'Africa. South Italy. Sicily maybe.' Like
Natalis; but there again I had the impression that a lot
of people in the racing world were from the big horse
districts. Maybe it was in the blood. 'He bought into

the Reds about the same time as Cammius took over the Whites.'

'He a driver or a businessman?'

'Businessman, definitely. If he's either.'

'Why "definitely"?'

'You've only got to look at him. He's no racing man, he's a clerk.'

'So why buy the Reds?'

'Mercury knows.' Cascellius shrugged and downed a mouthful of the Rhaetian. 'Probably he'd his reasons, but from the Reds' point of view it was a mistake.'

'Yeah? Why so?'

'Like I said, he's no racer. Not even a good business-man. The Reds are wallowing; they don't come in the first three one race in five. If it wasn't for Laomedon they'd be a joke.' Right. Laomedon. The Reds' lead driver and Felicula's ex-squire. 'Things get that bad, it's the faction master's fault.'

Uh-huh; even as a non-fan I could see that. And now I could account for the trace of contempt in the guy's voice. Cascellius was a Greens' supporter, and the Reds ran backstop for the Greens just as the Whites did for the Blues. If Pudens's team weren't pulling their weight then the Greens suffered too. And with the Pegasus/Polydoxus combination they'd have enough problems already.

Well, I'd got what I'd come for, or at least all I could take in at present, the morning was wearing on and I was itching to take a walk up on to the Esquiline, but we still had half the jug left and it would've been impolite to break away, especially after the guy had been so helpful. Besides, like I say one of my favourite pleasures is shooting the breeze over a jug. So we emptied it while we talked about the vegetable trade, family life and kids: he had six of them, not five after all, three boys three girls, in a tenement flat just inside the Subura. It sounded hell to me but he wasn't complaining.

'You need any more help, you know where I am, Corvinus,' he said as we shook hands before he went back to Mammo. 'I'd a lot of time for Pegasus as a driver. The Greens haven't been the same since they lost him. Good luck with the investigation.'

He wouldn't've taken any money – Cascellius's type never do – and I wouldn't've insulted the guy by offering it; but I had a word with the landlord and arranged for a complimentary jug of Rhaetian the next time he was in. Then I set off for the Virbian Incline.

8

I found Puden's house no problem. Like Cascellius had said, it was big, easily the biggest in the immediate area, and an address on the Esquiline isn't for those short of a gold piece or two. Which was odd: Cascellius had said that Pudens was a plain-mantle, and plain-mantles per se don't run to that size of property. The Roman social scene's broadened since old Julius opened up the Senate, sure, but all that means is that more new guys are climbing the ladder, and the values are still those of the old families at the top. These include having a purple stripe to your mantle, even if it's not the broad one a senior magistracy nets you. I'd've expected that Pudens, like at least two of his faction master colleagues, would've bought himself out of the plain-wool class years ago.

I knocked on the door: good oak panelling with brass nails. The slave who opened it was young and good-looking in a beefcakey way. He also wore a very natty red tunic that showed a lot of leg.

'Uh . . . the master at home?' I said. Chances were he wasn't, not at this time of day, and that was what I was hoping for: you can't barge in on a nest of conjugal felicity and ask to talk to the mistress privately about her extramarital sex life, which wasn't exactly what I had in mind but was the next thing to it.

''Fraid not, sir.' The guy was polite, anyway. 'He's at the stables.'

'How about the mistress?'

'Yes, sir. Only she's having her hair done at the moment. You don't mind waiting?'

'No problem. She doesn't know me: Marcus Valerius Corvinus.'

The slave's eyes flickered but neither his expression nor his tone changed. 'Very well, sir. I'll ask her if she's receiving. If you'd care to come in?'

He left me in the lobby, closed the door behind me and went off towards the atrium. I was impressed. Mistress of the house's beefcake-purchase or not – and I'd bet he'd been just that, unless Pudens exhibited certain unexpected proclivities – the kid's door-style couldn't be faulted, and for quality like that you pay through the nose. The lobby was impressive, too: big as a small room, with coloured marble panelling in the walls, a pricey bronze lamp-tree and a mosaic that covered a good chunk of the floor space. Not the usual hackneyed 'Beware-of-the-Dog' tat, either: a stage scene with musicians and dancing-girls that I'd bet hadn't come from a pattern book. Pretty good art work, what's more, in stones that were smaller than the standard type. All that meant a hefty price tag, but there was taste there as well, and a certain amount of originality. I was beginning to suspect that, if Felicula had had a hand in things, she might be rich but she was no low-class bubblehead.

The slave came back. 'The mistress will see you now, sir,' he said. 'If you'd care to follow me?'

We went into the atrium. The lady was in a chair by the pool, having her hair dressed by a maid. She was older than I thought she'd be – mid-thirties, maybe – but she was certainly a looker, in a hard, brassy way. Good body, too, what I could see of it under the silk mantle.

'Valerius Corvinus?' The voice fitted the looks: confident, brassy, with Aventine vowels that didn't take any prisoners. 'I'm pleased to meet you. Have a seat.' She turned to the slave. 'That'll be all, Decimus.' Cool and collected, with no overtones: beefcake the guy might be, but unless she'd been putting on an act for my benefit the relationship was straight mistress/servant. He bowed, pulled up a chair for me and left. 'You too, Melpomene. We can finish that later.' She waited until the maid had packed up her scissors, comb and curling-tongs and followed Decimus out.

I sat.

The lady adjusted the folds of her mantle; not nerves, I suspected, she just wanted to look her best. 'Now, Corvinus,' she said. 'I'm not going to pretend that I don't know why you're here. It's about Pegasus, isn't it?'

Well, that was direct enough. 'Yeah, it is,' I said.

'You'll notice that I'm not in mourning. You may find that a little callous, but Pegasus and I ended our affair some time ago. As far as I was concerned, anyway. I'm sorry he's dead, but I really don't think I can add to your knowledge of who killed him or why he died.'

I blinked. I'd been right about Felicula being no bubblehead. Aventine vowels or not, this was some smart and articulate lady. 'You, uh, seem pretty open about the relationship,' I said.

'It was no secret. If Gaius – that's my husband – didn't mind, which he didn't, then I don't see why I shouldn't be.'

'Right. Right.' I swallowed. 'Uh, you care to tell me exactly when and why it ended?'

'The when, slightly under a month ago. The why, no I wouldn't because it's none of your business.'

Well, that was me told. Still, she was within her rights. I shifted tack. 'Your husband didn't mind about Laomedon either?'

Pause; *long* pause, together with a look like someone might give a backed-up sewage drain. Finally, she said; 'You have been doing your homework, haven't you?' I didn't answer. 'No, he didn't mind. Nor did he mind about the man before Laomedon, and he won't mind about the next one, whoever he is. Gaius won't mind because he's a very nice man, a very nice man indeed, and he knows these affairs aren't important.' Jupiter! 'Let me tell you something, Corvinus, in the hopes that it'll satisfy your prurient curiosity. Gaius is my second husband, and I may not love him as much as he does me but I am very fond of him. I certainly wouldn't see him hurt, at any price. On the other hand, he is almost twice my age and not particularly well-preserved. That leads to certain discrepancies which we are both adult enough to acknowledge; hence the Laomedons and the Pegasuses.'

'Both racing drivers. I did wonder, lady, whether that might not be the reason why your husband bought into the Reds when he's no racing man himself. Would that have been on your suggestion?'

She flushed; the first sign of annoyance she'd shown. But then I was glad to see she could be rattled after all. 'I find that rather offensive, Corvinus,' she said. 'No, the suggestion wasn't mine, although I admit it's made things easier. Gaius has never been interested in racing, but he has led a very sheltered life and he has always been aware of the fact. A humdrum existence doesn't preclude the formation of fantasies, in fact it may positively encourage them. It's no detraction from my husband, quite the reverse, to say that given the opportunity he might choose to inject a little colour into his life before it's too late to do so. No pun intended. Becoming master of a faction – and marrying me – has served that function.'

Gods! I was dealing with a brain here and no mistake! This one might even have Perilla beat! 'Marrying you?'

She lowered her eyes, but I didn't miss the smile. 'I'm not exactly hideous,' she said mildly. 'And I am thirty-three years his junior. Also my background was . . . hardly humdrum.'

I remembered the mosaic in the lobby. That, and the low-class accent which she made no attempt to hide, plus the still slim body, all added up. 'You were on the stage?'

Her head came up. She was definitely smiling now. 'You're being generous, Corvinus. Thank you. No, I never played in mime, but I wasn't a prostitute either, if that was what you were thinking. Something in between. Before my first marriage I was a dancer.'

Uh-huh; that would explain Pudens's plain mantle. She'd be a Roman citizen, sure – the marriage wouldn't be legal otherwise – but the old prejudices still held, and any guy marrying into the entertainer class could whistle for a stripe, however much money he had.

'So what's your husband's background?' I said. 'Just out of interest.'

'He was in corn. Not a shipper, a broker.' She hesitated. 'He had a business in Panormus before he sold out and moved to Rome.'

Panormus. Sicily again. It was funny how Sicily kept turning up. 'And how did you meet?'

'My first husband – his name was Turranius and he was in the building trade – had died a few months previously. We had a mutual friend. It developed from there.'

Yeah; I could see how that might make sense. I didn't want to run Felicula down, or stereotype her, but the scenario was common enough to write itself: retired businessman fresh in from the provinces with stars in his eyes, nubile young widow looking for a bankroll to hook on to, pushy friend acting as go-between. It happened all the time. And why shouldn't it? Both parties got what they wanted: the girl had security and a sugar-daddy who'd pay the clothes and jewellery bills, the guy got an active bed partner who'd liven up his failing years and turn his septuagenarian pals green with envy. The sexual bit wasn't too rare either. Certainly, on her showing, anyway, the arrangement seemed to be happy enough. 'Okay. Tell me more about Laomedon,' I said.

I'd caught her off-balance. 'There's nothing to tell,' she said. 'He was my lover before Pegasus, that's all. We broke up six or seven months ago.'

'Your doing or his?'

The frost was back. 'Again, that's private, Corvinus. However, just to show you that I'm not totally devoid of vanity I'll admit that it was mine.'

Yeah; that fitted, and I would've guessed as much even if she hadn't told me: it chimed with what Typhon had said, and the whole Laomedon/Pegasus needle relationship indicated that the guy hadn't been too pleased about being replaced. Besides, this was a lady who did the dropping rather than one who was dropped. 'What's he like?'

'As a person?' She shrugged. 'A body. A very impressive one, mind you, which is why I took up with him, but that is as far as Laomedon goes. He doesn't have intellect, he has instincts.'

'He hated Pegasus, or at least that's the impression I'm getting. You think he could've killed him?'

She didn't answer at once, and I could see she was giving the question very careful thought indeed. Finally, she said; 'Yes. It's possible, under certain circumstances.'

'Such as?'

'On the racetrack, certainly. Especially if the opportunity arose suddenly; if he were in a position to force a bad crash, for example, with no danger to himself. Laomedon would do that without a second thought.'

'How about knifing the guy in the back in an alley?'

'Perhaps. As I say, Laomedon operates by instinct. Imagine a big cat – a lion or a panther – stalking a marked animal, waiting his chance and leaping. That is Laomedon. Yes, again it's possible. And the fact that the knife was in the back doesn't signify. For Laomedon the important thing would be the death, not how he achieved it.'

Well, that was pretty concise, not to say providing more proof, if I needed it, that there was a brain inside that beautiful head; and although I hadn't met the guy yet it rang true. Apropos of which: 'If I wanted to find him,' I said, 'apart from at the stables, how would I go about it?'

'When our affair began he rented a first-floor flat above a honey-seller's in a tenement on the south side of the old Flaminian Circus. Whether or not he still does I can't tell you, but I would imagine he's still there.' Her voice was matter-of-fact: she could've been giving me information about a casual acquaintance rather than an ex-lover. 'He had no reason to move, and he doesn't live at the stables. Also there's a cookshop-cum-wineshop next door that you could try. He goes there sometimes in the evenings.'

'Uh-huh.' I paused. 'Can you think of anyone else

who'd want Pegasus dead? Or a reason for killing him?
From the private side?'

'No. I told you. Our relationship was purely physical, and when it ended we had no further contact.
Now, Corvinus, I have things to do this afternoon,
so if you've quite finished perhaps you could allow
me to do them.'

A brush-off, but a polite one. I stood up. 'Sure, lady.
Thanks very much. You've been very helpful.'

'Don't mention it.' She was smilingly demure. 'Incidentally, I have a favour to ask of you.'

'Yeah?'

'No doubt you'll want to talk to my husband. I'd
ask you not to bully him, please. He does try so hard
to be the decisive world-weary faction master, but it
is a very fragile shell and you could break it easily. As
I said, I wouldn't want Gaius hurt, at any price. You
understand me?'

'Yeah,' I said. 'Yeah, I understand. I'll be careful.'
I hesitated. 'Uh, just one more question. The guys at
the stables said that Pegasus had been getting fixes
over the past couple of months. Lead sheets with a
flying dagger scratched on them. He ever bring up
the subject with you?'

'He told me about them, yes.'

'They worry him at all?'

'A little, although certainly not as much as they
would have worried Laomedon, say. Pegasus wasn't
unduly superstitious, but all drivers are leery of curses
to some extent. It would be unreasonable to expect
otherwise.'

'He didn't have any idea who might be sending them?'

'None at all. Not that I know of, anyway. Fixes aren't exactly uncommon in the racing business, Corvinus, especially where the top drivers are concerned. It isn't quite a case of familiarity breeding contempt, but any driver who devotes too much attention to them is bound to find his performance suffers, and most at least try to put them out of their minds.'

'Uh-huh.' Well, that was that. 'Thanks again, Felicula. I'm sorry to have disturbed you.'

'Not at all.'

I left.

So; what now? Sopilys was a definite promising lead, but even if he was working at the docks it was sixteen miles to Ostia, I'd need a horse to get there, and by the time I arrived it'd be time to head back again. Besides, I had my own Ostian contact who could trace him faster than I could. I hadn't seen Agron for quite a while, but he was still comfortably married to the Alexandrian boat-builder's daughter, his kid-count was up to five, and what he wouldn't know about the Ostian docks scene you could write on a sandal-strap and forget. When I got back home I could send a skivvy and save myself a lot of grief and wasted effort. Sopilys was someone I really had to talk to.

So was Laomedon. Even so, although there was still a fair chunk of the afternoon left I didn't particularly relish another trip over to the Mars Field side of town. The sky was clouding over again, too: I hadn't been lucky with the weather. Enough for one day. I set off for the Caelian and home.

On the way, I thought about that conversation with Felicula. She'd been helpful, sure, more than helpful, but I still wondered. First of all, ex-dancer or not the lady had a top-notch brain, and she was as cool as a Riphaean winter. Second, I only had her word for it – her very convenient word – that she and Pegasus hadn't still been an item at the time of his death; ditto for the fact that Pudens was a complaisant husband, both where Pegasus and Laomedon were concerned. Sure, that could well be true – I hadn't met the guy yet, so I had nothing to set against it – but on the other hand the lady could be spinning me a line: complaisant husbands aren't too plentiful in Rome, and the fact that when the affair with Laomedon started the guy had moved into non-faction accommodation might be significant. The warning – and it had been a warning – not to lean too hard on the Reds' faction master when I did meet him was ambiguous, too: yeah, she could be genuinely fond of him, but the request, bolstering up what would be a natural reticence in discussing the lady's amorous activities with her husband, could equally be an attempt to head off some embarrassing questions. Third, when I'd suggested her own ex Laomedon as a likely killer she'd practically fallen over herself to back up the theory.

So Felicula, much though I'd liked her, was most definitely still in the running. Why she would've done it – or had it done – was a separate issue. I doubted whether the motive was simple jealousy. There hadn't been any indication, so far anyway, that Pegasus was tom-catting – quite the contrary, if his feud with Laomedon was anything to go by – and having met the lady I was ready to take her at her own valuation. Also, a rich bubblehead who got her kicks from squiring one of Rome's top drivers might've had him stabbed out of pique if he'd given her the brush-off, but Felicula was no bubblehead; if she decided to kill someone, it'd be for a much less simple reason.

The rain started before I was halfway through the Carinae. By the time I hit Head of Africa I was soaked. I could've called in at Mother's, but why make matters worse?

Not that I knew at that point, of course, that even Mother's was preferable to what was waiting for me at home.

9

Bathyllus had the wine all right this time, but he was looking distinctly subdued: there was something . . . *internal* about his manner as he handed me the cup that just didn't square with the sarky, supercilious ray of sunshine that we knew and loved.

'Uh, hey, Bathyllus,' I said as I handed over my wet mantle. 'You ill or something, pal?'

He compressed his lips. 'No, sir.'

'A bereavement? Anything like that?' I didn't know much about Bathyllus's family, although he'd mentioned a brother in Thessalonica once. Not that I could imagine the little bald-head having anything as messy as a childhood. My guess was that the brother was a blind and he'd sprung full-formed from a broom closet, like Athene from the head of Zeus.

'No, sir.'

'Uh-huh. So what's the trouble? You lose your truss in the wash? The Watch on the point of nailing you as the Caelian Flasher? One of the kitchen maids is pregnant?'

He coloured up and gave me the ghost of a sniff, but the guy's heart obviously wasn't in it. 'No, sir. None of these things. Nothing at all, in fact.' He folded the mantle carefully, avoiding my eye. 'Did you enjoy your day?'

'Yeah. Yeah, it was okay.' I frowned as I moved towards the atrium. Jupiter, this was bad! I couldn't even wind him up any more! The gods knew what was bugging the little guy, but things were going beyond a joke. Still, if he wouldn't confide he wouldn't confide, and I've never believed in coming the hard-hearted master. 'Perilla at home?'

'Hmm?'

'Perilla. My wife. The mistress.'

'She's working, sir. In her study.'

'Fine, fine. Give me the jug, Bathyllus.' I paused. 'The *jug*, sunshine. Okay?'

I took it from his nerveless fingers and went upstairs. Perilla was at her desk with a writing tablet and half a dozen serious book-rolls arranged tidily in front of her. She looked up, smiled and lifted her chin for the welcome-home kiss. I set the jug and the wine cup on the table by the reading couch and stretched out.

'Bathyllus,' I said.

The smile faded. She put down her stylus. 'I don't know what's wrong with him, Marcus. He's been roaming the house like a ghost, you have to say everything twice, and he broke an ornament this morning. That little glass dolphin I bought in Antioch.'

I winced. Not because of the dolphin; I'd never liked that thing. But Bathyllus with a feather duster was pure poetry in motion. I couldn't've been more shocked if he'd taken a scrubbing-brush to the wall paintings. 'He won't talk to you either?'

She shook her head. 'Not a word. Do you think we should call in a doctor?'

'No. The guy isn't ill, as far as I can see. He just has something on his mind, that's all.' I took a swig of the wine. 'But we can't go on like this. The poor bastard's suffering.'

'So what do we do?'

I shrugged. 'The gods know. Whatever it is, it's serious. And it isn't getting any better. We have to find out.'

'How? He won't tell us.'

'Okay. So maybe one of the other lads can.'

Perilla chewed her lip. 'Is that ethical? If Bathyllus doesn't want to confide then we can't just go behind his back.'

'The hell with that. We can't help him unless we know the problem.'

I got up and went to the window. Perilla's study looked down on to the garden, which was the self-elected province of smart-as-paint Alexis. The rain had stopped, and sure enough there was the guy himself engaged in two-spit-double-mulching, or whatever Varro's *Gardener's Year* recommended for late March. If my young horticulturist had a second name it would be Conscientious.

'Hey, Alexis!' I shouted. His head lifted. 'Up here! The mistress's study, spit-spot!' He gave me an answering wave and left his spade in mid-mulch.

Perilla was still looking doubtful. 'It does seem too much like prying,' she said.

'Prying nothing, lady.' I filled my cup from the jug:

being in Perilla's study with all these books glaring down at me always gives me a nervous thirst. 'We have a seriously disturbed major-domo here. Everything's going fairly smoothly at the moment but it's just a matter of time before the place starts to fall apart. It's my simple duty as head of the household.'

'Well.' She sighed. 'I suppose you're right. How was your day, incidentally?'

'I'll tell you later. We've got more important things to think about at present than murder.'

We twiddled our thumbs while Alexis, presumably, washed the layer of topsoil off himself and dragged a comb through his hair: I'd said I wanted him spit-spot, but the guy had his own standards, and leaving half the Caelian on the stairs in his wake didn't play any part in them. Besides, even in his present weakened state Bathyllus would've had the guy's guts for truss strings. Finally, he knocked and came in.

'Yes, sir.'

There was no point beating about the bush. 'What's up with Bathyllus, pal?' I asked.

He looked at his feet and shuffled them. 'Er—'

Jupiter on a see-saw! 'Come on, Alexis! You know! Spit it out! That's an order!'

The guy swallowed painfully. 'I . . . ah . . .' His Adam's-apple bobbed again.

I was really alarmed now. Alexis was one of the best, hardly a slave at all. We had a good relationship going. If he was that chary about spilling the beans then the situation was Serious with a capital S. 'Look, whatever it is, however bad it is, it can be fixed,' I said. 'But we can't do anything until we know what we're up against.'

'Oh, no, sir.' Alexis coloured. 'It's nothing like that. It's just that he's . . . ah . . .' – he swallowed again – 'Bathyllus is in love, sir.'

I nearly dropped my cup. Beside me I heard Perilla gasp. 'He's *what?*'

Alexis was as red as one of his own radishes. 'With the housekeeper next door,' he said.

Oh, holy gods! '*Bathyllus?*'

'Yes, sir.' He glanced reproachfully at Perilla who was having a choking fit. 'It isn't funny, madam.'

Yeah; I'd forgotten that the kid had been smitten himself not all that far back. I'd wondered how the affair was going, but how Alexis spent his occasional free hours was none of my concern. I managed to keep my face straight.

It wasn't easy, mind.

'Titus Petillius's housekeeper?' I said; Petillius was our neighbour, a hefty Etrurian very big in the mantle-dyeing business. 'She's in her eighties!'

'No, sir. The new one. She arrived only a few days ago. Her name's Tyndaris.'

Oh, joy in the morning! The little chubby chap with the wings and archery set didn't put off, did he? 'What's she like?'

He hesitated. 'Large, sir.'

'"Large"?' Perilla was choking again. I passed her my wine cup and she swallowed.

'She's a middle-aged lady, sir, and quite . . . impos-ing.'

'How did this start?'

'Bathyllus went round to borrow some metal polish, sir.'

'I see.' Yeah; that was our Bathyllus. From such trivial beginnings do matters of great import spring. 'And is it . . . ah . . . reciprocal?'

'No, sir. That's the problem.'

'But she does know? That the little guy's' – I had to press my lips together for a moment – 'smitten?'

'No, sir. He hasn't talked to her since. He sent the polish back by one of the kitchen boys.'

I recovered my wine cup from Perilla – the lady had control of herself now, but she was still looking pretty pink – drained it and poured a refill. Then I sat back. Jupiter! I never thought I'd see the day! Forget flying pigs: Bathyllus in love merited a flock of six-legged polka-dot elephants. 'So what do we do?' I said.

They both looked at me.

'We help him, of course, Marcus,' Perilla said. 'He's obviously shy.'

Venus in a bathtub! 'Bathyllus? *Shy?* Lady, I've seen that little bugger chew up an ex-consul and spit out the pips just because he didn't wipe his sandals at the door!'

'Ex-consuls are not women.'

'He doesn't approve of women.'

'He clearly approves of this one.'

'That's a fat lot of good if he doesn't tell her!'

'Exactly.'

I frowned: maybe it was me, but that last little bit

of stichomythia sounded a bit of an anacoluthon. Or whatever. 'Run that past me again, lady.'

'It's obvious, dear. We have to bolster his self-confidence. Make him believe he can succeed. Perhaps engineer another meeting when the time is ripe.'

'Perilla, we're talking about Bathyllus! The bugger's got so much self-confidence he could walk across the Tiber without using a bridge!'

'Not where women are concerned. I keep telling you but you don't listen.'

'Men, women, what's the difference?'

Perilla sighed. 'Just trust me, Marcus. All right?'

I took another swallow of wine. 'All right. Have it your own way.'

'Thank you.' She turned to Alexis. The guy had taken to examining his boots again. 'We have to plan this very carefully, Alexis. Do you have any contacts in the Petillius household? Female ones?'

'Lysias has been seeing one of the laundry maids, madam.' Lysias was our coachman, and it was news to me. Life understairs was clearly a world in itself that I hadn't known existed. Not a very savoury one, either. Jupiter! I felt like we'd prised the lid off an Alexandrian bodice-ripper here!

The lady didn't bat an eyelid. 'Good. She may come in useful. Anyone else?'

'It's a bachelor establishment, but there're some female kitchen staff. I could ask Meton if he—'

'Not Meton,' Perilla said firmly. I nodded. Quite right; the further away that anarchic bastard was kept from this business the better, because he and Bathyllus loathed each other's guts and tossing a spanner into the works of the little guy's blossoming love-life would make his year. 'We'll just have to rely on the maid. What's her name?'

'I don't know, madam. I could find out if—' He cast a wistful eye on the door.

'Later,' Perilla said. 'Now, how do we bolster Bathyllus's confidence? That's partly your job, I think, Marcus. Masculine bonding.'

I blinked. 'What? How the hell do I do that, lady?'

'To begin with, you can stop making silly jokes about his physical size, his baldness and his truss. Encourage him to talk about things he's interested in.'

'Perilla, the little bald-head isn't—' I caught her glare and started again. 'Bathyllus isn't interested in anything but buffing up bronzes.'

'Have you ever asked him?'

'Uh . . . no, not exactly, but—'

'Then how do you know?'

Gods alive! I didn't deserve this! And life wouldn't be the same without its bit of Bathyllus-baiting. 'Lady, he's *Bathyllus*! If he ever gets deified he'll be the god of staff rotas! He hasn't got time for anything else!'

'Except now, presumably, next door's housekeeper.'

I groaned; you don't argue with Perilla, not in this mood. 'Okay. I'll try.'

'Good. Well done.' She smiled. 'That should serve as the first phase. And, Alexis, perhaps you could ask Lysias to have his girlfriend drop a few hints. Simply to break the ground.'

'Yes, madam.' The guy didn't look comfortable. 'Certainly, madam. And speaking of breaking ground—'
Another wistful glance, this time at the window.

'Very well.' Perilla glanced at me. 'I think we've done all we can at present, haven't we, Marcus?'

'Uh . . . yeah. Yeah, more or less.'

'You will remember, dear? About the baldness and so on?'

'Yeah. I'll remember.'

'Then we'll go down and begin putting the plan into operation.'

'What – now?'

'You were the one who insisted that something had to be done quickly. Oh, and Marcus . . .'

'Yeah?'

'No mention of the woman to Bathyllus, please. Or any allusion to her. The poor man's embarrassed enough already without having to suffer your heavy-handed jokes.'

I managed a sickly grin. This was going to be difficult, I could tell that now. 'Okay, fine,' I said. 'Let's get it over with.'

Lover-boy was standing in the atrium when we came down. Not doing anything; just standing. His eyes focused and he saw us. Perilla dug me in the ribs.

I cleared my throat. 'Uh . . . how's it going, Bathyllus?'

'Dinner will be another hour, sir. We hadn't expected you back quite so soon.'

'That's okay. No hurry.' I stretched out on my usual couch and set the jug and cup down on the table. Perilla lay down opposite. We needed a touch of strategy here. I pointed to the little marble statue of an old woman and her dog that we'd picked up in Athens and that now stood on a plinth by the pool and said casually; 'Hecale's looking a bit dull, pal. You want to give her a rub?'

'Yes, of course, sir.' He pulled a cloth from his belt – Bathyllus always carries one, just in case he meets an unexpected smear – and started in on the dog's back.

I gave it half a minute or so, then I said; 'Hey, Bathyllus, you remember Flatworm Lentulus?'

'Yes, sir.' Jupiter! I'd heard more life in a funeral oration!

'I bumped into him today in Market Square. We got talking about major-domos and I bet him a jug that you didn't have any hobbies or interests.' I noticed that Perilla had put her hand over her eyes and was moving her head slowly from side to side but I ignored her. 'That right?'

The cloth paused. 'Actually, sir, I play draughts. And I collect beetles.'

'Uh . . . beetles?'

'Yes, sir. I have eighty-three.'

'That's . . . uh . . . fascinating, litt— Bathyllus.' I took a fortifying swig of Setinian. 'Eighty-three beetles, eh? Quite a collection. What do you feed them on?'

'Oh, I don't feed them, sir. They're dead. I push pins through them and fix them on to sheets of papyrus. Or simply glue the smaller ones down. Then I label them.'

'What the hell do you do that for?'

That got me a glare from Perilla. 'According to Aristotle, Marcus,' she said, 'there are over a hundred varieties of beetle. I don't believe they've ever been properly classified. Bathyllus, that is really interesting!'

'I find it so, madam.' He moistened the cloth with his tongue and moved on to the dog's foreleg. 'Of course, many are quite different in colour or size, but you would be amazed how often on closer inspection identical examples turn out to be no such thing. Naturally, it's difficult to tell when they're scuttling around, particularly the very small ones, but once they're stuck down the individual characteristics positively leap out at you.'

'Right. Right.' I downed a gulp of wine. 'Now about draughts—'

'In fact, there have been occasions when I have myself thought that two specimens were completely identical, only to find on much closer inspection that they differed in one tiny particular. The respective lengths of the thorax and prothorax, perhaps, or the shape of the head.'

'Bathyllus—'

'The gem of my collection is an extremely large scarab beetle which was passed on to me by a friend who came across it on one of the Egyptian grain barges. The elytra and pronotum have a beautiful and very unusual golden sheen, while the mandibles are slightly less developed than one might expect on a scarab—'

'Bathyllus!'

'—although I haven't really had much opportunity to compare many examples. Yes, sir?'

'Uh . . . I think maybe that's enough polishing for the present, sunshine. Hecale's looking a lot brighter.'

'*Marcus!*'

That was Perilla. I ignored her: head-of-household duty was one thing, but if the lady thought I was going to sit through an hour-long lecture on bugs she was whistling through her ear.

'Ah. Yes.' Bathyllus looked down at the cloth in his hand as if it had magically appeared. 'Certainly, sir. I'll . . . go and check on the progress of dinner.'

'You do that, pal,' I said.

He wandered out. There was a frigid silence. Finally, Perilla said; 'Marcus Valerius Corvinus!'

'Yeah, yeah, I know.' I shifted uncomfortably on the couch. 'But if I'd let him rabbit on a minute longer my head would've dropped off. And given the slightest encouragement he'd've brought out all eighty-six of the fucking things and given us their life histories.'

'Eighty-three. And don't swear.'

'Whatever.'

'He was talking and you stopped him. Now that wasn't very clever, was it?'

I took a defensive swig of wine. 'Great. So we fix up a meeting with this Tyndaris and lover-boy out there whispers sweet nothings about beetles in her ear.'

'I found what he was saying very interesting.'

'Yeah, no doubt. But I'll bet this Tyndaris doesn't sleep with a copy of Aristotle's *Natural History* under her pillow.'

'That isn't the point. Bathyllus has to be weaned into conversing, and getting him to talk about his interests is the first step. Marcus, we discussed this!'

'Maybe so, but at the time I didn't know the guy was a crypto bugs nut. Where beetles are concerned you're on your own, lady. I'll do my best in other ways.'

Perilla sighed. 'All right, dear. Perhaps under the circumstances you should leave Bathyllus's interests to me. But you will be careful with him? More careful than you usually are, anyway?'

'Sure. No problem.'

'Fine. I suppose that's as much as we can reasonably expect.' I had my mouth open to protest, but she went on: 'So what happened this morning? Did you talk to the Greens' faction master?'

I told her about the interview with Natalis and the follow-on with Felicula. 'The Reds' driver Laomedon is looking a prime suspect. Certainly he's got the strongest motive, and characterwise he fits like a glove.'

'You haven't seen him yet, have you?'

'No. I thought maybe I'd call round at the Reds' stables tomorrow, talk to him and the faction boss Pudens. Also I'd like a word with the Whites' second, Uranius. He's an outside bet, sure, but I can't afford to write anyone off this early.'

'You think Pegasus was involved in something underhand?'

I freshened up my wine cup. 'I'd give you good odds, lady. When he was with the Greens, certainly, despite what Natalis said; maybe later, too, at least in embryo. If I can find this guy Sopilys we might be a bit further forward as to the what. It's too late today, but I'll send one of the lads out to Ostia first thing tomorrow morning, see if Agron can help.'

'You don't think perhaps Sopilys could be the killer himself?'

Yeah; I'd mulled that one over a couple of times. 'He had a grudge, sure. But he'd already punched the guy's lights out, so I'd guess he regarded the account as settled. Besides, Ostia's a fair way off. He'd've had to come special.'

'It depends on the strength of the grudge, surely. On what it involved.'

I nodded. 'True. Like I say, I'm not ruling anyone out. We're not at that stage yet.'

Bathyllus softshoed back in. I half expected the little guy to be carrying his bug collection, but he wasn't. I breathed again.

'A message from Meton, sir,' he said. 'He can advance dinner to ten minutes' time, if that would suit you.'

Well, at least he was sounding on top of things now. That little baring of the soul seemed to have done some good, anyway. Maybe Perilla was right. I stood up. 'Sure. We'll come straight through.'

'Very well, sir.' He hesitated. 'That scarab—'

But he wasn't getting a second chance. No way. I was already past him and heading for the dining-room. Bodice-rippers are one thing, but entomology before dinner is the complete pits.

IO

Next morning after breakfast I gave Alexis instructions on how to find Agron and what I needed from him and sent him off to Ostia: Alexis, because as well as being smart, which Lysias isn't, the kid can sit a horse without falling off, and that's more than most of my lot can. I'd've preferred to send one of the littermen – these lardballs can always do with the exercise – but a thirty-two-mile round trip on foot would've been pushing things and I wanted the message to arrive before next Winter Festival.

Meanwhile I set out myself for Mars Field and the stables; the Whites first, because they were nearest. I was lucky. Cement-Features was on the gate, and he recognised me. Not that that helped too much where the treatment was concerned; it just meant the suspicious look was more personal.

'The boss is down at the racetrack,' he said.

'No problem, pal.' I put on my best smile. 'I was looking for Uranius. He around?'

'Maybe.'

Jupiter! This coy secrecy could get on your nerves really quickly! 'You care to come down on one side of the issue or the other, friend?' I said. 'Or should I just pant with the uncertainty of not knowing?'

That got me a long, measuring stare while Cement-Features chewed his lip. 'You want to talk with Uranius, then I got to clear it with Hesper,' he said at last.

'Fine with me, sunshine. I'll wait here, shall I?'

But I was talking to a closed and bolted gate. I kicked my heels for a good five minutes before it opened again and Hesper himself came out. He stood back to let me through.

'How's it going, Corvinus?'

'Not bad.'

'You talk to Sopilys yet?'

'Uh-uh. Still trying to trace him. I found the Black Cat, though. Thanks for the lead.'

He grunted. 'Sisyphus says you want to talk to Uranius.'

'Who the hell's Sisyphus?'

'That's me.' Cement-Features was glowering away in the background. 'You want to make something of it?'

'Uh . . . no. Not at all. Good name, good name.' I turned back to Hesper. 'No big deal. It's just for the sake of completeness. Is he around?'

'Yeah. But he's with the horses. I'm too busy just now to nursemaid you like the boss said but I'll take you to the common-room and send him over, okay?'

'Fair enough.' Gods alive! You'd think I was just itching for a chance to poison the brutes' feed. Or maybe Hesper thought I could put a hex on them just by being in the same stall.

'Follow me, then.'

We went the same way as before, only this time not so far. He took me up the steps of one of the barrack blocks, opened a door and showed me in.

They certainly looked after their own in the factions. The common-room was just that: a big room with stools, tables and benches, even a bar counter at the far end, although there was no one behind it. Four or five guys were shooting dice at one of the tables. They gave me suspicious looks, but when they saw Hesper behind me they went back to their game.

'Okay, Corvinus,' Hesper said. 'You'll be fine here. I'll send Uranius over and join you as soon as I'm free.'

I shrugged. 'Suits me, pal. Whatever you like.'

Hesper nodded to the dice school and went out.

I chose a table as far as I could from the dice players – they were ignoring me anyway – and sat down. It was a good ten minutes before the door opened again and a little guy like a monkey walked in.

'Valerius Corvinus?' he mumbled.

'Yeah.'

'Name's Uranius. You wanted to talk to me.' He sat down. Monkey was right; the guy was clean-shaven, but everywhere else was covered by black hair so thick you could've used him for a doormat. The other thing I noticed was that he had no presence at all, none. The dice players hadn't even looked up.

'That's right,' I said. 'About Pegasus.'

I caught a flicker in his eyes as he sat down facing me. Yeah, well; he'd have to be a real fool not to realise he figured somewhere in the line of suspects.

'I didn't kill him.'

'I'm not saying you did.' I was mild. 'I just want to see the guy from your angle, that's all.'

'He was a bastard.'

Well, that was straight enough. I hadn't expected him to come out quite so strong, mind. 'No surprises there, friend. What kind of bastard, exactly?'

He put his hands together and bunched them. I'd been wrong about his having hair all over: there was a slave brand burned into his right forearm, and that the hair didn't cover. 'He treated me like dirt. You don't do that to your second, specially when you've taken his place as lead. You'd've thought the team hadn't had a first driver until he showed up. Ten years I've raced with the Whites, six as leader. Sure, I haven't notched up many wins, but I know my business, I'm good at it and I've got a record of placings. Pegasus arrives and it's six years out the window.' The hands gripped each other hard. 'All that's fact. You could've got it from anyone, but I'm telling you myself up-front. I've nothing to hide.'

'Yeah. Right.' I indicated the slave brand, delicately. 'By the way, you . . . uh . . .' I started again. 'That still valid, or have you bought yourself out? If you don't mind my asking?'

'It's valid.' Uh-huh. Interesting. 'I don't blame Cammius, mind; he had to jump at the chance of Pegasus when he was offered, and the man was a first-rate driver. Better than me, I'll admit it, better than anyone else on the sand just now. But he'd've wrecked the Whites from the inside, sooner or later. I saw it, Cario saw it, only Cammius wouldn't listen.'

'Cario?'

Silence. Finally he said; 'The boss's son. You haven't met him?'

'Uh-uh. I didn't know he existed.'

'He exists, all right. Have a word with Cario, Corvinus. He'll tell you about Pegasus.'

'Yeah. Yeah, I might just do that.' I hesitated. 'Uh . . . don't get me wrong, pal, but I assume you were here the afternoon Pegasus was killed? Just to clear things up, you understand?'

Another silence; a longer one, this time. Uranius had been talking normally, but now there was a definite shift in his eyes. 'Yes. That's right,' he said.

I kept my face expressionless: if the guy was as bad a driver as he was a liar then come the new season the Whites really had problems. However, there was no point arguing. 'Fine. And you wouldn't know who he was planning to meet at the wineshop?'

The eyes widened, then flicked away from mine for an instant. 'Was he planning to meet someone?'

'Yeah. I think so.'

'Then no. The answer's no.'

The door opened and he turned towards it with obvious relief: Hesper, back on nursemaid patrol. I stood up.

'It's okay,' Hesper said. 'Take your time.'

'Oh, I'd finished.' I glanced at Uranius. 'Unless you've anything else you'd like to tell me, pal?'

The Whites' new top driver shook his head. He was staring at his hands as if he thought maybe they might take an independent line from his brain, and above the sprouting black hairs the tips of his ears were pink. 'No,' he mumbled. 'Nothing else.'

Hesper gave him a sharp glance, then shrugged. 'Fine. I'll take you back to the gate, Corvinus.'

'Thanks for your help, pal,' I said to Uranius, but there was no answer. We left him sitting.

Hesper was frowning as we walked back. I kept the pace slow, because the guy obviously had something on his mind and was wondering whether to spill it. Finally he did.

'You give Uranius a bad time back there?' he said.

'Not particularly.'

He grunted. 'Looked like it to me.' I said nothing. 'Corvinus, I've known Uranius for years. He's a strange guy, deeper than you'd think to look at him. He has his moods but he's a fine driver. Not great, but competent. And he's straight, straight as a rule. I just want to make sure you have that clear.'

We'd stopped. Over by the stables they were mucking out again. 'He told me he was here the afternoon Pegasus was murdered,' I said. 'Was he?'

The frown deepened. Hesper opened his mouth to say something, then he changed his mind and laughed instead. 'Hold on. That was three days ago, right?'

'Right.'

'No, he wasn't here.' Then, before I could speak: 'He wasn't killing Pegasus either, though. He was nowhere near Iugarius.'

'Then why the hell should he lie about it?'

Hesper was grinning. 'I told you. The guy's deeper

than he looks, and he gets embarrassed easy. Four times a month, races permitting, he sings with an amateur glee club down on the Aventine. We used to give him a lot of stick about it, but it's important to him and the lads've accepted that. Admitting it to a stranger would be different.'

'And three days ago would be one of the days?'

'Right. When Pegasus was knifed Uranius was busy singing three-part harmony with his musical pals. So lay off him.'

I grinned. Jupiter! A singing driver! Well, I'd've lied about that myself. 'You happen to know where this glee club hang out?' I said. 'Just for the record?'

'Sure. They meet in a tenement flat next to the Temple of Queen Juno. Tenant's name's Marcus Silvius. He's the baritone.'

I made a mental note. It would check out, sure it would: it was too screwy not to. 'Fine. Thanks, Hesper.'

'Don't mention it. And don't mention it to Uranius, either, if you talk to him again. If he knew I'd told you the poor guy wouldn't know where to put his face.'

'You've got it.' We carried on walking. 'One last thing. Uranius mentioned a guy called Cario.'

'Right. The boss's son.'

'He wouldn't be around at present, would he?'

'No. But if you want to talk to him you'll find him at the Circus. He and Cammius'll be there all day, finalising arrangements for the Megalenses.'

We'd almost reached the gate. Cement-Features –

I couldn't think of him as Sisyphus – got up from his stool and stood glowering.

'Thanks again, pal,' I said to Hesper.

'No problem.'

We shook and I set off up the road towards the Reds' compound.

On the way I thought about Uranius.

He hadn't struck me as the murdering type, sure. Still, like Hesper had said, there was more going on inside that monkey's head of his than appeared on the surface, even allowing for the lie about being on site the afternoon Pegasus had been killed. He hadn't liked that question about who the guy had been meeting, for a start: there'd been something screwy there, although I couldn't put my finger on exactly what it was, and if Uranius was as straight as the stables master claimed then there shouldn't've been. I'd docketed that for future reference.

The fact that he was still a slave was significant too. A lot of the guys in the racing business – drivers included – are slaves bought and trained by the faction bosses, and most of them stay like that. However, for a lead driver there's always the possibility of a win – or maybe a series of wins, depending on the race and the drivers' prize money – netting him enough to buy himself back; after which time, of course, he can claim lead driver's wages from the faction. Buying your freedom's a watershed. Sure, faction bosses are usually happy to regard any prize money won by a slave as coming into the traditional 'pocket-money' category – what in a normal household would be covered by tips, Winter Festival cash and the like, and which may, if he's lucky, eventually mount up to enough for the guy to buy his freedom – but technically any money earned by a slave is his master's property, and they wouldn't be human if they didn't take advantage of it, at least to dock the slave of a percentage. Especially since in the process they're staving off the evil day when their number-one driver buys his independence. From the driver's point of view, of course, the thing's the other way round: buying your freedom, expensive though it is, means security, a rise in status and a huge hike financially.

The key phrase there is 'number-one driver'. Like I said, these guys – slave or free – are the cream; seconds come nowhere. When Pegasus had joined the Whites it'd hit Uranius as hard in the pocket as it was possible to get. By his own admission he was no ball of fire on the sand, but he'd've been slowly stashing away runner-up prize money to buy his freedom and make the break. With Pegasus running lead that would've stopped, because the second's job is to hinder the opposition, not drive to win. With the Greens and Blues, sure, a second is in with the chance of a place in the final three, but not the Whites and Reds.

All that meant that with Pegasus dead – and especially with this new flash horse of the Whites' – Uranius was back on the gravy train, where he had to be unless he wanted to stay a slave all his life. Soft, sensitive type or not, as far as motive was concerned the guy had it in spades.

*   *   *

I'd reached the Reds' stables, which lay just short of the Greens'. The guard on the gate took my name and request to speak to Pudens without a murmur.

'Straight on,' he said. 'The boss's office is in the centre of the main block after the granaries.'

He went back to picking his teeth.

'Uh . . . you mean I can just walk in?' I said.

That got me a stare. 'Sure. Why not? Go ahead.'

I did. Shit; I was an old enough hand at faction security by now to realise that, as far as the Reds were concerned, theirs was as loose as an Aventine brothel-keeper's morals. I must've passed ten, maybe a dozen guys between the gate and the main faction buildings and they didn't give me so much as a glance.

I found the office door no bother and knocked.

'Come in.'

Standard office furniture, with no fripperies, shoe-string stuff; we were definitely downmarket here. The guy behind the desk was a little elderly nondescript in a plain mantle. On the other hand, the man with him radiated aggression like a catapult at full stretch. They were both looking at me. I had the impression I'd walked in on an argument.

'Who the hell are you?' The standing half of the partnership was glaring at me. He may've been small, but what there was of him was solid muscle. Black, gleaming muscle polished with oil: I'd've guessed Numidian, or maybe even backwoods African. And he was wearing so many medallions and good-luck charms round his neck and wrists that I'd bet when he moved he'd sound like a foundry.

'Marcus Valerius Corvinus,' I said.

'Ah.' The plain-mantle gave a long sniff: it sounded like he had sinus problems on top of everything else. 'The man investigating Pegasus's death. It's all right, Laomedon.'

'Fuck that.' The black guy was still glaring at me. 'How did you get in?'

'I walked, pal. How else would I do it?' If this was the Reds' lead driver then I doubted if we'd end up soul mates. My hackles were rising already.

'You weren't stopped at the gate?'

I shrugged. 'Your gate guard didn't seem too worried. He gave me directions.'

'Holy Castor!' Laomedon turned on the plain-mantle. 'Pudens, I've told you a hundred times! No one gets past the gate until they've been vetted! And they don't fucking wander around like they own the place!'

'Valerius Corvinus wasn't wandering around,' Plain-mantle said mildly. 'He came directly here. That's so, isn't it, Corvinus?'

'Sure.'

'Then there's no harm done.' He put out his hand; I noticed that the fingernails were bitten and ink-stained. 'Rufrius Pudens. You've met my wife, I believe.'

We shook. The hand felt like a limp bag of bones. 'Uh . . . yeah. I called round yesterday.' I glanced at Laomedon, but he'd folded his arms and was looking down at the desk. If he'd been a five-year-old I'd've said the guy was sulking.

'Then she will have given you all the help we –

as a corporate entity – can provide. Pegasus had no connection with the Reds at any time; I scarcely knew the man, professionally or' – he paused – 'or otherwise.' Did his expression twitch? I wasn't sure. 'Welcome as you are, I'm at a bit of a loss as to what you're doing here.'

I glanced at Laomedon. 'Mainly I wanted a word with your lead driver, sir.' The black guy's head lifted and his eyes burned into me. 'If you wouldn't mind.'

There was a pile of wax tablets on Pudens's desk. He picked the top one up and put it down again. The pile shifted. 'No. Not at all. Quite . . . ah . . . quite understandable under the . . . ah . . .' His hand jerked, and the tablets spilled. One fell on the floor but he ignored it. 'You'd prefer to talk in private, naturally.'

'Yeah.' Certainly if Felicula's name was likely to come up. Which it was. 'If that's possible.'

'Of course. Of course.' He stood up. I'd expected him to be small, but stooped as he was he had a head's start on Laomedon. 'I'll just . . .' His hand fluttered. 'Laomedon, we'll continue our discussion when Valerius Corvinus has finished.'

Pudens wasn't watching the driver – he was already halfway to the door – but I was. Laomedon didn't say anything, but on his face was a look of pure contempt.

The door closed. Slowly, his eyes never leaving me, Laomedon walked round behind the desk and sat down in Pudens's chair. I'd been right about the medallions; the guy didn't so much move as clink.

I pulled up a stool. We sat staring each other out for a good half-minute.

'Okay, Corvinus,' he said at last. 'You have the ball.'

'You and Pegasus had been cutting each other up on the track ever since he took over from you with Felicula,' I said.

'Right.'

'You hated the guy's guts.'

'Right again.'

'Where were you late afternoon, three days ago?'

'Not on Iugarius.' He pushed the chair back and set his feet on the desk. Two more tablets slid on to the floor. 'Mind you, I wouldn't tell you if I was, would I?'

I had to smile. 'No, I don't suppose you would. Why do you stay with the Reds?'

He hadn't been expecting that. His eyes shifted. 'That's none of your business.'

'They're a joke. Pudens is a joke. You don't respect him as a boss or as a man. You could shift to the Greens, especially now Pegasus is gone. Sure, you'd start out as second, but you're too good to stay there. Or are you?'

'I'm good. Very good.'

'As good as Pegasus was?'

'Pegasus is dead. However good he was, now I'm better.'

'You think now you've another chance with Felicula?'

'That bitch can go to hell. Pudens is welcome to her, plus whatever stud she takes up with next.'

'Yeah? You've got another girlfriend?' His mouth

closed like a trap; and that was unexpected. I'd touched on something there. Only thing was, I didn't know how or what. I started again. 'Okay. Let's assume you didn't kill Pegasus. Who do you think did?'

'No one.'

I blinked. 'What?'

'You asked, Corvinus.' He grinned. 'I've answered. No one. Maybe he killed himself. Maybe it was an accident. Who the fuck knows? Who the fuck cares?'

'He was stabbed in the back. That was no suicide, and it was no accident.'

Laomedon shrugged. He was still grinning. 'Suit yourself. He's dead. That's all that matters to me.'

'Why did Felicula dump you?'

The grin faded. 'She didn't dump me, Corvinus. Nobody dumps me, boy. I walked.'

'That isn't how she tells it.'

'I said. She can go to hell.' He took his feet off the desk. 'So can you. Pegasus is dead, and that's all I care about. Now get the fuck out of my stables.'

'Your stables?'

His face was purple under the black. 'Piss off, Corvinus!'

We were both standing now. 'Did you kill Pegasus?'

'Not me. I wish I had.'

'Then you know who did.'

He opened his mouth – and stopped. Then he laughed. 'Maybe I do at that, boy,' he said. 'Maybe I do at that. But then, I'm not telling, am I?'

There wasn't anything more to say. I left, with my brain buzzing.

11

The Circus was just north of the Aventine, so I could kill two birds with one stone here: check up on this new guy Cario, as well as report in to Cammius, and maybe – if I was lucky – catch the glee club baritone Silvius to confirm that Uranius had been where he was supposed to be the afternoon of Pegasus's murder.

That talk with Laomedon had left me with more questions than answers. Sure, the guy had hated Pegasus so much you could almost see it coming out his ears, and Felicula had been right when she'd said that ninety-nine per cent of the bastard was on the surface; but there was still that one per cent to be accounted for, and whether he was the murderer or not by his own admission he knew more than he was saying. That needed thinking about.

The weather had picked up, it was another bright spring afternoon, and the stalls area in Cattlemarket Square was heaving with cheerful punters. There was a knot of them at the corner of the Altar to Unconquered Hercules – that's a popular place with street performers, because they get the crowd flow to and from the Velabrum – and I stopped off to see what the centre of interest was.

It turned out to be a dark-skinned man, maybe a native Egyptian, with a folding table and what looked like three thimbles. The thimbles were upside down and he was shifting them around, sliding them past each other into different places in the line almost faster than my eye could follow. I watched fascinated: I hadn't seen anything like this before, and from the attention the punters round him were giving they hadn't either. The only thing missing was a point to the performance. Sure, it was slick and I couldn't've moved my hands that fast myself, but where juggling's concerned Cattlemarket Square punters are a demanding audience, and anything less than four balls in the air at once with maybe a meat cleaver for variety won't draw even a passing glance.

Then the guy stopped shifting the cups and waited. One of the punters – a grizzled old tunic who'd been keeping a sharp eye on things – laid a copper coin on the table and tapped the middle thimble. The Egyptian lifted it, the old guy swore and the crowd laughed. He picked up one of the end thimbles, and there was a pea under it. The copper coin disappeared quick as a flash into the Egyptian's belt-pouch, he covered the pea with the thimble and started the routine again.

I grinned. So. It was a gambling game. Illegal, of course, outside the Winter Festival, and if the market patrol turned up the guy'd be in for a thumping, but I've never been against private enterprise and the odds seemed fair enough. I folded my arms and settled down to watch.

He was good, the Egyptian. With professional gambling, you've got to judge your punters to a hair: make them think they haven't got a chance and they give up and drift off; lose too often yourself and you might as well take up humping baskets of vegetables for a living. I reckoned the lose/win ratio was about four to one, which kept the audience and still netted a pretty fair return. The only thing was, I couldn't really see how the punter, given a reasonable sharpness of eye, should lose at all. The game wasn't like dice, it didn't depend on chance: you saw the pea go under, and whatever the guy did with his hands all you had to do was watch the thimble. Simple.

I moved forwards politely. At street level, Rome's a working-man's city, and tunics tend to remind pushy purple-stripers of that fact any chance they get, but the weather was still working its magic and the crowd let me through without too much cursing.

'You mind if I have a go, granddad?' I said to the grizzled tunic who'd been monopolising the betting.

'Nah.' He tightened the drawstrings on his purse with disgust. It wasn't empty, but I'd bet it'd got a lot lighter since he'd opened it. 'Go ahead, son. I'm not making anything of this. My eyes aren't what they were.'

I glanced at the Egyptian, although maybe 'Egyptian' wasn't right after all: he was the wrong shade of brown, for a start, and the features were unusual. 'Go ahead, pal.'

The guy lifted a thimble to show the pea. Then he whipped the thimbles around in a complex series of switches, crossing his hands over occasionally, sometimes shifting a thimble without actually moving it. He stopped.

This was money for old rope. I took out a copper coin, laid it on the table and tapped the left-hand thimble, the one with the pea underneath. The guy lifted it . . .

No pea.

The crowd laughed, and the grizzled tunic chuckled through his gums. Shit! I'd've sworn that was the one! There was even a tiny chip out of the rim that I'd marked when the pea went under. Only obviously it wasn't.

The 'Egyptian' grinned at me, lifted the middle thimble to expose the pea and pocketed my copper piece. 'You another try, sir?' he said.

'Yeah. Sure.'

I was watching a lot more closely this time. I lost again.

I lost five times in a row. The sixth I only won because I didn't bother following the pea and picked a thimble at random. The crowd loved it: they love anything where a purple-striper gets rooked.

'One more, sir?'

Well, fractured Latin or not he knew his business. He was too good for me, anyway; although I still couldn't see how he worked the scam. 'No, I'll quit while I'm ahead,' I said. 'Thanks a lot, pal. It's been very interesting.'

He gave me a grin with perfect teeth behind it. I put my purse away, let someone else take my place and moved out through the parting ranks to the square proper.

Most of the access gates to the Circus would be closed and locked, but the officials' entrance at the starting end next to the main processional adit was open, and the public slave on porter duty told me that Cammius and Cario were busy with the boss. I slipped him a copper or two from the few the pea and thimble juggler had left me with and asked him to let them know I was there and that I'd like a word when they were free.

'You mind if I sort of look around, pal?' I said. 'Any time I've been here I've been sitting up on the bleachers. I'd be interested to know what the place is like from the sand end.'

He gave a pointed look at my purse. I sighed, took out a half silver piece and handed it over. Sightseeing ain't cheap in Rome.

'Look all you want, sir,' he said. 'Your friends won't be finished for half an hour yet.'

'Fine, fine.' Sure, I could've sat it out in a wineshop – there're quite a few along the outside walls, in amongst the souvenir-sellers, the hot food outlets and the cheap and cheerful brothels – but like the latter concessions most're only open when there are games on, and I couldn't be certain that Cammius and his son would come and find me. Besides, like I'd said, seeing the place from the sharp end would be a new experience. I carried on through the tunnel and out into the sunlight.

The Circus on a non-race day looks even bigger

than it does full, which seems crazy but that's the way things are. Eerily quiet, too, although that's a lot more understandable: the absence of a hundred and fifty thousand yelling punters leaves a bit of a gap. The holding-boxes – what they call the Prisons – were shut up, but I walked along the white lane-lines the way the cars would go, towards the break line and the nearer turning posts at the end of the Spine. Seen from this angle it was impressive as hell. The Wart hadn't made too many additions, but there again he hadn't needed to because old Augustus and his pal Agrippa had spent a small fortune on the place when it burned down in the big Circus Valley fire sixty-odd years back. Later on, too: the huge obelisk in the middle of the Spine that he'd filched from Egypt might be nothing but a glorified sundial, but it must've cost a bomb to transport and erect. It just showed how much importance the demagogic old bugger placed on impressing the betting public.

I carried on up the Spine. Every so often, between the statues and the towers and the altars, there were basins. Those, plus the ten-foot ditch that ran the length of the seating tiers, would provide the water for the sprinklers to throw over the horses. I wondered where the sprinkler that Pegasus had killed had been stationed. Probably much further up, and on the other side.

I had to admit I was fascinated. Me, I'm no sightseer, but in all the times I'd watched races and wild-beast shows in the Circus since I was a kid I hadn't ever really *looked* at the place, and it was like knowing it inside out but seeing it for the first time, both at once; like the statue on a column that I remember goggling at across the width of the track when I was about five years old, that was the spitting image of my Capuan nurse. I'd half believed for years that it was actually her, and mentally I still called it Lusca. Now it turned out – from the inscription on the base – that it was of some goddess I'd never heard of called Pollentia. You live and learn. Mind you, they say natives know their own city least, and I suppose that's true. Certainly I wished I'd brought Perilla. The lady would've loved it.

I did the whole circuit, past the shrines of Murcia and Consus and the far posts with their Horse-scarer altar, then back the far side, past the fancy marble Couch of the Gods that Augustus had built next to the finishing line so the statues brought in from their various temples to watch the games could see the winner gallop by them towards the steward with the palm and the purse. It took me the half-hour, easy, and at the end of it I could've murdered a cup of wine. Still, I was glad I'd done it. For a start, I understood better where these racing guys were coming from. Sitting in the bleachers, you only see a small part, and you ignore that because you're watching the cars; down on the sand, with no audience or cars to distract you, and taking it slow, you got a different view. The Circus wasn't just a racetrack, it was a whole separate world, lovingly put together and cared for. I could understand, looking at it from this angle, how obsession could creep in.

I was just turning in by the Pavilion and the Eggs

when Cammius and a younger guy came out of the tunnel. Perfect timing. I gave them a wave and walked over.

'So, Corvinus.' That was Cammius. 'How're things going?'

'Well enough.' A lie: at this stage of the investigation I felt like I was swimming through glue, but I wasn't going to admit that to Cammius.

'Good.' The Whites' boss nodded towards the second man. 'This here's my son Cario.'

I'd've guessed even if I hadn't known. The other guy was a perfect younger version of his father: a chunky Spaniard with bristly hair that was black for Cammius's grey. Unlike Cammius, though, he was barbered within an inch of his life in the latest style, and his mantle was sharp Market Square best. He held out his hand, and I noticed the carefully manicured nails.

'Valerius Corvinus.'

No Spanish vowels. He could've given the Master of Blues Acceptus a run for his nasals. I knew the type: second-generation successful provincial, blade-about-town. Not an unpleasant youngster, though, from first impressions. We shook.

'I don't know about you, Corvinus,' Cammius said, 'but we've had a busy morning. There's a good wineshop round the corner, if you're interested.'

I grinned. 'Very. Lead me to it.'

'This your first time in the Circus?' Cammius said as we walked back through the tunnel. 'The sand bit, I mean?'

'Yeah. There's a lot more to it than I'd thought.'

'You should see it on a race day. Up in the stands, that's exciting enough, but down here' – he paused – 'there's a magic you wouldn't believe. I wouldn't trade it for anything.'

'Me neither,' Cario said.

I looked at him. The resemblance went a lot deeper than appearances: thirty years on, I could see, he'd be just like his father. They'd both been bitten by the racing bug, if 'bitten' was the word. It probably wasn't: a bite's superficial, and well-groomed society playboy or not the guy had racing oozing out of his pores.

'The wineshop's run by an old friend of mine,' Cammius was saying. 'He captain-ownered a pair of ships out of Tarraco, only he didn't have my luck.'

We rounded the Circus's Aventine corner. The wineshop was one of the shallow booths built into the superstructure, but it'd sprawled outwards towards the road in the form of benches and tables with orange trees planted in sawn-off Gallic barrels filled with earth. While Cammius went inside to talk with his mate and order the wine, I sat down with Cario at one of the tables.

'So you're looking into Pegasus's death,' he said.

'Yeah. That's right.' I was watching him closely. 'You didn't get on, I understand.'

'No. He was a bastard.'

'So everyone tells me.'

Cario grunted. 'He was a good driver, mind. The best. I'd've forgiven him a lot for that.'

'Like specifically what, for example?'

'He thought he was the gods' gift to the team.' His

lips twisted. 'Or rather, he knew he was the gods' gift to the team, which made it worse. Also—' He stopped.

I waited. Then, when nothing else came, I said, 'Also?'

'Nothing. Or nothing important. Forget it, Corvinus, the guy's dead and burned. Good riddance.'

'You're not interested in who killed him, then?'

'No. My father cares, but personally I don't. I've had this argument with him myself – with my father, I mean. Pegasus may've been the saviour of the Whites, but we're better off without him.'

'In what way?'

He shrugged and didn't answer. Well, I couldn't force the issue. I changed tack. 'Your new lead driver. Old lead, whatever. Uranius.'

His eyes sharpened. 'Yes? What about him?'

'He didn't like Pegasus either. And he had a reason, over and above being treated like a second-rater. He's still a slave. He was saving up to buy his freedom.'

'Uranius wouldn't've killed Pegasus. He isn't the type. Besides, he has an alibi. He was down on the Aventine the afternoon he was stabbed.' He paused, then added casually, or what he presumably thought was casually: 'Just like I was back at the stables, working with Dad on the accounts. If you're interested.'

Uh-huh. I glanced past his shoulder. Cammius was only a few feet away, carrying a tray with wine jug, cups and a plate of cheese and olives. If he'd heard that last bit – and he'd been close enough – he didn't comment.

'Crescens was busy, so I brought this myself,' he

said. 'It's not the Carthaginian stuff I gave you at the stables, Corvinus, but it's good Spanish, and that's the best. The cheese and olives, too.' I noticed he gave Cario an odd look as he set the tray down, and the younger guy coloured. 'Just the thing after a hard morning's business.'

'What were you doing exactly?' I said.

That got me a frown and a stare blank as a marble statue's. Jupiter! For all his friendliness, where the faction was concerned the guy was touchy as hell.

'It's only eighteen days to the Megalenses,' he said. 'That may seem a lot to you, but it isn't. There're things to discuss which are frankly no business of yours.'

Ouch. Still, I should've expected stonewalling where racing went. I was getting used to it.

Cammius sat and poured for all of us. I took a considering sip. Yeah, well: maybe it was a question of taste, but *the best* was exaggerating a little. I wouldn't've rated it alongside a more than half-decent Latian, although it wasn't much behind; and that's high praise where a wineshop wine's concerned. Certainly after a long, thirsty walk round the Circus I wasn't going to be too critical. The cheese and olives weren't bad, either.

'Now,' Cammius said. He sounded fairly genial again. 'How's the investigation going?'

I'd been hoping we'd avoided that topic. 'Uh . . . I'm assessing the suspects at present.' It sounded good, anyway. It was even true, in a way.

'Did you talk to Titus Natalis?'

There was real venom behind the last two words. I glanced up in surprise. 'Yeah,' I said. 'I talked to Natalis.'

'And?'

'He . . . uh . . . threw me out.' Talk about bathos! Well, that was what had happened, and there was no point in covering it up.

Cammius chuckled without humour. 'Bastard,' he said.

'I got the impression he didn't much like you either.'

'That's because I'm the one who's going to push his face into his own horses' droppings. Or I would've done, if everything had been equal. He's behind the murder, Corvinus. Don't ask me how, I don't know, but Natalis is behind it.'

'Come on, Dad.' Cario had been pretty quiet since his father had joined us, but there wasn't any shilly-shallying here. 'Natalis may play dirty at times, but he wouldn't go that far.'

'Natalis would sell his own grandmother to keep the Greens on top.' Cammius took a swallow of wine. 'He's got the edge now and he means to keep it. In the punters' eyes a loss for the Greens these days is practically a second Cannae. They've got out of the way of losing, and that's not healthy.'

'How do you mean, "play dirty"?' I asked Cario.

The young guy glanced at his father. Cammius nodded his permission. 'There've been a couple of incidents recently,' he said carefully. 'Oh, sure, on the track it's expected. But we caught one of their men trying to sneak in with a shipment of straw. He had a surgeon's knife strapped to his thigh. Then there was one of our own watermen, a new employee. He had a twist of powder in his purse.'

'We were lucky. Neither got past the gate.' Cammius was frowning into his cup. I didn't ask what the outcome had been. I'd bet, though, that the waterman at least hadn't left with a golden handshake. 'It happens, although not to us as a rule. Or to the Reds. The Blues – well, they're used to it, it's all in a day's work. And the Greens have the backing, which we don't. Messing with them's dangerous. You know what I mean.'

Prince Gaius. Or his agents, anyway. Yeah, I knew; you didn't have to be a racing man to make that jump. 'You think Natalis would go the length of murder?'

'Faced with Pegasus and Polydoxus at the Megalenses?' Cammius drank some of his wine. 'Yes, Corvinus. I'm sure he would. Whether he did or not's another matter. And he'd be in a position to get away with it, what's more.'

I thought of Valgius and his Watchmen. Yeah; he would, at that. 'How about Laomedon?' I said. 'The Red driver?'

That got me a sharp look, from both of them. 'Laomedon's a possibility,' Cario said slowly. 'For other reasons.'

'Pegasus was screwing his ex-girlfriend,' I said.

'So. You've found that out.' Cammius reached for a piece of cheese. 'Not that it would've been difficult. I've a lot of time for Pudens, but the poor man's no Adonis. And his wife's a wild one.'

'Incidentally.' I sipped my wine. 'You happen to

know what the situation is? Over at the Red stables?'

'It's a complete shambles,' Cario said. 'Laomedon tries to hold the place together, but he's fighting a losing battle. Morale's rock-bottom, and if Laomedon hadn't been the driver he is last season the Reds would've trailed every race.'

'Uh-huh.' Well, no surprises there: it was the impression I'd got myself. Pudens was no ball of fire in the business line, either. 'It must be pretty frustrating for the guy. Why doesn't he switch to Green?'

'He would if he could. He drove for them a while five or six years back. Started small, made it up to third driver, which is where he stuck because Natalis refused to promote him. Two years ago he got tired of waiting and left to be lead with the Reds.'

'Is that so, now?' I'd wondered why he hadn't picked me up on that one when I'd talked to him. 'Clash of personalities, right?'

Cammius chuckled. 'Say "collision" and you'd be closer to the mark. The story is he told Natalis what he could do with his team and walked out. Natalis doesn't forgive easy.'

I winced. Yeah, I could visualise the scenario because I'd met both men. Tact wasn't exactly Laomedon's strong suit – he'd act first and think about his career later – and Natalis was about as equable as a tiger with toothache. Putting them together wouldn't make for a happy relationship. 'Pegasus was driving lead for the Greens when Laomedon moved, right?'

'No,' Cammius said. 'He was their second. Then

two months later the lead broke his neck in the Plebbies and Pegasus was promoted. Natalis brought in an Antiochene driver called Nicetus to run back-up. He's the current Green number one.'

Interesting. 'So what about the Blues? Wouldn't Acceptus take Laomedon on?'

'He might.' Cammius topped up our wine cups but left his own half full. 'I wouldn't, myself, for the same reasons Acceptus doesn't snap him up. Laomedon's a first-rate driver, but he's also a fouler; he'll win any way he can, and that's not a popular attitude in the Colours. The games're risky enough as it is.' Yeah; I remembered Hesper saying the same. 'Also, he's no different off-sand than on. He's not a team person. If he can't be leader he won't play.' His lips twisted. 'His problem is, he thinks he's prime leader material and he isn't. Close, but not there. And that makes all the difference in the world.'

I nodded. Yeah, that summed the guy up nicely. Like I'd noticed before, Cammius was no slouch when it came to reading character. And it was interesting that he'd expressed himself in terms of a kids' game; there was definitely an immature side to Laomedon that might well make him more dangerous. 'So he's stuck where he is?' I said.

'Very much so.' The Whites' boss frowned. 'He's at the top of the tree, but with a team that's rapidly becoming third-rate, and he wouldn't take a demotion even if it was offered. His only other option would be to move to one of the big teams in the provinces – in Alexandria, say, or Antioch – but for a lead driver that's a one-way ticket, and as far as a career in Rome was concerned it'd be a dead end.'

'Right.' I looked up at the sun. I hadn't noticed, but it was getting late, almost halfway through the afternoon. And I still had the Aventine baritone to check up on before I headed back to the Caelian. 'Uh . . . pleasant as this is, gentlemen, if you'll forgive me I should be moving. I've got one more thing to do before home and dinner.'

'You have far to go?' Cammius asked politely.

'Not far. The Caelian. But we have a touchy chef.'

Cammius smiled. 'Really? You're lucky. They're the best kind. I'm afraid I spend so little time at home myself that mine would be surprised to see me eight days out of ten. But then I am a widower, I have no ties, and there's so much to do at the stables that it's usually not worth the trip.'

'Yeah, right.' I got up. 'Thanks for the wine.'

'You're welcome.' He glanced at Cario. 'We should be going too. It was nice to run into you, Corvinus. Good luck, and keep us informed.'

'Yeah. I'll do that. See you later.'

Cario raised his cup. I left.

12

All that needed thinking about, and I mulled it over as I headed up Public Incline on to the Aventine towards the Temple of Queen Juno and the tenement where Uranius practised his part-singing four times a month.

It was looking good for Laomedon, very good indeed: judging from what Cammius and Cario had told me the guy had another prime motive to fit in with the jealousy angle, although that, of course, might've been enough in itself; from what I'd seen and heard of him, the Reds' lead driver was pure, simple beefcake with a mind so one-track you could use it to draw lines, and if he had knifed Pegasus then I'd bet a sturgeon to a stuffed mussel that where reasons were concerned we didn't need to go beyond good old-fashioned spite. All the same, the existence of a professional grudge shortened the odds pretty considerably. It would've gnawed at the egotistical bastard like the pain from a bad tooth, especially since after his spat with Natalis Pegasus had got the lead driver's job; and when Pegasus made his shift to the Whites and Laomedon's replacement slipped into the top slot with the Greens that would've made matters worse. It was like a series of movements the guy with the thimbles and the pea could've made. If Laomedon had stayed where he was he'd've been the Greens' lead driver; at least, that was what he'd believe. Instead, he was stuck with the deadbeat Reds and going nowhere fast. With the size of his ego that would make a go-getter like him pretty bitter. Add Felicula to the pot and you had the recipe for a murder just waiting to happen.

On the other hand, I doubted if the guy had the brains actually to mastermind a killing, and in that case there was another angle that might be worth thinking about. If Cammius was right, then career-wise Laomedon might be between a rock and a hard place and know it, but he was still with all his faults and shortcomings currently one of the best drivers in Rome. It wasn't his fault the Reds were rubbish. Like it or not, and *pace* Cammius, no faction boss can afford to write someone like that off altogether. Which suggested an interesting scenario, and one that merited more than a little attention for its own sake.

Okay, where did it take us? Background: the Whites, with their Pegasus/Polydoxus combination, are looking like serious challengers for the new season. One of the other faction masters – let's call him for the sake of argument Natalis, because that bastard is already out to wreck the Whites – approaches Laomedon with a deal. If Laomedon does the faction boss's dirty business and zeroes Pegasus, he'll take him on as lead . . .

I frowned. Uh-uh; it didn't work. No way did it work. Sure, going by what Cammius and his son had said, Natalis had his knife into the Whites, and from my own experience of the guy I wouldn't trust him further than I could spit, but there were too many points against. First, the Greens already had a perfectly good lead in their Antioch import, and by all accounts in the long term Laomedon would be a poor replacement. Second, Natalis and Laomedon had already had a major run-in and I couldn't see the Green boss being prepared to kiss and make up, especially since he could be fairly sure the same problem would come up again. Third, like I say, chummy wasn't exactly the greatest brain in the world and personally I'd think twice before I entered into any sort of clandestine agreement with him because as sure as eggs are eggs the bastard would blab.

So not Natalis. A bummer, sure, but the theory didn't need him specifically. If we were talking faction bosses, how about Acceptus?

Despite first appearances, the Blues guy was more probable. Sure, I didn't know how he weighed in on the moral side, but otherwise the thing had possibilities. First of all, he had no hatchet to bury: Laomedon had never driven for the Blues, he had a clean sheet. Second, more important, from what I'd gathered from that confab at the Whites' stables when Cammius and Acceptus had had their little run-in the Blues team wasn't precisely shining at present. Sure, Cammius had said that Acceptus would've hesitated to take Laomedon on because of his reputation, but the fact remained (we kept going back to this) the guy was one of the best drivers in the business. That, combined with the chance of scuppering what he obviously saw as the Whites' pretensions, might've tipped Acceptus's scales. And, I'd take my holy oath, traditional alliance or not Acceptus was out to do the Whites down just as much as Natalis was.

As a theory, it had its holes, but it was worth keeping in mind. And pure as the driven snow was something Laomedon most decidedly wasn't.

I'd got to the top of the first Aventine slope, parallel with the Temple of the Moon. This is real tenement country: high-rise flats as far as the eye can see, with washing strung between the balconies either side of the road. Me, I've never been much of an Aventine fan. It's got nothing to do with the fact that it's a downmarket district; compared to the Subura, which has a lot worse slum areas than Rome's southernmost hill, I just find it drab. Sure, there're nice bits and the people're okay, but generally once you've seen one street you've seen them all. The Aventine is pease porridge to the Subura's spice cake.

The Temple of Queen Juno would be off some-where to the right. I took a convenient alleyway that looked like it wouldn't peter out and headed towards the river side of the hill.

One guy I hadn't thought much about was Cario. Typhon had singled him out with Uranius as a leader of the anti-Pegasus lobby, and what I'd seen of him confirmed it. Still, he'd made no bones about the fact, and he seemed straighforward enough. There were only two question marks over him as far as I could see: one, that reticence when I'd asked him what he had against the dead man apart from the effect he had on the team; two, that he'd been pretty quick off the mark supplying an unsolicited alibi for the afternoon Pegasus had been killed. Me, I tend to be suspicious when someone defends themselves before they're attacked, and in essence that was what the guy had done. Added to which, his behaviour when he noticed that his father might've overheard suggested that he'd deliberately told me a porky and knew he'd been caught out. Mind you, at that point Cammius himself hadn't exactly been beyond suspicion either: if you twisted my arm and forced me to give a straight opinion, I'd say that he had heard and decided to let the lie go. Whatever their various motives, there was something screwy there, that I'd bet on. What it was, and how serious it was, I didn't know, but I hadn't finished with Cario; not by a long chalk.

The Temple of Queen Juno was just up ahead. Hesper had said the block was next to it, but like I say if the Aventine's got lots of anything it's tenements, and there were two or three contenders. I chose one at random that had a vegetable-seller's at street level and asked the lad with the cabbages if he knew a Marcus Silvius. I was pretty certain that I'd get a yes: one thing the Aventine has in common with Rome's other poorer parts is that everyone knows everyone else. With the number of people your average slum landlord manages to cram into his gimcrack property you'd expect anonymity, but it doesn't seem to happen that way. If I'd asked the same question on the Pincian or the Caelian I'd probably just have got a blank stare, even from the guy's next-door neighbour.

'Sure,' the cabbage-seller said. 'Third floor up, right-hand door.'

'Would he be in at present, do you know, pal?' I said. There was still a fair-sized chunk of the afternoon left, and tenement-dwellers tend to be working men with jobs to go to.

'Oh, Silvius'll be in, sir. He hasn't got much option.'

Odd answer, but evidently the gods were smiling. 'Fine,' I said. 'Thanks, friend.'

I climbed the stairs. Like most of the high-rises I've ever been inside, it smelled of stale urine and staler cabbage soup, with overtones of nappies, and the graffiti artists had been busy on the walls. The usual preoccupations: sex and sport. This was obviously a Green neighbourhood: I passed two or three terse and unflattering phrases about the Blues and several longer ones saying how great the Greens were. One, obviously out of date, even mentioned Pegasus. I reached the third landing and knocked on the right-hand door.

There was a pause, followed by a sort of shuffling, rolling noise. The door opened on to nothing.

'Yes?'

I looked down. The guy's face only came up to my navel. Then I realised why. He wasn't a midget, he just stopped at the knees. My scrotum contracted in sympathy.

'Uh . . . Marcus Silvius?' I said.

'That's right.' A strong voice. Educated, too.

'Marcus Valerius Corvinus. I was told you run a singing group.'

'Indeed.' He'd been looking a bit wary; now he relaxed.

'You . . . uh . . . mind if I come in?' I tried to control the queasy feeling in my stomach. Deformities of any kind always make me feel sick, and no legs was a total new one on me. It was a beaut, though; if you can use the expression for something like that. 'I've a few questions.'

'Not at all. Glad of the company.' He put the palms of his hands flat on the floor and pushed backwards. Yeah; that accounted for the rolling noise: he was sitting on a wooden cart. Clever. Not that it'd help him with the steps, which explained the guy downstairs's comment. 'Close the door behind you.'

I did, and looked round. It was a bigger flat than you normally find in these places, and a couple of doorways off indicated at least three rooms. There was a lot of furniture, too, far more than a tenement flat usually boasted, or even a proper house. Chairs and stools, mostly. And everything was waxed and polished till it shone.

'Have a seat,' Silvius said. He parked himself so that his back was against a wall. I noticed there was a low table next to him with what ought to've been book-rolls on it, but one was open and there were only a few lines of text, with symbols above them. He must've seen me look in their direction because he said, 'Just a song or two I'm working on.'

'Right. Right.' Perilla wasn't into music, but she had

a few books of annotated Greek lyric poetry and I'd come across that sort of thing before. Smart buggers, those musicians. I lowered myself on to a chair and tried not to look at the shiny rounded stumps jutting out below the hem of his tunic. 'That'd be for the glee club, yeah?'

'I prefer to call it a performers' circle. Or maybe a choir.'

The last word was Greek. I looked at him in surprise. He wasn't a Greek himself – not with a name like Silvius – and you don't expect to hear Greek in an Aventine tenement. Not anything barring the commoner swear words, anyway. 'You're a musician?'

'I play the flute, yes, but not well. Mostly I compose for voice.'

'Professionally?'

'No. Not any more. Not for many years now, in fact, since my accident.' He smiled. 'A carriage ran over my legs, Valerius Corvinus, since you're no doubt wondering. But I'll spare you the details.'

I swallowed as my scrotum shrank another inch or so. 'Uh . . . yeah. Yeah, right. Thanks.'

'I used to compose and perform for the emperor's mother.'

'*Livia?*' Jupiter, I hadn't known the poisonous old bitch had been all that interested in music! 'You worked for Livia?' Well, that was something we had in common. I just hoped he'd done better out of it than I had.

'For quite some time, yes. She had a good ear. And, although I shouldn't really say it, a very fine contralto voice, even in her latter years. Untrained, of course, and she didn't exercise it much, naturally. It's such a pity that singing is so frowned upon in Roman aristocratic circles, isn't it? I always feel there's a great deal of stunted talent among you purple-stripers.'

I almost forgot the tightness in my crotch. Sweet gods! There was something for the grandchildren! The empress Livia singing in the bath! Still, I supposed, you never knew when the artistic temperament was liable to break out, even in the top families. Rumour had it that Prince Gaius wasn't averse to a bit of dressing up, for a start.

Silvius was watching me carefully, a half-smile on his lips. 'You're surprised?' he said. 'About the empress?'

'Sure I'm surprised! You were, uh, part of the household?' I put that one delicately. Most private musicians were bought in with the help. On the other hand, if he was Livia's freedman I'd've expected him to be a Livius rather than a Silvius, with his original slave name tacked on the end, which is the way these things go normally.

'No. I was never a slave. In fact, I come from quite a good family. I own the deeds to three farms near Mutina jointly with my brother, and the income from these – plus the empress's small pension – is more than adequate for my needs.' He hesitated. 'I also talk too much, as you've no doubt noticed. Forgive me. Now what can I do for you? I assume it has something to do with the group. You're thinking of joining us, perhaps?'

'Uh . . . not exactly. You know a guy called Uranius?'

'Certainly; our *basso profundo*. He's been with us almost from the start. We have two tenors, plus Uranius and myself. I sing baritone and also, of course, compose and direct.'

'You have four meetings a month, right?'

'Three.'

Something cold touched my spine, but I kept my voice level. 'Only three?'

'Yes. At fairly irregular intervals because the group have other commitments. We meet on the afternoons of the fifth, eighteenth and twenty-fourth days of every month. There was a fourth meeting on the twenty-ninth, but six months ago one of our tenors contracted a regular obligation for that date and we were unable to agree on a substitute.'

'Uh-huh.' There was something out of kilter here, sure, but I could worry about that later. At least the twenty-fourth – the afternoon of the murder – checked out. 'And Uranius was at the last meeting? The one on the twenty-fourth?'

'No. I'm afraid he missed that one.'

'*What?*'

'By arrangement. He'd told us on the previous occasion that he would be otherwise occupied.'

Holy Jupiter! 'Just let me get this straight, pal. Uranius told you on the eighteenth that he couldn't make the meeting of the twenty-fourth because he had another appointment?'

'Appointment I wouldn't know about. He just said he'd be busy and I assumed it had something to do with his work at the racing stables. He's a professional charioteer, you know. Quite a famous one.'

'Yeah. Yeah, I know.' My brain was humming. Dear gods! There went Uranius's alibi! And not only that; he'd known for at least six days prior to the twenty-fourth that he wouldn't be able to make the meeting and hadn't let on to anyone what his alternative plans were. 'He make a habit of missing sessions, or was it a one-off?'

'It happens, now and again. In everyone's case, excluding mine, although Uranius is always very conscientious about warning me in advance. Sometimes we rearrange the date or cancel, but mostly we go ahead with just the three of us. Which we did on that occasion.' The guy's voice had taken on an edge. 'Valerius Corvinus, I've been very patient. What exactly is this all about? Uranius isn't in trouble, is he?'

'No. No.' I hoped he couldn't read the lie on my face, but I wouldn't've bet on it. 'He probably was at the stables right enough.'

'Then perhaps you could answer my first question. What's your interest in my friend Uranius's movements?'

Well, there wasn't any reason not to tell him. 'I'm looking into a murder. One of the other White drivers. A guy called Pegasus.'

Silvius sat back. 'Ah,' he said. He didn't look happy.

'You've heard of him?'

'As a driver, certainly. From Uranius, too, yes. Not a very nice man, as I understand.'

'Most people seem generally agreed on that, yeah.'

'And he was killed – presumably – the same afternoon as our practice?' I didn't say anything: given the circumstances, it was a logical assumption to make. 'Corvinus, you're very lucky. If I'd known that fact before you arrived I would have lied to you with absolutely no compunction whatsoever. As it is, I'll tell you categorically that Uranius wouldn't harm anyone. He may not look it, but he is a very gentle man. A *gentleman*, indeed.' His lips twisted. 'Slave or not, Uranius is a gentleman. Now if you have no further questions . . .'

The atmosphere had turned definitely chilly, and I had the distinct feeling that I'd outstayed my welcome. 'I'm sure it'll all work out,' I said, getting up. Like hell I was. 'Gentleman' or not, if Uranius hadn't been over on Iugarius shoving a knife into Pegasus then where had he been? And why the big secret? 'In any case, I won't take up any more of your time. Thanks a lot, friend.'

'Time is something I have a great deal of, certainly too much to worry about anyone taking it up. And I don't believe I want your thanks. Nor do I consider us friends.'

'No.' I felt, suddenly, tired. 'No, you probably don't, on either count. But I appreciate the help anyway.'

He didn't answer. I let myself out and closed the door after me.

Okay; so Gentleman Uranius wasn't off the hook yet,

not by a long way. Still, I'd been impressed by how far Silvius had been prepared to go to defend him, and it certainly chimed with all the other reports. Despite the business of the phantom rehearsal, I'd be almost ready to call the guy a red herring and throw him back, only on the evidence of my interview with him I'd bet a flask of imperial Caecuban to a worn copper piece that he had something to contribute. To do with the case, I mean, not some little personal secret he was keeping schtum on for reasons of his own. I'd used the word 'appointment' with Silvius. That hadn't been intentional, but maybe my subconscious had been working: we still had the problem of who Pegasus had been planning to meet in Renatius's. If Uranius had known six days in advance that he'd miss the choir practice . . .

No; that horse wouldn't run. They may've got on as well as two dogs over the same dinner dish, but Pegasus and Uranius were both Whites drivers; they saw each other every day, or they could've done, and if one of them wanted to talk to the other then there wouldn't've been any reason to make clandestine arrangements. Unless of course Uranius had somehow suckered Pegasus into thinking he'd be meeting someone else . . .

That thought stopped me, but I put it to one side for the present. Ah, hell; we'd get to the truth eventually, and there was no point theorising in a vacuum. The fact remained that the guy was hiding something, and I couldn't rule him out until I knew what it was.

I'd have to have another little talk with Uranius.

13

The weather was still holding when I got back to the Caelian. Bathyllus was outside the front door, buffing up the knocker. He did a double-take when he saw me.

'You're early, sir,' he said.

'Yeah. It's getting to be a habit.' Well, another trip uptown to the stables would've put me in grave danger of missing Meton's dinner deadline, and I'd done enough for one day. Besides, I had my domestic responsibilities to consider. 'Uh . . . how are you, sunshine?'

Bathyllus gave me what only amounted to a quarter major-domo power sniff. 'Much as usual, sir. Shouldn't I be?'

Hell; I wouldn't get a better chance, despite Perilla's warnings. 'Since you mention it, little guy—'

I stopped. Bathyllus wasn't listening. The cleaning rag drooped from his hand and he was staring past my shoulder with an expression on his face like a calf with a belly-ache. I turned round.

The door of the next house – Petillius's place – had opened and a woman had come out. Alexis hadn't been kidding: large was right, and it was the first word that came to mind. Housekeepers don't come small as a rule – the kitchen pickings are too lavish – but this one would've tipped the scales at two hundred pounds, easy. She didn't so much walk towards us as roll in state, like Cleopatra's barge coming into dock.

'Afternoon, Bathyllus,' she said. 'Lovely weather, isn't it?'

I glanced at the guy. You could've used his face to roast chestnuts, and he was hissing slightly. 'You, uh, want to answer the lady, pal?' I murmured. 'Quickly, for preference?'

The hissing stopped, but the colouring went up a notch. He swallowed and gave a sickly grin. I winced: grins and Bathyllus just don't go together. 'Yes!' he squeaked. 'Delightful! Quite spring-like!'

Oh, Jupiter in a bucket! Whatever chat-up lines Paris had used on Helen when she'd come sailing out of the Spartan royal palace I'd bet a sturgeon to a sardine that that wasn't one of them. I nudged our Trojan hero manqué in the ribs, but it seemed that was all we were going to get this side of the Greek Kalends.

'Uh . . . you're Tyndaris, right?' I said. 'Petillius's new housekeeper?'

'I am, sir.' She dimpled in three of her four chins. Not a bad looker, by any means, facially; there was just a hell of a lot of her. Twice what there was of Bathyllus, for a start. 'And you're Valerius Corvinus, no doubt. Master's mentioned you several times.'

Yeah; probably, from the brittle brightness of her tone, with the prefixed phrase 'that wine-soaked bugger next door'. If we got on okay with our new neighbour above the level of the bought help it was largely because of a live-and-let-live policy. Petillius might be a big, jolly, florid-faced man who'd double the clientele in a month on looks alone if he ever took on the running of a wineshop but he was a convinced water-drinker with a down on wine that would've beaten Demosthenes's hollow. The first time I'd seen him our kitchen brigade were loading up the cart with a month's worth of empty wine jars bound for disposal on Pottery Mountain, and the look I'd got would've fried a rissole. First impressions count. Ever since then, the best I'd been able to expect was a slight nod. Blink, and you'd miss even that.

'So, Tyndaris,' I said, 'how're you settling in?'

'Very well, sir, thank you. Being in Rome's nice. I was in Baiae last. A nice town with very nice people, sir. Quiet out of season, but nice, you know?'

Ouch. 'You, uh, made many friends here? So far?' Next to me it sounded like Bathyllus had taken to gargling. I ignored him.

'Not yet, sir. But I've been out and around shopping, and I've seen quite a bit of the place. Quite a change from Baiae.'

'Yeah. I'd imagine it would be.' Especially the nice bits around Suburan Street. On the promenade at Baiae you didn't have to watch where you were putting your sandals and at the same time keep an eye out above for falling tenements.

'I like them porches you have here with the pictures.' She beamed, and the four chins jiggled in sympathy. 'Lovely, they are. Baiae has a picture porch, of course, but it isn't near as grand and the pictures aren't as nice. I call in whenever I'm down the market and sit for a while. The master doesn't mind. "So long as it's culture and not the size of the men's whatsits that interests you, my lass," he says, "you can look at all the paintings you want." Says it every time.' The chins jiggled again. 'He enjoys a good joke, the master. You can't help but laugh.'

'Right. Right.' I nodded. Gods alive! Well, to each their bag, and if the lady enjoyed looking at coy nymphs and muscle-bound heroes while she was out buying the spring greens that was no concern of mine. However, it did give me an opening. 'Ah . . . how about bugs?'

Her face clouded. 'Bugs, sir? How d'you mean "bugs"?'

Bathyllus's gargling ended in a choke. I studiously kept my eyes away from him. 'Beetles. That sort of thing. You, uh, interested in them at all? On the collecting side?'

'No, sir.' I had the distinct impression that the lady had taken a sort of mental shuffle backwards, and I sighed inwardly. Add a word to that prefixed phrase above: '*mad* wine-soaked bugger'. Well, it'd been an outside chance. A shared love of beetles might have brought two lonely hearts together. 'I can't say as I've ever really thought about it much.' She cleared her throat nervously. 'Now, if you don't mind I'll be getting on. I've a few things to buy for dinner.'

'Yeah. Yeah, right. Uh, nice meeting you, Tyndaris. Wasn't it, litt . . . Bathyllus?'

Finally I looked at our major-domo. He was still puce, which with his bald pate made him look like a dyed egg, and he still had his manic grin.

'Mph!' he said. Very illuminating.

'I'll say good-day, then. Enjoy your afternoon, sir. Bathyllus.' Over her shoulder, Tyndaris gave us both a look that could've come straight off one of her paintings; maybe the one in the Octavian Porch with the nymph Daphne fleeing Apollo. Given that the nymph Daphne was built like two hippos squeezed into the one skin and that she thought the god had been overdoing things with the prophetic herbs.

I watched until she'd rounded the corner. Then I took Bathyllus's arm in a firm grip.

'You and me, pal,' I said, 'are going to have a little talk.'

I frog-marched him into the atrium. No sign of Perilla, but maybe that was just as well.

'Sit,' I said, pointing to the lady's usual couch.

'Really, sir, I don't see why—'

'*Sit!*'

Bathyllus sat.

'Sir, I don't see why I should be subjected to—'

'Shut up, Bathyllus.' Jupiter! It was worse than having a huffy teenager glaring back at you. Or maybe one of Perilla's huffy philosopher mates, it came to the same thing. 'You're in love with this Tyndaris woman, right?'

'Well, sir, ah I ah that is er I wouldn't exactly say ah—'

'Right.' I stretched out on my own couch. I'd've killed for a jug of Setinian, but that would've meant letting the little bugger temporarily off the hook while he fetched it. 'I'm glad we've got that settled. You think you're going to make an impression goggling at her like a fucking carp with laryngitis?'

'Sir, carp don't get—'

'Shove it, sunshine, you know what I mean. That wasn't a rhetorical question. I want an answer.'

It was a long time coming. Finally he said, without the ghost of a sniff, 'No, sir.'

'Great! Now we're getting somewhere! So what do you propose to do about it?'

Pause; *long* pause. Then, when I'd almost given up waiting: 'Absolutely nothing, sir.'

I stared at him. 'You're kidding!'

'No. The lady is so far above me that—'

'No arguments there, pal. She's got quite a bit on you both sides too.' I saw him wince. 'Yeah, okay. Bad joke, poor taste. But that's hardly positive thinking, is it?'

'I've told you, sir. I have no intention whatsoever of engaging the lady's affections. Should that be remotely possible.'

'Why not?'

He goggled. 'You don't mean, sir, that you would countenance—'

I held up a hand. 'Bathyllus, listen to me carefully, because I'll only ever say this once, right? I'll make jokes, I'll slag you off, but slave or not you're family. That counts. So if you're serious I'll give you all the help I can. Understand?'

He was quiet for a long time. Then he said quietly, 'Yes, sir. Thank you, sir.'

'Fine. So are you? Serious, I mean?'

'Yes, sir.'

Gods! Me, I'd've run a mile, but who knew what strange, lascivious thoughts ran through that fevered brain? 'Okay. Let's take it from there.' I reached for a non-existent wine cup. Bugger. 'The main problem as far as I can see is approach. Up to now you've come across with all the force of a wet dishtowel. At least, judging by how today's little meeting went. Right?'

He swallowed and nodded.

'On the other hand, she seemed friendly enough when she came up to us, so maybe I'm being over-critical. I – ah – understand that wasn't your first encounter.'

'That is correct, sir. I called over a few days ago to borrow some metal polish.'

'And?'

'Nothing else, sir. Only the metal polish.'

Jupiter on skates! 'No, Bathyllus I meant, what happened then?'

'I borrowed the metal polish, sir.'

The gods give me patience. 'You didn't talk to the lady? Not at all?'

'I identified myself, sir. And I said that I would return it as soon as possible. Which I did.'

'Right. Right. Very commendable.' Count to ten,

Corvinus. Scratch that; make it twenty. 'But you didn't, uh, have any sort of conversation? Like for example asking her where she was from and how she was enjoying her new job? Simple, everyday, basic things like that?'

'No, sir.'

'But you were already, uh, smitten?'

'Yes, sir. Very much so.'

Priapus in a marrow patch! We'd an uphill struggle here, I could tell that now. 'Uh, Bathyllus, pal, forgive me for asking you this, but, uh, have you had, uh, anything to do with women at all in your life? I mean, uh, privately, as it were?'

'Oh, yes, sir. There was a girl in Brindisi, before your father bought me.'

That was promising. Maybe Bathyllus wasn't as sexually naïve as I'd thought. A cosmopolitan town, Brindisi. 'And?'

'She was the one who introduced me to beetles, sir. We spent many happy hours looking for them.'

Shit. 'That's all? The whole story? The two of you, uh, *beetled* together?'

'Yes, sir.'

'What happened to the girl?'

'She married a bricklayer, sir.'

'Uh-huh. And nothing else happened? In the, uh, interim period? Nothing whatsoever?'

'No, sir.'

I sighed. Well, at least we were one step ahead of the game this time: after my own conversation with Tyndaris I was pretty sure we could scratch the beetles.

All the same, I felt a bit like Hercules must've done when he had his first sight of the Augean stables. 'Okay,' I said. 'This is what we do . . .'

Perilla got back half an hour later. She was carrying a pile of solid-looking book-rolls.

'Oh, hello, Marcus,' she said. 'I didn't realise you were in.' She leaned down for the welcome-home kiss. 'Have a good day?'

'Not so's you'd notice.' I hefted the jug that I'd finally got Bathyllus to bring me and topped up my wine cup. 'Book shopping?'

'That's right. Critias in the Argiletum sent round to say he'd acquired a full copy of Ephorus of Cyme's *Universal History.*' I shuddered. Yeah, well; like I say, to each his bag. 'Why's Bathyllus looking so cheerful?'

'We had a talk.'

She set the books down on the table. 'Ah.'

'"Ah" is right, lady. The air is cleared. And I've seen Tyndaris.'

'*Really?* What's she like?'

'Large.'

'Marcus—'

'You haven't seen her, I have. The word is apt and comprehensive. She's also got a thing about paintings. That's where you come in.'

'Marcus, dear, I'm sorry but you are not making sense.'

I explained. 'Tyndaris likes calling in at the porches when she does her shopping for the pigs' trotters. I've suggested to Bathyllus that you give him a sort of crash course on what's what and where it is, and the next time she goes he tags along and impresses the pants off her.'

Perilla smiled. 'Not literally, I hope.'

I grinned. 'Yeah, well, maybe not. But it's a start. What do you think?'

'I think it's brilliant.' She kissed me again and lay down on her couch. 'I'll start making a list right after dinner. Now. How is the case going?'

'The plot thickens.' I took a swallow of wine and told her about my interviews with Uranius, Laomedon and Cario. Also with the choirmaster Silvius.

'You think either of them could've done it?' she said. 'Laomedon or Uranius, I mean?'

'They're both possibles, sure. For different reasons.'

'No more than possibles?'

'Perilla, I don't know. Not yet. Characterwise, between the two I'd put my money on Laomedon. He checks out perfect all round: he hated the guy's guts, he was jealous as hell of him for all sorts of reasons, he's capable of murder, at least the physical side of it, and for all I know he had the opportunity. On the other hand I get the impression the bastard's too thick and too arrogant to carry a plan through off his own bat without tripping himself up or boasting about it later. He's got beans to spill, sure, he may even know who the killer was, but I wouldn't like to bet he'd have the nous to do it himself.'

'Unless he was working with someone else. Some-one with more brains.'

'Right. That's a possibility. There again, I could be underestimating the guy completely. Under that beefcake exterior may pulse the brains of a criminal Aristotle.'

'Brains don't pulse.'

'Whatever.'

'Very well. What about Uranius?'

'Uranius is the opposite. He thinks too much. Sure, he lost out to Pegasus even more than Laomedon did, but he hasn't got the killing feel to him. That's the impression I got, and that's what everybody's been telling me. A nice, quiet guy, wouldn't say boo to a mouse.'

'Quiet men can commit murder, given the proper incentives. And he did lie about where he was the day Pegasus was killed.'

'No argument, lady. On either count. For that matter, though, I'd say Cammius's son was lying too, and that's just as strange because at the time he had no need to.'

'Hmm.' She put her chin on her hand. 'It could've been an instinctive defence mechanism.'

'A which?'

'He was simply responding to what he subcon-sciously assessed as an implicit accusation.'

'Uh . . . yeah. Yeah, right.' Jupiter! That was *Latin*? 'Anyway, although he was open about disliking the dead guy he was pretty cagey over some of the details.'

'What kind of details?'

'That I'm not sure of. He clammed up too soon. Something to do with how Pegasus behaved in the team.'

'In that case we could be back to the bribery and corruption theory here, with Cammius and his son conspiring at the murder.'

'It's possible.' I sighed and took a long swig of wine. 'Everything's possible. You ever get the feeling you're swimming through porridge, lady?'

Perilla smiled quietly. 'Oh, you'll get there in the end, Corvinus,' she said. 'I have every confidence.'

Before I could answer, Bathyllus soft-footed in. Perilla had been right: the little guy looked a lot more like his old self.

'That's the dinner gong, is it, sunshine?' I said.

'Not yet, sir. But Alexis is back from Ostia, if you wanted to see him.'

I sat up. Hell; so much had been going on that I'd forgotten I'd sent him over that morning to check on Sopilys. 'Sure,' I said. 'Tell him to come straight in.'

Our sharp gardener looked pretty whacked, which was understandable: it's a long way to Ostia, even on horseback and with a good road. I held up the wine jug and raised an eyebrow, but Alexis shook his head. Par for the course: Alexis isn't one for wine, even when he is knackered.

'So. How did you get on?' I said.

'I saw your friend Agron, sir, and we went down to the docks together and asked around. No problem. Sopilys was working as a stevedore on the main wharf. If you want to meet him tomorrow, late morning or early afternoon, he'll be delighted to talk with you.'

'"Delighted"?'

'His own word, sir.' Alexis hesitated. 'I don't think he liked the dead man very much. He doesn't have much time for the master of the Green faction, either.'

'Is that right, now?' Well, it wasn't too surprising, if the guy had been fired. And a disgruntled Green eager and willing to talk his heart out was just what I needed. 'You ask Agron if he had time to split a jar?'

'Yes, sir. He'd be happy to. He suggests you go to his flat first thing and he'll take you to Sopilys himself.'

'Great.' Well, that was tomorrow taken care of. I still had Uranius to talk to, mind, but that could wait a couple of days. And it would be good to see Agron again. 'You've done marvels, pal. Thanks a lot.'

'Don't mention it, sir.'

'By the way, you may've noticed that Project Bathyllus is off and running. And I've met the Tyndaris female.'

'Really?'

'Yeah.' I kept my voice neutral. 'Matters are in hand involving the mistress and a guide to Rome's artistic treasures.' I glanced at Perilla and she grinned back. 'Only talking to the little guy I get the impression that where women are concerned he could do with a bit of preliminary coaching in basic conversational skills. Like stringing two consecutive words together and not grinning all the time like a demented chimp. Maybe you could handle that side of things for me, before we turn lover-boy loose on an unsuspecting world.'

'Lysias would be better, sir. He's . . . he has the experience.'

'Fine. Tell him not to overdo it, though. We don't want to create a monster.'

'No, sir.'

At which point the little bald-head himself padded in and announced dinner. Cheerful was right; he was practically whistling. Ah, well; it was spring, after all, and tastes vary.

All the same, as I carried my wine cup through to the dining-room I tried very hard not to think of the physical practicalities. It wouldn't've been fair to Meton's cooking.

14

I'm no horseman. I can ride okay, but being on top of a horse isn't exactly my idea of a great time, and I travel slow for preference; so even setting off just after dawn when the roads were quiet it took me a good three hours to get to Ostia.

Rome's port is foreign ground. I don't have much to do with the town at all, nor do most city-Romans unless they've got connections with ships or the grain trade; and where the Ostians and Rome are concerned to a lesser extent it's the same. Sure, there's any amount of coming and going between the two places, but that's mostly on the business side. When it comes to mixing socially, the fourteen miles of Ostian Road's enough to keep city and port largely different worlds. You don't even get the gang fights that flare up regularly between, say, the Eleventh District boys and the Transtibbies from across the Sublician Bridge, although it does happen occasionally on race days when the bargees come into town by the cartload wined up and looking for aggro. Think ships, trade and grain and you've got the place in one. Sure, it isn't exactly run-down, particularly around the theatre where Augustus did a bit of fancy building, but what with the old harbour silting up and most of the heavy stuff barring corn going from Puteoli it's not exactly thriving, either.

Agron's place was in a street of high-rises on the edge of town just shy of the Sullan Wall. He'd done pretty well for himself since I'd first met him years before when he'd been Varus's sister's gopher, and although he still lived in a first-floor flat he owned the whole tenement, plus the boat-building yard he'd inherited from his Alexandrian father-in-law. I'd met his wife Cass a few times: a big-boned, handsome woman very much into housework, cooking and kids. The last count, there were five of these, but Cass seemed to run a permanent crèche for the other tenement mothers, so I was never quite sure which ones were the little Illyrian-Egyptians.

I slipped one of the streetwise kids you always get hanging around tenements a couple of copper pieces to mind the horse and climbed the stairs to the first floor. Forget the usual breathe-through-your-mouth trick; there were no nasty smells, the walls were graffiti-free and the steps had been scrubbed until they shone. I'd bet the stairways further up were the same, too, because Cass believed in the direct approach where slovenly tenants were concerned, and any poor bugger who didn't measure up to her standards'd be out on his ear so fast his head would spin. Cass was a lady you didn't cross.

It was noisy, though. Whatever was going on on the first-floor landing made a free-for-all cat and dog fight sound like a slack afternoon in the Pollio Library.

I turned the corner of the stair just as a screaming midget hurtled round it and threw herself at the space beneath my bottom rib. I doubled up, but she didn't slacken speed, just pulled her head out of my breadbasket and carried on past me like nothing had happened.

'Hey, Corvinus!' I looked up gasping. Agron was shaking off half a dozen five-year-olds like they were puppies. 'Good to see you, boy! How's the lad?'

'I may never play the double-flute again.'

'Shame. You were getting good, too.'

I propped myself against the door jamb and waited for the pain to ease. 'You and Cass opened the junior branch of the Ostian gladiators' training school, pal?'

'It's a birthday party for a neighbour's eldest. That was her you just met, by the way.'

'Fine. Tell the kid from me she has a great future with the legions knocking holes in city walls.'

He laughed. 'You want to split that jug before we go and see your friend?'

'Inside or out?'

'I wouldn't do that to you, Corvinus. There's a new wineshop just opened round the corner that serves a fair Massic. Oh, and they've got a nice smoked Caedician, if you're interested.'

With me it's wine, with Agron it's cheese. Which reminded me. I took out the straw-wrapped parcel I'd picked up on a quick detour past the fancy food shops in the Velabrum and stowed away carefully in the horse's saddlebag. The birthday girl had dented it a bit, but that just served the bastard right for throwing wild parties. 'Forget the Caedician,' I said. 'Here. Enjoy.'

He opened the parcel like it was made of gossamer, looked in and sniffed.

'Sweet gods! That's a Lesoran! A *whole* Lesoran!'

'Yeah.'

'A whole *fresh* Lesoran!'

'Congratulations. You win the nuts.' The guy knew his cheeses, I'd give him that. And he had an expression on his face like mine would be with a thirty-year-old Caecuban.

'But you can't *get* fresh Lesoran in Rome!'

'The guy in the shop swore he'd had it brought over from Gaul by trireme. Now how about that Massic?'

'Sure.' He was holding the straw-wrapped cheese like it was spun glass. 'You've got it.'

'Just remember to bring him back sober, Corvinus.' I looked up. Cass was standing in the doorway like a Praxitelean Juno, with a one-year-old in the crook of her arm. Probably sprog number five, but I wasn't taking bets. 'Otherwise you're both in trouble.'

Ouch. Like I said, that is one lady you just do not mess with, if you know what's good for you. Not more than once, anyway. The last time we'd come back plastered I'd got my head to play with and Agron had slept on the living-room couch for a month. 'Uh, right, Cass. Yeah. No problem.' I glanced at Agron. He grinned weakly and shrugged. Time for the master-stroke peace offering. 'Ah . . . I've got something for you too. Or for the kids, rather.' I produced the second parcel from my cloak pouch.

Or what had been a parcel. The human battering-ram had scored a direct hit, and the pastries and candied fruit inside had got seriously bent. 'Oh, sh— . . . bother. They're, uh, a little shop-soiled.'

Cass took the papyrus-wrapped bundle, looked inside and made a face. 'So I see,' she said. 'Never mind. Off you go and enjoy yourselves. Late lunch when you get back. Pigeon pie.'

Agron glanced at me. 'That okay with you, Corvinus?'

'Yeah. Great.' I meant it, too: Cassiopeia's pigeon and egg pie with cinnamon would've had the gods passing up on their ambrosia. She'd given Meton the recipe, but the result just wasn't the same, and with Meton rolling the pastry that's high praise. Agron might be seriously under his wife's thumb, but there were definite compensations.

'Oh.' The lady paused in the doorway to the flat. 'Before you do go, Alexis didn't mention if you'd be staying the night. It's no problem, you can bunk down in the living-room with the kids.'

I looked at the specimen she was holding. It had a look of terrible concentration on its face and it was making a horribly familiar grunting noise.

'Uh, no,' I said, edging away from the danger zone. 'That's okay. I, uh, have to be getting back.'

'You're sure?' Agron said.

'Oh, I'm sure. Thanks for the offer, though.'

The atmosphere on the landing was growing thicker by the second. I made it to the safety of the stairwell just in time.

*   *   *

We had the jug, and Agron made inroads on his cheese. Then we set off for the harbour.

I was glad I'd asked the big Illyrian to track down Sopilys for me. Ostia may've lost quite a bit of trade these past fifty years, but it's still the main port of the capital of the world, and that means a hell of a lot of wharves and a hell of a lot of shipping. Which in turn means a small army of stevedores. If I'd tried it cold, finding the guy wouldn't've been easy.

'That's him over there.' Agron pointed to a little runt in an oversize tunic leaning against a pile of hides and chewing a hunk of bread. We'd timed it well: the Ostian stevedore gangs work in shifts and we'd obviously hit his lunch break. 'You won't want me butting in, Corvinus, so I'll leave you to it. See you back at the gates, okay?'

'Right. Thanks, pal.' I strolled towards the guy. 'Hey, Sopilys?'

He looked up, and I saw his eyes take in the broad stripe on my mantle. The jaws stopped working and he grinned.

'Marcus Valerius Corvinus, right?' he said.

'Yeah.' I held out my hand and we shook. 'So. My lad Alexis tell you what this is about?'

'Sure. That bugger Pegasus. Your slave says some-one put a knife into him.'

'Right.'

He lowered the bread and spat neatly over the side of the wharf into the scummy water. 'Couldn't've happened to a nicer person. I hope the bastard's frying in hell.'

Well, at least opinions were pretty consistent on that subject, anyway. I wondered if Pegasus had had a sweet grey-haired old mother, and if so whether her view would be any different. Possibly not. 'I understand you had a fist-fight with him before he left the Greens,' I said. 'Care to tell me what it was about?'

'I might.' He looked pointedly at the fold in my mantle where I kept my purse and took another bite out of the bread hunk.

I sighed: Alexis's *delighted* had obviously been a relative term. 'No problem, pal. A silver piece?'

He chewed and swallowed. 'Make it five.' I'd been leaning against the hides next to him. Now I straightened. Sopilys never moved. 'Information doesn't come cheap, Corvinus.'

'That depends on the information. Two.'

'Five. Last offer. Pay up or ship out.'

I shrugged. 'Okay. Five it is. If the information's worth it.'

'Pegasus was on the game.' His teeth tore at the bread.

'Uh-huh. What sort of game would that be?'

He laughed, spraying me with wet crumbs. 'There's only one game in the racing business. He was selling races.'

Yeah, well, I'd expected as much; still, it was good to have it confirmed. 'Who to?'

'You ever hear of a man called Eutacticus?'

Shit; not another name! 'Uh-uh. Who's Eutacticus?'

'Runs a betting cartel and takes a cut from most of

the freelance touts. The smart ones, that is. Those that aren't smart end up cut different.'

I nodded. Right. I might not know Eutacticus, but I knew the system. Technically, betting – any kind of betting, barring private wagers – is illegal in the city outside the Winter Festival: a hangover from the good old strait-laced Republican days when a man stuck to his plough and left fast women, fancy food and the like to degenerates like the Greeks. Witness the guy in the market with the thimbles. In practice, just like they do with tax collecting and public sector building, the state licenses a small number of cartels to run a book at the racetrack in exchange for a flat fee paid to the Treasury. The guys heading the cartels may not appear in the social calendar, but with a hundred and fifty thousand punters packing the Circus on race days and just begging to throw their money away most of them could buy out King Croesus without straining their bank balances, and as far as street clout's concerned they have it in spades. They also tend to have all the moral sensibilities of Suburan alley-cats.

On the other hand, they're just the cream. Below them there's room and to spare for private enterprise to take an interest, and since stamping on unlicensed touts just isn't a practical option for the authorities some of the bigger and less scrupulous cartel bosses run their own policing system; for which read 'protection racket'. No one loses, everyone wins, and if there are corpses tucked away behind the concession stands then the city judge turns a blind eye because they're just a necessary part of the system.

The whole business is rotten, sure, but it does the job. Not that that made the buggers at the top any nicer people. I'd bet this Eutacticus was a real peach.

'So how did the scam work?' I asked.

Sopilys shrugged. 'The usual. Eutacticus tips Pegasus the wink when he's to lose. Not every race, that wouldn't be in anyone's interest because it'd push the betting down and Pegasus'd get the reputation of being a second-rater. The losing's easy. Getting away with it without being spotted by your faction boss, that's the tricky thing. Pegasus was good at that.'

'Until he was spotted.'

Sopilys reached down, picked up a small flask of wine and took a pull at it. Then he wiped his mouth with the back of his hand. 'You want to tell the story yourself?' he said finally. 'Or do you want to hear what really happened? It's your money. You choose.'

Touchy as well as venal. Still, he had a point. 'Yeah, okay,' I said. 'Go ahead, friend.'

'No, he wasn't spotted. I told you, the guy was good – he'd have to be, with Natalis's eye on him – and he didn't take risks. Eutacticus is no fool either. They only worked the scam three, maybe four times a season. Eutacticus'd wait until the odds rose and the heavy money was laid on, then he'd give the bastard the nod and that would be it. He'd clean up and Pegasus would find a nice little nest-egg in a drop somewhere.'

'So what went wrong?'

Sopilys grinned. 'I went wrong. I was the guy's groom. One day I caught him cutting a trace.'

'And you told Natalis?'

'There's no profit in splitting to the boss, Corvinus, and that bugger's near enough to skin a flint. Pegasus and me, we . . . came to an arrangement.'

I was beginning to see daylight here. 'You soaked him in exchange for keeping your mouth shut.'

'Not soaked. I wasn't greedy. With what he was getting he could afford it.' He took another swig from the wine flask. 'I kept to my side of the deal for two months. Then two days before the Augustales the bastard suddenly shafted me.'

'Uh-huh. And how did he do that?'

'You ever hear of something called cassia senna?'

'No.'

'It's a plant, comes from Africa. Inland Africa, not the province. Dry leaves and pods, with the leaves being the real buggers. They stink to high heaven, but you soak them in water, pour the water over a handful of raisins and leave them to steep. Feed the raisins to a horse and the result's like a bad colic. Only thing is, after it's eaten them the horse pisses orange.'

'You've lost me, pal. What good would that do Pegasus?'

'I told you. He was smart. A colic, sure, any horse can get that naturally, but the orange piss is a give-away that the brute's been doped. The stable vet spotted it straight off. He goes running to Natalis, who blows his wig and orders a search of the stable lads' belongings, because stable staff're the first and obvious suspects, right? And guess where they find a dinky little bag with a couple of fucking cassia senna leaves inside?'

'You're saying Pegasus set you up?'

'Sweet as a nut. Natalis pulls me into the office by the balls and an hour later I'm out on the street and lucky still to be walking. Fifteen fucking years I worked for the Greens and it was all gone. One afternoon, that's all it took.'

'You didn't tell him about Pegasus? Natalis, I mean.'

'Sure I told him. The bugger might've reckoned on me clamming up, but I'd nothing to lose. I gave Natalis the whole boiling, A to Z.'

'And?'

'And nothing. He didn't believe me because, like I said, Pegasus'd been careful to keep his nose clean.' Sopilys shook the wine flask, put it to his mouth and drained it, then tossed it over the side of the wharf. 'Bastard! The lads did, though, by hell they did! When I got the bugger outside the Cat the next night and beat the shit out of him they stood back and let me do it.'

Well, that cleared up that little problem. It showed that Sopilys was probably telling the truth, too: although I'd bet Pegasus hadn't been any more popular with his Green team-mates than he was with the Whites, he was still the lead driver, and it takes a lot of animosity for that to get ignored. 'You, uh, happen to have any idea why Pegasus left?'

Sopilys shot me a look. 'Why should I?'

'It's a fair question,' I said equably. 'Considering the guy transferred to the Whites less than two months later.'

'Corvinus, by that time I'm here in Ostia unloading barges. I don't have the contacts no more, and after the way I was treated I don't have the fucking interest, either. I'll tell you one thing, though: it wasn't for the reason you're thinking.'

'Is that so, now?' I leaned back. 'And just what would I be thinking?'

'That Natalis sussed the bastard himself and threw him out.'

Ostian stevedore or not Sopilys was no bonehead. There was a brain behind these shifty eyes. 'Okay. You care to tell me why that's definitely not an option?'

'First off, the only meet between the Augustales and the time he left was the Plebbies, and Pegasus won his race hands down. Drove like a dream with no wobblers, right?' I nodded. 'Second, more important, the guy wasn't sacked, he transferred. Sitting back and letting him do that wouldn't't've been Natalis's style, especially since the two of them rubbed each other's bristles up the wrong way. If he'd caught Pegasus throwing a race – especially if it looked like it was no one-off – he'd've pegged the bastard out for the vultures before you can spit.'

Fair point; and Natalis had more or less told me the same thing, on general principles, when we'd talked. Which raised a very interesting question in itself . . .

'Fine,' I said. 'One last thing. This Eutacticus guy. Where would I find him, now?'

Sopilys grinned. 'Oh, you don't want to do that. You really don't.'

'Five silver pieces, remember? I could make it eight.'

The grin faded. Sopilys licked his lips nervously and his eyes flicked to mine and away. 'Corvinus, listen,' he said. 'I'm serious here. Telling you what happened's one thing, especially if it pisses on that bastard Pegasus's bones, but he's dead and the scam's dead. No use stirring it. And Eutacticus is bad news, believe me. The worst.'

'Ten. I'll find him whether you tell me or not. Only if you don't when I do see him I'll make sure he knows your name. Understand?'

No grin now, not a vestige; the guy was sweating. 'Castor! You wouldn't—'

'Just give me an address, pal, then I'll pay you what I owe you and get out of your life.'

'You tell Eutacticus I blew the whistle and I'm dead. I'm not kidding, Corvinus.'

He wasn't either: the guy was scared shitless. 'Peach' was right. 'I won't tell,' I said. 'You've got my word for that. But I need the address.'

It was a close thing. For a while I didn't think he was going to bite, but ten silver pieces is a lot of gravy to a bargeman. Sopilys's eyes shifted again and he lowered his voice. 'Okay,' he said. 'We have a deal. He has a big place on the Pincian. Near the south-east corner of the Pompeian Gardens. But look, Corvinus—'

'Great. Thanks, friend.' I took a half gold piece out of my purse and handed it to him. 'Oh. And if you happen to think of anything else in future that might be of interest you let me know, okay?' I gave him Agron's address.

'Fuck that. There isn't any more. Or if there is I can't help you with it.' He slipped the coin into his pouch. If he was grateful for the bonus it didn't show.

'And if you're planning to mix with Eutacticus, friend, then you don't have no future.'

I winced. Well, we'd cross that bridge when we came to it. 'Right. Thanks again. I'll see you around.'

The lack of a reply was eloquent enough; and I could feel his eyes on my back all the way to the dock gates.

I picked up with Agron and we went home for Cass's pigeon pie and another jug; the kids' party had broken up by then, thank the gods, and the flat was pretty peaceful apart from the big guy's own brood plus two or three leftovers who were playing Romans and Carthaginians round the table. I packed it in before they got round to refighting Zama, collected my horse from the neighbour's garden next door where Agron had parked it and started back for the big city.

Not a wasted day, by any means. Sopilys had confirmed one theory – that Pegasus had been involved in a scam before he left the Greens – and given me a couple of unexpected leads. This Eutacticus guy was a mixed blessing. Sure, if I wanted to fill in the background to the scam – which I'd have to do before I ruled it out as a contributing factor to Pegasus's murder – then I'd have to talk to him; only from the colour Sopilys had turned when the bugger's name came up that wasn't something I was looking forward to, not without a half-dozen beefy lads with clubs at my back as an insurance policy. Like I say, these cartel bastards live on the edge, they've got more clout, practically speaking, than a decade's-worth of ex-consuls, and they play hard. If they didn't, they wouldn't last five minutes.

The other lead was less straightforward. I'd taken Sopilys's point about Pegasus having walked as an argument against Natalis having rumbled him, sure I had. There were things, though, that didn't quite fit. Natalis was no fool: he'd been a driver himself, he was a Green to the bone and I'd bet he knew his faction better than a father knows his kids. So if the lads who'd been with Pegasus that night at the Black Cat had believed Sopilys's version of the doping story enough to stand back and let the ex-groom thump him then Natalis couldn't've been totally blind to the possibility that his ace driver might be a rotten apple. Added to which, Sopilys had told me himself that he'd been lucky, the day he was sacked, to leave the premises without a few bones broken. If Natalis was the sort of guy to take an attempted poisoning personally – which again according to Sopilys he was – then that just shouldn't've happened. Only if you were working on the theory that the Greens' boss had pulled Pegasus's plug a month and a half later then it must've happened not just once but twice.

Put all that together and something smelled. I didn't know yet what it was, but I'd find out. One thing I'd bet on, though: Natalis knew more than he was saying. And taking that with what Cammius had told me about the Greens' attempts on their crack horse Polydoxus that was interesting as hell.

15

The next day was the twenty-ninth – the day my musician pal Silvius had told me had been the date for the fourth monthly glee club meeting before it had been scrapped – and I was up bright and early for my stake-out of the Whites' stable. Sure, I could've got Uranius into a corner and tried twisting his arm over where he'd been going for the last six months when his mates thought he was singing bass on the Aventine, but from my brief conversation with him I doubted if that'd get me anywhere. Guys like Sopilys could be bought and the Laomedons of this world might bluster but they'd crack under pressure. Uranius was something else, the stubborn, silent type. One got you ten that he'd simply clam up, and short of accusing him directly of shoving the knife into Pegasus, which I didn't want to do because I didn't think he'd done it, I hadn't all that much comeback.

Which left the sneaky approach. I might be unlucky, of course – I didn't *know* that he was working to a fixed programme, and even so he might be innocent as a newborn babe – but the chances were that if I let him loose and watched where he went then I'd have the answers I needed.

If Uranius was running true to form he wouldn't be setting out much before noon, but I couldn't risk missing him so I got myself over to Mars Field with plenty of time to spare. My main problem was cover. Mars Field is what it says, a lot of empty space, and even on the edges buildings aren't too plentiful. Apart from the stables themselves, the stretch of road that overlooked the Whites' gate was a virtual blank. The best I could do was an old rain cistern set a dozen yards back from the kerb and fifty yards shy of the gate on the other side that'd probably been used for watering stock when this part of the city had been virgin farmland. Not perfect by any means, but it screened me from the Whites' guard and from any passing pedestrians. The sight of a purple-striper skulking in the bushes might prompt a few awkward questions, and you could only get away with leaning nonchalantly against a tree-trunk and whistling for so long before someone got suspicious.

At least the weather was good. Standing around twiddling my thumbs in the rain has never been my idea of a morning well spent.

It was a long wait right enough, but finally just after noon Uranius came out, nodded to Cement-Features and came walking towards me. I let him pass, then tagged along behind at a safe distance. Inside the city proper at that time of day the streets are heaving, but even though it does connect with the Aemilian Bridge Triumph Road's comparatively empty; of foot traffic, anyway. The last thing I wanted was to have him turn round and see me following.

For the Aventine, you turn right at Marcellus Theatre and go through the old vegetable market to Cattlemarket Square and Public Incline beyond. Uranius didn't. He kept on going. On to Iugarius.

My scalp was prickling. Renatius's wineshop was in the next block, and coincidences like that just didn't happen.

Tailing the guy was money for jam. Wherever he was going, he obviously wasn't worried about the secrecy angle, which might've persuaded me that the whole thing was innocent after all if I hadn't known he'd had six months to lose any nervousness. Still, I couldn't afford to get cocky. The road was pretty full now with the usual city-centre mélange of donkeys, mules, litters and pedestrians – we were past Renatius's and almost within spitting distance of Market Square – so I narrowed the gap to just three: an old biddy with a string bag almost as big as she was and full of onions, a tunic carrying a load of assorted kitchenware on a pole, and a plain-mantle so fat that if Uranius did happen to glance behind him for starters he'd have four horizontal feet of blubber to spot me through.

Then the old biddy suddenly decided to stop for a breather. She set the bag down next to her, effectively blocking the pavement, and after the resulting confusion I realised he wasn't ahead of me any more.

Shit. I pushed past the woman as politely as I could, jumped the bag, elbowed past the kitchenware man and Tubby Titus, took the next corner into the side street at a skid and was just in time to see Uranius disappear into the entry of a low tenement fifty yards further down.

I stopped. Okay; so what did we do now? As far as I could see I had three options. I could wait for the guy to come back out, or I could go home and nail him later at the stables, or I could follow him in. There wasn't much point to the first, and I'd had enough of hanging around for one day. Ditto for the second, which just meant putting things off.

That left the third . . .

Whatever god looks down on footsore sleuths was smiling. A seriously crinkled old biddy who could've been the sister of the one who'd blocked Iugarius had just disgorged from the tenement entrance and was stomping her single-minded way towards me. I stepped out in front of her.

'Sorry to bother you, grandma—' I began.

'Then don't, son.' A pair of rheumy eyes set above a nose that could've belonged to an unlucky prize-fighter glared up at me and a seriously bony elbow caught me in the ribs. 'And watch where you're stand-ing.'

Jupiter! I skipped aside and walked backwards while she plodded on up the pavement like a single-minded warthog. 'Uh . . . yeah. Right. Only that guy who went inside a moment ago. You happen to see which flat he was after?'

'I ain't blind. And I've the dinner to buy.'

'First floor? Second?'

'Second. Theogenia's.'

'Great. Thanks a lot.'

'You're welcome. Now bugger off.'

I stepped off the pavement into the gutter and watched as she crossed the road, pushed her way between a couple of loungers on the far side and disappeared round the corner. She didn't break stride once. Why the legions bothered with battering rams and tortoises when they could recruit little old ladies with string bags and lethal elbows I didn't know.

Second floor. And a woman by the name of Theogenia. Yeah, well, maybe *innocent* wasn't so far out after all. Certainly it might explain the secrecy.

I took the stairs two at a time, reached the second landing, chose a door at random and knocked. A minute or so later it was opened by an unshaven guy holding a dead chicken up by the feet. The mind boggled.

'Yeah?' he said.

'Uh . . . Theogenia's flat?'

'That's the one opposite.'

'Right. Thanks.' I was talking to the woodwork. I crossed to the door on the other side of the landing and tapped. There was a shuffling noise, the door opened and a frail old woman peered out.

'Yes?'

'Uh . . . your name Theogenia?' I said.

'Yes. What can I do for you?'

She had to be eighty, at least. Okay; so scratch the romantic interest. 'I'm looking for a guy called Uranius.'

Her eyes shifted. 'I don't know anyone called—'

'Lady, I don't want to cause any trouble, right? I just want to talk to him, and I know he's here.'

She hesitated and glanced behind her. Then she said; 'Very well. You'd best come in.'

She stepped back. There was only one room, with a bed, a low table, a dresser and a couple of stools. Uranius was sitting on one of them. He looked up at me, his jaw sagging.

Sitting on the other stool and overhanging it considerably on both sides was a girl. She wasn't a looker, that was sure. A wall-eye swung in my direction, and her face would've done service for the back of a cart. Behind me, the old woman closed the door and shuffled over to the bed. She sat down and stared at me in silence.

Uranius had finally managed to get his mouth closed. 'What are you doing here, Corvinus?' he said.

'I was meaning to ask you the same question, friend.'

The Whites' lead driver shrugged. 'It's no business of yours,' he said, 'but this is my fiancée Galatea.'

'She is *what*?' I said, when he told me the next bit.

'Titus Natalis's daughter,' Uranius repeated. He was actually blushing.

'So what the hell's she doing in an Iugarius tenement?'

'It's the only way we can meet.'

Gods alive! The Greens' faction master's daughter and the lead White driver, eh? Things were beginning to make sense. Complicated sense, sure, but still . . .

'He, uh, doesn't know, then? About the engagement?'

'Daddy would kill me,' the girl said simply. She

might not have anything going for her in the looks department, but she had a nice voice. 'He'd certainly kill Uranius. Literally.' She stretched out her hand and took his. 'He thinks I'm visiting my old nurse – that's Theogenia here – which of course I am.'

'There's been no hanky-panky.' The old woman spoke for the first – and what turned out to be the only – time, and from her tone I'd've bet she was hell over eating up the spinach. 'I haven't left them alone for a minute. And she's always been a good girl.'

'Nursie, *please!*'

Jupiter! the star-crossed lovers' bit. It was Bathyllus all over again. Maybe they were putting something in the water. There wasn't another stool, so I leaned against the wall for support. 'So this has been going on for the past six months, has it?'

'That's right,' Uranius said. 'We met the first time by accident. I'd seen Galatea on and off at the racetrack with her father. Then I bumped into her in Critias's bookshop in the Argiletum and we got talking. It sort of . . . took off from there.'

'Meeting at Theogenia's was my idea,' the girl said. 'I've visited Nursie' – she paused, then went on more carefully – 'my nurse Theogenia once a month for years, ever since Daddy gave her her freedom. We didn't have to make any special arrangements. And when Uranius's fourth choir practice meeting was cancelled it seemed the perfect opportunity to get together regularly without anyone knowing.'

Critias's bookshop. Where Perilla had found what's-his-name's *Universal History*. Yeah, well, I'd known that Uranius was a pretty strange guy for a slave, so I supposed literacy and a taste for reading weren't too far over the top. 'Uh . . . *Galatea*? That's an unusual name, isn't it, for a freeborn woman?'

As soon as I said it, I felt like biting my tongue off. For these two, the words 'freeborn' and 'slave' would have definite and unpleasant connotations. Freeborn women – especially ones from rich families – don't marry slaves. It's a legal as well as a social no-no: loss of citizenship's only the start of the problem. And from what I'd seen of him, like the lady had said, Titus Natalis wasn't the sort to give a fatherly blessing to the alliance. Star-crossed lovers was right.

The girl had reddened. 'It's just a nickname. Daddy gave it to me when I was a child. He's from Sicily, you know.'

Galatea. The nymph the Sicilian cyclops Polyphemus was stuck on. Yeah, well, given the current situation and Uranius's physical appearance, if not the lady's, that had a certain irony to it in itself. Who says coincidences don't happen?

'Galatea's father wants her to marry into a purple-striper family.' Uranius was squeezing the girl's hand. 'He's got . . . ambitions. But we thought . . . we thought maybe—'

'We thought if Uranius could earn enough to buy his freedom it would at least be a start,' Galatea said. 'Certainly it would remove the legal barrier. Daddy's not as hard as he seems, not where family's concerned. There's always the chance that I can . . . bring him round eventually.'

And now with Pegasus dead and the Whites on the up-and-up all that was back on the cards, I thought, and caught myself guiltily. Shit, no; that was pure kite-flying. Uranius was no killer. No way, nohow, never. Anyway, I'd bet when the bastard was getting himself stabbed in Renatius's alley he'd been here swapping sweet nothings with his fiancée under Theogenia's eagle eye. Which reminded me. I turned to Uranius.

'When we talked at the stables I asked you if you knew who Pegasus was planning to meet at the wineshop. You said you didn't know. You, uh, like to change that answer now, maybe?'

His eyes flickered. 'No.'

I sighed. 'I'm sorry, but you're a bad liar, pal. I knew that at the time and I know it now. So who was it?'

'I told you the truth, Corvinus. I didn't know Pegasus was meeting anyone. And he wasn't likely to take me into his confidence, was he?'

I couldn't leave it there. The guy had beans to spill, that was sure, and whatever they were they were important. 'Okay. But you saw something. Or someone. Now look, Uranius, I really don't want to hassle you but I have to know, right? So cut the prevarication.'

He hesitated and glanced at Galatea.

'Go on,' she said quietly. 'Tell him.'

Uranius swallowed and nodded. 'All right. I'd been here and I was on my way back, walking along Iugarius. There was a crowd outside Renatius's wineshop and a couple of slaves were carrying someone out of the alley on a stretcher, but I didn't stop to see what was going on because I was late. I'd gone about a hundred yards when someone banged into me from behind and almost knocked me over, then kept on running.' He paused. 'He was pretty distressed. I doubt if he even saw me. He certainly didn't look back.'

The hairs on my neck rose. 'But you recognised him, right?'

Another swallow. 'Yes. I did. Of course I did.'

Long silence. I waited.

Galatea squeezed his hand. 'Uranius? Marcus Corvinus is right. He has to know.'

Uranius looked at me. The guy wasn't happy, that was sure. 'It was the boss's son,' he said. 'Cario.'

16

It was too late in the afternoon to go all the way back up to the Whites' stables that day, and besides I needed to think this through before I confronted Cario. The guy had questions to answer, sure he did, but at least the air was a lot clearer. I could scratch Uranius from the list of suspects, anyway. I'd confirmed the timings with Theogenia quietly on my way out, and our lovesick Whites driver had a cast-iron alibi: all that poor sap was guilty of was covering up an affair that, if it had come to light, would've at best split the pair and at worst left him dead in an alley of his own. Galatea had been right on that count: her father wasn't the type to accept a slave as a son-in-law, not when he had the entrée into high society through Prince Gaius and his pals, and although as far as looks went she wasn't much of a catch Daddy's bank balance would be a pretty strong incentive for any poverty-stricken noble. Added to which, I'd bet that if and when he did find out about the engagement Natalis would have both the ruthlessness and the contacts to terminate it with extreme prejudice forthwith.

So. Home. I left the tenement, carried on up the road until it joined with Tuscan Street and then headed for Circus Valley and the long hike up the Caelian. I could've murdered a jug of wine, but that could wait until I got in. Also, although it hadn't been a particularly strenuous day a lot of it had involved just standing around, and I was physically and mentally knackered. Besides, there was the Bathyllus situation to check up on. Before I'd left that morning Perilla had said that the next stage of the operation was all ready to roll: she'd put together her cultural guidebook for the little guy to mug up, Lysias had had a word in the perfumed ear of his next-door girlfriend, and arrangements had been made for our shy major-domo to tag along with his two-ton inamorata on her daily shopping trip. He'd be back by now, hopefully bright-eyed and bushy-tailed, and ready with his report. That I was looking forward to with a sort of horrible fascination.

There was no sign of him when I got in, just one of the kitchen skivvies doing duty as a door-slave. I stripped off my mantle, sent the kid scurrying for a jug of Setinian, and went through to the living-room. Perilla was on the couch with Ephorus of Cyme. I gave her the usual kiss.

'Bathyllus not back yet?' I said.

'No, Marcus.' She laid the roll aside. 'I'm getting rather concerned. Mind you, the list I gave him was quite exhaustive.'

'Didn't you tell him to spin it out? It's the only courting ammunition the guy's got. If he fires it off all at once next time it'll have to be the bugs.'

'Spinning things out entails having other things to

talk about in the spaces, dear. I think that may be Bathyllus's problem.'

'Yeah. Right.' I stretched out on my own couch.

'So. How was your day? Did you find where Uranius goes when he isn't where he should be?'

'Uh-huh.' I told her about Galatea and Theogenia's flat.

'But that's dreadful! The poor girl!'

'It's the way the world works, lady. There's nothing you can do about it. Personally I think that if she has the idea that Uranius buying his freedom will change Daddy's mind for him she's whistling through her ear.' The skivvy came in with the magic tray. I poured a belt of Setinian, downed it in one and refilled the cup. Nectar! 'We had one more plus. Cammius's boy Cario has jumped a couple of notches up the suspect list. Uranius saw him running away after the murder.'

Perilla frowned. '*Right* after the murder? But I thought you said that Uranius was with his girlfriend at the time.'

'Not right after the murder. Uranius was passing when the Watch were doing their little tap-dance. He saw Cario a couple of minutes later when the guy was haring in the direction of Triumph Road.'

'Then the timing's wrong, surely. If Cario were the killer then he would have been gone long before that.'

I took another swig of wine. 'Not necessarily. From what Uranius said he was seriously panicked. That argues some involvement, for a start. And he could've been hanging around in a blue funk before he decided to go back to the stables.'

'At a run?'

'Why not?'

'Corvinus, that isn't very likely, is it? Either he'd take to his heels at once – in, as you say, panic – or he'd have had sufficient time to recover and would walk back sensibly. And if the killing was premeditated, as you said you believed it to be, then for the murderer to draw attention to himself by running when there was no need would make even less sense.'

I thought about that for a moment. Yeah. Right. The lady had a point. Two points. 'Even so, he must've been involved somewhere along the line, Perilla. Innocent men don't run away when they see a corpse being carried out of an alley. Besides, he knew the guy. If he'd asked one of the ghouls who it was and been told Pegasus – which he would've been – he'd surely have made himself known to the Watch. And the clincher, naturally, is that he told me categorically and unsolicitedly that he'd been at the stables when the murder happened.'

'There's no such word as *unsolicitedly*.'

'Whatever. You know what I mean. Killer or not, the bastard's in it to his eyeballs.'

'Oh, I agree. He's certainly a prime candidate for the person whom Pegasus was waiting to meet. In fact, that would explain why he ran.'

Yeah; I'd been thinking much the same myself. If I'd had a secret appointment with someone and turned up for it only to find the guy had been stiffed by a person or persons unknown half an hour before then I'd be pretty jittery too. Especially if—

I stopped.

'Hey, Perilla,' I said. 'Pegasus was the Whites' driver, Cario's the Whites' boss's son, right?'

'Yes. So?'

'We've been round this way before, with Uranius. If one of them wanted to talk to the other one then why the hell not do it at the stables? Why this complicated cloak-and-dagger shit with a non-faction wineshop?'

She had on her prim look. 'I don't know, Corvinus. You tell me. And please don't use bad language where it isn't necessary.'

Well, that was an improvement on her usual blanket prohibition, anyway. 'Because whatever the purpose of the meeting was it was strictly under the rose. Where the Whites were concerned, I mean. They wanted privacy, they didn't want to be seen talking, and they certainly didn't want to risk being overheard by their faction mates. That suggests a conspiracy of some kind involving the faction. When he drove for the Greens Pegasus was selling races, and leopards don't change their spots. One gets you ten he was set to work the same scam with the Whites, and Cario was involved.'

'Marcus, Cario is the son of the Whites' faction master!'

'Sure he is. All the same, I know Cario's sort. Jupiter, I used to *be* one. Young tearaways who run around with the fast crowd get through money like it was going out of fashion so they're always broke. What's the odds that Cario and Pegasus were cooking up a scam between them for the Megalenses?'

She was frowning. 'Such as what?'

'Gods alive, Perilla, I don't know exactly! Probably Pegasus was going to throw his race, let Cario clean up on the outside bets and split the profits.'

'You really think that's likely?'

'Why not? And it would explain the wineshop.'

'Not altogether. It was still a very public place, and Pegasus, at least, would be sure to be recognised. As indeed he was. If what they were discussing was connected with racing then surely they would have chosen a safer venue.'

'There may have been reasons. I wouldn't dismiss the possibility out of hand just because of that, and it's the natural assumption to make.'

'Very well.' She tugged absently at her earlobe. 'Let's say they were planning what you suggest. You've met Cario, Marcus, I haven't. Do you think he's capable of something like that?'

I was on a roll here, and I had my mouth open to say yes. Then my brain finally kicked in ahead of it and I stopped.

The honest answer was no. I'd been spouting pure moonshine, and I knew it. The guy might be a sharp-dressing blade-about-town, but he was a racing man like his father and a White to the bone. Cario wouldn't throw a race for cash, and he wouldn't do down the Whites; no way, never, it just wasn't in him. Also unless he was the best actor I'd ever come across he'd genuinely hated Pegasus, and hate doesn't fit well with partnership. Last, the Megalenses would've been Pegasus's first drive for the faction. Even if the guy was a crook – and there was no argument there – he would've wanted to settle in, establish his faction street-cred, especially having just come down the ladder from the Greens. He wouldn't've thrown his first race even if he could be almost sure of not being caught, not just for the sake of a few side bets. The game wasn't worth the candle.

She was right about Renatius's being too public a place to discuss a racing scam, too. That put the lid on it. The scam theory was all wrong. There were just too many negatives for it to be tenable.

'No,' I said. 'No, maybe not.'

'Then why the meeting? If it was Cario?'

I took another swig of wine. 'Search me, lady. Sure, I'm ninety-nine per cent certain that Cario's our boy there, but that's as far as I go. The rest'll have to wait until I—'

'Good afternoon, sir.'

I turned round in surprise. Our wandering major-domo had finally returned to the fold, and he'd done his usual trick of pussyfooting in on my blind side. 'Hey, Bathyllus! How's the lad?'

'Very well indeed, sir,' he said. 'Madam.'

I could believe it. The little bald-head radiated health, goodwill and smugness. He was almost – shock, horror! – smiling. 'Okay,' I said. 'Unbutton your lip and give! How did things go with Tyndaris?'

'Absolutely splendidly, sir. And the mistress's little *vade-mecum* was invaluable.'

'So let's have the blow-by-blow account. Where did you go?'

'We bought some pork chops, sir, in the meat market. Pork is very reasonable at present, seemingly. Then we went to the vegetable market and purchased—'

'Bathyllus.'

'Yes, sir?'

'No preliminaries, please. Just the salacious bits.'

'There were no salacious bits, sir.'

Yeah, well; I hadn't really believed there would be. Just checking. 'Okay, sunshine. Whatever. But skip the shopping list, right?'

Bathyllus sniffed. Great! I hadn't heard a real one of these for days! The little bugger was on the mend, right enough! 'If you insist, sir. The lady had only recently been to the Octavian Porch so she suggested we visit Apollo's temple on the Palatine. The Danaids and their husbands, sir. Sculpture rather than painting, of course, but she expressed a liking for art in the round. Fortunately the mistress's booklet came up trumps and I was able to hold my own in a most stimulating conversation.'

'Uh . . . *stimulating*?'

'Yes, sir. Extremely so.'

Jupiter on wheels, what had we unleashed? On both sides. And the Temple of Apollo, for the gods' sakes! If you were to name just one venue in Rome that was favourite for sexual assignations, the Danaid Porch in Apollo's temple would be the lad. Maybe it was that long line of scantily clothed female and unclothed male figures that did it – forty-nine of them, if the artist had followed the myth; I'd never counted myself – but the place acted on the male-female libidos like a barrel of oysters and a bushel of asparagus. Which raised interesting questions about Tyndaris's own motives. If she'd been the driving force, as it were, then Bathyllus was home and dry; any female who took a male companion round the Danaid Porch was sending a message so clear you could read it in the dark with your fingertips. 'You care to go into details, pal?'

'We inspected the statues, sir. I drew parallels with the work of Hagesandrus, Athanadorus and Polydorus which Tyndaris questioned, and this in turn led to quite a spirited exchange concerning the nature of—'

'Right. Right. That's enough.' Jupiter! Besides, Perilla had opened her mouth to say something and I'd just bet it would've been erudite and ten miles off the point. 'What happened next?'

'We went for a fruit juice, sir. To a little place on Tuscan Street. We sat there for some time, which explains my lateness.'

This sounded more promising. 'You talked?'

'Tyndaris did most of the talking, sir. It transpires that she's a widow, from Ephesus originally. Her former partner was a coach-driver who died in unfortunate circumstances. She wasn't very clear about these but I understand they involved a bull which had escaped from a slaughterhouse.'

'Uh . . . yeah. Right.'

'Her then master's family moved to Baiae some five years ago. He managed one of the hotels on the seafront but gave it up when his wife died. That was last year, sir. Three months ago he inherited a little property in Fidenae. He moved into it but was compelled to make cuts in his household and so sold Tyndaris to a dealer in Rome. Whence of course she came to our neighbour Petillius.' Bathyllus blushed. 'I have the impression, sir, that she's quite a lonely person.'

Fascinating stuff, fascinatingly told. Still, from the sound of things the boy had done good, certainly a lot better than I would've given him credit for. And *lonely* had a promising ring to it. 'So have you, uh, arranged any sort of follow-up?'

The blush deepened. 'She asked me if I would give her a hand tomorrow morning with a little pickling, sir. If that is all right with you. Petillius, it seems, is extremely fond of pickled pig's trotters.'

Yuch! Even so, each to his own. And at least Operation Bathyllus had got off to a flying start. 'Well done, litt— . . . Bathyllus. He's done wonders, hasn't he, Perilla?'

'Marvellous.' The lady beamed.

Bathyllus was blushing so hard now he looked like a Spring Festival egg. 'Thank you, sir. Meton says dinner will be served quite shortly, but I left instructions for the hypocaust to be stoked and you should have ample time to bathe if you wish. Can I bring you some more wine in the meantime?'

'No, that's okay, pal.' Well, his day out had certainly brightened up the little bald-head: usually the question about the wine had a sarcastic edge to it and was accompanied by a pointed glance at the level in the jug and a disapproving sniff. I didn't know how long this new all-sweetness-and-light version of our major-domo would last, but it made a pleasant change from the sarky little bugger we normally had to deal with. 'The bath sounds good, though. Just what I need.'

'Very well, sir. I will give the appropriate instructions. A fruit juice, madam?'

Perilla smiled and shook her head. Bathyllus bowed and soft-shoed out.

I waited until he was out of earshot. 'Mission accomplished, lady, would you say?'

Perilla was still smiling. 'It would seem so, Marcus. Quite definitely. Success may, however, take a little getting used to.'

'Yeah, right.' Never a truer word was spoken. I took another gulp of Setinian, topped up my cup from the jug and stretched to my full length with a satisfied sigh. Bowing, even! Somewhere over the Capitol flying pigs were looping the loop. 'Never mind. Enjoy it while you can.'

17

Next morning I was back at the Whites' stables. The place was getting to be a real home from home, and when I walked up to the gate Cement-Features even gave me a grin and a half-salute.

'You want to see the boss you're out of luck, Corvinus,' he said. 'He's in Ostia raising hell about a late grain shipment.'

'No problem. Is Cario around?'

'Sure. He's in charge today.' He turned round and yelled through the open gate: 'Thrax! Hey, *Thrax*!' A wizened old guy with no teeth and a rake lounged out. 'Take Marcus Corvinus here over to admin, right?'

Grunt.

Obviously security wasn't relaxed even when the boss was out. Still, I expected that now. I followed the Thracian and his rake past the line of stables – most of the horses looked to be in at present this time, but then it was earlier than it had been on my first visit – and through the workshop quarter to the admin block. He opened the door that gave on to the big entrance hall and stepped back to let me through.

There was no one around but a snotty-nosed kid with a mop swabbing the floor tiles who gave me a long, slack-jawed stare and then bent to his executive duties like nothing else existed in the world. He looked about eight, but he was probably twice that physically and half of it mentally. One of the sprinklers, no doubt. In a job that consists solely of running out at a team of galloping horses and throwing water over them brains aren't a priority; quite the reverse, in fact. For an off-duty sprinkler mopping floors is a naturally related secondary activity that doesn't require much in the way of additional skills. He'd've already mastered the concept of the bucket, for a start.

I'd assumed the Thracian gopher had followed me in, but when I looked behind me he wasn't there. I stuck my head out of the door again. Our toothless ball of fire was already lugging his rake back in the direction of the gate at a pace that would've shamed an arthritic tortoise. Shades of my old pal Daphnis before he metamorphosed into the obnoxious financial whizz-kid he now was.

A literal race, the Thracians, or possibly just bloody-minded. Cement-Features had told him to take me to the admin block. He'd taken me to the admin block. Finish, end of story. Shades of Daphnis was right: that lazy bugger would've done exactly the same in his heyday. Maybe they were distant cousins. I went back inside, grinning, and knocked on the door of Cammius's office.

No answer. I knocked again, waited, then pushed at the door. It was locked. Bugger.

I turned to the sprinkler. 'Hey, son.'

I got the slack-jawed stare again. 'Yeah?'

'You happen to know where Cario's gone?'

He leaned his mop against the wall, drew his forearm slowly across the base of his nose and blew hard at the same time. I winced. 'Yeah. Practice track.'

'He say how long he'd be?'

The kid shook the results of his rhinal ablutions off his arm. 'Nah.'

'You want to take me there?'

'Got the floor to do.'

Impasse; we had a real eager beaver here. Still, I admired the kid's devotion to duty, even if it did spring from the lack of sufficient brain to pave more than a one-track mind. I took a copper coin out of my purse and held it out.

He might be thick, but he wasn't stupid. The coin disappeared into a dirty fist before I could blink.

'Okay,' he said. ''S this way. Round the back.'

We went outside and turned left, towards the rear wall.

'Uh . . . you're a sprinkler, right?' I said.

'Yeah.' The kid was plodding along with his eyes fixed straight ahead like an ox ploughing a furrow. Watching him gave me a queasy feeling in my stomach. *Thick* didn't quite cover it after all; there was definitely something missing there. I've never been happy around people who're one bun short of the dozen, and I suspected that my guide of the moment didn't even make it into double figures.

'One of you kids was killed at the last Plebbies,' I said. 'By your ex-lead driver Pegasus.'

'Yeah.' Gods! For all the life in his tone I might as

well've been talking about a lost mop! That sort of thing I just can't handle. The hairs rose on the back of my neck.

'You happen to remember his name?'

'Sure. Pylades.'

'Know anything about him? Where he was from? Who his family were?'

A shrug. 'He was jus' a sprinkler.'

He was just a sprinkler. Shit. The poor little bugger could have that inscribed on his tombstone. If he had one, which I doubted. 'You know of any particular friends? Here in the faction or outside?'

Another shrug. It could've indicated a no, but I wouldn't've bet on it. I'd guess we were working at the very edge of his intellectual capabilities here. Still, at least I had a name, that was something. You never knew what might be relevant.

We'd been walking past a line of storage sheds that faced the back wall of the compound. Now these gave out on to open ground.

''S the practice track there.' The kid pointed, and before I realised it he was off and running back the way we'd come.

'Hey!' He stopped and looked round. I opened my purse, took out a silver piece and flung it to him. 'Thanks a lot, son!'

His right hand whipped up and plucked it from the air in a single, effortless motion. Nothing wrong with his reflexes, anyway. Well, there wouldn't be, would there? In his line of business if he were as slow physically as he was mentally by now he'd be dead.

He opened his hand, stared down at the coin and his jaw dropped. I gave him a wink and turned away.

To a sprinkler a silver piece is a once-in-a-lifetime tip. I just hoped the poor bastard would live long enough to spend it.

The practice ground was a short version of the Circus track with a turning post of padded timber at each end. These last would be the most important feature: any competent driver can manage a pair of horses on the straight, but it takes real skill to do a controlled U-turn from the gallop, and that doesn't come without a hell of a lot of work on the part of both the man and his team. It was in use. The car was up the far end – it'd just rounded the further-away post and was on the return lap – but I recognised the crouching driver even under his safety helmet: Uranius. Right. So the lead horse, the one on the inside, would be the famous Polydoxus.

The beast was fast, even I with my non-racer's eye could see that, a gleaming black-coated, tight-muscled beauty with a mane that streamed behind him like smoke in the wind. And he wasn't just a galloping horse; you could see the *pleasure* in every stretched muscle and the way he pushed his head out against the bit, like he was running ahead of himself and straining to catch himself up just for the fun of it. The other horse was keeping pace, sure, but you could tell it was him who was call-ing the tune. It was the difference between watch-ing a man who was good at his job but was just going through the motions and another who lived it naturally.

'Corvinus! What the hell are you doing here?'

I looked away from the galloping horse. Cario was coming towards me, and he didn't look too pleased.

'I went to the office but it was locked up,' I said. 'I got the cleaner to bring me.'

He took my arm, frowning, turning me round. 'The kid had no right,' he said. 'He should've come on his own. Standing orders.'

'That was my fault. I twisted his arm. And I got the impression original thought isn't exactly his forte.'

The frown lifted a bit, and Cario grunted; he wasn't a bad lad and I'd guess he wasn't a hard one, either. 'Yeah, well,' he said. 'No harm done, but rules are rules. Even he should've known better. We'll go back now, if you don't mind.'

I shrugged. 'Sure.' I glanced over my shoulder. The car had reached the nearer post, and as I watched Uranius pulled the horses in and brought it round in a controlled skid, sweet as a nut and with less than a hand's-breadth between the inside wheel and the base of the turn. 'That's Polydoxus on the inside, right? He's a beaut of a horse.'

'He is,' Cario said shortly, and pulled me on. 'Now. What can I do for you?'

'You can tell me what you were doing on Iugarius the time of the murder.'

Cario stopped dead. His eyes flickered. 'I wasn't anywhere near Iugarius. I was here. I already told you.'

'That's not what Uranius says.'

'Uranius?' He shot a quick look towards the track. The car was up to full gallop again, streaking for the far post. 'Uranius wasn't there either. He was down on the Aventine.'

I shook my head. 'Uh-uh. Wrong. He saw you running back towards Triumph Road. You nearly knocked him over.'

I thought that the guy was going to deny it but the silence went on too long for that to be a viable proposition. He didn't say anything else, though, just kept on going.

I caught him up. 'Come on, Cario,' I said. 'It's too late for this. Give, okay?'

He stopped again. We faced each other. He was scowling but he'd lost a lot of colour.

'All right,' he said finally. 'Yes. I was there.'

'Because you'd arranged a meeting with Pegasus.'

He nodded. 'But I didn't kill him. I swear that. I never even saw him.'

'You care to tell me what the meeting was about?'

I got the long silence again. Then he shrugged. 'Sure. Why not? It doesn't matter much now. In the office.'

We walked on without saying anything more. In the admin building the kid was pushing his mop around again. He gave us a frightened look, but Cario ignored him. He took a bunch of keys from his belt, unlocked the office door and went in. I followed.

Cario sat down behind the desk. I pulled up a stool. 'Okay,' I said. 'Let's have it.'

His mouth was set in a tight line. 'I'd been running around with some young purple-stripers.' His voice was toneless. 'We . . . some of us thought it'd be fun to go round the streets of an evening taking purses. Over the Winter Festival there was a bit of trouble. A death.' I didn't say anything, just waited. 'It was an accident. I wasn't directly involved, but the man had some sort of seizure while Le—' – he paused – 'while one of the others was holding him. Next thing we knew he was dead. We left him and ran. That's the whole story.' He looked full at me. 'I'm not proud of myself, Corvinus.'

'Uh-huh. And Pegasus found out, right?'

'I don't know how. There were no witnesses, but yes, he found out. He . . . threatened to tell my father. And the authorities. Unless—' He stopped.

'Unless you paid him not to.'

'Right. Or that was part of the price, anyway. Dad would've told the city judge's office himself. There's been . . . this wasn't the first time, although the others weren't so bad. And Dad's straight that way. He'd've stood by me, but he wouldn't've covered things up.'

'So Pegasus was blackmailing you.'

A nod. 'I gave him fifty gold pieces. That was supposed to be the end of it, but ten days ago he told me he wanted another fifty.' Ten days ago. That would be four days before the murder. 'Dad gives me an allowance, or pays me a pretty generous salary, rather, but, well' – he shrugged – 'that goes. You know how it is. I haven't got that kind of money spare. I had to borrow twenty of the original fifty as it was. And it wouldn't've stopped there. I couldn't ask Dad for the cash without telling him why I needed it, so I had to do something.'

'You arranged to talk to him.'

'Right.'

'Was Renatius's your choice or his?'

'His.'

'Any particular reason?'

Cario shrugged. 'None that I know of. We couldn't talk here for obvious reasons, not with Dad around. I wanted it to be somewhere public in case he turned nasty, and I reckoned I'd need a jug of wine in front of me so I insisted on a wineshop. Any wineshop. He suggested Renatius's and I agreed. It was close but not too close, and there wasn't much of a chance of bumping into someone I knew there.'

Fair enough. 'You said that the money was only part of the price. What else was involved?'

'Pegasus wanted a bigger say in what went on. He'd got round Dad – Dad's no racer himself, and to be fair to the guy he knew the business inside out, especially where the Greens were concerned – but I was being difficult.'

'Care to tell me why?'

'Because right from the start I hated the bastard's guts, and I didn't trust him. It was that simple.'

'But your father did? Trust him?'

'Sure. It was one reason why he took him on in the first place, barring the driving, of course. Like I say, he knew the business inside out and he was no fool. Neither is Dad. Having Pegasus on the team gave us another edge, I don't deny it. That was what made it worse. I felt I was being squeezed out already, and I didn't like it.'

Well, at least he was being honest, and that impressed me. If Cammius was no fool then neither was his son; he must know that he was giving me yet one more good reason to think he was the killer. What he'd said took the heat off Cammius as a possible suspect, too, if he'd ever been in the running. My ears had pricked up when he'd mentioned Pegasus's ambitions where the faction was concerned, but from the sound of it Cammius hadn't minded; quite the reverse. Which fitted in with what I knew of the old guy. If we were thinking along the lines of *cui bono* then Pegasus's death hurt him there as well. Besides, we were in a whole different ball game from the situation over at the Reds' place. Cammius was in firm control of his faction, and although he might not have the long-term all-round experience of, say, Titus Natalis he was too much respected and too strong a character for Pegasus to mount any sort of take-over.

'Okay,' I said. 'You want to tell me what happened the day of the murder? In detail?'

Cario laced his fingers together. He was looking a lot calmer now, but from the way he was twisting his signet ring I knew that appearances were deceptive. 'We arranged to meet at Renatius's, like I told you,' he said. 'Only something came up, a problem with one of the horses, and I was kept back. When I got to the wineshop there was a crowd outside, or rather outside the alley next to it. I asked a guy what was going on and he told me that Pegasus had been found knifed. I panicked and I ran. Maybe I passed Uranius on the way, but if so I can't remember.' He spread his hands. 'That's all, Corvinus. That's all there was. I swear it.'

'Anyone else know about the meeting?' I knew the question was pretty pointless, but it had to be asked.

'No. Not from me, anyway.'

No surprises there; I'd've been surprised if he had let it out. And I already knew that Pegasus hadn't blabbed. I leaned back on the stool. Cario's story fitted; too well for reasonable doubt, anyway. More, I recognised the truth when I heard it, and Cario wasn't lying, not as far as I could tell. 'You didn't see anyone else you knew? On the way?'

Cario gave a lopsided grin. 'Corvinus, believe me, at that point I couldn't've said what day it was. I haven't been so scared in my life.'

Yeah; I'd believe that too. So: we were back to raking among the suspects. Still, although I reckoned we could scratch Cario for the moment the fact remained that the guy had a cast-iron motive, he'd been in the area at the proper time and the only reason he'd admitted it was that he'd been rumbled. If he was a red herring then I wasn't throwing him back altogether, just letting him swim around on the hook until I found a better prospect.

'By the way,' he said. 'What was Uranius doing on Iugarius?'

'Hmm?'

'He doesn't usually get back from the Aventine until a lot later and Iugarius isn't on the usual route.'

'Oh, the practice session finished ahead of time. And he had business in Market Square.' I wasn't going to betray Uranius's confidence. It was too important that the existence of the affair with Natalis's daughter didn't get out. 'So he said, anyway.'

'Right.' Cario nodded, not really interested. He smiled suddenly. 'I'm glad I told you,' he said. 'It's been worrying me.'

'Yeah.' I got up. 'Well, thanks a lot. You want to see me to the gate?'

'No, I think I can trust you. It's the least I can do.'

I left. The kid with the mop had moved a few tiles further on. He didn't look up as I passed.

18

Okay; so where did we go next? The Whites' stable was played out for the moment. That left the Green and the Red connections. The one guy, though, that I really had to talk to because he'd be able to fill in the background to Pegasus's life of crime with the Greens and possibly give me the reason why he'd shifted to the Whites, was Sopilys's bugbear Eutacticus, the crooked cartel manager. Not that that little meeting was something I intended to rush into; even without Sopilys's warning I'd've thought twice before heading gaily up to the Pincian and knocking on the bastard's door, not without taking out some sort of insurance first. Something along the lines of half a dozen of my beefiest slaves and a note dropped to my old pal Gaius Secundus currently at the Mint but attached to the city judge's office saying where I'd gone and how long I was likely to be there. The powers-that-be might turn a blind eye to cartel monkey business where unlicensed touts were concerned, but a missing purple-striper was another matter. I didn't think Eutacticus would mess with a Roman noble, however little actual practical clout he'd got; not unless he felt himself threatened, of course, and that was something I'd be very careful to avoid. However, there was no point in taking risks. All I intended doing at this juncture was making a quick reconnaissance, just enough to get the guy's actual address so I knew exactly where I was going, then clearing out until I'd made proper arrangements.

Triumph Road cuts across the north-west corner of the city, ending up at the Aemilian Bridge. Too far west, in other words. The best way to the Pincian was to go back a little towards the centre, take a left along the south side of the old Flaminian Circus, then join Broad Street halfway between Capitol Hill and the Saepta. After that it was a straight line north along the far side of Mars Field towards Augustus's mausoleum and the start of the Flaminian Road proper. A fair hike, sure, but it had to be done some time: this was something I didn't want to delegate. Besides, I still had half the morning left, it was a beautiful day and good weather for walking.

I was going past the row of upmarket tenements that front the line of the old racetrack – the Flaminian's been out of use for years now, and most of it's built up – when I remembered something. When I'd talked to Felicula she'd told me that Laomedon rented a flat on the Flaminian's south side and used a wineshop there as his local. She hadn't given me a name, but wineshops couldn't be too plentiful along this stretch and I might as well check it out while I was in the area. Besides, if I was going to take a hike out as far as the Pincian I owed myself a bit of lubrication first.

There was only one contender: a tight little place

with roses growing up the wall and two or three well-scrubbed tables out front. The only visible customers were a couple of guys chatting over a jug, but we were still two hours shy of lunch so that was about par for the course. A good time to ask questions, too, because the landlord'd be free to answer them. I nodded to the two punters and went in.

Nice place, at first glance anyway; I'd have to remember it. The inside tables and benches were just as clean and scrubbed as those outside and there was a fairly well-executed humorous mural on the side wall, of three baboons picking grapes and operating a wine-press. No other bodies; I was on my own.

The guy behind the counter gave me a smile. 'Yes, sir. What'll it be?'

I looked at the board. 'How's your Privernian, pal?'

'You like to taste it first?'

Good sign. No wineshop owner'll offer you a free taste of his best vintage if the stuff's rotgut. 'No, that's okay. Just pour me half a jug.'

'Fine.'

While he was lifting the flask out of its rack I leaned over the counter and said: 'You happen to know a guy called Laomedon? Drives for the Reds?'

'Sure.' He pulled the straw bung, reached for a half jug and poured. 'Lives just up the road. He's in here quite often. Or he used to be.'

'Uh-huh.' I glanced up at the board again, checked the price, took out my purse and laid the coins on the counter.

The flask went back into its housing. He set the jug and a cup in front of me and scooped the money into his palm. 'You a friend of his, sir?'

'I've met him.' I took a sip. Not bad; not bad at all. The price was fair, too. I'd have to remember this place right enough. 'You a Red supporter yourself?'

'Nah.' He grinned. 'I've never been much interested in the cars. Not a betting man, either. I don't have the time or the inclination.'

One of the guys from outside stuck his head through the door. 'Hey, Maior! Another jug out here!'

'On its way.' The landlord hefted a different flask from the one with the Privernian and filled a fresh jug from the shelf. ''Scuse me, sir.'

I waited until he'd delivered the wine and brought back the empty jug. 'He's a popular customer, is he?' I said. 'Laomedon?'

The man grinned. 'Not so's you'd notice. A bit of a blow-hard, gets on some of the lads' wicks sometimes. Me, I don't mind. I just pour the wine and keep my mouth shut.'

I sipped. I didn't have any firm plan here, not as far as questions were concerned. I was simply feeling my way. Still, Maior seemed quite happy to stand chatting until the cows came home, which was fine with me. 'He's had the flat for a while?'

'Since before my time, anyway. Not that that's all that long. I took the place over two years back come the Spring Festival. He had it then, that's all I know.'

'He married?'

Another grin. 'Not so's you'd notice.'

'Girlfriends?'

'What do you think? He's a racing driver.'

'Yeah. Right.' I took a swallow of wine and topped up the cup to cover my next question. 'I heard he was friendly with his boss's wife. Felicula.'

The grin faded. For the first time the guy looked suspicious. 'You something to do with the factions, sir?' he said.

'No. I'm just interested in Laomedon.'

'And why would that be?'

The tone wasn't hostile, but it was guarded. I weighed the options and chose the truth. 'One of the other top drivers was killed six days ago.'

'Pegasus? Yeah, I heard about that. Stabbed, right?'

'Right. I'm . . . looking into it. Privately.' I might as well show my credentials, even if they were slightly bogus. 'On behalf of the Whites' master of faction.'

Maior whistled. 'You think Laomedon did it?'

'No. I'm just checking leads and he's on the list.' Pretty near the top, now, I'd reckon, with Uranius and Cario gone, but there was no point spreading that one around. 'Would it surprise you if he had done? You've known the guy for two years.'

He glanced over my shoulder at the open door, then leaned his elbows on the counter. 'Laomedon's a bastard,' he said quietly. 'That's just my personal opinion, mind, and it doesn't go beyond these four walls. Sure I'd believe he killed the guy. If I had a copper piece for every time he's bad-mouthed Pegasus in here I could retire on the proceeds. But as far as knowing anything about a stabbing goes, no, I can't help you.'

'Pity.' Bugger; I'd hoped blow-hard Laomedon might've slipped in a boast or two in his cups. Or at least – because he'd hinted that he knew who had done it – let out something that might help. Well, that was that. I still had the wine.

'Anyway,' Maior went on, 'like I said he hasn't been in all that often recently. I haven't seen him more than three or four times since he took up with that new girlfriend of his.'

I'd been lifting the cup to my lips. I set it down. 'Yeah?' I said. 'Who would that be, now?'

'Egyptian woman.' Maior's eyes shifted slightly. 'Name of Serapia. Properly stuck on her, he is, from what he's said when he has been in. She's a laster, too.'

'"Laster"?'

'Most of them only last a month or so at the best. She's been going four.'

The back of my neck was prickling. 'She local?'

'No. That's why he isn't in much these days. She has a shop on the Sacred Way. Lives above the business.'

'What kind of shop?'

The shift in the eyes was back. 'Medicinal supplies,' he said tonelessly. 'So I understand.'

Something cold touched my spine. Medicinal supplies, eh? Sure, Rome's doctors had to get their raw materials from somewhere, but three times out of five anything that called itself a medicinal supplies shop turned out to be as dodgy as a back-street import-export business. And on the Sacred Way, too.

There're a lot of very respectable properties along the city's oldest road – some blue-blood patrician houses, for a start, that've been there since Cincinnatus cut his first furrow – but you get a few other old-established firms as well; in fact, firms belonging to the oldest profession in the world, where Cincinnatus probably slid in the back door while his wife was busy at her distaff. And where you get brothels, you get whacky herb shops. They go together like nettles and dock-leaves, and much for the same reasons: you catch things, you gotta cure them.

More to the point, from my view, the ladies – and they were usually ladies – who ran these places didn't believe in over-specialisation. They could turn their hands to anything in that line, and most of them branched out into areas that might be dubious but were perennially popular. Including the one that required thin lead sheets, an iron pen, basic literary skills and a nasty imagination.

Egyptians are especially good at that sort of thing; in fact, they're known for it. And with a name like Serapia I doubted that Laomedon's girlfriend was a pillar of the established religious community.

One got you ten the lady dealt in fixes.

Click.

I put a lining on my stomach before I left with Maior's bread and cheese special (the cheese was good, too, a mature Vestinian that Agron would've loved) and headed on for the Pincian. I was sorely tempted to turn right instead of left when I hit Broad Street and check out Serapia's whacky leaves shop, but that could wait for another time. You don't change horses in mid-stream, and I was halfway to the Pincian already.

Wise decision. Like I said, it was a beautiful day for walking, and it got even better. Once I was past the Saepta and Agrippa Field the crowds slackened off; not that this part of town's ever all that crowded anyway. The narcissi were out at the edges of Mars Field to my left and the sun glinted on the chichi residences set into the hill slopes of the Quirinal to the right and the Pincian straight ahead.

You don't get tenements in this part of Rome. Nor, consequently, the riffraff that go with them. The Broad Street region is one of the priciest in the city, and what residents pay for is space and privacy. They don't frequent wineshops, either – or not the cheap and cheerful sort I patronise, anyway. Seventh District wine drinking is a sedate and definitely upmarket affair, and the local equivalent is likely to be closer to an expensive private club, probably with bath suites attached so the well-heeled punters can sink their cups of Falernian – *real* Falernian, thirty years old, at least – in the pampering company of half a dozen nubile slave girls who cater for their every whim. Or, of course, nubile slave boys if their tastes run that way.

I found one of these places on Pincian Road itself, between the Gardens of Pompey and Lucullus. I thought at first it was an urban villa – one of these countryside-in-the-city places with picture galleries by the mile and ornamental gardens you need a map to get round – but there were tables on the manicured lawn inside the fancy wrought-iron gates and a small army of waiters carrying trays of snow-cooled wine flagons and saucers of peeled grapes. I went in. I might be wearing a purple-striped mantle, but after a morning hoofing it over a large part of the city I wasn't looking too impressive, and the guy who came over looked like he was within an inch of ushering me out at the end of a long pole.

'Yes, sir,' he said. 'What can we do for you?'

'Uh . . . you got a wine list, pal?' I said. First things first; the Pincian's a long way from the Flaminian Circus, and Maior's Privernian was only a fond memory.

He sniffed. 'Yes, sir. Of course, sir.' He reached into the belt of his natty primrose tunic and produced a scroll that wouldn't've disgraced one of the encomia that provincial cities send to the Wart on his birthday. I unrolled it and read.

Two minutes later I was still reading. I needn't've bothered asking. I could've demanded any premier cru wine between Tibur and Naples and I'd be asked to name the year. I'd've got it, too, so long as it wasn't any later than the death (or whatever) of the Divine Augustus. The prices matched. For what they were asking for a jug, at Renatius's I could've bought the whole flask.

There again, Renatius's cellar didn't boast any stocks of thirty-five-year-old Velletrian. I ordered a half jug together with some olives and Lucanian sausage and settled on to one of the crimson-upholstered couches in the portico. I got some curious stares from the sharply dressed punters in the group to my left but when I tipped them a wink and a leer they suddenly lost interest and went back to discussing shipping costs and the *dreadful* mess poor old Quintus was making of his new import tax nonsense.

Primrose came back with the wine and nibbles. Forget the terracotta jugs you find in most wineshops, or the chipped Samian they bring out sometimes when you've ordered a wine at the top of the board. This one was silver, and it came nestling in a snow-filled wine cooler with a running band of nymphs and satyrs round the middle. The Lucanian sausage was neatly sliced, with a dinky little silver knife beside it and a fingerbowl and napkin on the side in case you did happen to get a spot of grease on your fingers. While I watched, the guy lifted the half jug from the cooler with a napkin of his own like he was taking a sacred object from a shrine, poured the Velletrian into a matching cup, nudged the little dishes of olives and sausage into a more aesthetically pleasing relationship with the whole, inspected the result critically and stepped back.

'Will that be all, sir?' he said.

'Yeah.' I reached for my purse, took out too many of the contents and handed them over. 'No. One more thing, pal. You know if a guy called Eutacticus lives around here?'

The conversation round the next table stopped dead. Perilla uses a phrase sometimes, *the cynosure of all eyes*. I'd never been absolutely certain what it meant, but now I knew. If I'd asked whether it was okay to strip off and do a belly dance on the lawn the looks I was getting would've been the same.

'Ah . . . yes, sir.' Primrose's fine-chiselled features set like concrete. 'I believe a gentleman of that name does live just up the hill. The house with the tritons on the gates. You can't miss it.'

'Fine. Fine.' He scurried off as if I'd lit a fire at his tail. I gave my neighbours another leer and a wink and they quickly went back to discussing high finance. Then I sipped the wine. Beautiful. Better than beautiful. Mind you, it should be at the price.

You don't hurry thirty-five-year-old Velletrian. It took me a good hour to finish the half jug, and by that time the sun was well past its mid-point. I speared the last slice of sausage – it was *Lucanian* Lucanian; what else? Even I could tell that – balled up my napkin and strolled to the entrance, chewing. I could feel eyes on my back all the way.

Primrose was right; I saw the house with the triton gates straight ahead of me almost at once. It was a beaut, gleaming white marble frontage with a terraced ornamental garden in front sweeping down to the perimeter wall. It even had a brook running past it, with waterfalls. Profits in the betting business must be sky-high, right enough.

There was the usual guy on the gate, sitting to one side on a folding stool picking his teeth and communing with nature. There were also, however, two very large tunics who looked like they might spend their free time arm-wrestling gorillas. I didn't give much for the monkeys' chances, either. They glared at me like I'd spat in their salads and flexed their very considerable muscles.

Not the time for socialising, obviously, and anyway I'd got what I wanted for the moment. I carried on walking, giving them a nod in passing but getting as much response from the marble tritons. My back burned all the way up the road.

I was sweating when I turned the bend out of sight of the house. Jupiter! Maybe that had been a mistake. Still, it was done now, and at least I knew where Eutacticus hung out. I carried on past Lucullus Gardens then took a right at the next road and headed towards High Path and home.

Bathyllus was waiting for me with the usual tray. I took off my mantle and sank a quarter-pint of the Setinian. After the Velletrian it tasted thin, but you can't live on these heights all the time.

'All right, Bathyllus?' I said. 'How did the pickling expedition go?'

'Very successfully, sir.' The little bald-head was looking sleek, and I noticed a scent of after-shave powder in the air. 'We got quite chatty over the trotters.'

'Great! You're making giant strides.'

'I'm not sure Tyndaris's master absolutely approved of my presence, however. On his visit to the kitchen to investigate the sounds of hilarity he did make several adverse remarks concerning over-fraternisation.'

Ouch. Knowing Petillius I could imagine what these might be: he'd probably suspected a full-blown orgy below stairs with the wine flowing like water. But *hilarity*?

Bathyllus???

'Uh . . . this "chatty" you mentioned involved quite a bit of laughter, then, did it?' I said carefully.

The little guy looked shocked. 'Not on my part, sir!' I breathed again. At so much as a chuckle from our major-domo the world would end because humanity would have nothing left to hope for. 'That was Tyndaris. She has an extremely lively sense of humour.'

I'd imagine the lady would have a pretty effective laugh, too, to reach all the way from the servants' quarters. Probably the kind that knocks pigeons off their perches at fifty yards and stuns passing bullocks. For the first time I felt a twinge of sympathy for our water-drinking neighbour. Still, this didn't augur well, on any account. A house-owner is responsible for the behaviour of his domestics, and the last thing I wanted was an irate Petillius hammering on my door to complain that our head slave was instigating a cachinnatory disturbance. Especially since I suspected that our coachman was already squiring one of the guy's maids. 'Ah . . . maybe you and Tyndaris should keep it down a little in future, pal,' I said. 'Or bring her over here on the next occasion, if Petillius doesn't mind.' That was another unwritten law of relations between neighbours which this time worked in my favour. Slaves don't have much of a social life to start with, they're not allowed by law to contract proper marriages, and consequently most house-owners turn a blind eye to a certain amount of coming and going between households. If this produces the odd unexpected small bundle nine months later then that's life: the situation is usually resolved amicably, and at least the girl's master can chalk up a free addition to the menage. With Petillius, of course, you couldn't make that assumption, but the chances of Tyndaris presenting him with an end-of-year bonus courtesy of our Bathyllus were so close to zero you couldn't work them out on an abacus.

'That might be possible, sir,' Bathyllus said. 'The lady did express an interest in my non-slip polish for marble tiles and I suggested a demonstration. I will put it to her tomorrow.'

'Fine. Fine. Just both of you watch your step, okay? And I don't mean on the tiles, either.'

'I haven't the slightest intention of venturing out on the tiles with Tyndaris, sir.'

I gave him a sharp look, but his face was as bland as ever. Jupiter! I must've misheard that one, or else it had been a fluke. Bathyllus wouldn't recognise a play on words if it bit him in the knee, and he sure as hell never made any. The only other explanation was that Tyndaris was charming him out of his shell; but if so I wondered what sort of monster was hatching. 'Uh . . . right.' I said. 'Good, Bathyllus.' I took a settling swig from my cup. 'Is the mistress around?'

'Yes, sir. In the garden, talking to Alexis.'

I went out. Perilla was in the far corner, the sunless bit where Alexis keeps his compost. She turned round.

'Oh, hello, Marcus,' she said. 'Alexis was suggesting a rockery here.'

I gave her the coming-home kiss. 'A what?'

'It's just an idea of my own, sir.' Our smart-as-paint gardener was blushing. 'A pile of big stones planted between the spaces with small perennials. I thought if I could find some of these Rhaetian mountain varieties they would do very well. Perhaps *aquilegia caerulea* or *hepatica angulosa*. Both of these would take shade, and—'

'These things can grow on *rocks*?' Jupiter! You learn something new every day.

'No, sir. Not exactly. You fill the spaces with earth. The plants grow between the stones.'

'Why not just make a pile of earth and be done with it?'

'They're mountain plants, sir. I thought it might lend a bit of . . . verisimilitude. And the plants would grow better in something approaching their natural environment.'

'That being a mountain, right?'

'Yes, sir.'

I sighed. 'Alexis, I don't know how far we are above sea level on the Caelian but we're a hell of a way under Rhaetia. And mountains at the bottom of the garden I can do without. How high does this pile of rocks have to be before it constitutes a "natural environment"?'

The kid gave me a wild look. 'Uh . . . only two or three feet, sir. I never said that—'

'Yeah? And that's a mountain?'

'Not exactly.' I noticed with interest that the guy

was starting to sweat. 'It sort of replicates the natural growing conditions in which—'

'Marcus, I think we can trust Alexis to know what he's doing,' Perilla said quickly. She took my arm. 'Come back inside and tell me how the case is going.'

I shrugged and followed her. Artificial mountains for plants. Jupiter! They'd be raising beans in water and farming fish next.

Bathyllus had put the wine jug on the table within easy reach of my couch. I topped up my cup and settled down.

'So,' Perilla said, lying down opposite me. 'Did you have a word with Cario?'

'Yeah. He was the guy who set up the meeting, all right. But he isn't the killer. Or at least I don't think he is.' I told her the tale.

'You're sure he didn't do it, Marcus?' she said when I'd finished. 'Yes, I know that I said the timing doesn't match, and it doesn't, quite, but blackmail is too strong an incentive to ignore simply on that account. The story of his being involved in the accidental death during the mugging puts him in the wrong, certainly, but again you only have his word for it that the incident actually happened. And Cario didn't admit to arranging the interview with Pegasus until you gave him no option.'

'He didn't have to tell me Pegasus was blackmailing him at all, lady.'

'He had to tell you something to explain the meeting. Blackmail is an obvious excuse. And he was careful that the story should reflect worse on Pegasus than on himself; furthermore, that it would be difficult to confirm.'

Yeah; I hadn't thought of those aspects, and to be fair I couldn't fault them. 'So you think Cario's guilty after all?' I said.

'No, not necessarily. Of course not. But I wouldn't discount the possibility on the evidence available.' Perilla twisted a lock of hair. 'One thing, though. If he isn't it calls a major element of your theory into serious question.'

'Yeah? What's that?'

'That the murder was premeditated. If Cario is innocent then ipso facto Pegasus wasn't lured to the wineshop by his killer. The crime could have been committed on the spur of the moment by anyone passing at the proper time.'

Shit; she was right. That was something else I hadn't thought through. Of course, it would mean that whoever killed the guy had to have been in the area for reasons of his own and seen his chance. That left the field open again. There was always Uranius, naturally; again, I only had his word for it that the murder had already been committed when he passed the wineshop, and the timing was so tight that it was well within the bounds of possibility he'd left the old nurse's flat slightly earlier than he'd claimed or she'd remembered. Added to which, with marriage to Galatea as a possible prize he certainly had a motive. All the same, I couldn't believe in Uranius as a killer; no more than, when push came to shove and *pace* Perilla, I could believe in Cario. So who else hated Pegasus enough to kill him, was capable of a sudden, spur-of-the-moment murder, and had a plausible reason for being on Iugarius?

'Laomedon,' I said.

Perilla looked at me. 'Pardon?'

I sat up. 'We're back to Laomedon, lady. He has a new girlfriend on the Sacred Way, and he spends most of his free time at her place now. If he were going from there to the stables or vice versa he'd have to go along Iugarius. He could've spotted Pegasus going into the wineshop, or better into the alley for a piss. And a quick spur-of-the-moment knife in the back would be just his style.'

'What's this about a girlfriend on the Sacred Way?'

I told her what I'd learned at Maior's. 'She deals in suspect substances, and you know what that means. Remember the fixes? It all ties in.'

'Laomedon denied killing Pegasus point-blank. And you told me you believed him, because he didn't have the intelligence to lie convincingly.'

'True, but he also said—' I stopped. Oh, shit. Oh, gods.

'Marcus?'

'Laomedon claimed – or good as claimed – that he knew who the murderer was. On the other hand, he suggested that no one had killed the guy. Maybe he was right on both counts.'

'Corvinus, you are *not* making sense!'

'Sure I am, lady. His girlfriend's a witch. Or the next thing to it.'

Perilla's mouth set in a line. 'Marcus, dear, we've

been through this before,' she said. 'There are no such things. Witches do not exist.'

A good woman, Perilla, and clever as they get, but sometimes her mind is so closed against the obvious that you can knock all day and still not get an answer. Me, I wondered if anyone had told the witches. Time for a little diplomacy. 'Yeah, well. Maybe they don't. Still, the woman's worth talking to, right?'

'Of course she is. I'm not denying that. I only said—'

'Fine. Fine. We'll leave it there.' I paused. Then another thought struck me; not a very pleasant one. 'Uh . . . Perilla?' I said.

'Yes, Marcus?'

'You, uh, you wouldn't happen to be, like, free tomorrow morning yourself, would you?'

She grinned. 'All right, Corvinus,' she said. 'I'll come with you.'

I breathed a quiet sigh of relief. There're times when having a closed mind at your elbow is reassuring.

19

Serapia's place was on the Head of Africa side of the Sacred Way in what was still called the Cerolian Marsh, although that had been drained and built on when Cato was in rompers. Suitable location, given her line of work: a natural penchant for marshes and damp groves where the sun don't shine is pretty well part of the job specification. The shop was at the end of a rubbish-choked alley off the way itself, on the ground floor of one of these anonymous old buildings that looked like they'd been thrown together in an afternoon round about the time of King Tarquin from whatever came to hand and then left over the next five hundred years or so to fall down again. 'Shop' was a misnomer: most shops are no more than three-walled rooms open on the street side so the customers can see what's on offer. This one was just a low plank-wood door in a crumbling brick wall.

The door was closed. I hesitated with my hand on the latch.

'Uh . . . maybe this isn't such a good idea after all, lady,' I said.

Perilla sniffed. 'Don't be silly, Marcus.'

'Yeah, well.' Silly or not, even with Perilla in tow

to give me moral support this was one interview I definitely wasn't looking forward to. Eutacticus'd be bad enough, but at least with him all I'd have to worry about was being belted on the noggin with an iron bar and given a free swim in the Tiber. Not that I'm super-stitious, you understand, but these ladies you don't mess with, and if you do have to you watch your step.

I was more than half hoping that there was no one at home, but the latch lifted easily. I pushed the door open.

The first thing I noticed was the smell. Not that it needed much noticing, mind: it came billowing out with an in-your-face, elbows-spread attitude you couldn't ignore, and it could've come straight off one of Alexis's mulch piles. I gagged.

The second thing was the darkness. Whatever pur-pose the place had originally been designed for – maybe just storage, or somewhere to keep the family pig – it sure as hell hadn't involved being able to see more than a yard in front of your face. The only light there was was what we'd brought in with us, and there wasn't all that much of that, either.

'Come in, Valerius Corvinus.'

Oh, shit. A cold hand clutched at my gut and squeezed. It was like being inside a cave underground. The floor was beaten earth, the ceiling-joists – they couldn't't've been much more than a foot above my head – were screened by hanging bunches of herbs, and all I could see either side of me were baskets piled high with what I hoped were dried fungi. And the smell was making me sick.

'Go on, Marcus,' Perilla murmured from just behind me. 'There's nothing to be nervous about.'

Yeah, I thought, tell that to my stomach, lady. 'Uh . . . Serapia, right?' I said into the darkness.

'Laomedon's told me so much about you.' One of the shadows at the back of the shop moved. 'Don't be nervous. I don't bite. Who's your friend?'

She was young, from the sound of her voice, but that was about all I could tell. 'Ah . . . my wife Perilla,' I said.

'Good morning, Serapia,' Perilla said brightly. 'Do you enjoy sitting in the dark or could we have a little light, perhaps?'

The woman chuckled. 'Of course,' she said. 'Wait a moment.' The shadow moved again, I heard the click of flint on steel and a spark jumped. She blew on the tinder until it flamed, then lit a spill. 'There.' The lamp wick caught. 'That's better. We can see each other now.'

I wasn't sure that I wanted to. Perilla or not, the hairs on the back of my neck were telling me to turn round and get the hell out while I was ahead.

Just then something long and smooth slid over my sandalled foot and kept on sliding, turning my bones to water. I glanced down and wished I hadn't.

'Oh, shit!'

'*Marcus!*'

Another chuckle. 'Ignore Phaedra, Valerius Corvinus, she's only interested in mice.' Sweet holy gods! 'You wanted to talk to me. Very well. Go ahead.'

She was sitting on a bench against the far wall,

watching us. She was a looker, that was sure, I could see that even in the light from the single oil lamp: mid-twenties, no older, black hair – not just dark, but glossy-black – falling free round a face that could've belonged to one of the old Egyptian princesses. Not the Greeks, the other ones, before Alexander took over the country. She held herself like a princess, too, chin high and pushed forward, eyes like knives, totally assured.

I cleared my throat and took a step forwards. 'You . . . ah . . . you were expecting me?'

She shrugged. 'Laomedon said you were asking about Pegasus. You're intelligent, thorough and persistent. You had to come sooner or later.'

Well, that was fair enough, and the answer impressed me more than if she'd claimed it was the result of some mumbo-jumbo. Still, it didn't make me any happier. I had the uneasy feeling that she'd ducked the question, and her use of my name when I first came in hadn't sounded like guesswork, even if she had missed out on Perilla. 'Then you know why I'm here?'

'To find out if we – or I – had anything to do with that man's death.' The general tone was neutral, and pleasant enough, but the hint of pure venom in the phrase *that man* set warning bells ringing.

'And did you?' Perilla asked.

Serapia's eyes rested on her: a long, appraising look with a mind at the back of it. No fool, this woman. 'Of course,' she said. 'I killed him myself.'

'Really?' Perilla's tone expressed no more than mild interest.

'Oh, yes. He deserved to die, a thousand times over.'

The calm admission should've rocked me, but it didn't because I'd come more than half expecting it and now, having met the lady, I'd believe it. Even so, I swallowed. 'Uh . . . the fixes, right?' I said.

'I sent a knife after him, and it finally caught up. Report me to the city judge's office if you like. Frankly I don't much care.'

'Oh, how nice,' Perilla said. I glanced at her worriedly: that lady just didn't know when to keep her mouth buttoned, did she? 'Not that I think we'll bother.'

I cleared my throat. 'That was, uh, quite a favour to Laomedon,' I said.

'I didn't do it for Laomedon. I did it for my brother.'

That jolted me momentarily out of my fear. I stared at her. 'Your *brother*?'

'His name was Pylades. Pegasus killed him at the Plebeian Games.'

Oh, shit; the sprinkler who'd got himself run over. I thought back to what the landlord of the Flaminian Circus wineshop had told me. Yeah, right; he'd said that Laomedon had taken up with Serapia four months ago, which would put the start of the affair some time in December, a month after the Plebbies. The time matched, sure, and it couldn't be coincidence, but I couldn't see the connection between the two. 'So how did Laomedon fit in?' I asked.

'Hatred, Marcus,' Perilla said quietly. 'She needed it for the curse to be effective. As much as she could get.'

Serapia looked at her, her eyes wide with surprise. 'You've studied magic, madam?'

'No. But it's logical.'

'Magic is always logical. You're right, of course. Two are far stronger than one, and Laomedon hated Pegasus almost as much as I did. I searched him out and used him. With his knowledge and permission, naturally. You must always have permission.' She shrugged. 'It was easy, especially since he believed.'

'Yes,' Perilla said drily. 'I can see how that would be quite important.'

I swallowed at the tone; she had more guts than I did, sure, I'd admit that, but there's a big difference between nerve and stupidity, and she was straying a bit too close to the line for my taste. Chancy bitches like Serapia you don't sass, if you've any sense, whatever you happen to believe. The risk just ain't worth the candle. 'You like to tell us the whole story, lady?' I said.

Serapia turned her eyes on me. 'There's nothing to tell,' she said. 'Pylades was twelve. He wanted to be a racing driver. He joined the Whites as a sprinkler, meaning to work his way up to his reins. He lasted two months and six days. Then Pegasus murdered him.'

'It was an accident,' Perilla said.

'It was murder.' The strong chin jutted. 'I was watching and I saw. Pegasus had time to choose between running my brother down and losing position. He chose the first. Which is more important? A child's life or a race?'

'So you decided to kill him.'

'I decided to execute him. My mother was a witch. She taught me the knife. She said it never failed if you hated enough, but I wanted to make sure. I found Laomedon, persuaded him to sleep with me.' A small smile. 'Not difficult, that part. Then I told him about Pylades, and the knife. Asked his permission to borrow his hate and use it to kill Pegasus.'

'This knife,' Perilla said. 'How do you send it, in actual fact?' There wasn't anything but curiousity in her voice. She could've been asking about some new Greek mechanical gizmo. The hairs on my neck rose another notch.

Serapia's dark eyes glinted in the flame of the lamp. 'You're interested, madam?'

'Academically, yes.'

'Academically.' She smiled her small smile again. 'So. Very well. You must let the power build. Perform the proper rite three times when the moon is waxing.' Yeah; Hesper had told me that the fixes had come at monthly intervals. 'The knife flies with the third time.'

'And what would the proper rite be, exactly?'

'A joining, after the lead sheets are delivered. Where two work together the sexual act has great potency. Especially when the two wills are equally strong for the desired effect.'

'I see,' Perilla said. 'Thank you.' Cool as a cucumber. Me, I was sweating. Jupiter! I'll never understand that lady!

'That satisfies your academic interest?'

'Yes.'

'No more than that? You could be a witch yourself. You have the power and the ability. I can tell.'

'Oh, I doubt it.' Perilla gave her bright, brittle smile. 'And it really is all rather silly, isn't it?' Ouch! 'Well, Serapia, we won't take up any more of your valuable time. No doubt you want to grind your wolf's-bane or whatever you witches do at this hour.' She turned. 'Marcus?'

I jumped. 'Yeah?'

'If you've quite finished, dear, I think we'll be going.'

'Uh, yeah. Right.' I backed towards the door. 'Thanks a lot, Serapia. It's been . . . interesting.'

The dark eyes rested on mine. I had the impression the woman was laughing, but she made no sound and she didn't answer. Somewhere in the shadows something slithered: Phaedra, looking for mice. At least, I hoped so.

The door was behind me. I turned and was through it as fast as if I'd been greased.

'Well, Marcus,' Perilla said.

We were sitting outside a wineshop by the Temple of Jupiter Stayer of the Host. I'd sunk three straight cups of wine and my hands were still shaking. Perilla had some camomile concoction flavoured with honey. 'Well what, lady?' I said.

'That was fascinating.'

I shivered. Not the word I'd've chosen. Serapia had been one scary lady. 'You convinced now?'

Perilla sniffed. 'Of course not. It was complete

nonsense from beginning to end.' I stared at her. 'Corvinus, you really don't believe anyone can kill by magic, do you?'

'Uh—'

'It just isn't rational. Oh, I don't deny she was persuasive, even impressive, if somewhat theatrical, although I suppose her customers expect that sort of thing. She may even believe she has the power herself. However, I think it far more likely that if Serapia did kill Pegasus – which she may well have done – then her own hand was on the knife at the time.'

'Laomedon was convinced.'

'From what you've told me of him, dear, Laomedon isn't the world's most powerful intellect. I'm sure he was convinced. That doesn't make his opinion any more valid.'

I took a deep breath. 'Okay. So how do you read it?'

'But it's obvious!' Perilla took a sip of her drink. 'Serapia hated Pegasus. She knew the way to the Whites' stables, and if she was capable of pinning lead curse sheets to the gate on three separate occasions and remaining undetected then she was certainly capable of following the man and murdering him when the opportunity arose. There is absolutely no need to bring in all this silly supernatural nonsense. I assume a woman could have managed the actual killing? Physically, I mean?'

'Uh, sure, but—'

'There you are, then. It's only a possibility, of course, but she had as good a motive as anyone, and the mechanics of the murder present no problems. There's only the question of opportunity. I suggest you have another word with Laomedon. Ask him if he can account for Serapia's whereabouts at the actual time of the murder. If he can't then we can take it from there.'

'So why the business with the curse at all? Why not just ice the guy and be done with it?'

Perilla sighed. 'It's a question of mentality. The woman obviously enjoys making a show of power, to herself as much as any. Supernatural power. All that silly business with the darkness and knowing your name and the snake was so terribly staged, wasn't it? If she'd been a normal person then yes, she would have done as you say, but she isn't. So she goes through the motions of cursing the man – openly, as far as Laomedon is concerned – then, unknown to him, she commits the physical murder. Pegasus dies mysteriously of a knife in the back at the appropriate time, as per the curse, and her reputation as a witch is confirmed. Not just in Laomedon's view – and anyone else's, including yours – but perhaps more importantly in her own.'

I sat back. Jupiter! I was out of my depth here. A simple, straightforward knifing in an alley I could understand, but this mentality stuff left my brain hurting. 'Uh – all that makes sense, does it?' I asked. 'I mean, just a yes or no would do, lady, and I'll take your word for it.'

Perilla smiled brightly. 'Yes, dear. Of course it does. Whether it's what really happened, though, is quite another matter. That's up to you to find out.'

I topped up my cup and took a swig; the wine was working its own customary magic and I was beginning to feel more in charge of myself now. The lady might have something, but personally despite her guarantee I wouldn't be taking any bets. Also, I couldn't shake off the worry that she might've shown herself just a little too much of a smartass for her own good, because Serapia hadn't struck me as any kind of con artist, and like I say you walk carefully where these bitches are concerned. Still, she was right about one thing. Another talk with Laomedon wouldn't go amiss. 'I might just take a walk up to the Reds' stables now, in fact,' I said. 'You want to tag along or are you going home?'

'Oh, I'll go home. I have things to do, and I can get a litter in Market Square.' She grinned. 'Also, perhaps you've had your hand held enough for one day.'

I didn't answer. Maybe Serapia had been right about one more thing too: if Perilla did ever take up witching then she'd have the rest of the sorority beat hands down.

I saw Perilla off in her litter, then carried on up Iugarius towards Triumph Road and the stables.

I couldn't dismiss scary Serapia and her curse; not completely, not hand on heart, despite what Perilla had said, because whatever the truth might be you don't junk a lifetime's assumptions in five minutes. On the other hand, I couldn't just blow the whistle and call it a day, not if there was any reasonable doubt in my mind that I'd solved the case. Which there was. Perilla had achieved that much.

Besides, the curse solution stuck in my throat. Not that I ruled it out as impossible, let alone dismissed it out of hand; far from it. But it left too many questions unanswered, and when push came to shove I couldn't believe that there hadn't been a human hand holding that knife.

I gave Cement-Features on the Whites' gate a wave as I passed and carried on to the Reds' compound. This time there was no one on the gate at all. I hammered with my fist until finally someone came and unbarred it.

'Laomedon around this morning, pal?' I said to the guy; the intellectual counterpart, from the looks of him, of my superfast Thracian rake-man.

'Yeah.'

I waited. Nothing. 'Uh . . . could you maybe sort of suggest where exactly he might be?' I said.

'Search me, friend.' The guy moved aside. 'He's in here somewhere, that's all I know. You want to look, you go right ahead.'

So the Reds hadn't modified their laissez-faire attitude to security any in the four days since I'd been here last. I went in.

It took me a good ten or fifteen minutes to find him. He was outside the wheelwrights' workshop talking to one of the workmen. When he saw me he nearly had an apoplexy. The workman made himself scarce.

'Hey, Laomedon,' I said. 'How's it going?'

'They let you in again?'

'Sure. No problem. It's understandable; the way your team's performing poisoning the entire stable could only be an improvement. If anyone felt inclined to make the effort.'

He went an even deeper shade of purple. 'Fuck you, Corvinus.'

'I've talked to Serapia.'

The purple faded. 'What?'

'Your girlfriend over on the Sacred Way. I know about the curse. Murder by witchcraft is still a crime on the statute books, pal, and as an accessory you're just as much for the high jump as if you'd stuck the knife in yourself. More so. With an ordinary killing you might strike lucky and get away with confiscation of property and exile. Witchcraft means the chop.'

I was guessing, sure: I didn't have the slightest idea what the penalties involved were. But I'd decided on this approach on the way over, and it came up trumps. Forget purple now; you could've matched the guy's colour with the skin on six-month-old milk.

'You can't prove anything,' he said.

'Sure I can. Like I say, I talked to Serapia in the presence of a witness. She admitted the whole thing. Seemed quite proud of herself, in fact. That should be all the city judge's office needs.'

'Corvinus, I—'

'Of course, if you were to help me clear up a few matters I could drop a word or two in the right ear.'

Long silence while Laomedon's razor-sharp brain took that on board and worked out the meaning. I could almost hear the grinding of rusty cogs. 'Like what?' he said at last.

'First, you wouldn't tell me where you were at the time Pegasus was killed. You care to do that now?'

His brow furrowed. 'But Pegasus was killed by the curse. That's the whole—'

'Sure. Just for the sake of completeness.'

'I took the afternoon off. I was with Serapia, in her flat above the shop.'

'Fine.' He wasn't lying, I'd swear to that. He wouldn't think it mattered now. Okay; scratch Perilla's mentality theory. I couldn't say I was sorry to see that one go. 'Right. Second. Pegasus had a couple of scams going. I thought maybe you being in the racing business you might be able to help with some inside information.'

He gave me a crafty look. Or a look that he meant to be crafty, anyway. 'Maybe. That bastard was always on the look-out for scams. So what're the two you know about?'

There wasn't any reason not to tell him. 'He was selling races when he drove for the Greens. To a guy called Eutacticus.'

'The cartel boss?' Laomedon sniggered. 'Yeah. I knew that. Wasn't anyone in the racing game who didn't.'

I frowned. 'Score Natalis for one, pal. When I suggested it to him he practically gave me my head in my hands.'

'I'm talking about drivers, Corvinus. You can't fool a driver out there on the sand, not where throwing a race is concerned. We know each other's form too well. One of us pulls back when he shouldn't or zigs on the straight when he should've zagged and lets the man behind through, it gets noticed. Sometimes it's a genuine mistake, sure, but if it isn't you can spot the difference. Besides, we all do it. Or we would do if we got the chance.'

'So why didn't anyone tell Natalis?'

'Holy Castor, you don't listen, do you? It happens all the time. Live and let live. We cover for each other. Any guy who split would be a danger to the rest because it might be any of them next. So they make sure he's run his last race, one way or another. End of problem, and the word soon gets around among the new drivers. Besides, Natalis is a boss, and bosses are the enemy. So long as the driver's careful and not too greedy, and there's no proof, what the bosses don't know don't hurt them. Even I wouldn't've split on Pegasus. Not for his good, for mine. Now. What was your second scam?'

'Pegasus was blackmailing Cammius's son. Young Cario. Trying to edge him out of the admin side of the Whites.'

Laomedon went very still. 'You sure about that?' he said.

'Cario told me himself.'

The Reds' driver laughed. 'Castor! The scheming bastard! Well, I suppose one colour's as good as another, and maybe he thought the odds were better.'

'What's that supposed to mean, pal?'

'He was angling the same way for the Reds. It was why he took up with Felicula. At least, that was the original idea. Me, I've had experience of that lady and she's no pushover where men are concerned. I could've told him at the time but it was more fun seeing him find out for himself.'

My scalp tingled. 'Hang on. You're saying that Pegasus started an affair with Felicula to get control of her husband's faction?'

'Sure. In through the back door. Me, I wouldn't've thought of it for one minute. I'm a driver, not a pen-pusher, and I don't want to be no boss. The only interest I had in the lady was the obvious. Pegasus was different, he had ambition coming out of his ears. He didn't want to stay no driver the rest of his life.' He sniggered. 'Never mind Felicula. The one Pegasus really wanted to get into bed with was Pudens. Then he'd kick the old bugger out.'

Oh, Jupiter! 'You sure about this?'

'Sure I'm sure. The bastard told me himself. Said give him a few months and he'd be my new boss and tear up my contract. I laughed in his face. Some hope! Not with that lady!'

I leaned back against the workshop wall. Sweet gods! This was a new twist and no mistake, and it needed a lot more thinking about than I could give it at the moment. Certainly it raised questions about Felicula. I'd assumed that she was out of the case completely, but from what Laomedon had just told me she – and possibly Pudens – might well turn out to be centre stage.

Laomedon was looking at me anxiously.

'Hey, Corvinus?'

'Yeah?'

'Serapia must've told you about her brother. And Pegasus was a complete bastard, crooked as hell. He deserved to die. You really going to report us to the city judge?'

I could've laughed myself. The muscle-bound tough guy was standing there like a schoolkid up for a telling-off by the teacher.

'Maybe not,' I said. Strangely – or maybe it wasn't all that strange – I felt a whole lot better for the news. 'Or not yet, anyway. You see, I don't think you two were responsible after all.'

I left him standing open-mouthed, staring after me, and walked towards the gate.

20

As I walked back down Triumph Road I was thinking hard. So. Pegasus had had ambitions. That in itself didn't come as any surprise. Some drivers go on driving – and winning – until they've got grey in their hair, by which time if they've reached the top of the tree and been sensible on the way up they have enough prize money put aside to retire and open a wineshop or buy into some aspect of the horse business. They're the lucky ones, though, and there aren't many of them: you don't see many guys still on the sand past thirty, successful ones, anyway. Either they're dead or their edge is gone and they're on the skids with younger men taking over. If they stick with the reins they're headed nowhere down a blind alley, like Laomedon. The best they can expect when their luck and skill run out is a stables job that pays peanuts, and eventually a seat in the corner living on memories and handouts.

The really smart ones are the ace drivers who think ahead past the easy money, quit at their peak and work or buy their way into the business side of things. Guys like Titus Natalis. Good drivers who're also boneheads are two a penny in the factions, but a driver who knows the sand and has more between his ears than padding can go far. Maybe not as far as Natalis – top man with the top team – but set up for life and with a comfortable old age to look forward to. Rome isn't the only place with a racetrack, far from it, and out in the provinces there're a lot of seriously rich wannabe town councillors who know that the way to a voter's heart is through his race-card and would fall over themselves to bag a prime Rome-trained racing man as faction head.

The operative word there is *trained*. Racing's a business like any other. Your average driver knows the sand, sure, but – like Laomedon said – he's no pen-pusher. And to be in the market for faction boss you have to know the non-driving side. The only way you can do that is to get experience, and the only way you can do *that* is hook a deputy's job. Preferably one where the actual boss is happy to let you run things while he swans around in the social limelight.

I reckoned that this was what Pegasus had been doing with the Reds. Or hoped to do, rather. From his angle the situation was perfect: a ramshackle faction with a boss who was a joke and could be twisted round his little finger. The way Laomedon could've worked it, if he'd been the type. The Reds might be bottom of the ladder, but they were still a Roman team, and as far as kudos went that put them head and shoulders above anything out in the sticks. Besides, crook or not, the guy had been no slouch. I'd've bet that if he had oiled his way to the top then he could've turned them round and built them up into contention . . .

Only that was where I stuck. Sure, Pegasus would've

made a good deputy, even managed to be the real power behind the throne, but in terms of that scenario there was no way he could ever be the actual boss. And that, I knew, would niggle him because Pegasus wasn't the type to play second fiddle. Cammius had taken over the Whites because he'd made his pile as a merchant and had the gravy to buy them from the wastrel who'd had them before. Natalis had been subbed by Prince Gaius and his pals. Acceptus was just plain rich to begin with. Pegasus, on the other hand, might be doing okay as far as prize money went but he wouldn't've had enough in the bank even to cover the starting bid. Assuming Pudens was willing to sell, which I'd bet he wasn't. He wasn't on his financial uppers like the ex-Whites guy, either.

Which left the sneaky approach.

That was on the cards from the first, of course. Unlike Laomedon, Pegasus wasn't a Reds driver, so he didn't have the connection with the faction which was the first requirement for a take-over. That, naturally, was where Felicula came in. The guy's train of thought was obvious: like Laomedon had said, he was slipping in through the back door. If he could get Pudens's wife on his side he'd be home and dry. Work on the faction boss through her, negotiate a contract that gave him a slice of the action and it was only a matter of time. Only, like Laomedon had said again, it didn't work.

I was level with Tiberius Arch now. I wasn't headed anywhere in particular, but a wineshop would be good and the nearest was in the direction of Iugarius. Thinking while you're walking is fine, but nothing beats a jug and a seat in the sun where you can watch the world pass while you do it. And my mouth was dry as a camel's scrotum.

On the other hand, just taking up with Felicula and expecting that a few sweet nothings breathed in her ear would give him the key to the kingdom didn't sound like Pegasus's style at all. The guy had been a lot smarter than that. He was no puffed-up Laomedon, and he must've known before he made his move what kind of lady he was dealing with. Not the sort, certainly, that would hang on his neck and do whatever he wanted at the first flex of his manly biceps. From what I'd seen of her – and from what Laomedon had told me – Felicula had a mind of her own, she was no fool and she ate men for breakfast. Plus, adulteries aside, she seemed genuinely fond of her husband and completely happy with his position as faction boss. The chances of Pegasus persuading her to team up with him and ditch Pudens were about equal to an elephant making consul. And the implications of *that* were that before he made his move Pegasus had to make sure he had more methods of persuasion than straightforward sex. It was just a question of working out . . .

I stopped.

Oh, Jupiter!

Leopards don't change their spots. He tried it later with Cario, for the same reason. Why not with Felicula?

One got you ten that Pegasus's second lever was blackmail. And what's the best – in fact the only – way to get rid of a blackmailer?

Right. Felicula had just shot to the top of the suspect list.

I carried on walking. I wasn't all that far shy of Marcellus Theatre by now, and the crowds were thickening by the minute. I could always pass up the seat in the sun aspect of things and head for Renatius's. Today was obviously a thinking day, and Renatius's was a good place to think in. Assuming Charax and his loud-mouthed cronies weren't in residence, of course.

The main drawback to that theory, naturally, was that the actual events didn't back it up. According to Felicula, the affair had ended about a month ago, well before the guy was murdered. If Pegasus had been blackmailing her, or trying to do it, anyway, and she'd decided on a final solution then I couldn't see her giving the guy the brush-off first. That would really be asking for trouble. The obvious strategy was to lull him into a false sense of security and then put the boot in when he least expected it. Also, just before he died he'd put the bite on Cario. That would suggest, as Laomedon had said, that he was shifting targets from Red to White. And that didn't point to a successful blackmail ploy where Felicula was concerned at all.

Hell.

Unless . . .

I slowed. Unless the idea of muscling in on the Reds came later, at the end of the affair. That cleared up the first problem, anyway. Felicula, like I say, was one tough-minded lady, and maybe Pegasus had under-estimated her, or overestimated himself. Probably both together. The two of them had settled down into a nice cosy long-term sexual liaison and he'd got overconfident. At that point – don't ask me how – he'd stumbled on a secret that he reckoned was big enough to serve as a lever to prise her away from Pudens. Only, like I say, he's miscalculated. Felicula calls his bluff and throws him out on his ear . . .

The next bit was tricky. I needed to explain why a) Pegasus shouldn't then blow the gaff in revenge or b) Felicula hadn't zeroed the guy straight away in self-defence; because neither of these two things had happened. Tricky, but not impossible. The strength of blackmail is in the threat. Once Pegasus let the secret out – whatever it might be – he'd've shot his bolt and made himself a serious enemy, both for nothing. Me, I'd think twice. Better to keep it in reserve and hope the victim'll see sense, maybe even agree to a negotiated settlement. As far as b) went, I could see that, if Pegasus had suddenly come up with the blackmail idea out of the blue, the lady's immediate reaction might've been to show him the door: we don't all think straight away in terms of murder. It would only be later when she thought the thing through that she might decide he'd be better off dead. Of course, that way she'd be running a risk. When a woman gives a lover the metaphorical chop and then less than a month later the guy gets chopped for real, then the authorities may just get to thinking that . . .

I froze. Oh, sweet gods, hang on! Oh, almighty and ever-loving Jupiter! Corvinus, you bloody, bloody fool!

I didn't have to explain anything, because there was nothing to explain. When Typhon had told me about the affair originally he'd spoken like it had still been going strong when Pegasus died. When I'd mentioned it to Cammius at the wineshop near the Circus he'd implied the same. Finally, if Laomedon had known the lady had broken off relations he would've made some snide remark to that effect at some point. He hadn't, not once. In fact, the only evidence I had for a split had come from Felicula, and even then she'd covered her back by saying the affair was only over as far as she was concerned.

We were in a whole different ball game. When Pegasus had died the two had still been an item, at least as far as he knew. There wasn't any reason for him to blow the gaff. And blackmail, like Perilla had said, is a prime motive for murder. Felicula was definitely on the hook.

People were staring at me. I moved off quickly.

So. It was a question now of what Pegasus had on the lady. Not the fact that they were lovers: that was common knowledge, and Pudens might be a sad stick of celery but he wasn't blind. Besides, when I'd talked to him he'd taken the link between his wife and the dead driver and its implications on board without a murmur. There wasn't any reason not to accept that husband-wife relations were just what the lady had told me they were.

Okay; so what else had we got? Scratch bringing up the dire and dreadful secret of Felicula's past. That might weigh with some guys – dancers, strippers, mime actresses and the like are among the lowest of the low, socially speaking – but it clearly wouldn't come as any news to Pudens. The lady had obviously been up-front on that score when she married him, and the fact that she wasn't embarrassed about mentioning it to a total stranger and even included a reference to it in the house decor put it completely out of court. Which left another kind of dire and dreadful secret altogether.

Pudens wasn't Felicula's first husband. That'd been – if my memory served me correctly – a builder by the name of Turranius, who'd died. Shortly afterwards through a mutual friend she meets Pudens, who's lately come from Sicily, and they tie the conjugal knot. Fairytale stuff, right? Poor but beautiful widow marries rich merchant and they live happily ever after. Or, if you prefer the more cynical but probably truer version: poor but beautiful widow hooks rich old patsy. Myself, I don't judge; like I say, in that sort of situation each party comes out ahead in different ways and it's no one's business but theirs.

So far so good. Only let's say that what I got from Felicula was a sanitised version. She didn't tell no lies, sure, but she didn't tell the truth either. Emended scenario: Pudens arrives in Rome from Sicily where he's made his pile in corn, Felicula sees him, gets smitten, lines him up and puts the mutual friend on the job. Eventually they meet and marry. Happy ever after, end of story.

No mention this time, notice, of the builder.

Me, I'd like to know at what point in the sequence

fly-in-the-ointment Turranius dies. And how he dies.

I was at the junction with Iugarius now. I could've carried on along it towards Renatius's, but I didn't. I turned right towards the vegetable market and the stall of my racing-world informant Cascellius.

He was there, selling a couple of bunches of spring onions to another of the ubiquitous bag-ladies.

'Hey, Corvinus!' he said. 'How's the murder investigation going?'

'Not bad.' I glanced at the next stall. Mammo, the old girl with the teeth, was firmly in residence. 'You care to split another jug, pal?'

'Sure. Always willing. It's lunchtime, anyway.' He came out from behind. 'Same place okay?'

'No problem.'

We made our way to the wineshop in the alley with the plane tree and the washing. I ordered a jug of Rhaetian, plus some bread, sausage and cheese.

'So,' Cascellius said. 'What's the question this time? I'm assuming there is a question?'

'Yeah.' I grinned. 'It has to do with the Reds' boss's wife. Felicula.'

His bovine face clouded. I'd forgotten that he didn't approve of that lady, although maybe that was an advantage in the circumstances. 'What about her?'

'She was married before. To a builder, guy named Turranius.'

'Right. So?'

'He died.'

'Right again.'

'You happen to know how?'

'No.'

Bugger. Well, maybe that had been expecting too much. 'Any idea who would?'

He chewed that one over for a while. Finally he said, 'You could try his place. It's under new ownership now, of course, but there'll be someone there who'll remember him.'

'Great!' It seemed that I'd struck lucky after all. 'Where would that be, exactly?'

'Out beyond the Aventine, on the old Ostia Road.'

A fair hike, but I had the whole afternoon in front of me and under the circumstances I'd risk Meton's displeasure for once. 'And who's the owner these days?' I said.

'Oh, now.' Cascellius frowned. 'You've got me there, Corvinus. I've no idea. But you can't miss it. It's on the right, just before Pottery Mountain.'

You can't miss it. I groaned mentally. Shit; I'd heard that one before. The old Ostia Road ran next to the Tiber and its wharfage, and it was just bristling with builders' yards, sawmills, cement works and small construction firms in general. It'd be like finding a needle in a haystack. Maybe an afternoon was optimistic. Still, it couldn't be helped, and it was a lot better than nothing.

The waiter came with the wine and the food. Cascellius moved aside while he set it down. I poured the wine and sank half my cup in a oner. Beautiful.

'All right.' Cascellius chewed on a piece of bread. 'Tell me what's happening.'

He deserved that, at least. I gave him the highlights of the case so far, up to but not including the business with Felicula. That part was *sub judice* for the present: I could be doing the lady an injustice, although I doubted it, and until I had some definite proof I'd keep my suspicions to myself. Maybe he had some inkling from my question – there's no way to make an enquiry about the manner of death of an ex-husband sound innocent – but if so he didn't pursue the matter. He was interested in the curse, though. And in Eutacticus.

'You watch that one, Corvinus,' he said. 'He's bad, bad news.'

'Yeah, I know.'

'Maybe you don't know well enough. Guy who used to come into the Cat, hailed from over Gabii way, set himself up as a tout. Nothing big, wouldn't take bets of any more than a silver piece and always paid out on the nail. Last his wife saw of him, he was being taken off between two of Eutacticus's heavies. She found him the next day kicked to death in an alley next to the temple of the Sun.'

'No sweat, pal. I'm not interested in his current betting scams. I just want to have a word about Pegasus.'

'That might be one word too many. Eutacticus keeps his eyes open, and he doesn't like people taking an interest in his business at all. Full stop.' He bit on a slice of sausage. 'Take it from me. Be warned.'

'I'm a purple-striper. He won't fool with the aristocracy.'

'I wouldn't count on that. The last I heard he was

getting to be bosom friends with the senior consul.'

'Vitellius?' Yeah, that made sense. By reputation, our new first magistrate – under the Wart – was a big racing fan. He wasn't too honest, either. Even for a consul.

'Right. You watch the Blues next season. Vitellius is one of their biggest backers.' Cascellius extracted a piece of gristle from between his teeth. 'What's the betting they make a sudden and miraculous recovery?'

I stared at him. 'You serious?'

'One hand washes the other, Corvinus, and friendships go two ways. Let's just say I wouldn't be surprised if the Blues started winning races again. In any case, take my advice with Eutacticus and don't trust your purple stripe.'

I topped up the cups. Yeah, well; maybe he was right. After all, like Sopilys had said, whatever scam Pegasus had had going it was history now. Maybe I'd give Eutacticus a miss unless I really had to see him.

I hadn't missed the implications of that line on Vitellius and the Blues, either.

21

I left Cascellius finishing off the wine and headed for the old Ostia Road. This wasn't a part of the city I was familiar with. Like I say, the stretch of Tiber bank south-west of the Aventine is mostly industrial, or rather an area where bulk shipping plays a big part because it's within easy reach of the barges that bring the heavy stuff up from the port: corn for the city granaries, building materials like brick, stone, cement and wood. The southern part serves as the city dump, particularly for the thousands of earthenware wine and oil jars the population get through in a year. That's been going on for the last few centuries, and Pottery Mountain's the result. It's just what it says: a mountain of old jars that've been piling up, probably, since before Brutus threw out the Tarquins. Turranius's yard might prove tricky to locate, but Pottery Mountain posed no problems.

Tricky was the operative word. Cascellius had said that Turranius's old place was on the right just shy of the mountain, but apart from a mega-large concern taking up two or three acres that looked like it would be a major government contractor all I could see were a line of timber yards, and they were on the other side of the road. I'd have to ask again.

Outside one of them was a tunic planing a length of plank. I went up to him.

'Excuse me, friend,' I said. 'I'm looking for a builder's yard that used to belong to a guy named Turranius. You happen to know where that might be?'

He stopped and wiped his brow. 'Sure,' he said. 'That's Anterus's across the street.'

I looked. Above the double gates of the mega-large concern was a sign that said in letters two feet high: *Gaius Cornelius Anterus: Building Contractor*. I did a double-take. 'Uh . . . *that's* Turranius's yard?'

'Up until five or six years ago it was. Only Turranius I know of around here.'

'He have a wife called Felicula?'

The man shrugged. 'Search me, pal. But if you're looking for Turranius's then that's the place.' He carried on planing.

'Right. Thanks.' I crossed the road, my brain whirling. Shit, this didn't make sense; it didn't make sense at all. Not as far as the scenario went, anyway.

There was a guy on the gate. He'd been watching me with interest – not a lot happens down by Pottery Mountain, and you have to make your own amusements – and he stood up.

'Afternoon, sir,' he said politely.

'Uh . . . the boss in?'

'No, sir. Just the manager. Can I ask your business?'

'I wanted to talk to someone about the, uh, former owner.' I was looking beyond him. Jupiter! The place was huge! 'That was Turranius, right?'

'Yes, sir. Before my time, but Turranius it was.

The manager should be able to help you. He was here before Cornelius Anterus bought the business.'

'Fine. And where would I find this manager?'

'In the office, sir. Just go straight ahead. His name's Simo.'

I walked through the gate and down the central avenue. Huge was right, busy, too: the place positively hummed, and there were more slaves around than you could shake a stick at. Over to my left, a group of them were polishing coloured marble slabs; the stuff you see in those fancy houses on the Janiculan where the super-rich owners haven't even heard the word veneer and wouldn't've touched it with gloves on. Next on down was a guy chiselling the square holes into a matching set of column drums. Marble again, but white this time, and solid, not the usual cheapo variety with the marble-dust facing. Pricey as hell. Of course, Anterus, whoever he was – obviously, from the name, a freedman of the Cornelii, or more likely second or third generation – could've taken the firm into the luxury bracket himself, but I doubted it. This set-up had long-established class written all over it.

I found the office and knocked. Inside was a dapper little guy in a neat orange tunic sitting behind a desk studying what looked like architect's plans. He looked up.

'Yes?'

'Uh . . . Simo, right?' I said.

'Indeed, sir.' He smiled. 'Don't tell me. The Palatine Library extension. Everything's in hand. We should be able to begin work in—'

'Uh, no. No. My name's Marcus Valerius Corvinus. I came to ask about—'

'Valerius Corvinus?' The smile changed to a frown. 'I don't think we have anything on the schedule for a Valerius Corvinus, sir. Would this be a private contract? Or merely an enquiry? I'm afraid we're fully committed for the next—'

'No. It's not business. I was told you might be able to help me with some information. About the former owner.'

'Sextus Turranius? I'm afraid he's dead, sir. Has been for several years.'

'Right. Yeah. I knew that. In fact, that's what I was hoping you could help me with.'

He was still frowning. 'In what way, sir?'

'You happen to know how he died?'

'Certainly. I was present at the time myself, as it happens.' He stood up. The architect's plan rolled itself back into a cylinder. 'Forgive me, sir, but before we go any further can I ask what your interest is?'

'I'm, uh, investigating a murder. Of a racing driver. Guy called Pegasus.' I could see that the name didn't mean anything to him; not a racegoer, then. 'He was a . . . friend . . . of Turranius's widow. At least, if I've got the right Turranius. Lady called Felicula.'

His mouth set in a line. 'Felicula was certainly Sextus Turranius's wife, sir,' he said, 'but I can't see what that has to do with—'

'No hassle, pal,' I said quickly. 'I'm just checking angles. Filling in the background.'

'Indeed.' He sat down again, rolled out the plan

and weighed it at the corners with four small blocks of marble. 'And you want to know how her husband died. Surely it would be better, if you really think the information is important, and I cannot think why, to ask the lady herself?'

'I, uh, didn't want to do that.'

He stared at me for a long minute. Then he said, coldly; 'Sextus Turranius died in a. fall from some scaffolding. He was inspecting a repair to the pediment of the Temple of Mars the Avenger, and he was alone at the time. The Lady Felicula was at home and had never to my certain knowledge visited the site. She and her husband were the happiest and most loving of couples, and I personally find your implications offensive. Now good-day, sir.'

Ouch. Still, I couldn't leave things there. 'You say you were present. So he wasn't alone.'

'I meant alone on the scaffolding itself, sir. And there were several people present at the time. Myself and at least five of the workers. On the ground. We were all witnesses, and it was a complete accident. The master leaned out too far and overbalanced.' He hesitated. 'Sextus Turranius was not a young man, sir, but unfortunately he insisted on taking a personal interest in any work in progress. He was extremely conscientious, a first-class craftsman in his own right, and I had nothing but admiration for him. Or for his wife.'

I sighed. Well, that was that. Not even Pegasus could make a case for blackmail out of an accidental fall from a set of scaffolding. 'Right,' I said. 'Thanks a lot, friend. Sorry to disturb you.' I turned to go. Then another thought struck me. 'Oh. By the way. I assume there were no kids from the marriage?'

'No, sir. There was . . . a considerable age difference, as I told you.'

'And Felicula was the only heir?'

'Yes. She was.'

This bit was tricky. However, although the guy obviously disapproved of me he was being helpful by his lights, so I asked the question anyway. 'You have any idea what Turranius's estate was worth? Once this place was sold?'

'Not for certain, sir. But I would guess somewhere in excess of two million.'

'Two *million*?' Jupiter! One million was the property qualification for a broad-striper!

'Yes, sir. Sextus Turranius had other investments besides the firm. Two million would be a conservative estimate.'

'Uh, fine.' My brain was buzzing. 'Fine. Thanks, pal. You've been very helpful.'

'Don't mention it. But, Valerius Corvinus—'

'Yeah?' My hand was on the latch of the door.

'Let me just say one thing before you go, in case what I've told you is at all unclear. I was privileged to know the Lady Felicula for several years, since her marriage, in fact. She is a very charming lady, and she certainly had no hand in the death of her husband.'

He didn't wait for a reply, just turned back to his architect's plans. I left.

★   ★   ★

So. Scratch any suspicious circumstances surrounding Turranius's death. If there had been any other work-men with him on the scaffolding, or if it'd collapsed while he was up there, I might've had my doubts. With two million at stake Felicula could well have afforded to rope in one of the guy's employees as her hit-man, but by all the evidence the fall had obviously been the silly old bugger's own fault.

That was a point in itself, of course: Turranius had been a silly *old* bugger, and if this had happened six years ago then Felicula could only have been in her late twenties. Take that fact along with Pudens – another silly old bugger if I'd ever met one – and we still had the familiar scenario of the hard-nosed little gold-digger. At her age, with a husband already more than halfway into the urn, she could afford to wait. Especially with the fringe benefits. I didn't know whether Turranius had been as accommodating over the lady's extramural activities as her current husband, but if the guy was as wrapped up in his business as Simo implied then she'd certainly had enough free time on her hands. My guess was that history was simply repeating itself.

Which didn't, of course, mean that Felicula was a murderess. Gold-digging's no crime on its own, not even a moral one in my view, and from the sound of things, apart from the question mark over her sex life, she'd been a model wife to Turranius, too. I couldn't get her there, not on present evidence, and if I couldn't then neither could Pegasus.

I couldn't get her in terms of the scenario, either. Forget the poor but beautiful widow, the first part anyway: when she'd married Pudens the lady had been seriously rich in her own right. Two million plus is a lot of gravy, and she hadn't struck me as a particularly big spender. Of course, there were people – men and women – who could never have enough, and that might explain why she had chosen Pudens to marry when she'd doffed her widow's whites, but still . . .

Hell's teeth! There had to be something else. Pegasus had had some sort of hold over her, that I was sure of, he was that kind of person. But I couldn't, now, think for the life of me what it was.

Unless, of course, there had been a husband *before* Turranius; one who'd also died. Simo's last little speech had suggested the lady had been married for some time, but even so late twenties were late twenties; they left space for another old codger and to spare. And that one Pudens *wouldn't* have known about. Any girl can lose one geriatric husband to bad luck, but two in a row's pushing it. And if I discovered I was husband number three, I'd be watching what my very charming wife put in my gruel . . .

Maybe the scenario wasn't all that far out after all. I just had to go a little further back.

The sun was well into its last quadrant as I approached the Arch of Drusus and Germanicus (why the Wart had let himself be persuaded to erect a monument to that bastard I didn't know; cynicism, probably) and I put a bit of zip into my steps. I still had a long way to go to the Caelian, and I might've been blasé about missing dinner when I was back there at the wineshop but Meton wasn't mocked; not with impunity, anyway. It was getting busier the closer I came to the Aventine: no wheeled traffic yet, naturally, but there were a lot of pedestrians and a few litters. One – a double one – was parked at the side of the road, with the four litter slaves and two outwalkers standing beside it. Maybe one of the chairmen had bust a sandal-strap.

I was almost on them when I realised something was wrong. The outwalkers looked familiar. They were big guys with the muscles bulging out of their tunics. I slowed.

Too late. One of the guys came forward, with the second close behind on my other side. They moved together with me between them like the two halves of a rock sandwich. My shoulders grated.

'The boss wants to talk with you, Corvinus,' the first guy said.

Oh, shit. No prizes for guessing who the boss was. And I recognised both of them now: the pair of gorilla-wrestlers who'd been stationed outside the gate of the house on the Pincian. I made a fist of my left hand and swung it hard and low at the first guy's groin . . .

His own right hand moved down so fast it blurred, catching mine and holding it. 'No need for that, pal,' he said quietly. 'We don't want no trouble. Just get in the litter, okay?'

The second tunic had gripped my right arm with fingers you could've used to lift the column drum in Anterus's yard. I couldn't've moved if I tried.

I managed a shrug. 'Fine.'

'That's good. Keep up the co-operation and you won't get hurt.' He let go and moved aside.

The litter was empty. I sat down on one set of cushions and Laughing George squeezed in opposite, shutting the curtains behind him. The four litter lads took the strain and we were off. *Strain* it must've been: I'm not light myself, and the guy must've weighed half as much again. If we reached the Pincian without one of them doing himself a permanent injury they could count themselves lucky.

'Uh . . . we're going to see Eutacticus, right?' I said.

No answer. Laughing George had obviously shot his conversational bolt and he was sitting there with a face that was pure granite. Hell; so much for planning. When – if – I talked to the cartel boss I'd envisaged a lot more back-up than I actually had at present, which was zero. Perilla didn't know where I was. She didn't – and something cold touched my spine – even know about Eutacticus, because I'd been careful not to mention him. The lady would only have worried.

Like I was doing now. I kept thinking of Cascellius's pal, the one from Gabii who'd been found kicked to death in an alley . . .

The long silent trip to the Pincian wasn't pleasant.

We got there eventually. The litter guys set us down, Laughing George opened the curtains, climbed out and waited for me to disembark. The house was even more impressive from close up: a marble-porticoed monstrosity with a flight of steps that would've put the Temple of Jupiter Capitolinus to shame. Not that I was much interested in architecture at that precise moment.

'Go ahead, Corvinus,' Laughing George growled. 'We're right behind you.'

A comforting thought. I went up the steps trying to fight back the cold feeling in my gut, with the gorilla-wrestlers at my heels. The door-slave gave us a look as blind as Homer's and opened up.

The hall inside could've come straight from one of the Wart's Capri villas, only it was bigger and probably cost more.

'Straight through and up the stairs. The boss is in his study.' Still Laughing George. The other guy hadn't spoken. Maybe he couldn't.

'Is that so? All this and culture too. What's he doing, pal, writing an ode?'

'Don't be smart, Corvinus. Just walk.'

I walked. At the top of the stairs was a panelled door between a pair of matching bronzes that would've had my stepfather Priscus drooling.

'Stop there.' Laughing George pushed past me, knocked and waited.

'Come in.'

LG opened the door and moved aside.

22

I went in. The study was fitted out in keeping with the rest of the place: way over the top. Maybe comparing it with the Pollio Library is an exaggeration, but there were still a hell of a lot of book-rolls in the cubbies round the walls. Perilla would've loved it.

Not that the guy on the couch looked much like a reader. I couldn't imagine him chucking his kids under the chin, either, or shooting the breeze with his wife over the pork rissoles of an evening. I couldn't imagine him doing anything, except maybe lying in the shallows of some river with his nostrils above the surface pretending to be a log and waiting for some poor bastard to use him as a bridge.

'Sit down,' Eutacticus said.

Laughing George and his mate took me by the elbows and plonked me down on the other couch. Then they stepped back to just within grabbing distance.

'Marcus Valerius Messalla Corvinus.' That came out slow and consideringly, like he was chewing it.

'Uh . . . yeah. All four of me.'

I could feel Laughing George shifting slightly in his number twelve sandals, but the guy's expression didn't change. 'Don't make jokes, Corvinus, please,' he said. 'I won't tell you again.'

I swallowed. 'Right. Right.'

'I'm told you were asking about me recently. And that you're making enquiries into the death of a charioteer.'

'Right.' Jupiter! Maybe I'd died and been reborn as a parrot.

'I don't like enquiries.'

I was going to say, *tough*! but I changed my mind. This bastard wasn't a bastard who enjoyed backchat. I didn't say anything.

'On the other hand, in this instance my conscience is clear.' He showed his teeth in a quick grin. I thought of logs. 'And what is more important in respect of your continued good health I didn't personally approve of Pegasus's death myself.'

'Uh . . . yeah?'

'We had quite a good relationship while that gentleman drove for the Greens. You're probably aware of that fact already. Our association might have been in abeyance temporarily, but it still existed. Very much so. I looked forward to its resumption when he had settled in with his new faction, and I don't take kindly to losing an asset. Not kindly at all.' He was staring at me with a look that would've done credit to a jaundiced wolverine. 'Whoever killed Pegasus did me no favours. I just wanted to make sure you understood that, in case the results of your . . . investigation led you to think otherwise.'

'So you don't know who did it?' I said. Well, it was

worth asking, and at least my neck seemed safe. That was a relief, anyway.

'No. Not at the moment.' Without taking his eyes off me he reached his little finger to his mouth and carefully picked between two teeth with the nail. 'But I'm making enquiries of my own, and when I do that person is going to be very sorry. Very sorry indeed.' He inspected the nail and wiped it on his mantle. 'No one kills in the racing business without my knowledge and approval, Corvinus, not for any reason. Certainly no one kills against my interests. If the murderer is lucky you'll find him first.'

'Or her.'

He made a wheezing noise. It could've been a laugh but I wouldn't've taken any bets. 'Or her, as you say. I don't make distinctions. In either case they're dead meat.' My stomach went cold, not so much at the words as at the way he said them. 'So you'd better move quickly. However, as far as your . . . enquiries . . . into the late Pegasus's sideline activities in the racing sphere are concerned, I expect those to end as of now. They're none of your business. You understand me.' It wasn't a question, and he didn't wait for an answer. He looked past me at Laughing George. 'I'm finished. Take him out and . . .' He paused fractionally. The lips twisted in a smile. 'Let him go.'

Bastard!

'Yes, boss.' A hand big as a ham lifted me to my feet.

'Oh, and Corvinus?'

My mouth was dry as old leather. 'Yeah?'

'My thanks for putting me on to the fact that Pegasus wasn't killed for his purse. I owe you one.' The thin lips twisted again. 'A small one, so don't start getting big ideas. You can consider that letting you leave here with your ribs intact constitutes part of the repayment.' He turned away. 'Goodbye. Have a pleasant walk to the Caelian.'

The sun was almost beneath the horizon of Mars Field as Laughing George closed the gate behind me and I set off back down Pincian Road. My stomach still felt like someone had tied a knot in it. Well, that had been a nasty little experience and a half, and I reckoned I was lucky to get out the other end with all my bits still attached, especially after Eutacticus's penultimate parting shot, because I wouldn't bet more than evens that his crack about the ribs had been a joke. Humour clearly wasn't that bastard's bag. Or not the brand of humour that I appreciated, anyway.

Glad to be outside and undamaged as I was I didn't much relish the thought of any more walking. Today had been a long, long day and I was whacked, even without the last interview, if that's what you'd call it, too whacked even for a wineshop. Not that I had to walk, of course; now the restriction on wheels within the city boundaries had been lifted until dawn I could take a carriage from the rank at the Saepta. Besides, I needed space to think.

I took the first one in the line, gave the guy directions

and settled back against the cushions. Look on the bright side, Corvinus. At least I'd talked to Eutacticus. Or been talked at, rather. And I'd learned two things. The first was a simple confirmation, if I'd needed one, that Sopilys hadn't been spinning me a line and Pegasus had actually been up to no good with the Greens; the second, far more important, was proof that he'd had plans to do the same with the Whites. That little nugget of information was interesting, and I thought about it and the implications for quite some time.

Then there was the question of Felicula. We weren't finished with that lady yet, no way, not by a long chalk. The most likely person to know whether she'd been married before Turranius, of course, had been Simo the building site manager, but the idea hadn't occurred to me until I'd left the yard and I didn't think the guy would prove too helpful a second time round, even if I did trek all the way back down to Pottery Mountain. Maybe Cascellius could help, although I doubted it: Cascellius's knowledge of Felicula wouldn't go back that far, and if even Pudens didn't know – which I'd bet he didn't, and couldn't've done for the scam to work – then I was stuck that side as well. There was always the public records office, sure – that would have the documentation of an earlier marriage, if it existed, on file – but I didn't even consider taking that route. For a start, I didn't have any idea of date or name of husband, and for another thing I didn't know whether either he or the lady had been a Roman citizen at the time. If not, then I could whistle for a record; if so, I'd still be twiddling my thumbs waiting for the clerk to find the document at next year's Winter Festival. Assuming, like I say, it existed in the first place. I sighed. Maybe the best plan would be to cut the knot, confront Felicula herself and see where it got me.

It was fully dark when we pulled up outside my front door. I paid off the carriage and was reaching for the doorknob just as Bathyllus opened up with the tray in his hand. Janus in spangly tights, how that little bugger does it is a complete mystery. Ours, however, not to reason why, just be grateful. I sank the first cup of life-giving fluid in one and held out for a refill.

'Sorry I'm late, Bathyllus,' I said. 'Problems you do not want to know about.'

'Yes, sir.' He closed the door then held the cup long enough for me to get rid of my travel-stained mantle. 'Ah . . . you have eaten, have you?'

Uh-oh. This sounded bad. Miss a meal in the Corvinus household without giving three days' prior warning in writing and you have a major diplomatic incident on your hands. 'Meton's, uh, annoyed, right?'

'When I last went down to the kitchen he was cleaning the skillets, sir.'

Bad news; *bad* news. Skillet-cleaning is a job for the skivvy, and Meton was strictly the culinary demiurge type. Our touchy-as-hell chef was into seriously put-upon mode, and my chances of getting so much as an omelette out of him were about as good as a snowball's rolling through Hades. 'Dinner was . . . ah . . . something particularly good, then?'

'Sea urchins in rosemary-flavoured wine and poached tunnyfish steaks with a sweet cumin sauce, sir. He went to the fishmarket at dawn specially.'

Oh, bugger; worse and worse. That wasn't the sort of stuff that took readily to a reheat, and the guy even objected to warming up leftover bean stew for lunch. Also, knowing Meton, he'd've put in more time choosing the shellfish and tunny than the Wart spent on the Armenian problem. 'Never mind. I wasn't hungry anyway.' A lie, but hassles after the day I'd had I just didn't need. 'How's Project Tyndaris going, incidentally?'

The little bald-head coloured. 'Extremely well, sir. I called round just after lunchtime and invited her here tomorrow for the tile-polishing demonstration. She was delighted. *Most* gratifying.'

'Fine. Fine.' I relieved him of the wine jug and carried it through to the living-room.

'Marcus, where on *earth* have you been?' Perilla was lying on her couch with a writing tablet and stylus. 'Meton's livid.'

I kissed her. 'Yeah. I've heard.'

'We waited as long as we could before starting dinner but we had to give you up. You look absolutely exhausted. What happened?'

'Long story, lady.' I stretched out on the couch. Jupiter, that was good! 'I talked to Laomedon. Serapia's probably in the clear, but we've got another two or three new front runners.' I told her what the Reds' driver had told me about Pegasus's designs on the faction. 'That opens up a whole fresh angle. One gets you ten that the bastard was working on Felicula to get his foot in the door with her husband. Blackmail.'

'Pegasus had some sort of hold on the woman?'

'Yeah.' I filled my cup. 'At least, I think so. I don't know for sure, let alone what it was, but it seems likely. And I'd bet good money that their affair didn't end when she said it did.'

'Hmm.' Perilla put the writing tablet aside and laid her chin on her hand.

'I thought maybe it might have something to do with her ex Turranius, but I checked and that's all above board. Turns out he was rich as Croesus and Felicula got the lot, but he died in an accident.'

'A genuine accident?'

'Sure. The guy fell from a set of scaffolding in front of half a dozen witnesses.' I sipped my wine. 'He was on his own at the time, so there was no funny business. Problem is, I can't see what else Pegasus could've had. Unless there was a prior marriage we don't know about that ended the same way.'

Perilla was frowning and twisting her hair. 'I don't suppose you could be approaching things from the wrong direction?' she said.

'How do you mean, lady?'

'I'm not altogether sure myself. But from what you told me Felicula does seem genuinely fond of her husband and it is reciprocal. If Pegasus had become a party to some secret in her former life then it would have to be something major before it would threaten a split in the relationship. And if she is financially independent then that factor wouldn't come into things.'

I shifted on my couch. 'I'd call murder pretty major, myself.'

'Marcus, you're overpostulating here. For that theory to work, you need both an earlier husband and a convenient death. There's no evidence at present for the existence of either, and until there is perhaps it might be better to think in other terms.'

'Yeah? Like what?'

'We know quite a lot about Felicula. She used to be a dancer, she was previously married to a builder who left her a very wealthy widow. She loves her husband and has a good relationship with him. Correct?'

'Sure.'

'Now what do we know about Pudens? Apart from the fact that he's Master of the Reds and Felicula's husband?'

Gods! Well, sometimes you have to humour them. 'One, he's pretty well-heeled; he must be, to run the Reds. Two, he's Sicilian, or at least he moved from there. Panormus, specifically. And three, he made his money in the corn business.'

'One, you've just told me that Felicula is rich in her own right and is also fully in favour of her husband's involvement with the faction. Why should he be the one who pays the bills? Two, the only evidence you have for Pudens being Sicilian, or a former resident of Sicily, comes from Felicula. She in turn probably derived it from Pudens himself, since they only met after he had moved to Rome. And three . . . well, the same argument applies. You have no *objective* evidence for his past life whatsoever, except what he told his future wife.' She paused, then said quietly; 'Marcus, when you get right down to it we don't really *know* anything about Pudens's antecedents at all.'

I sat very still. Shit, the lady was right. Even Cascellius hadn't been able to give me any concrete information about him. And blackmail was all about antecedents . . .

'You think we should take a closer look at Pudens?' I said.

'That would certainly be an obvious course of action, if only for purposes of elimination.'

'Okay. But how?'

'Wasn't Quintus Lollianus in Sicily at one time? You could begin by checking with him.'

Yeah; now that was a distinct possibility. Lollianus was an old pre-Perilla mate of mine and we'd had him and his wife round for dinner once or twice since we'd moved back from Athens. He was big in Aqueducts and Sewers these days but he'd done his two-year junior finance officer's stint as an aide to the Sicilian governor. And since as far as the Roman administration's concerned Sicily is first, middle and last all about corn, any major Sicilian corn dealer would inevitably come to the finance officer's notice. Lollianus might well know Pudens. Or not, as the case might be, which would be interesting in itself. Score one for the grapevine. 'Good idea, lady,' I said. 'I'll see him tomorrow.'

'You mentioned two or three new possibilities. Felicula was one. Who were the others?'

'Hmm?' I was still thinking about Pudens. 'Oh, the other two go together. Cammius and Cario.'

'Marcus, we've been through both of these already!'

'Uh-uh. Like I said: together, not separate. And there's new evidence.'

'Where from?'

This was the bit I'd been dreading. 'Uh . . . a guy called Eutacticus. That was why I was late home. He's . . . ah . . . a cartel boss. Lives up on the Pincian.'

'Oh, Corvinus!' Perilla was looking at me like I'd said I'd been selling my body to sailors under the arches of the Sublician. Which didn't surprise me: everybody in Rome knows about the cartel bosses. They just don't talk about them.

'No problem, lady. We had a very pleasant chat. He confirmed that Pegasus had been throwing races when he drove for the Greens and that he had plans along the same lines with the Whites.'

'He *told* you that?'

'Uh . . . yeah. It was no skin off his nose. The guy's dead and the scam's buried with him.'

'I'm sorry, dear, but I don't believe you. Not about Pegasus cheating on his faction. About the pleasant chat. You're hiding something.'

Oh, hell. 'Jupiter, Perilla, just drop the psychic stuff, okay? I'm fine. No bones broken.'

She sat up. 'No *what?*'

'Perilla, will you just listen?'

'Don't you *ever* get involved with people like that again! Marcus, they are *dangerous*!'

She was telling me something I didn't know? 'Okay, okay,' I said. 'Just leave it, will you?'

Silence. *Long* silence. 'Very well,' she said at last. 'What about Cammius and Cario?'

Gods! That had been a nasty one. I took a restorative swig of Setinian. 'We know now that Pegasus was definitely planning to throw a wobbler with the Whites. *Definitely* being the operative word; we've moved beyond theory here. Cammius must've had his suspicions about why a top driver should've left the Greens. He would've had to be blind or a fool if he didn't, and Cammius isn't either. Agreed?'

'Agreed. But—'

'Wait a minute, lady. I've got the ball. Let's say Cammius found out somehow that Pegasus meant to play the same game with him and decided to cut his losses. He gets his son Cario to decoy the guy on to neutral ground – remember, we only have Cario's word for it that Pegasus is blackmailing him – and one or the other of them kills him.'

'But—'

I held up a hand. She subsided. 'If the blackmail part is true then it gives Cammius an even stronger motive, and as his son Cario has it as well, over and above straight exposure to the authorities for the business of the guy with the apoplexy. Pegasus was trying to worm his way into the running of the Whites. The faction's Cammius's baby, and his son's out of the same mould. Neither of them would take that lying down. From their point of view Pegasus is a liability in all sorts of ways. He has to go for the good of the team. Murder arranged as per the above.'

Perilla was staring at me. 'Have you finished now?' she said. You could've used her tone of voice to ice prawns.

I blinked. 'Uh . . . yeah. Yeah, that about covers it.'

'Very well. Now you listen to me. First: you said yourself that Cammius viewed Pegasus as the only hope for the Whites. Under these circumstances killing him would not only be stupid, it would be completely senseless. If Cammius found out – and could prove – that Pegasus was planning to, as you put it, throw a wobbler then it would make far more sense to confront the man and change his mind under threat. Marcus, we have been through all this!'

'Yeah, but—'

'Second: you told me that Cammius welcomed Pegasus's input to the running of the faction. Again, that makes sense because Pegasus had far more experience of the racing world than he did, and on these grounds I would admit a motive for Cario but not for his father. Added to this, Cammius strikes me as an extremely strong character. Had he been another Pudens then I would accept your point; as it is, it is highly unlikely that he would allow himself to be sidelined by one of his drivers. If the situation did become insupportable he could simply fire him.'

'Uh, right, but—'

'Third: I admit he may have been pretending, but you said you were convinced that he was unaware of any meeting at the wineshop; in fact, he specifically asked your help in discovering who the other person was. If he already knew that Pegasus's contact had been his son, and that the meeting had been set up between them to decoy Pegasus into a position where he could be murdered, then such behaviour is not only irresponsible, it verges on the imbecile. And that word, I think, could usefully be applied to the theory as a whole.'

I winced. Well, I had to admit it was a fair analysis. The lady didn't take prisoners, either. 'What if Pegasus was blackmailing Cammius?' I said. 'In that case, sacking wouldn't be an option.'

'Over what?'

'Jupiter, Perilla, I don't know!'

'Exactly. Well, then: does Cammius strike you as a person particularly open to blackmail?'

'Uh . . . no, but—'

The lady sighed. 'Corvinus, why don't you go to bed?'

I grinned. 'Is that a proposition, lady?'

'No, it isn't. Your brain's tired. Have an early night and make a fresh start in the morning. Unless of course you want to beard Meton in his den first and see what you can scrounge. I didn't ask if you'd eaten, but I assume that even if you have it wasn't much.'

'I'll pass on that, thanks.' Uh-uh, no way, never, certainly not in my present weakened state. With a wasted dawn trip down to the fishmarket as the

bone of contention I wasn't going near Meton for a
month. Besides, it does you good to miss out on a meal
occasionally, or so the doctors say. Hunger sharpens
the intellect. In which case I was going to be one of
the smartest men in Rome come breakfast time.

Ah, well. She was probably right as usual. I was
whacked, and an early night sounded really good. I
got up, stretched, kissed the lady and padded off to
hit the mattress.

23

I was up the next day bright, early and bushy-tailed. Knowing Lollianus, the lazy bugger wouldn't be strolling in to work until the sun was well up and running so I had time for a long and leisurely breakfast catching up with Perilla on humdrum domestic matters. Like the Tyndaris situation. That, as Bathyllus had said, seemed to be going pretty well. The little guy had blossomed like a rose, and according to the lady he was in and out of next door like nobody's business. What Tyndaris saw in him, mind, I couldn't see myself for the life of me, but they seemed to be becoming an item. A platonic item, sure, but if that suited them – or Bathyllus, at least – then great. Today was the day of the tile-polishing expedition. I was sorry I had to miss it.

I left for the Aqueducts and Sewers Department around mid-morning. The weather had settled down and we had a beautiful spring day. Lovely for walking. I took the long way round to Market Square: up Head of Africa and left along the northern base of the Palatine. The hawkers were out in force selling twisted sesame bread, pastries and dubious rissoles. I passed them by – even a seriously disgruntled Meton couldn't do anything to bread, fruit and honey, and I was already stuffed – but at the corner of New Street there was a guy with a trayful of cheap flashy bracelets and I bought one for Bathyllus to give to Tyndaris. The little bald-head would never think of something like that for himself, and I'd bet a gold piece to a kick in the teeth that it'd advance his case a hell of a lot more than a gift-wrapped recipe for non-slip tile polish.

Aqueducts and Sewers are attached to the Temple of Venus Cloacina at the Market Square end of the Sacred Way, just in front of Aemilian Hall. I stopped a clerk and asked for Lollianus.

'He's in his office, sir,' the clerk said. 'I'll take you.'

'Hey, Marcus.' Lollianus was parked behind a desk with enough wax tablets to keep Perilla going for a year. 'How's it going?'

'Not bad.' We shook. Maybe it's the effect working somewhere like Aqueducts and Sewers has on you, but Quintus Lollianus was a long way now from the sleek young wineshop crawler he'd been fifteen years back. He had *senior administrator* written all over him from his carefully covered premature bald patch to his Cordoban leather sandals. A nice guy, though, so long as you kept him off sediment traps.

He waved me to the visitor's chair. 'You having problems with your drains or do you want to tap in free to the Aqua Claudia?'

I grinned. 'Neither. I wanted to pick your brains. If you've got ten minutes to spare.'

'Sure. Pick as long as you want. The clerks do all

the work anyway, I just sign the documents and handle any grief that's tossed in our direction.'

I doubted that. If I called him lazy earlier I wasn't being serious: these tablets weren't just for effect, and even when he'd had all his hair and no paunch Lollianus had been a conscientious member of the establishment. In embryo, at any rate. 'It's about Sicily,' I said. 'You were there as quaestor thirteen or fourteen years back, right?'

He nodded. 'When old Paullus was governor. I haven't been back since, though, so if you're asking about anything more recent—'

'No, that should just about do it.' Pudens had been in Rome for six years plus, and he was no spring chicken. If he'd been in business before that then he and Lollianus must've overlapped. 'You have much to do with the corn side of things?'

'Sure. I was finance officer, Marcus. Of course I did.'

'Fine. You ever come across a dealer called Gaius Rufrius Pudens?'

Lollianus's brow furrowed. 'The Reds' faction master? He was in Sicily?'

I nodded. 'In Panormus. Or so I was told.'

'Then you were told wrong, pal. At least, I never met him. And in two years I met most of the guys in the corn business and heard of the rest.'

'You're sure of that?'

'Not a hundred per cent. If he was before my time, or after it, then I wouldn't know. But certainly thirteen years back there was no Rufrius Pudens around.

Not in Panormus, certainly, that's definite. I was stationed there.'

Oh, hell: Perilla had been right, there was something screwy about Pudens. 'You don't know anything about him at all?'

'Apart from the fact that he's the Reds' boss, no. And not too good a boss either, from what I hear. He could've been in the corn business, sure, maybe in Africa or Tripolis, Egypt even, but he wasn't in Sicily. Not at that time, anyway.' Lollianus was frowning. 'Hey, Marcus, you okay?'

'Yeah. Yeah.' We were on to something here, I could feel it in my gut. 'Look, Quintus, can you put me on to anyone who might be able to give me definite information about these places? Same sort of time, or maybe a bit later. Anything up to six or seven years back.' It was a long shot; if Pudens had lied about Panormus he could just as easily have lied about the business he'd been in. If any. Sicily apart, corn meant the African coast and the Nile, but if Pudens hadn't been in corn at all he could've come from anywhere between Hercules's Pillars and the Parthian border. Still, Africa, Tripolis and Egypt were the obvious starters.

'I can't think of anyone offhand, but I'll ask around.' The guy was still frowning. 'What's this about?'

Well, I had to tell him something. Especially since he seemed ready and willing to help. 'It's complicated. Basically, I'm looking into the death of the Whites' lead driver. Pegasus.'

Lollianus's eyes widened. 'Yeah, I heard about that.

Stabbed in an alley somewhere, right? You, uh, think Pudens might be involved?'

'Pal, I don't know. I just don't know.' I wasn't hedging, either. What Lollianus had just told me had pulled the rug right out from under, and I needed to think. 'Let's say it's a possibility, one I hadn't considered up to now. Only keep it under your hat, okay?'

'Sure.'

I got up. 'I've got to go. Thanks for your help, Quintus. I owe you one.'

'No problem. Any time. And I'll let you know if I come up with anyone who can help with the African side. Regards to Perilla, right?'

As I left, he was already reaching for the wax tablet on the top of the pile.

I needed to think, very badly. There was a wineshop I sometimes used on the Argiletum opposite the west end of Aemilian Hall, and that was the closest, so I parked myself at one of the outside tables and ordered half a jug of Massic.

What the hell was going on? I'd seen Pudens, and the guy was a total rabbit. Felicula herself had said he'd led a sheltered, humdrum life before they'd married, and I could believe it. If anyone had told me he was covering up a murky past then I'd've looked around for the minders.

Only, obviously, he was. And unless Felicula had been lying to me – and I couldn't imagine why, on this account, she'd want to – then she knew nothing about it either.

It cleared up the blackmail question, anyway. Forget Felicula; Pegasus's target had been Pudens himself. No wonder that Uranius had said the guy was so confident about taking over the Reds, if he had the faction master in his pocket. And I'd bet that Pudens was a pushover . . .

Except, of course, he hadn't been. Pudens was still master of the Reds, and Pegasus was dead.

The implication was unmistakable. Pegasus had put the bite on Pudens, then allowed himself to be lulled into a false sense of security. When he was least expecting it, the worm had turned and Pudens had killed him . . .

I frowned and took a large swallow of the Massic. No. Hell, that didn't make sense. Murky past or not, for a guy like Pudens to kill Pegasus was about as likely as a dormouse biting the throat out of a tiger. He just didn't have the oomph. I'd as soon suspect my stepfather Priscus, and that, believe me, is saying something. If it had been Mother or Felicula, now . . .

Oh, sweet Jupiter! Just hang on, Corvinus! Hang on!

Why not? I knew, from personal experience, that the lady had a protective attitude towards the old buffer, and also that she was smart, streetwise and no shrinking violet. What was to prevent it being a corporate venture involving the two of them? Stage one: Pegasus, having somehow pulled the smelly tunic from Pudens's dirty laundry basket, approaches the guy, threatens to reveal all and demands a slice of the

Reds. Pudens spills the beans to his wife. Stage two: both of them, working together, smooth Pegasus's heated brow. Pudens promises him the earth as soon as it can be arranged, Felicula takes him into her bed and keeps him happy that way. Maybe she even pretends that she's on his side and, when he does edge Pudens out, he'll have her and her two million into the bargain. Stage three: having got the guy suitably conned, they set up the murder. It wouldn't even be necessary for one of them to do the actual killing themselves. Rome's full of entrepreneurs who'd slit their own grandmother's throat for a handful of silver pieces, and as an ex-dancer Felicula would have the contacts among the city low-life to hire a professional.

It would work, sure it would. More, it made sense; it explained, for a start, why Felicula had lied to me about the affair being over, because she'd still need her lover to be docile and compliant right to the moment he got his in Renatius's alley. Of course, it meant that Felicula already knew her husband's guilty secret if she hadn't known it previously, but that was no barrier. Whatever it was, it can't – to her – have been all that important. Certainly not important enough to outweigh her relationship with her husband . . .

Which led me to the next question, the one that won you the nuts.

What could Pudens possibly have to hide that he wouldn't want to become common knowledge? That he might even be prepared – in Pegasus's view anyway – to give up the Reds for? And that he and Felicula would be ready to cover up by murder?

The obvious answer was something criminal, but that I just couldn't see. The picture of Pudens zeroing a business rival, say, or selling secrets to the Parthians, or disappearing into the blue with a few sacks of gold coins from someone else's safe just didn't gel. He wasn't the type; no way was he the type. It had to be something else. So what?

I filled my cup and took a long swallow. Okay; let's play this Perilla-style: what did we know – actually *know* – about the guy? He was an ineffectual geek. He was master of the Reds and he was—

I stopped, and played that thought back. I couldn't fault it. If that wasn't the right answer then it should be.

Holy gods! It was simple! It was so, so simple! And it explained Sicily completely.

I left the rest of the wine on the table. I had some more walking to do: all the way over to the Esquiline.

It was time I had another word with Felicula.

The lady was at home, sitting in the garden. Her smart-as-paint young door-slave showed me through and bowed himself off.

'Valerius Corvinus.' She set down a book-roll on the table beside her. It looked like a play. 'You're a surprise. How can I help you this time?'

'Pudens isn't your husband.'

Her face froze. 'What?'

'You aren't married. And Pegasus found out. Now tell me I'm wrong.'

Long silence; too long. 'Corvinus, you are either drunk or mad or both. We've been married for almost six years.'

'You want me to go down to the public records office and check?'

Our eyes locked. Finally she looked away. 'No,' she said. 'That won't be necessary.'

There was a cast-iron chair off to one side. I lifted it over and set it down facing her. She didn't move.

'How did you know?' she said.

'Guesswork. Pegasus had to have something on one of the pair of you. If it wasn't you then it had to be your—' I stopped. 'It had to be Pudens. Then I found out he'd never lived in Sicily, or not as a corn dealer, anyway. After that it was just a matter of considering possibilities.'

She turned back to face me. 'We're as good as married. And it's none of your business.'

'No argument, lady. To the first, anyway. It doesn't bother me. I'd imagine it doesn't bother you either.' I paused. 'Pudens, now . . .'

'My husband' – her eyes challenged me over the word – 'is a very conventional man. Yes, for people to know that we aren't legally man and wife would hurt him deeply. It would also, despite what you think, hurt me. As I said, we're as good as married. The absence of a document doesn't affect things.'

'So why didn't you? Do it properly, I mean?' Her lips were set tight, so I answered my own question. 'Because he's got a wife already, right? Somewhere other than Sicily.' I waited. Nothing. 'Oh, come on,

Felicula! I'm not prying, I'm not being judgmental, but I have to know exactly what's going on. Six years ago the guy made a break with his old life and came to Rome. Did he change his name or just lie about where he'd been living before?'

'Neither. Or, as far as the second one goes, not officially. Why should he? He hasn't, as you seem to be implying, committed a crime.' You could've grated cheese with her tone. 'His wife lives in Leptis.' Tripolis; right. I'd been on the right lines after all. 'She's a dreadful woman: cruel, domineering, totally selfish. Gaius was married to her for over thirty years and hated every minute of them. You've met him, he isn't a forceful person. You can understand how much pressure he would have to be under before he snapped.'

Yeah, I could. We were getting the biased Pudens-eye view of the other lady, sure, but I doubted it was all that far off the mark. 'Why didn't he divorce her?'

'I told you, Corvinus. Gaius is very conventional, or perhaps that's the wrong word. He has his own standards and way of looking at things, and at the same time he is deeply sensitive to other people's opinion. For him, divorce wasn't an option. It still isn't.'

'So he cut and ran instead?'

'If you like. He simply . . . went. He took half the money in his bank account, which wasn't much because Gaius wasn't a very wealthy man, and sailed for Rome. He left his wife the rest of the money plus the house and business. There were no children to complicate matters.'

'He was a corn dealer?'

She smiled for the first time. 'Not in any grand way. A small wholesaler. He supplied grain to bakers.'

'Uh . . .' I hesitated over the next question, but she seemed to be loosening up. 'Forgive me asking, Felicula, but why Pudens? I mean, why did you take up with him?'

She looked at me. 'Because I liked him,' she said simply. 'And he loves me.'

'He's thirty years older than you are, he has no money of his own and he's got nothing going for him. I'm sorry, lady, but that doesn't make sense.'

She shrugged. 'That depends on your definition of what is sensible. I have enough money myself, more than I can ever need or spend. Gaius is a lovely person, I saw that as soon as I met him. And I've always been attracted to men who are much older than me. Not in the sexual sense, I don't mean that at all. Sex, as I explained to you before, is a different matter altogether. Just to . . . live with.'

Jupiter! Perilla with her 'mentality' would have a field day with this lady! Mind you, in a way I understood what she was getting at. Maybe it had something to do with compartments. 'He never thought there might be a chance he might be recognised here in Rome? Before Pegasus, I mean?'

'There was always that possibility, of course, but it wasn't likely. I told you, Gaius wasn't an important man in Leptis. He lived all his life in a working-class part of the city, and he didn't go out much. The only people who would know him were his customers, and they were locals. The chances of one of them ever coming to Rome, let alone seeing him here were remote in the extreme. Besides' – she shrugged again – 'if any of them did recognise him and take the news back then what did it matter? As I said, Gaius hadn't committed a crime. Leaving his wife wasn't even desertion. She was far better off financially than he was.'

'Why doesn't his wife divorce him?'

'Perhaps she already has. Gaius wouldn't know. But it wouldn't make any difference to him if she did. He still wouldn't marry me.' She hesitated. 'You see, *Gaius* considers himself married, and as I say he has his own ways of looking at things. He can be quite stubborn when he likes.'

Gods! They were a pair, these two. But I couldn't've mistaken the fondness in the lady's voice at that last bit. 'Okay,' I said. 'Now we come to Pegasus. He found out. How?'

'I don't know, Corvinus. I honestly don't know. There are lots of Africans and Tripolitanians in the racing business, Laomedon for one, although he's certainly from Hippo, not Leptis. One of them might have been responsible. Or perhaps it was someone who knew Gaius when he arrived, before we met. Or Pegasus may have smelled a secret and dug the answer out in ways of his own. That last wouldn't surprise me. Pegasus was good at finding out things, especially things people didn't want known.'

'He was blackmailing you, right?'

'He went to Gaius first, threatening to tell me. He

didn't know at that time that *I* knew. After he did, he simply threatened to spread the story around.'

'This was just before he was killed, wasn't it?'

'Yes. About a month before. That was when I broke off our affair, of course.'

'Uh-huh. You, ah, sure you did that, lady? Absolutely sure?'

That got me a long, slow look. 'I'm not in the habit of sleeping with men who are trying to blackmail my husband, Corvinus. Yes, I'm perfectly sure.'

'And yet Pegasus didn't do what he'd threatened to do? Make the story public?'

'We reached an agreement.' Her lips tightened. 'Meaning I paid the bastard.'

'He didn't want a share of the Reds?'

'He did. But he got money instead. A great deal of money. That made up for it.'

'Until you had him killed,' I said quietly.

There was a long, long silence. Finally, she said, 'No.'

'No what?'

'I didn't kill Pegasus, or have him killed. Neither did Gaius. Perhaps I would have done before too long – I would certainly not have had any moral scruples about it – but I didn't. In a way, I'm sorry because I would have very much liked to.'

I wasn't a hundred per cent sure if she was telling the truth or not, but she sounded convincing as hell. And her story certainly hung together, too closely for me to point a finger and say 'That's a lie.' Well, there wasn't much more I could do here but give her the benefit of the doubt until events demanded otherwise. I stood up.

'Fine. Thanks for your time, lady.'

'Corvinus?'

'Yeah?'

'A question for you. Pegasus was a bastard. A complete bastard. Whoever killed him did the human race a favour. So why do you persist? Why not leave things alone?'

Fair point. And I didn't have an answer for it, either. Not even to myself.

24

So where did we go from here?

The short answer was 'home'. If Pudens and Felicula were a washout – and my gut feeling was that they were – then we'd just run out of front-line suspects. In these circumstances, when a bout of solid, basic rethinking is on the cards, then home's as good a place to be as any.

Pudens had come as a surprise, but for me the one that really took the biscuit was Felicula. If I needed a lesson warning me of the dangers of prejudgment then I'd just had it. Not that the mistake had been totally my fault. Gods alive! The lady wasn't just unusual, she was unRoman. For a rich widow to marry (or whatever) outside her class wasn't all that uncommon, but ninety-nine times out of a hundred the guy would be a piece of low-life beefcake, certainly younger and probably with razzmatazz by the bucketful; or she'd go the other way and hitch up with some flashy spendthrift with a pedigree the length of a book-roll but without a silver piece to pay the Ferryman. What she didn't do – nohow, no way, never – was go for a total loser from a provincial back street old enough to be her father and with all the panache of a plate of boiled cabbage. Which was exactly what Felicula had done. I couldn't get my head round that at all.

It just showed you: love's a funny thing.

What I would have to remember to do, though, was send a runner over to Lollianus at Aqueducts and Sewers telling him to call the search off. I'd been lucky there, at least. The chances of one of his senatorial pals having come across a back-alley grain merchant in the less salubrious parts of Leptis were so slim you couldn't've used them for a doorstop.

I walked down Virbius Incline and turned into Patrician Street and the Carinae. Well, at least Meton couldn't complain this time: it wasn't even the middle of the afternoon yet. Maybe the case just needed a while to settle. There were angles I hadn't tried, loose ends to follow up, see where they led, especially where the big boys, the main faction leaders, were concerned. Them I hadn't really considered up to now; not because they weren't likely, but there'd just been better goods on offer. Natalis was the obvious prime candidate, sure, but if what Cascellius had hinted about the Blues' increased chances for next season was anything to go by then Acceptus was in there with a shout as well. I wasn't stuck yet.

Bathyllus was buffing up our doorknob when I got back. He was wearing his smug look, together with a natty lemon tunic and a dab of scented hair-oil. Scalp-oil. Whatever. He was also humming.

Frightening; really frightening.

'Hi, sunshine,' I said. 'Tyndaris been?'

'Yes, sir. She came round shortly after you left.'

'Success?'

'The lady was good enough to say my polish was a marvel. I gave her the remainder of the batch and she copied down the recipe.'

'That's great. Onward and upward, right?' I moved past him. 'Oh, by the way, I got a little something for you on New Street.' I took out the bracelet and handed it over. 'Choose an appropriate moment to give it to her.'

The little bald-head flushed. 'That's extremely kind of you, sir. I'm . . . ah . . . invited over later to share the household's dinner. I'll present her with it then.'

'Good thinking, pal.'

'Did you have a pleasant day yourself, sir? Can I get you some wine?'

'Yeah. No hurry, litt— . . . Bathyllus.' Jupiter! I'd never get used to this supersolicitous new major-domo of ours. Love's a funny thing, right enough. 'Just bring it through when you have a moment.'

'The mistress is upstairs, sir. In her study.'

'Okay. Let's have it there, then. Oh, and Bathyllus, send a skivvy round to the Aqueducts and Sewers office at the Temple of Venus Cloacina. My compliments to Quintus Lollianus, and would he call off the search. He'll know what I mean.'

'Yes, sir. Right away.'

I took off my mantle, bundled it up on the hall bench and went up to Perilla's study. She was up to her ears in book-rolls, holding a wax tablet and chewing on a stylus.

'Oh, hello, Marcus,' she said. 'You're back early.'

'Yeah.' I moved the stylus aside and gave her the usual kiss. 'What's going on?'

'Just updating my catalogue. We really must get some new cubbies put in along that far wall. I'm having to use each one twice already.'

I lay down on one of the two reading couches. Me, I like my study on the bare side; books just clutter things up. Perilla's was like a corner of the Pollio Library, and she'd more paper and ink stacked than I'd use in a decade. How she could work under conditions like these beat me completely. 'I understand Bathyllus's floor-polishing went down a storm.'

'Yes.' She glanced at the title-tag on a roll, made a note in the tablet and pushed the book into one of the cubbies. 'You were absolutely right about Tyndaris, though. She is quite large and decidedly . . . overpowering.'

'You think there're any developments there? I mean . . . *real* developments?'

'They seem to be getting along famously. And Bathyllus is really coming out of himself. I was amazed.'

'He's going next door for dinner tonight.'

'Yes, I know. I was there when she asked him. He's quite excited about it.'

I grinned. Gods! *Coming out of himself* was right! The last time I'd seen Bathyllus get excited about anything was when we had the atrium pool relined. And the lady was certainly pulling out all the stops.

'So how was your day? Did you talk to Lollianus?'

'Uh-huh.' I told her about Pudens and Felicula. 'We

were close there, lady, but I don't think we won the nuts. We'll have to think again.'

'You're sure they didn't do it?'

'Not absolutely. But she sounded genuine, Perilla. Me, I wouldn't risk any bets.'

'Hmm.' She laid the wax tablet on the desk and sat down on the couch facing me. 'So where does that leave you?'

'Basically with the two big faction bosses. Titus Natalis and Gaius Acceptus.'

Perilla frowned. 'I hate to have to say this, but what about your cartel owner? What was his name? Eutacticus.'

My guts twisted: that that bastard was responsible for Pegasus's death, despite what he'd said, was a scenario I didn't even want to think about. If the evidence came, it came, but I wasn't going to go looking. 'He's a possibility, sure,' I said carefully. 'The guy's a complete crook, he wouldn't scruple over murder, and I only had his word for it that Pegasus was still willing to play ball, but he sounded real enough. And if Pegasus was prepared to sell out the Whites the way he did the Greens then Eutacticus would have no reason to have him killed.'

'Very well. So. Natalis and Acceptus.'

I shifted into a more comfortable position on the couch. 'Natalis is the more likely. He certainly has the stronger motive. First, he had a standing grudge against Pegasus. Maybe just because, like he told me, the guy had walked out on him and joined the opposition, but there might've been another reason. I just can't believe Natalis didn't know anything about the throwing races scam. He's no fool, and he'd been a driver himself so he'd know what went on backstairs. That being so, he can't've misread the signs among his own team when the lads with Pegasus at the Black Cat let Sopilys punch his lights out. Second—' I paused; Perilla had opened her mouth and closed it. 'You wanted to say something, lady?'

'No, dear. It's just that—' She hesitated, then shook her head. 'Never mind. Carry on.'

'Okay. Second's the fact that the combination of Pegasus and that new horse Cammius has been rearing suddenly put the Whites into contention. Either on their own wouldn't've counted all that much, but both together did. Cammius told me the guy had already had a crack at the horse; hitting the driver would be the logical complement. Natalis is no angel, he's got used to winning, and with Gaius and Macro behind him he can afford to take risks. If—'

There was a tap on the door and Bathyllus came in with the wine. 'Here you are, sir,' he said. 'And I took the liberty of bringing the mistress some of Meton's cold lemon and honey punch.'

'Right. Right, thanks, Bathyllus.' Original thinking as well as politeness? Tyndaris was working wonders right enough. I looked at the tray. Jupiter! The little guy had even given us napkins! Freshly ironed! In rings! 'Just set it down, pal.' He did. 'Uh . . . speaking of Meton. He, uh, okay today? I mean, in himself, like?'

'He was talking of meatballs and boiled turnip for dinner, sir. With apples and custard to follow.'

I swallowed. Well, we'd just have to sit this one out. 'I see. Fine, fine. That's all, Bathyllus.'

'Thank you, sir.' He left.

I caught Perilla's eye. 'Meatballs and boiled fucking *turnip*?' I said.

The lady sniffed. 'Don't swear, Marcus. It's your own fault. And remember, I have to eat it too, and I'm not fond of turnip either.'

'At least you like apples and custard. The bastard knows I *hate* apples and custard.'

'You said "if".'

'What?'

'You were talking about Natalis being able to take risks, dear. You said "if".'

'Uh, yeah. Right.' I got my mind into gear again. 'If Natalis did ice Pegasus then he might feel his back was covered. Maybe with justification. We still haven't gone into that funny business with Valgius and the Eighth District Watch, and that points the finger at Natalis if anything does.'

'Marcus, if Prince Gaius and Sertorius Macro are involved in this business then I think you should drop it. I told you so at the time.'

'Too late for that now, lady. We'll just have to see what the future brings.'

She sighed. 'Corvinus, you are your own worst enemy. You know that, don't you? What about Acceptus?'

'He's the tricky one.' I passed her her cupful of Meton's lemon and honey aberration and took a swig of my own Setinian. 'At the start I just had a gut feeling about him, but the guy's beginning to show glimmers of form. He didn't like the idea of the Whites taking an independent line, to begin with, and he wouldn't've shed any tears when Pegasus got chopped. The main thing, though, is he's got big backers of his own.'

'He's master of the Blues faction. They're one of the two leading teams. Of course he has backers.'

'Sure, but according to my pal Cascellius one of them's our new consul. And *he* has suddenly become bosom friends with Eutacticus.'

Perilla was quiet for a long time. Then she said, 'Oh. Oh, I see.'

'Right.' I swallowed a mouthful of wine. 'Vitellius's reputation isn't exactly sweet-smelling to begin with, and you can bet whatever the two of them talk about at dinner up there on the Pincian it isn't flower-arranging. Acceptus is definitely on the list.'

The lady had lifted her cup. She hesitated, then set it down again. Very wise. 'Marcus,' she said. 'Can we go back to Natalis for a moment, please?'

'Sure.'

'Tell me what you said right at the start. About not believing something.'

I frowned. 'Uh . . . I said I couldn't believe that Natalis hadn't known Pegasus was throwing races, or at least suspected he was, because—'

'Because he'd been a driver himself. And that he couldn't have overlooked or misinterpreted the incident outside the wineshop. Yes, that was it. I completely agree. So doesn't it strike you as odd that not only did he not accuse Pegasus of malpractice to his face at the time but he denied categorically to you that there had been any? Especially since he and Pegasus didn't seem to have parted on friendly terms, and Pegasus was moving to an opposition team. After all, why shouldn't he give him what amounted to a bad reference, even on suspicion? It didn't matter any more to him.'

I had my mouth open to answer, but I closed it. Gods, she was right: when you came to think about it it didn't make sense at all. And certainly the Natalis I'd met hadn't been any kind of soft touch. 'Go on,' I said. 'You have the ball, lady.'

'I think the reason was that Pegasus's move to the Whites was engineered. By Natalis himself.'

I picked up my cup and took a slow sip. 'Perilla, that doesn't add up,' I said. 'Eutacticus admitted that Pegasus was cheating on the Greens. And he was Natalis's best driver. Why the hell give him to the Whites?'

She shook her head. 'No. That's not what I meant. Of course Pegasus was throwing races. What I'm suggesting is that Natalis caught him, but instead of firing him or whatever the normal procedure was he made him a proposition. Pegasus would have to leave the Greens, but there would be no mention of the real reason. Instead, he would be allowed to move – specifically – to the Whites, on the under- standing that he would become a sort of agent-in- place. Possibly only temporarily, until he had repaid the debt.'

I sat back. Shit. It fitted; it fitted like a glove. It explained Natalis's atypical blindness and generosity, for a start: he wouldn't've wanted to prejudice Pegasus's chances of Cammius taking him on by giving the guy the boot, and under the circumstances any hint of skulduggery would be a bad idea. It also – and this struck me like a dash of cold water – explained his behaviour the day I'd gone to see him. I'd been well on my way to being pitched out on my ear when he'd suddenly changed his mind and agreed to see me after all. And what had done the trick was that I'd used the word 'scam' . . .

I'd meant a straightforward racing scam, of course: the kind Pegasus had actually had going with Eutacticus. But Natalis didn't know that, or at least he couldn't be sure until he'd talked to me, because Pegasus was involved in two scams. One was his own, but the second was Natalis's. And that was the one he'd really not want to be public knowledge.

Sweet gods, it was beautiful!

Perilla was watching me. 'Marcus?' she said. 'What do you think?'

'Yeah,' I said non-committally. 'Yeah, it would work.' Never, ever let the lady know how smart she is. Life can get unbearable. 'You might just have something there. How do you mean, "repay the debt"?'

'But that's obvious. The debt was Natalis's overlooking of his deal with Eutacticus. And once Pegasus had the run of the Whites' stables he could dispose of the horse. What was his name? Polydoxus.'

Silence. You could've heard a spider scuttle. Oh,

gods! Holy, ever-living gods! The lady had cracked it. Cracked it right down the middle.

What's more, if she was right – and I'd bet a dozen of Caecuban to one of Meton's lemon specials she was – then Lucius Cammius had just shot back up into the number one spot.

25

I went round to the Whites' stables after breakfast the next day. I'd thought things over very carefully, and decided that the best way to handle this was to confront Cammius himself and see which way he jumped.

My old pal Cement-Features was on the gate, and he grinned at me.

'Who is it this time, Corvinus?'

'The boss, if he's in.'

'He's in, but I can't guarantee he'll see you. With the Megalenses coming up we're running around like blue-arsed flies in here. You can try, though. Hold on and I'll send a gopher to check.'

'Fine.' He went back inside and I kicked my heels for a minute or so. Then a thought struck me. I waited until he came back. 'Uh . . .' Hell; what was the guy's proper name? Something to do with rocks. Tarpeius? Prometheus? Oh, yeah. Sisyphus. 'Hey, Sisyphus.'

'Yeah?'

'You're the regular gateman, right?'

'Sure. There's another guy who spells me, plus the nightwatchman, but ten out of the twelve daylight hours I'm it.'

'Cario told me you'd had some trouble a while back. Attempted sabotage.'

Cement-Features scowled. 'Yeah. Couple of jokers trying for the horses. We nailed the bastards good.'

'You involved both times?'

'Uh-huh.'

'When was this, exactly? You remember the days?'

The scowl deepened and he ran a hand over his stubbly chin with a rasping noise like a file on granite. 'Now you're asking, Corvinus. Exactly, no. The first time was well after the Plebbies, round about Winter Festival. That was one of our own watermen.'

'He'd been with you a while?'

'Nah. New boy.'

Oh, yeah; Cario had said that. 'He come recommended?'

'They all do. No one joins the faction who can't be spoken for from the inside. Standard practice.'

'Who by?'

A shrug. 'Can't tell you that. But he'd be a brother or a cousin or something of one of the other lads. Hesper'd know. He's in charge of that side of things.'

'How did you spot him?'

'In this business you get a nose for buggers like that. He looked nervous, like. I stopped him and frisked him. He was carrying a packet of powder under the belt of his tunic.' Cement-Features sniggered. 'He won't try that again in a hurry.'

'He's still working here?'

'What d'you think? Nah. And after what me and

the lads did to him he won't be working nowhere for a while.'

'He say who gave him the package?'

'Stranger in a wineshop. Paid him ten silver pieces with another twenty promised.' He spat. 'Ten silvers! For doping a horse! Cheapskate.'

'How about the other guy? The one with the surgeon's knife who sneaked in with the hay delivery?'

'Right. That was – what – about a month later.'

'You knew him?'

'Uh-uh. The fodder merchant'd taken him on as muscle a day or so previous. He didn't know him either.'

'Cario said he was a Green.'

'Yeah. He was one of their lads. A mucker-out.'

'He tell you that himself? About being a Greens' employee, that is?'

'Eventually.'

I winced. 'He's still with the Greens?'

Cement-Features sucked on a tooth while he gave me a slow stare. 'No,' he said at last. 'That particular bastard didn't make it. Complete accident. After we'd finished questioning him we gave him back his knife but he tripped on his way out and took it between the ribs. Sad, but then he shouldn't've been carrying it in the first place, should he? Dangerous things, knives. We sent the body back to Natalis with our compliments.'

Uh-huh. Well, I'd known they didn't pussy-foot around in the factions, and I supposed the man had known the risks. Still, it sent a shiver down my spine.

Just then a little ratty guy poked his head round the gate. 'Boss says he'll see Valerius Corvinus for ten minutes,' he said.

'Right.' Cement-Features turned back to me. 'You're on, Corvinus. See you later.'

'Sure.'

I followed Rat-Face through the compound to the admin block. No sign of my little pal the floor-scrubber this time, but Hesper was just coming out of the office.

'Hi, Corvinus,' he said. 'You on your way to talk to the boss?'

'Uh-huh,' I said.

'Make it short, right? With the Megalenses coming up we've got things to do.'

'No problem. Uh . . . Hesper?'

'Yeah?'

'Any chance of a word later? A very brief word?'

He frowned. '"Brief" brief, sure.' He glanced at Rat-Face. 'I'll be down at the paint shop, okay? Bring him there.'

Rat-Face nodded. I knocked and went in.

Cammius was sitting behind the desk. He looked up. 'Good morning, Corvinus. I'm sorry, I can't spare you much time but—'

'Just the answer to one question'll do,' I said. 'You knew Pegasus was still working for the Greens, right?'

I thought he'd blink, at least, but he didn't. What I got was a long, expressionless stare. Then he said, very quietly; 'Close the door, please. And sit down.'

I did. 'Well?'

'Pegasus severed relations with the Green team after the Plebeian Games. You know that.' There was ice in his voice.

I ignored it. 'Officially, sure. I'm not talking officially.'

'Then I don't understand what you mean.'

'I asked you before whether you knew why Pegasus had split with Natalis. You said you didn't. I think that was a lie.'

'Go on.'

'Was it?'

'You have the floor, Corvinus. I'll say my piece later.'

The stare was making me nervous. Cammius's eyes had never wavered. 'Okay. Pegasus had a scam going with a cartel owner called Eutacticus. Natalis found out he was throwing races and showed him the door.'

'Natalis admits this?'

'No. But the race scam is a fact, and after the Sopilys incident he'd've been a fool if he didn't at least suspect it. And Pegasus leaving just at that time can't've been coincidence.'

'All right. Carry on.'

'The next bit's guesswork, sure, but having met Natalis I'm fairly certain of my ground. Natalis and Pegasus do a deal. In exchange for hushing up the scam, and maybe a promise of a return to the faction later, Pegasus agrees to transfer to the Whites. Only he'll still be working for Natalis. Once he's snugly burrowed into your faction and been accepted as a White he'll – as my wife put it – repay his debt by poisoning or otherwise taking out that fancy horse of yours.'

I stopped, expecting some sort of reaction from Cammius, but all I got was silence and more of that constant, unblinking stare. I could've been talking about the price of carrots down in the market.

'Trouble is,' I went on, 'I couldn't see you being a fool, either. You must've known, or at least suspected, why Pegasus had made the switch, and probably worked out the reason behind it. My guess is that you kept your eyes peeled, maybe fed him a bit of rope, gave him what he'd think was a fair chance at Polydoxus. Then, when he took it and you had your proof, you queered his pitch somehow without him knowing it'd been intentional, lay low and then at the first opportunity murdered him. Sure, he was a loss, a big loss, but he was more of a liability, especially taking into account all the trouble he was causing inside the faction; with the horse safe, you could always wait for another driver who'd be straighter and more amenable.' I folded my arms. 'So. How am I doing, pal?'

You could've cut the silence with a saw. Finally, Cammius said; 'Very well indeed. Congratulations, Corvinus. I can see I've grossly underestimated you. You're quite right.'

Jupiter! 'You mean you admit it?'

'Up to a point, yes.' Gods, the guy was calm, I'd give him that. And the stare still hadn't wavered. It was like being drilled through with an auger. 'I did know why Pegasus had left the Greens and suspect him of being Natalis's plant. Also, yes, I gave him the opportunity to kill Polydoxus while keeping him under observation. But no, I didn't murder him. That wasn't necessary.'

'You care to tell me why not?'

'Pegasus might have been rotten, but he was no fool either. You know the penalty for killing or attempting to kill a racehorse. He wasn't a slave, so he'd have avoided crucifixion, but it's still death, and I doubt if Natalis would've used his influence with the prince under the circumstances to have the sentence commuted, let alone cancelled. Nor, as a failed agent, would he have been very welcome back at the Greens' stables. Once I had my proof I put all these points to him. He was a first-rate driver, and like you said he would've been a huge loss. Killing him, one way or the other, would've been a waste. Also, unlike Natalis, I'm not a vindictive man, and as I say he was no fool. We reached an agreement. I'd forget about the attempt on Polydoxus if he'd behave in future and act as my agent against the Greens.'

'Uh-huh. And when was this agreement made?'

'About five days before his death.' He paused. 'You can confirm all this with Cario, if you like. He was present as the second witness at Pegasus's failed attempt on the horse.'

Shit; it held together. I felt like crying. 'So you turned him?'

'Indeed. Not that it did either of us much good in the end.'

'So why the hell didn't you tell me this before?'

Cammius's face set. 'Because it was faction business, Corvinus, and secret. It still is. I wouldn't be telling you it now if you hadn't worked most of it out already. Also' – his lips twisted – 'I put a high value on my own neck.'

'This is why you were so sure the last time we talked that Natalis was responsible for the guy's murder?'

'Of course. I couldn't give a reason because that would've meant letting you into the secret. But it can't be anyone else.'

Yeah; I'd go for that solution myself. One got you ten Natalis had found out somehow that his blue-eyed boy was rumbled; maybe he'd heard about the failed attempt on Polydoxus and put two and two together. Certainly if Pegasus had been turned then he'd changed from asset to severe liability pretty smartly. Sure, skulduggery's endemic in the racing game, but the cardinal rule is never get caught. Like Cammius had said, even though they're not often applied – they don't need to be, with the factions exercising their own sanctions – the penalties for a charge backed by proof are pretty swingeing, and even Prince Gaius would think twice before putting his oar in. Chopping Pegasus might seem drastic, but Natalis wouldn't have the luxury of choice.

Not that I'd be shedding any tears: I'd hoped that bastard might be involved somewhere. It looked like I'd got my wish.

Cammius was watching me. 'Corvinus?'

I blinked and refocused. 'Yeah?'

'If you're not going to haul me off to the city judge's office then I really do have things to do. That ten minutes was generous, and you've already used them up.'

'Uh . . . right. Right.' I stood. 'Thanks for your time.'

'Don't mention it. It's been . . . an education. You're going to the race meet at the Megalenses?'

'Sure. Probably.'

'Send round here first. I'll give you and your wife passes for the owners' row. Oh – and put your money on Polydoxus. Even with Uranius driving he's a winner.'

'Yeah. Fine. Thanks a lot.' I stopped. 'Oh, by the way, I was going to ask Hesper, but maybe you know yourself and I won't have to bother him. The waterman who was caught with the whacky powder four months or so back. Sisyphus on the gate says he was probably related to someone else on the team. Can you tell me who?'

'No. Or not offhand. Hiring non-driving staff is Hesper's concern. He's master of stables. You'd best ask him.'

'Right.' I hesitated. 'Uh . . . no hard feelings? Over the accusation?'

'None at all, Valerius Corvinus. As I said, your ingenuity impressed me. And under different circumstances you could've been right.'

I believed him. There was steel there, right enough. And where his faction was concerned, Cammius was no man to cross.

Rat-Face was sitting on the steps when I came out, and without a word he led me round to the paint shop. Hesper was standing talking to what was obviously the guy in charge because he wasn't actually doing any work himself. There were three cars parked outside the shed with a couple of skivvies with paintbrushes slopping away. White paint, of course, although I noticed that one of the skivvies was working on a line of gold beading that ran round the edge of the driver's platform.

Hesper looked up. 'Two minutes, Corvinus, okay?'

I nodded and moved over to inspect one of the cars. Jupiter, it looked flimsy! The framework was thin enough to begin with, but the screen at the front and sides was no more than lath, and without the yoke-pole I could practically have lifted the whole thing off the ground with one hand. Sure, when I was a kid – like any other kid in Rome – I'd wanted to be a charioteer, but you wouldn't get me on one of these things now, not with four powerful racehorses up front, because they'd hardly notice the weight. No wonder so few drivers reached old age. What made it worse, of course, was that to manage four sets of traces without them tangling the guy had to tie them round his waist, which meant that if the car did come a smash he went with the horses, with nothing bar his leather helmet and the knife at his belt to cut the reins standing between him and the next world. I shuddered. Buggers like Laomedon and Pegasus might be well paid, but they earned every copper piece.

'Have a useful talk with the boss, Corvinus?'

I glanced up. Hesper had finished his business and was coming over. 'Yeah,' I said. 'You could say that.'

'So what was it you wanted to ask me?'

I told him. 'No hassle. I'm just checking angles.'

'The little bastard was a cousin of one of the lads over in the wash-house.' Hesper was scowling. 'Not the laundryman's fault, he recommended the boy in good faith and he's been with us for years. If you want to talk to the kid, though, I doubt if you'll get any more than we did at the time. It's the usual story. Stranger came up to him in a wineshop, promised him more money than he'd ever seen in his life to slip a powder into the horse's drinking water. Happens all the time, but the old hands know the risks and they keep clear.'

'Which horse? Polydoxus?'

Hesper nodded. 'Yeah. Normally he'd be off limits to new staff, but it wouldn't be difficult to get round that.'

'You mind if I talk to your laundryman?'

'Suit yourself. Name of Philematius. I'd take you over but I've things to do. You coming to the race?'

'Yeah. Cammius is giving me a couple of passes to the owners' row.'

'Fine. I'll see you there. Oh, and put your shirt on Polydoxus. That beauty's going to leave the rest standing.'

I followed Rat-Face to the laundry. Like I say, racing stables are like one of these big, self-sufficient villas you get out in the country. All the basic facilities and services are somewhere on site, sure, but I'd thought that at least they'd send their smalls out. Nothing doing. They even had the big fullers' vats of piss. I wondered if it had to be human, or if they got the horses to contribute.

Luckily, Philematius wasn't one of the poor buggers tramping the vats, and they were downwind. He was a nondescript guy, thin as a rake, with a nose that looked like it ran a permanent drip. When I went over he was pegging up a row of tunics to dry in the spring sunshine.

'Yes, sir,' he said. 'The boy's my aunt's son. He'd been on at me for months, and I got him a place just before the Plebbies. I was mortified, sir. He's a good lad, but just not very clever. He didn't know what he was doing.'

'There any chance I could talk to him?' I said.

Philematius hesitated. 'I suppose so, sir. He wouldn't be able to tell you much, though. The man who gave him the powder was a complete stranger. I'd warned him, but you know youngsters, he wouldn't listen.'

'Yeah.' I paused. 'Uh . . . what happened to him afterwards, by the way? Exactly?'

'He got off lightly. Both legs and one arm broken.' I winced, and he saw me do it. 'No, no, sir. He was lucky. Hesper fed half the powder to a sick mule and it died. He could have fed the rest to Stephanus, but he didn't although he was well within his rights. He's a good man, Hesper.'

Oh, gods! Still, if they'd handed the kid over to the authorities he'd've got the chop anyway. The same applied to the Greens' mucker-out. 'Stephanus is the lad's name?'

'Yes, sir.'

'Where can I find him?'

'The tenement directly opposite the entrance to Pompey's Theatre. Fourth floor, right-hand door. His mother's name's Leuce.'

Practically within spitting distance: Pompey's Theatre is just up from Tiberius Arch. It wouldn't put me out much to check. 'Right. Thanks,' I said.

Rat-Face took me back to the gate.

26

I found the tenement and went up to the fourth floor. The place was pretty run down, even for tenements, with rubbish stacked on the landings, gaping holes in the plaster that showed the lath beneath, and an even stronger smell than you usually got, which is saying something. The door looked like it'd been put together from planks taken from a cannibalised cart. I knocked. A thin, middle-aged woman in a threadbare tunic opened up.

'Yes?'

She looked washed-out; not just washed, but wrung dry, like every bit of colour had been leached out of her, physically and mentally. I could smell boiling cabbage.

'Uh . . . you Leuce?' I said.

'Yes.' That was a whisper; there wasn't even a scrap of interest in it.

'Your nephew Philematius sent me. I need to talk to Stephanus.'

'He's inside.' She stepped back. Not even the obvious question 'What about?' The eyes were blank.

I went in. Compared to this room, the landing had been in top-notch shape. There was a brazier in the middle with about a spoonful of charcoal burning in the basket. On top of that was the cabbage pot. Apart from the cooking arrangements the furniture consisted of two mattresses, a couple of shelves, mostly empty, and a chair. The kid sitting in the chair had a sort of twisted look to him. He must've been late teens – he'd've needed to be, to get inside a wineshop – but he looked about twelve.

'Stephanus?' I said.

His head came round slowly. His eyes had the same washed-out expression as his mother's. 'Yeah. That's me.'

The woman had sat down on one of the mattresses. She picked up what could've been a dishcloth, turned her back to us and started darning.

'My name's Marcus Corvinus,' I said. 'I'm investigating Pegasus's death.' A shrug. I waited, but there wasn't anything else. 'The Whites' master of stables told me you'd been caught trying to poison one of the horses. He said you'd been duped into it by a stranger in a wineshop. You like to tell me the story in your own words?'

'Nothing to tell. The man gave me the powder and ten silver pieces on account. I was stopped at the gate. Finish.'

'You ever see the man before?'

'Nah. He was one of the Greens. That's all I know.'

'He tell you that?'

'Uh-uh. I asked him straight out, first thing. He didn't answer, but he was annoyed as hell. He was a Green, all right.'

'Okay, let's take it from the start. You were in the wineshop—'

'Nah. Or only for a minute. It's old Sosius's place round the corner. I only went down there to deliver a bit of Ma's mending. He was waiting for me when I came out.'

Well, at least he was talking. 'What kind of man was he?' Another shrug. 'Old? Young? Big? Small? Well-dressed?'

''Bout average. Just a man.'

Hell. 'What did he say? Exactly?'

'He asked if I'd like to make thirty silver pieces.'

'And you said?'

'What d'you say to that? I just looked at him. Then he took out a purse and showed me. So I asked him what I had to do. He brought out the package.'

'He told you to put the powder in Polydoxus's drinking water.'

'Yeah. Just that. It would've been easy. Security's tight before a race, but we were into the slack season between the Plebbies and the Festival. I could of done it no bother.'

The woman turned round and stared at him, but she didn't say anything. Then she went back to her stitching.

'He tell you what it would do?'

'Nah. But I'm no fool. It was only a horse. And thirty silver pieces would've got us out of this dump.'

Well, I couldn't argue with that: the two of them could've lived for a year easy on thirty pieces of silver. If you can call it living. 'What then?'

'He gave me ten on account, said I'd have the rest when the job was done. Then he walked away.'

'You didn't see him again?'

'Nah. Next morning I turned up at the stables as usual. The bastard on the gate must've nosed something because he grabbed me straight off. Once they'd found the package that was it. I thought they'd kill me, but they didn't.' He looked down at his twisted legs and grinned. 'Shoulda done, though. The arm's okay now, but with these I'm not going nowhere.'

'You didn't call in a doctor?'

He looked at me; just looked. Sweet gods, we were in a different world here, and I should've known better than to ask. There ain't no doctors in the tenements. I pulled out my purse; too late now, of course, but late's better than never. There were eight silver pieces and some coppers. No time for penny-pinching. I emptied the lot into his lap. 'Thanks for your help,' I said.

He fingered the coins. I turned round. The woman was staring again. I moved towards the door, trying to make it look like I wasn't desperate to get out.

'Hey.'

My hand was on the latch. 'Yeah?'

'I don't know if it's any good, but the guy who gave me the powder had a tooth missing.' His finger pointed to his top jaw, just right of centre. 'That one there.'

'Fine. Thanks,' I said. I opened the door. 'By the way. How old are you, son?'

That got me another grin; a proper one, this time. The cash seemed to have perked him up. 'Today's my fourteenth birthday.'

Oh, shit. I left.

*　　*　　*

Once outside in the clean air I stopped to think. What now, exactly? The tooth business had been an unexpected bonus, but I doubted if anything would come of it. If I'd been able to persuade Natalis to parade his staff one got you ten that one of the buggers'd have a missing incisor, but that wasn't a viable option. As far as the case was concerned, I was up against a brick wall. Sure, the evidence pointed pretty straight to the boss of the Greens, but I didn't see how I could get any specific proof.

At times like these, all you can do is try a little cage-rattling and see what jumps up. Natalis was the obvious first target, but there was no harm in dragging a stick across Acceptus's bars as well. Like I'd said to Perilla, although the Blues guy might not have form so far he was getting there.

If I hadn't cleaned out my purse I would've gone round the corner to Stephanus's wineshop and thought about tactics over half a jug of wine. As it was, we'd just have to play things by ear. I set off back towards Triumph Road and the Greens' stables.

Socrates the troll was manning the gate, if 'manning' is quite the right word here. He didn't look too happy to see me, which was fair enough since I'd punched him in the balls on the last occasion.

'Is Titus Natalis coming out to play?' I said.

That got me an uncomprehending scowl. 'What?'

Yeah, right; maybe it had been a bit overambitious semantically. I tried again. 'The boss in?'

'You got an appointment?'

Three syllables! Wow! Education is a wonderful thing. 'No, but—'

'Then eff off.'

Well, life is never easy. Still, unless the guy was down at the Circus bribing the slaves who operated the starting gates to monkey with the mechanism, I was going to see him. Time for the first gentle shaking of the cage. 'Take the greasy little bugger a message,' I said carefully. 'Tell him I know about the scam with Pegasus and Polydoxus. And you'd better be back here and nodding before I can count to a hundred, pal, because if you're not the next stop's my friend at the city judge's office.'

He stared at me, his jaw working, and I reckoned I was about a fingernail's breadth from being mashed to pulp against the door jamb. I stared back. 'One . . . two . . . three . . .'

He turned. The gate slammed behind him and I could hear the bar clang into place. Yeah, well, that should just about do it. If I listened hard I could probably catch the screams of rage from here.

I'd reached ninety-four when he came back. 'The boss'll see you,' he said.

'Fine.' I went in past him.

He hadn't moved. 'One thing I want you to remember, Corvinus,' he growled. 'From me, personal.'

'Yeah? What's that?'

'The boss ever wants you stomped, you are fuckin' stomped. And I'll laugh while I do it, right? Now follow me.'

We walked the hundred yards to the admin block in

silence. The troll knocked on the office door, showed me in and then closed it behind me. Well, at least this time I wouldn't have him breathing down my neck. And it meant that Natalis wanted the interview to be private. Good sign.

He was sitting behind the desk screened by the huge gold chariot and horses monstrosity. If I'd thought Socrates had been unfriendly, the big guy was just bouncing with love and goodwill compared with Natalis. The glare I was getting would've roasted chestnuts.

'Sit down, Corvinus,' he growled.

I gave him my best smile, pulled up the fancy tooled Cordoban leather chair and sat.

'Now. What the hell is this about?'

'You had a deal going with Pegasus. You planted him on the Whites, the idea being that he'd get rid of Polydoxus from the inside.'

There was a long silence. Finally, he leaned back in his chair. 'That's garbage,' he said.

I shrugged. 'Okay. So throw me out and I'll take the story to the city judge's office.'

You could've heard an ant cough. The little piggy eyes measured me. Natalis might've been an ace driver at one time, but he was running to fat so fast it was a sprint.

'You've got no proof,' he said at last.

Uh-huh. At least we were making progress here: *garbage* to *no proof.* I didn't want to split on Cammius, but I needed the handle. And I hadn't made him any promises. 'Sure I do,' I said. 'He was seen having a go just before he died.'

That rocked him. He covered well, but I'd caught the flicker. 'Yeah? Seen by who?'

'Two witnesses.'

'You're lying. Cammius found Pegasus messing around with his top horse, he'd have his balls on a griddle. Or he'd've killed him himself. My guess, that's just what he did.'

'Cammius didn't want Pegasus, he wanted the guy who put him up to it. Killing Pegasus wouldn't be in his interests.'

'Is that so, now?' Natalis showed a sudden flash of teeth. 'Pity the bastard's dead and can't talk, then, isn't it?'

I crossed my legs and gave him another of my very best smiles. 'Oh, no. Quite the reverse. The fact that he's dead sort of points the finger pretty neatly.'

The grin faded. 'How do you mean?'

'Pegasus's wasn't the first attempt on Polydoxus. There was a kid called Stephanus after the Plebbies that some bastard suckered into trying to smuggle poison inside the Whites' compound. Then there was one of your muckers-out. His name I don't know, but he tried to do the job with a surgeon's knife. I reckon the city judge might just take these two incidents into consideration when he's calculating the *cui bono* of Pegasus's mouth being shut. And you, pal, are it.'

If I'd thought the guy was angry before, now he was livid. Forget roasting chestnuts; the look I got would've melted rock. He glanced behind me at the door, and I wondered if he was going to yell for Socrates, in which case I was in real trouble. Rattling cage bars can have its drawbacks, especially if you're on the wrong side of them at the time. He didn't, though. Instead he leaned forward as far as he could go. 'Fuck the city judge, Corvinus,' he said quietly. 'He doesn't matter. Fuck you, too. There'll be no case, not ever. There'll be no case because—' He stopped, and his jaw snapped shut.

Silence. The pause lengthened as we stared at each other over the speeding metal horses. Light dawned, and not too pleasantly, either. Shit; he might as well have finished the sentence because we both knew what the ending was going to be. And looking at him I knew he knew I knew.

There'd be no case because Pegasus had been killed in the Eighth District, where Titus Valgius the Greens-fancier was Watch commander and had the backing of Sertorius Macro. Who, in his turn, was the local stand-in for the arch-Greens-fancier Prince Gaius. And barring the Wart himself – and probably not even him, now – against that egotistical bastard there wasn't no court of appeal; nowhere, nohow, never . . .

I was up the creek without a paddle. Hell, without a sodding *boat*! Knowing that Natalis was guilty wasn't enough; *proving* it wasn't enough. If I wanted his hide pinned up in Market Square then I'd have my work cut out.

I stood up. Well, I'd got my wish, although 'rattled' wasn't exactly the word I'd use for the master of Greens at this precise moment. And I'd also got a confession of sorts. For what it was worth.

'Fine, pal,' I said. 'But it doesn't rest there. I'll just have to see what I can do from the other end.'

'You do what you like, Corvinus.' He'd sat back again. 'Just don't come crying to me if you find yourself up an alleyway of your own one of these days. And you can tell your friend Cammius that if he wants to mess with the big boys then he can take his chances as well. Now get out of my office. I'm busy.'

I left.

Well, that had gone down a bomb. Still, I hadn't been completely bluffing. Nobbling racehorses – let alone murdering drivers – is a serious business, and in race-mad Rome it isn't taken lightly; not where there's any sort of proof, anyway. There were a lot of powerful vested interests, and they weren't all in favour of the Greens. Also, I doubted that Gaius was personally involved in any of this, or even knew about it: the bastard was on Capri sucking up to the Wart, and say what you liked about the old devil Tiberius was no racing fanatic, and by his lights he was fair. Looking the other way was one thing, but when it came to pulling Natalis's chestnuts out of a very public fire even our crown prince might think twice about what it might cost him in goodwill. Macro, too. The city had had enough of the arbitrary use of power: Sejanus had only been dead for three years, and people – especially the ones with broad purple stripes – had long memories. Gaius and his city rep might have clout by the bucketful but they were still being careful how they used it.

So. Maybe taking things from the top down wasn't such a bad idea after all. Certainly it was worth a shot. And the logical place to start was with the bastard who'd tried to bury the case originally: the Eighth District Watch commander, Titus Valgius.

No time like the present. I set off down Triumph Road for Iugarius and the city centre. The Eighth District Watch headquarters were on Tuscan Street, just behind Julian Hall. Valgius hadn't exactly struck me as the conscientious type – not like my pal Decimus Lippillus over at Public Pond – but this late in the day he should be in his office. If I could needle him into some sort of investigation then maybe we were in business again. Certainly the situation had changed; I had a lot more hard evidence, for a start, and if I could persuade Cammius to go public over the attempts on Polydoxus then I'd got Natalis by the short hairs.

I hesitated as I drew level with Renatius's wineshop. Sure, my purse was empty but it'd been a long morning, it was past noon and I could murder a cup of wine with a bit of bread and cheese for ballast. At least Renatius would give me credit. I went inside.

Charax and his bone-idle cronies were in residence; in fact, they didn't look like they'd moved since the last time I'd been here. He raised his cup.

'Afternoon, consul.'

Jupiter! For the Charaxes of this world life is one long party. I gave him a nod and walked over to the counter.

No Lucius this time; Renatius was on his own. 'Hey, Corvinus!' he said. 'What can I get you?'

Maybe I'd better nail my colours to the mast right away; especially with drain-mouth Charax there to angle for free drinks. 'Uh . . . I'm financially embarrassed today, pal,' I said. 'Half a jug of the usual and some bread and cheese on the slate?'

'Sure, no problem.' Renatius grinned, hefted the flask and poured the Spoletian into a half-jug measure.

'Know the feeling, consul,' Charax said cheerfully. 'Disappointment in the City, right? Life can be a real bitch.'

His pals sniggered. I sighed. 'Shut up, Charax.'

'Right, sir. Shutting up forthwith. Beg your pardon for any umbrage caused.'

Renatius was cutting bread. 'So,' he said. 'Any news on the Pegasus front?'

'I'm looking into it,' I said cautiously. 'You hear any more yourself from what's-his-name? The Watch guy with the penchant for purses?'

'Delicatus.' He arranged the slices on a plate, added a wedge of cheese and pushed it over. 'Nah. Bugger's never been near me since. Not that I expected it. We've had quite a few gawpers, though, nosing down the alley. These ghouls give me the shivers. It isn't even as though they come inside for a cup or two to pay their ticket.'

'Yeah.' I filled my own cup and took a long swallow of the Spoletian. Beautiful. Like I say, Renatius doesn't run no Pincian club, but his wine's honest and after a hard morning's cage-rattling it slipped down like the best Caecuban. I started to relax.

'Hey, Corvinus!'

Hell; Charax again. I didn't even turn round. 'Yeah?'

'Renatius here tells me the bastard who did it holed up where we're working. Atellius's place just across the street. That be right, now?'

'Uh-huh.' I topped up my cup. 'Probably, anyway.'

'Only it was a funny thing. When we went back some bugger'd spoiled the wet plasterwork.'

I stiffened. '*What?*'

'Sure. Dirty great slather like he'd put his hand against it with his weight behind him. You reckon that was your boy?'

Jupiter! I faced him. 'It could've been.'

'That's what I thought. Well, when you catch the bastard tell him he owes us for another half-hour's smoothing time.' His sycophantic cronies laughed.

I went back to my wine. It didn't matter that they'd destroyed the evidence, sure – one hand-print's much the same as another – but it showed that that part of the theory checked out. Whoever had murdered Pegasus had waited his chance in the tenement across the road. Cool customer was right.

'You think you will catch him, Corvinus?' Renatius said.

'The gods know.' I took a swig of the Spoletian, then bit into the cheese and followed it with some of the crusty bread. 'If I'm lucky.'

'I'd go for one of the Greens myself,' Charax said.

My jaws stopped moving. 'Yeah, Charax? And why would that be?'

'These tricky sods're capable of anything.' Oh. Right. The Accusation on Principle: our cowboy builder friend was an ardent Blue. He wouldn't even touch cabbage. 'With Pegasus gone the Whites are shafted for the Plebbies. Then there's the business with Valgius. It makes sense.'

I almost choked on my cheese. Gods! Under that apelike skull pulsed a brain after all!

'You got the solution to the Parthian question as well, Charax?' Renatius had poured himself a cup of wine and was sipping it. One of the cadre of pals declared UDI and sniggered.

Charax ignored both of them. 'You mark my words. Minicius Natalis is the lad, sure as eggs is eggs. I'm not saying he used the knife himself, the bugger's too fly for that, but he was the mind behind it.' He paused. 'What they call the grey eminence.'

'The what?' That was the UDI man.

'The grey bloody eminence, you dork. The power behind the throne.'

'You mean like Prince Gaius?'

Charax set down his cup and grinned. 'Ah. Funny you should say that, my son. Now that's another thing . . .'

But my ego had taken enough of a bashing for one day. Perilla was bad enough, but if sodding Charax was going to solve the case from basic principles in five minutes flat while he was taking a break from not renovating tenements then I just didn't want to hear him do it. I bolted the rest of my cheese and bread, swallowed down the Spoletian and went for the door.

27

Titus Valgius was out to lunch when I got to the Watch-house, and from the jaundiced look on the desk squaddie's face when he told me I had the impression that he hadn't put in much of a morning before that. Not altogether unexpected, and at least I had Renatius's bread, cheese and Spoletian inside me to compensate for lost time. I sat on a bench and twiddled my thumbs until he came rolling in.

'Rolling' was right, or the nearest thing to it. Wherever the guy had been they obviously served their lunches liquid and he'd had at least a jug. Not that I had any quarrel with that – I'm all in favour of lunch in a cup – but layabouts like me are one thing, servants of the Senate and people of Rome are another. Getting pissed on the company's time just isn't the Roman way.

I stood up and he blinked at me like a constipated owl. Or maybe a constipated hippo would be nearer the mark. Whether or not he'd had anything solid down his throat in the past couple of hours the bugger clearly didn't stint himself at other times, because you could've used his mantle to gift-wrap a German beer barrel. If Valgius was fighting the flab then he'd lost the equivalent of Cannae.

'Who the hell are you?' he grunted.

You can take an instant dislike to some people. This bastard was about as simpatico as an enema. 'The name's Marcus Valerius Messalla Corvinus. I ran across your stooge Delicatus at Renatius's wineshop eight days or so ago when he concealed evidence in a murder case.'

Valgius goggled. I glanced sideways at the squaddie. He was staring past us at the wall, and you could've carved your initials on his expression.

'In my office,' the commander of the Eighth Watch said softly. 'Now.'

Well, at least I'd sobered him up. He led the way. It was like following a grain barge into dock.

'Office' was a misnomer, if I ever heard one. The gods knew how he got away with it, but the room was fitted out like a cat-house reception hall. There was a desk in the corner, sure, but it had that untouched look that things have when they're only for appearances sake. The really lived-in part had a couple of velvet-upholstered couches with gold beading, a bronze table that looked like it'd started life somewhere east of Ephesus, a wine set that could've belonged to old Julius's millionaire pal Crassus and enough drapes, hangings, soft-pile rugs and fripperies to fit out a queen of Palmyra's boudoir.

It also smelled of scent.

'Uh . . . nice place,' I said.

'Sit down,' he snapped, then lowered himself on to

one of the couches. It creaked. He reached for the wine jug, poured a cup – one cup – drank and set the cup down. 'Now. What the devil is this all about?'

'The murder nine days ago. Of the Whites' charioteer, Pegasus.'

'That's done and settled with. Pegasus was stabbed by person or persons unknown. Motive robbery.'

I resisted the urge to ask how more than one person could've inflicted a single stab wound: the guy would only have concluded, quite rightly, that I was taking the piss. 'Come off it, pal! He wasn't robbed. I saw the body myself before your squaddies arrived. He still had his purse.'

'That's not what my man Delicatus says. Or the two officers who were with him.' I was getting a look that would've made a cobra take up crochet. 'Furthermore, I understand your claim was not corroborated by any of the other people present. And, Valerius Corvinus, don't you dare call me "pal"!'

Uh-huh. Well, at least the fact that Delicatus had reported the incident showed that he hadn't been playing a lone game. Not that I thought it was likely: he'd be a fool to try any funny business without the backing of at least his immediate boss. 'The purse was there, *friend,*' I said. 'Delicatus knew it, his squaddies knew it, and by extension you know it. And the only reason I can see for pretending otherwise is to bury the case, which is exactly what's happened. And that leads naturally to the question why.'

Valgius hadn't looked like he could inflate any more without bursting, but he did. He wasn't just a hippo in a mantle now; he was a purple hippo. 'Are you accusing me and the men under my command of perverting the course of justice?'

'Yeah. I'd say that was a fair inference. What do you propose to do about it?'

His mouth opened and shut; that he hadn't been expecting, and it'd rocked him. We stared at each other for a good half minute. Then he said, more calmly now, 'What proof do you have that the man was murdered? For anything other than the cash he had on him, that is?'

'First, it was premeditated. The killer had followed him to the wineshop and waited in the empty tenement across the street until he came out. I have the evidence of the workmen in the wineshop that he left his handprint on some wet plaster.'

'That doesn't show premeditation. Any ordinary thief could have done the same.'

'Second, he was involved in a scam with Minicius Natalis the master of the Greens faction to get rid of the Whites' champion racehorse Polydoxus.'

The piggy eyes shifted. I'd been waiting for that, and I didn't miss it. 'You can prove it?'

'I can't, but the Whites' master Lucius Cammius can. He caught the bastard in the act.'

There was a long pause. Valgius passed his tongue over his lips. 'That's a very serious allegation,' he said. 'Natalis is a prominent man. To suggest that he would countenance any shady business is—'

'Look, *pal.*' I leaned forward. 'You asked for proof. I'm pointing you in the right direction. Officially. The very least you can do is take it as grounds for reopening the case. Or opening it, rather, because hitherto thanks to you and your goons there hasn't been a fucking case to reopen. You want to take the whole thing to the city judge, that's fine with me. But if you do you'll have to explain why the fact that it's Titus Natalis who's at the sharp end should make a difference.'

He was rattled now. The jowls were shaking up and down like a scared pig's. 'Natalis isn't entirely devoid of influence. The Greens have very powerful backers who—'

'You a betting man, Valgius? Because that's what it comes down to. What you're betting on is that when the shit flies off the shovel Macro and his boss Prince Gaius will step in and blow the whistle. Me, I'd go the other way. They might've done at the start, but things've moved on since then. And if they don't then when Natalis is pegged out for the crows you'll be down there with him. That I'll see to personally. You want to risk that, you can go right ahead.'

He was looking grey. 'Very well, Valerius Corvinus. You may . . . have a point. Certainly your . . . allegation regarding the attempt on the Whites' horse gives rise to . . . some doubts.' He gulped for air. Bugger; that was all I needed. For the Eighth District Watch commander to peg out in his office and Delicatus to come back and find me standing over another corpse was a complication I could do without. 'Leave it with me. I'll . . . have a word with Titus Delicatus. There may have been . . . a misunderstanding. Also with Lucius Cammius.'

'Fine.' I stood up. 'I'll expect developments. And if there aren't any, *friend*, then I'll be paying the city judge's office a visit myself.'

I left him reaching for the wine jug.

Well, that had been pretty satisfactory. I'd had to break confidence with Cammius, mind, but it'd been the only way to get things moving again. The main thing was I'd slapped a couple of substantial punches into Titus Natalis's midriff. The master of the Greens wouldn't like that; he wouldn't like it at all.

I was grinning as I came down the steps back on to Tuscan. Enough for one day. I thought about going back to Renatius's and having the other half of the jug, but maybe home would be a better idea. Besides, Charax'd still be there, and I found that guy wearing. The little bout of cerebration had come as a surprise, though. Who would've thought the lead-swinging bastard had it in him? Especially the bit about Natalis being . . .

I stopped. Wait a minute. Wait just one minute.

Grey eminence. Charax had described Natalis as a grey eminence. Meaning, in this context, that the guy might have been behind the murder but it wouldn't've been his hand on the actual knife.

Right. So much was obvious, sure. Natalis wouldn't be the real murderer. A wealthy public figure like him, especially one who had any number of gorillas on call, wouldn't do his own killing, no way, it was too risky and just too *infra dig*.; that was so self-evident that I hadn't even put it into words inside my own head. The thing was, though, precisely because I hadn't done that I'd missed out on the next logical step, the one that Charax had made. There had to be a hand on the knife. If Natalis did arrange the killing, then who was the actual killer? If I could find him and get him to talk then I had the bastard cold . . .

'You going to stand there all day, squire, or would you maybe consider moving?'

'Hmm?' I glanced round. A guy with a handcart piled high with cobblestones was waiting to get past, and waiting none too patiently. 'Oh, yeah. Yeah, right.' I shifted, and he trundled on his merry way muttering. I fell into step behind.

So who could it have been? My pal the troll on the gate would be prime: he was the right type, and his threat earlier that day suggested at least a part-time role as hit-man. Putting the frighteners on him might be difficult, but if he was the real killer – and the chances were good – then I reckoned it was worth a shot.

In that context there was another angle worth looking into. If I were Natalis, I'd want things as tight-wrapped as I could get them. Sure, having one of his own men do the job would be easy to arrange, but there were risks. He'd still have to make sure that there was no comeback, especially if things didn't go as smoothly as he expected. Which meant he had to be certain that, when the body was discovered, there wouldn't be any awkward questions asked like who done it and why. And *that*, naturally, meant squaring the local Watch.

If the murder had happened somewhere like Public

Pond where Lippillus was in charge the scenario would've been as likely as a flying pig: faction master, clout with the ruling junta or not, Decimus Lippillus'd've had the bastard clapped up at the first tentative approach so fast his eyes would water, and the same went for any of his squaddies because if that conscientious little dwarf caught any of his men on the fiddle he'd have their giblets. The Eighth District was a whole different ball-game. Even if I hadn't had prior warning that their commander was crooked as a stepped-on snake that interview with him would've sent every bell ringing. Whatever had paid for the fancy stuff in his office it hadn't been a Watchman's salary, which was probably the idea of having it there on display as a hint to clients that he enjoyed the finer things in life. One got you ten that Valgius was on the make. Which raised interesting questions vis-à-vis the murder of Pegasus.

Okay; let's try the scenario. Natalis has just discovered that his agent-in-place with the Whites has been blown and he decides to get rid of him fast. The trouble is, a straightforward killing's risky because he knows – has to know, for the killing to be on the cards at all – that Lucius Cammius has just caught the bugger trying to poison or whatever his horse, and worse that Cammius knows who's responsible. That being the case, if Pegasus is found stiff under dubious circumstances the chances are pretty fair that shortly afterwards Natalis will find himself handed the double whammy of attempted equicide and conspiracy to murder the beast's driver.

And because he's guilty of both the charges will probably stick.

So what can he do? He's got two options. One is to make the death seem natural. Tricky, even if he could get away with it. The second is to go for a simple, straightforward murder but make sure in advance that it won't be investigated. That's the one Natalis chooses. He does a deal with Titus Valgius to the effect that Pegasus will be decoyed into the Eighth District and—

I skidded to a mental halt. Oh, shit! That didn't work! It couldn't work, no way, nohow, never. Natalis hadn't decoyed Pegasus anywhere. The only reason for the guy being in Renatius's at all that day was to meet Cario re the blackmail. And if Natalis hadn't been responsible for bringing him there then a deal made in advance with Valgius didn't make sense. Sure, in the event he'd been lucky: from his point of view the Eighth District as a location for the murder had been perfect because Valgius had covered it up anyway, but it couldn't've been prearranged.

Bugger! I felt like crying.

Unless, of course . . .

Begin again. Assume there *was* a deal, because it fitted with everything bar the Cario business: Valgius was a Greens' sympathiser, he was bent as a hairpin, the Eighth isn't all that far from the stables so as a venue it wouldn't arouse any suspicions, and Natalis could be sure that if Pegasus was decoyed there and chopped any subsequent investigation wouldn't get past the starting gate. All that side of it was okay.

The problem only came with Cario; and that was really no problem at all because *Pegasus had chosen the meeting place.*

I hadn't wondered about that at the time, when I'd talked to Cario at the Whites' stables, because it wasn't all that remarkable. Now I did. Cario had insisted on a wineshop as the actual rendezvous, but it had been Pegasus who chose Renatius's. Sure, it might simply have been because like I say the Eighth District's slap next to Mars Field, but there could've been another reason: that Pegasus already had an appointment somewhere in the area and he was killing two birds with one stone. And if that was the case then we were in business again. When Pegasus was working undercover for Natalis they must've met somewhere on a regular basis to exchange information, and the Greens' stables themselves would obviously be out. The Eighth was a strong possibility; maybe even – because Valgius was a Greens' fan and would be willing to turn a blind eye in exchange for a sweetener or two – the Watch-house itself. All Natalis would have to do would be to send Pegasus a message by whatever route they used arranging another meeting. Then when he was safely inside Valgius's territory . . .

Something cold clutched at my gut. Oh, sweet gods, I could go further! If what I'd just thought of was right then no wonder Valgius had been shitting bricks at the end there. I'd had his balls properly in a vice, only I hadn't known it. Suppressing evidence was bad enough; that could lose him his job, at least. Knowingly providing a venue for the sort of clandestine meetings that Natalis and Pegasus were having was positively actionable, but even that might not be the worst he was guilty of. That particular crime was, if not murder itself, then at least like Natalis conspiracy to murder. And that could get him the strangler's noose.

How could Natalis make sure – one hundred per cent sure – that his pals in the Watch would play ball and see Pegasus's death got the lack of attention it deserved? Simple: he could have them zero the bastard themselves. Better still, he could see to it that the actual killer was the investigating Watchman.

I couldn't be certain, no way could I be certain, but I'd risk a better-than-evens side bet that the guy who'd actually knifed Pegasus was Valgius's stooge Titus Delicatus.

Right; so what did I need? First, a tie-in between the master of Greens and the Watch commander. Valgius was a Greens' fan, sure, and I'd wager after talking to the guy that he had itchy palms on general principles, but I had no proof of actual *connection*. Second, more than I'd got so far on Delicatus. He was bent right enough, and hand-in-glove with his boss – I knew that from the purse incident – and from what Renatius and Charax had said he had a certain reputation locally to live down to; but it was a fair step from there to murder. I wasn't unaware, either, of the size of the potential can of worms we'd got here. Sure, even nowadays with the imperial checks and balances in place corruption's part and parcel of public life – it's practically a Roman tradition, from provincial governors down – but a District Watch that's rotten at the core would merit more than a wink and a head-shake. If Valgius and his subordinates in the Eighth District were directly involved then the case had just moved up a notch in importance from a simple stabbing to something with much darker implications.

I could put the thing to my own friendly Watch commander, of course. Decimus Lippillus was on the inside, he'd know about any dirt that happened currently to be sticking to any of his colleagues. That, though, was the problem: Valgius was a *colleague*, and however bent the guy was professional ethics would be a factor. Asking Lippillus to pull the bastard's plug just wouldn't be fair. Besides, where dirt, slander and rumours were concerned, especially in the higher social strata, I had another option. I grinned to myself. Maybe I should have a word with my old pal Caelius Crispus.

He wasn't going to like it, mind.

28

Crispus worked out of the Justice Department, which just showed you that if the old biddy who plies the loom of fate has a sense of humour it must be pretty warped. Or in her case maybe woofed. Whatever. We went a long way back, certainly a lot further than the slimy little bugger took pleasure in calling to mind, and over the years we'd developed a sort of hate-hate relationship which, on his side, probably involved the fantasy of pissing into my urn. He didn't like Perilla, either, which I suppose given the nature of their past associations wasn't too surprising. Think of Orestes's views on Allecto the Fury and you'll get the picture.

On the other hand, I had a sneaking respect for the little rat. By his own lights he was the total dedicated professional who lived for his art; or maybe *craft* would be a better word in Crispus's case, because the guy's area of expertise was dealing in scandal. Which, of course, explained why he'd got as high as he had. Corruption being part of the good old Roman governmental system, when it comes to wangling appointments and moving up the ladder what you know about who can be as important as who your great-grandfather was, and Crispus knew a hell of a lot about the people at the top, mostly things that if they ever got out of the cupboard would have the buggers on the first ship to the Black Sea and ten years of cabbage dinners. Or at least meant no more party invitations and social distancing that would've made a flea-ridden baboon with halitosis look like Deb of the Year. I often wondered why, knowing what he knew, the guy hadn't been found floating in the Tiber with his throat slit years ago, but then maybe he had his own system of failsafes in place. If the momentary satisfaction of squashing a bug would result in your name featuring prominently the next day on the billboards outside the Senate House then you'd think twice, or at least make damn sure you had a bag ready packed and somewhere sunny in mind.

I'd intended to cut through the Velabrum on to Racetrack Road and home. Now I turned round and headed back up to Market Square. The afternoon was wearing on, but if I was lucky I could still catch Crispus before he hung up his tablet and stylus for the day.

The Justice Department has two sections, one dealing with the city itself, one with Italy and foreigners in general. Crispus was part of the second: an acting rep for the foreign judge. I'd been to his office before a couple of times, but admin officers move around more often than you'd change your tunic, so I checked with the guy on the desk.

'I'm sorry, sir, but you've just missed him,' he said.

Bugger! I could come back, of course, but I'd already gone out of my way to speak to him and I'd set my heart on it. Maybe I could catch him up at whatever particular den of iniquity he was infesting these days. 'You happen to know where he's gone, pal?' I said. 'It's quite urgent.'

The slave hesitated. He was one of those pretty-pretty types you get in the civil service with carefully curled locks and eyelashes that were just a shade too black to be natural. 'He – ah – usually calls in at the Grot for an hour or two after work, sir,' he said. 'You may find him there.'

'The Grot?'

'Narcissus's Grotto.' Was that a delicate blush? 'It's a bath-house.'

Uh-huh; Narcissus's Grotto, eh? That sounded like a fairly Crispus-type place. 'And where would that be exactly?'

'Near Quirinus's temple. Between the Mucial Hill and the Quirinal.'

The other side of Augustus Square; not very far, in other words. 'Fine,' I said. 'Thanks, friend.'

'No problem, sir.'

I left the Justice offices and headed for Quirinal Valley. I wasn't much for public bath-houses myself, especially the kind Crispus would patronise, but it'd been a long, gritty day and a good steam would be welcome. I hadn't got an oil-flask and scraper with me, but no doubt I could hire them from the . . .

I stopped dead. Oh, hell; hell's sodding teeth. Baths aren't pricey, as a rule, but whatever this one charged it'd be more than I'd got currently in my purse. Shit; how embarrassing. Well, we'd work something out.

*   *   *

Narcissus's Grotto was an unprepossessing place wedged between a couple of upmarket tenements, but whoever ran it had made some attempt to tart up the façade with marble stucco and the guy on the door was dressed to the nines in a sharp lavender tunic. He gave me a big smile when I went in.

'Good afternoon, sir,' he said. 'That'll be two silver pieces, please.'

I blinked. That I had not expected. 'Two silver pieces? For a *bath*?'

He shrugged in a take-it-or-leave-it way and went back to polishing his nails. Impasse.

'Uh . . . truth is, pal,' I said, 'I've come out without any cash on me. If you'll just let me through and give me some oil and a scraper I can call in tomorrow and—'

The smile had slipped. He set down the bit of pumice. 'I'm sorry, sir, but the house doesn't allow credit.'

Hell. Well, I'd have to fall back on Plan B and good old aristocratic cheek. 'You've got a customer in there by the name of Caelius Crispus? Works for the foreign judge?'

'Yes, sir. He arrived half an hour ago. But I'm afraid I can't—'

'Just take him a message from me, okay? My name's Marcus Valerius Messalla Corvinus, and I need to talk to him. If he'll pay me in then great; if not, no problem, tell him my wife and I will see him in his office first thing tomorrow morning. You got that?'

'Yes, sir, but—'

'Just do it, friend.' I gave him the full purple-striper stare, complete with flaring nostrils. 'And be particularly careful to mention the wife. Right?'

While he soft-shoed off into the inner regions I leaned my back against the counter, whistled through my teeth and examined the fittings. Public bath-houses vary. You get them all over the city, of course – only the more well-appointed private houses have their own bath suites, and even then you have to be close enough to an aqueduct to tap in to the water supply – and they go all the way up from the cheap and cheerful where a copper coin gets you a towel and a seat on a sweaty wooden bench to the pricier sort like Agrippa's Baths at the edge of Mars Field where they even have in-house gymnasia and a restaurant. This one clearly had pretensions. It may not have been big, from outside appearances anyway, but the decor of the lobby put me more in mind of an exclusive private club. A rather suspect private club, which along with the name, the swingeing entrance tab and the fact that Crispus was a regular didn't come as any surprise. The mural facing the counter took up the whole wall, and it showed a young man gazing down into a pool set in a grove of trees outside a cave. Tastefully done, sure, but where the young man was concerned it didn't leave much to the imagination. The phrase *well-hung* comes to mind. The trees weren't fig trees, either.

The attendant came back. 'That seems quite in order, sir,' he said. 'If you'll allow me just a moment I'll fetch you your towel, scraper and oil.'

'Fine.' I paused. 'The gentleman, uh, make any comment in particular, sunshine? When you gave him the message?'

'No, sir.' A sniff. 'Nothing I would wish to repeat. You'll find him in the hot room. The changing facilities are straight ahead at the end of the corridor.'

Nothing he'd wish to repeat, right? Well, that made sense, at least. I collected my things and went off grinning.

Pretensions was putting it mildly: the hot room was marble-tiled and marble-benched, and although there were no murals the owner had fitted it out with a scattering of pricey full-size bronzes of young athletes. Most were groups. I took one look at the nearest and decided to give detailed art appreciation the go-by. Whatever events these guys were entered for they didn't appear in the usual Olympic canon, and the poses would've made even Tyndaris's eyes water.

There were three or four punters in residence doing boiled lobster and guppy impressions. Wearing only towels as they were I couldn't tell their exact status, but they had the well-fed look of important broadstripers. They gave me one corporate glance and then ignored me.

Crispus was sitting on his own in a corner, looking like a stewed rat minus the hair. A definitely furious stewed rat.

'Corvinus, you bastard!'

'Hey, Crispus.' I went over and sat next to him. He edged further into the corner. 'How's it going?'

'You owe me two silver pieces!'

'Yeah. Sorry about that. Although I did give you an alternative.'

'Fuck that. One of these days I'm going to dance on your grave.'

'Come on, pal! I bring a little excitement into your life and this is all the thanks I get.' I looked around. 'Nice place. Maybe I should come here more often.'

He gritted his teeth. 'Just exactly what do you want this time?'

'Why should I want anything? Anything more than a bath, anyway. This is quite a find. Nice surroundings, friendly people—'

'Corvinus, I've had a long, hard day and I'd just like to relax, okay? You know and I know that I'm going to end up telling you whatever the hell you want to screw out of me, so let's get it over with. Then you can leave me in peace and go back to that bitch of a wife of yours. So no jokes, no threats. Just ask your question.'

Spoilsport. I quite looked forward to these little chats. Ah, well. 'Titus Valgius,' I said.

'The Market Square District Watch commander?' His brow furrowed. 'What about him?'

'He takes bribes, right?'

Crispus glanced sideways at the lobster guppies, but they were obviously having enough problems just breathing to bother listening in. Not that I was surprised. Two silver pieces for a bath was sheer extortion, sure, but the management certainly didn't cheesepare when it came to keeping the furnace stoked. The Grotto's hot room could've doubled as an antechamber to Hades, and I could feel my brain beginning to simmer already.

'Valgius is . . . flexible, yes.'

Jupiter! If the guy was 'flexible' in Crispus's terms then you could fold him up and slide him under doors. 'He have any dealings with Minicius Natalis?' I said. 'The Greens'— *ouch*!'

Crispus had gripped my leg. Hard. And whatever services Narcissus's Grotto offered they can't've included nail-clipping. One of the lobster guppies opened one eye, sniggered and then went back to the slow gasp.

'For the gods' sakes, Corvinus!' Crispus hissed.

'That sensitive a question, eh?' I gently unprised his clutching fingers.

'Look, we can't talk about this here. If you really want to discuss it then there're some private massage rooms. I'll give you ten minutes, max, and then you can piss off.'

'Uh . . . private massage rooms?'

He was already getting up. 'Sure.' He grinned evilly. 'What do you think your two silver pieces were for? We can mix business with pleasure.'

We left the lobsters to it, skirted the cold plunge and went down a cedar-panelled corridor to a small suite of cubbies discreetly tucked away at the rear of the building. A couple of little Nubian boys wearing nothing except smiles got up from their stools but despite his threat in the hot room Crispus jerked a thumb over his shoulder and they made themselves scarce. 'In there,' he said.

I'd been expecting something out of the steamy rolls of an Alexandrian bodice-ripper, but inside the nearest cubby there was just an ordinary massage table. Covered with a sheet of genuine Coan silk, sure, but for two silver Warts the customers were entitled to a little shameless luxury. Still, I let Crispus have the table while I sat on a folding stool.

'Now what the hell is this about?' Crispus said.

'You really want to know?'

'*No!* Forget I asked.'

I grinned. 'Okay.'

He wasn't grinning now, and I didn't think the sweat was entirely due to the management's heating arrangements. 'Corvinus,' he said, 'listen to me. Minicius Natalis is bad news. Seriously bad news. If you're going to ask me anything – *anything!* – about that bastard then I want your solemn assurance it'll go no further. Much as I'd like to see someone twist your head off by the ears I have no desire to go the same way. Clear?'

'Sure it's clear. No problem.'

'Fine. Now you've got ten minutes before I go back and finish my well-deserved bath. Start asking.'

'Like I told you, I want to know if Natalis and Valgius are an item, and if so—' I stopped. Crispus was sniggering. 'What's so funny, pal?'

'"Item." You could be right where Valgius is concerned, but not Natalis. Or if he is that way inclined I hadn't heard about it.'

My eyebrows went up a notch. That was one little nugget I hadn't expected. 'Okay,' I said. 'I'll rephrase that. They have some sort of deal going? Some criminal quid pro quo?'

Crispus shrugged. 'Maybe,' he said. 'Nothing definite that I know about, although it wouldn't surprise me. Natalis would sell his own sister to a cat-house if it benefited the Greens, and Valgius is so crooked he could meet himself coming back.'

'Examples?'

'He works a deal with the moneylenders round the Square. He turns a blind eye when they charge interest rates above the legal limit and he and the lender split the difference fifty-fifty. Then there's the protection racket.'

'Protection?'

'Insurance against burglary. The Eighth isn't much of a residential district, even along Tuscus and Iugarius. For a monthly sub to the Watch, proprietors can be sure they'll find their properties intact when they turn up with the keys in the morning. Funny thing is, it's the ones who don't pay who find the padlock forced and the stock gone.'

'Uh-huh.' Nice little earners, both of them, with the advantage that they'd provide a steady, regular income. 'How does Valgius get away with it?'

'Who's to complain? The moneylenders are making more than they would normally and Market Square has a lower breaking-and-entering record than any of the other districts. Everyone wins except the borrowers, and they're the sort that would have trouble raising cash legitimately in any case, so they're not beefing. Not publicly, anyway. Besides, Valgius has his own insurance policy. He's hand-in-glove with Macro, and you know what that means.'

Yeah, I'd sort of got that impression. Maybe from the evidence of my own talk with the guy *hand-in-glove* was putting it a bit strongly, but they evidently had a good everyday working relationship. Which reminded me. 'His sidekick Delicatus. How much is he involved in all this?'

That got me another snigger. 'Delicatus? Well, you might call him a full sleeping partner, Corvinus. Very much so. Now there the word "item" is appropriate.'

I sat back. '*Delicatus?*' I said.

'Sure. Valgius likes it rough, and they've been an item for years. Delicatus is the hit-man of the team. Hard to Valgius's soft, no pun intended. There isn't often much trouble – like I said, Valgius has things pretty well sewn up – but every so often he needs a little muscle. Delicatus is it.'

Gods! Talk about a can of worms! Still, at least it showed that if Valgius had been directly involved in Pegasus's murder he had the back-up to make it work. 'Okay. So let's go back to Natalis. What can you tell me about him?'

He hesitated.

'Come on, Crispus, give!'

'All right. But you get the safe version, okay? Safe for both of us.' Interesting: you didn't often find Crispus pussyfooting around a guy's reputation. Like all the best professionals, he took a pleasure in his work for its own sake, and once you had him going he was as gossipy as a Suburan grandmother with a drink in her. 'Like I say, he's got the faction in his bones. Started out with the Greens as a driver. When that career finished he clawed his way up into second place in the faction admin; at which point the previous master conveniently died of stomach cramps and Natalis's rich pals – notably including our current crown prince – subbed him to buy into the top spot.' Crispus slipped a hand under his towel and scratched his balls. I looked away. 'He wasn't "Natalis" then, of course, just plain Titus Minicius from Leontini. Or Olympius, rather, because he'd kept his driving name.' Yeah; I remembered that Cascellius had told me all that. Not the bit about the previous faction master, though, and that was interesting enough, if you like: convenient deaths by stomach cramps always get my attention, especially when it's been made clear that what I'm getting is a sanitised biography in the first place. 'Once he'd done his deal with the nobs he dropped the driver's handle, took the third name and started moving into society. Got himself a fancy house on the Esquiline and began really to build up the team.'

'Paying off his backers' investment, right?' I said.

'With interest. Natalis is no slouch, Corvinus. He knows his stuff, and he's a first-rate businessman. He used his connections to corner the market in prime horseflesh from Africa and Sicily, pulled in the top-notch drivers and creamed the opposition six ways from nothing. That was on the legal side, of course.'

'Meaning there was another?'

Crispus grinned. 'If you've got the clout and the money that bastard has, there's always another side. His backers like to win just as much as he does, none of them have any more scruples than a Suburan brothel-keeper and racing's never been a game for gentlemen. I won't go into details. Let's just say that if there's a corner to be cut Natalis'll cut it, and anyone who gets in his way will find themselves sliced in the process. There isn't much comeback, either.'

So; nothing new there. Still, I had other angles to cover, and with Crispus in a talkative mood I couldn't afford to waste the opportunity. 'How about the opposition? The other faction masters?'

He cocked an eye at me. 'Pass. I'm no racing fan. Ask someone else.'

'We're not talking racing here, pal. All I'm interested in is the dirty laundry, and there you're an expert. Let's start with Gaius Acceptus.'

Crispus shrugged. 'He's clean, as far as I know. A pusher, likes to win, which is why he chose the racing business. Good family, distantly related to the Sempronii, elder sister married to the junior consul. Also he's—'

A cold finger touched the back of my neck. 'Hang on right there, Crispus. Acceptus is related to Lucius Vitellius?'

'Sure. Brother-in-law. He and the consul are bosom buddies.'

The cold feeling intensified. Shit; I'd heard that phrase before in relation to Vitellius, although the other half of the friendship had been my cartel pal Eutacticus. The connection might be pure red herring, naturally – links among the top families are so convoluted that if you tried to plot them the result would leave a cat's cradle nowhere – but its existence raised a few very interesting questions about friends in common. Certainly it pulled Acceptus further into the middle of things. And the back of my neck was itching like hell. 'Tell me more,' I said.

'We agreed ten minutes. Your time's almost up.'

'Crispus, you bastard!'

'Okay.' He sighed. 'About what, specifically?'

'I'll settle for the consul.'

'Dirty laundry? Corvinus, I have a dinner engagement tonight. That amount of time we do not have, and some items even you wouldn't drag out of me with a hook.'

'Okay. Just what's connected with racing, then. I understand the guy's a fan of the Blues.'

'Is water wet?' Crispus snuffled. 'How do you think he got his wife in the first place? They may have fallen off recently but the Sextilii were giving their names to the year in Rome when Vitellius's four-times great-grandpa was turning second-rate leather into third-rate shoes. And consul though he may be the bastard's father only made it to quaestor.'

Jupiter! Snobbery, no less! Crispus never ceased to amaze me. I didn't know much about his own family antecedents, but I'd bet the nearest his father had got to a magistrate's chair was six feet in front of it on a charge of petty larceny. 'I was also told he was one of the faction's biggest backers. Financially, I mean.'

Crispus nodded and scratched his balls again. 'Right. He is. But it goes beyond money. He's round at their stables every chance he has. A charioteer *manqué*. Pretty good, too, from all accounts.'

'How about the dirty laundry? Where does that come in?'

'There're stories,' Crispus said cautiously. 'Like the time he was foreign judge three or four years back and fixed the Apollinares in the Blues' favour.' Yeah; the Apollinares are praetorian games, and as president the foreign judge has the last say in course disputes. 'And the wife business is relevant. Very relevant. Like I say, the Sextilii have the name, but they're not exactly rolling in cash. The rumour is that an interest in how the faction was run in exchange for some generous funding came as part of the marriage settlement, and Lucius Vitellius isn't one to lose out where a bargain's been struck.' He grinned mirthlessly. 'None of that family is. They're a hard, bad bunch, Corvinus. The eldest, Aulus, ate himself to death the year of his consulship, Tiberius threw Brother Quintus out of the Senate for peculation and Publius was chopped for getting involved with your friend Sejanus. Lucius has kept his nose clean in public so far but that's through cleverness. That bastard's the worst of the lot, take it from me. Certainly not someone to mix with.'

'He's friendly with the cartel boss Eutacticus, right?'

Crispus stopped scratching. 'Who told you that?'

I shrugged. 'Is it true?'

'It might be.' He was cautious. 'They're birds of a feather. Both crooked, both dangerous.'

'How about brother-in-law Acceptus? They got a triangle going there? A scam involving the Blues? Maybe pushing up their chances for next season?'

Crispus swung his legs off the table. 'Corvinus, you've had your time,' he said. 'Now just fuck off and leave me alone, okay? What I said about Vitellius goes double for Eutacticus. Maybe the three have got a scam, maybe not, I don't know and I don't care. Only if I were you I wouldn't lift any rocks to see what crawls out, understand?'

Well, I couldn't complain; I'd done pretty well out of the bastard for one day, and he'd given me quite a bit of food for thought. Especially the link between Acceptus, Vitellius and – possibly – Eutacticus. And maybe Natalis was the front runner, but the Blues boss was hard on his heels. 'Yeah, okay, pal,' I said. 'You've been a great help. I owe you one.'

'You owe me two. Two silver pieces.' He paused, and the evil grin was back. 'Unless of course you want to see it as my treat? Get your money's worth, as it were?'

I beat a hasty retreat to the changing rooms.

29

Thanks to an undignified sprint down Head of Africa that got me various complaints from sundry punters and a jab in the kidneys from a vengeful bag-lady armed with an outsize loaf, I made it back in record time. Bathyllus was at the door with the wine jug and cup.

'Uh . . . what's the dinner situation, sunshine?' I asked. With Meton firmly locked into unstable mode the question had a certain urgency.

'The mistress is in the dining-room, sir.' He took my mantle. 'I've just served the main course.'

Oh, bugger! Well, it could have been worse, and I didn't regret nailing Crispus while the iron was hot, as it were. Also, the little guy wasn't whispering, which would've been a really bad sign. I gulped down a swallow of Setinian, bagged the jug from the tray and went through.

'Marcus!' The lady looked up from spooning greens. 'Where have you been?'

I leaned over, kissed her and settled on to the couch. 'Yeah, yeah,' I said. 'I know.' I gave the contents of the table a quick summing glance. Not bad; no boiled turnip or chopped beef hash, anyway.

Quite the reverse: quails with what looked and smelled like an almond and ginger stuffing, a ham and dried apricot ragout and a side dish of spiced broccoli. Our draconian chef had obviously decided to heap coals of remorseful fire on our heads. 'I got caught up with Caelius Crispus.'

'Ah.' She sniffed, and the sniff spoke volumes. 'How was he?'

'Almost chatty.' I reached for a quail. 'I think the guy may be maturing.'

'Like an old cheese, you mean?'

'Yeah.' I grinned. 'Something like that. So how's life on the home front?'

'We had Tyndaris round demonstrating a cleaning fluid for copper involving flour, egg whites, salt and vinegar. A quid pro quo for Bathyllus's tile polish. He became quite excited.'

'Uh-huh.' Jupiter! If things went on like this then we'd have the cleanest, smartest house in the city. Plus the most manic major-domo. Still, if it kept the two of them happy I was all for it. 'Developing nicely, right?'

'She certainly seems taken. They're planning another shopping expedition tomorrow. I understand Tyndaris wants his help in choosing a new tunic and sandals.'

I almost dropped my spoonful of stuffing. 'Gods! She wants *Bathyllus*'s help?' Where women's fashion was concerned I wasn't too hot myself, but Bathyllus had as much idea of colour co-ordination as a prawn.

'I had the impression she's already chosen them, dear. Tyndaris is not stupid.'

Well, I'd certainly second that. In the pursuit of Bathyllus, the lady was showing the degree of strategic and tactical sense that had got Alexander the length of the Indus. Clearly in her eyes the little bald-head had something going for him, although I couldn't for the life of me see what. Animal magnetism, though, was something it definitely wasn't, unless we were talking hamsters. I filled my wine cup.

'So what did you want with Crispus?' Perilla asked.

Between spoonfuls, I gave her a brief run-down of the day's activities. 'We're moving into a different league here, lady. Certainly there are some big names cropping up, which suggests that there's a social angle involved. The old purple-striper mutual support club. And that makes things difficult, because breaking into that particular world at that particular level ain't easy.'

'Hmm.' Perilla shared out the last of the broccoli. 'You haven't actually met the junior consul, have you, Marcus?'

I grinned. 'Uh-uh.'

'Only his wife's quite charming.'

I paused, my wine cup halfway to my lips. 'You know her?'

'Very well. If you hadn't been so eager to go off drinking on the afternoon of the murder you'd have seen her yourself. She read us quite a good epigram in the style of Callimachus.'

Oh, shit! The poetry klatsch that had driven me to Renatius's! 'Sextilia was here?'

'She comes to all our meetings. The poor girl's

culture-starved, and it gives her an outing. Mind you, it can't be easy being married to a foot-fetishist.'

I goggled. 'A *what*?'

'Crispus didn't tell you? I'm surprised. Lucius Vitellius has the most *amazing* collection of women's shoes, Marcus. Worn ones, I mean. The gods alone know where he gets them from, certainly Sextilia has no idea and she's never had the courage to ask, but—'

'Hold on, lady!' I sat up on the couch. 'Never mind the salacious details. This is important. You're saying you're a friend of Sextilia's, yeah?' First the below-stairs revelations, now this. Different worlds was right. Maybe I should stay in more.

'Oh, yes. As I said, through the poetry group. I can't promise that you'll meet the consul himself – they don't see much of each other, to tell you the truth, what with one thing and another – but Sextilia is quite another matter. If you're really interested.'

I took a steadying gulp of wine. Gods! You live with a lady for getting on fifteen years and she still manages to surprise you. Not that, in Perilla's case, I should be surprised, only like every other man in Rome I tend to discount the female grapevine. Added to which, Perilla's never been part of the honey wine and cake set. Still, I suppose poetry and poets are different. 'Yeah,' I said. 'Yeah. You could say that.'

'Fine. Then I'll arrange it.'

'You, uh, think she'll be willing to talk? I mean, if Vitellius is involved then—'

Perilla had set down her spoon. 'Marcus, Sextilia

has very few illusions about her husband. They lead quite separate lives, and frankly I'm surprised that she didn't divorce him years ago. At present he is engaged in an affair with a freedwoman whose saliva he mixes with honey to make a throat lotion, and that sort of behaviour does tend to produce a certain . . . jaundiced attitude in a wife.' She sniffed, picked up the spoon again and helped herself to more ragout. 'On the subject of Lucius Vitellius's peccadillos your main problem, dear, may be getting her to shut up.'

Well, you live and learn. It made me wonder, though, about the high divine destiny of Rome. Personally, I wouldn't bet that any empire that elected a women's footwear-fetishist who smeared his neck with spit to one of the two top administrative places was going to get anything from the gods but a belly laugh. Shit knew what other little idiosyncrasies the guy had, but if they ran along the same lines then for the next nine months we were being governed by a total nut. 'How does—'

Bathyllus soft-shoed in. 'Are you ready for dessert, sir?'

'Uh-huh.' Despite the numerous sidetracks, the table was looking pretty empty. Praise where praise is due, and I can crawl in a good cause. 'Tell Meton from me that was delicious. Especially the broccoli.'

'I'm sure he'll be very gratified, sir.' Bathyllus hesitated. 'He told me to tell you he wasn't quite certain how you'd react to the spice mix.'

'Yeah? How so?' I had noticed that it wasn't the usual sauce, but then Meton did ring the changes occasionally, and this one was a winner. He wasn't usually that diffident, either. If Meton liked one of his new creations then ipso facto any adverse comment advanced by the actual consumer was tantamount to blasphemy. If you were really unlucky, it merited a personal visit so he could explain the reasoning behind the choice of ingredients and quantities while toying with a cleaver.

'He . . . ah . . .' Bathyllus hesitated. 'Seemingly he had the recipe from your mother's chef, sir.'

Oh, gods! I stared at him. 'He *what*?'

'The broccoli. It was one of Phormio's recipes. Rather a special one, sir, as I understand. He'll be delighted that you and the mistress enjoyed it.'

I glanced at Perilla. She was dabbing at her lips with a napkin and looking pretty green. I didn't feel all that good myself. Hell! What had we eaten? *What had we eaten?*

That 'react' had me worried, too . . .

Well, the damage was done, and barring the old feather-down-the-throat routine it was too late now for an answer to be of any more than academic interest. No doubt we'd find out in time; probably, knowing Mother's hyperinventive chef Phormio, around two in the morning. And Meton had done it quite deliberately. Chefs always trade recipes, but between these two there abided a deep and implacable professional hatred. If our little ray of culinary sunshine had used one of Phormio's aberrations on us then it was with malice aforethought. The fact that it had turned out edible only compounded his crime, because it meant we'd actually eaten the stuff.

One of these days I'd beat that devious, egotistic-al, sadistic bastard's skull in with his own omelette pan.

I sighed. Ah, well; there was no point in making a fuss because that would be playing into the bugger's hands, and it wasn't our little bald-head's fault any-way. To give him his due, if he'd known beforehand Bathyllus would've warned us. 'Just serve the fruit and nuts, Bathyllus,' I said.

'Yes, sir.' He turned to go.

'Ah . . . one more thing.'

'Yes, sir?'

'A point of information. Tunics. How do you feel about bright green ones with an orange belt? For women, I mean?'

'Very fetching, sir.'

'Right. Right.' I closed my eyes briefly. 'That's all, pal. Oh, and kick Meton for me in passing, will you?'

'Yes, sir.' He left.

There was a long silence. Perilla cleared her throat. 'You really think that the junior consul could be implicated?'

'It's an outside bet.' I took a long swallow of wine and filled my cup from the jug. Setinian may not be on the Hippocratic canon as an antidote to poison, but at least if you drink enough of it fast enough you stop worrying about what's going through your gut and when it'll trigger the 'evacuate' mechanism. 'A very outside bet. Those links between Vitellius, Acceptus and Eutacticus don't look healthy, but I'm just checking angles. My real money's on Natalis and his crooked Watch pals. That bastard did it, right enough. It's just a matter of getting proof.'

'Why don't you talk to Decimus Lippillus?'

Fair suggestion. Yeah, things were moving that way. I hadn't wanted to involve Lippillus, but if anyone could give me the inside edge on Valgius, Delicatus and the sins of the Eighth District Watch then that clever dwarf was the lad. And if for some reason he didn't know what was going on then since he was in the business himself someone should tell him. 'Okay, lady. I'll drop in on him tomorrow. Unless Phormio's whacky herbs do for me in the interim.'

'Don't overdramatise, dear. I'm just as annoyed with Meton as you are, but Phormio hasn't actually poisoned anyone yet. Besides, you said yourself that the broccoli was delicious, which it was.'

'Tell me that again when you're heaving your guts out in the small hours.'

'At least the case is officially open now. You've done that much. Valgius can't ignore your threat to go to the city judge.'

'Yeah.' I took another belt of Setinian. I'd been wondering about that. Perilla was right. Since our interview earlier that day Valgius would be running scared, but I had the bastard by the short hairs. Keeping the lid on a non-existent case was one thing; ignoring a direct, official approach was another. Valgius might drag his feet where an investigation was concerned, but he had to be seen to be doing something, and something was better than nothing. I wasn't going to be too popular with Lucius Cammius, though, because Valgius's obvious first step was going to be to question the guy about the attempts on his horse, and from what I'd seen of the factions they preferred to settle their own scores in their own way. Still, that couldn't be helped. 'I'll have to keep an eye on Valgius. Maybe that's something else for Lippillus.'

Just then, Bathyllus tooled in with the dessert tray. I glanced at it suspiciously, but Meton seemed to have shot his bolt with the broccoli and the dishes contained nothing more potentially noxious than dried fruits, stored apples and nuts rolled in honey and poppy seeds. At least, it all *looked* innocuous.

'Would you care for more wine, sir?' Bathyllus said.

'No, that's okay, Bathyllus.' I reached for one of the dry fruits, sniffed and nibbled. Pear. Definitely pear. Or it tasted like pear. I laid it down; gods, I could get paranoid here. 'Love life going well? I hear you and Tyndaris are off on another jaunt tomorrow.'

He blushed as he cleared away the empty dishes. 'Yes, sir. Her master gave her some money for the Megalensia and she asked me to accompany her to the clothes stalls in Cattlemarket Square. Also, there are some interesting friezes in the porch of Ceres's temple which she wishes to see.'

'Fine. Fine.' I poked at a nut. 'How's Petillius taking this, by the way? Everything okay there?'

'I haven't actually seen him, sir. Not since the . . . ah . . . kitchen incident.' Oh, yeah, the below-stairs Saturnalia that the old guy had gatecrashed. 'But

Tyndaris doesn't seem to think there are any problems. He's quite an indulgent master, sir.'

Yeah; that was putting it mildly. Me, I'm happy to leave the bought help alone so long as life goes on at its easy, comfortable pace – a disgruntled slave can do more harm in five minutes than a drunk rhino in a pottery warehouse, and keeping the buggers gruntled as far as possible seems only common sense – but I'm the exception. Or I thought I was. Letting your new housekeeper trail around the city looking at pictures is Indulgence with a capital I, while handing out tips at festivals isn't exactly common practice. Most slaves can reckon on cash boxes for the Winter Festival, sure, with maybe a small extra sub at the Matronalia and Compitalia, but that's about it. I was coming to the conclusion that I'd misjudged our neighbour. Beneath that bloated, oenophobic exterior beat the heart of a philanthropist. 'Great. Well, enjoy, Bathyllus.'

'Thank you, sir.'

'And if you should see any good truss shops on your wanderings, then—'

'*Marcus!*' Perilla snapped.

'Yeah. Right. Sorry, it was just a slip. That's all, sunshine. Have a good day.' Bathyllus exited, and I stretched: the long day was catching up on me. 'Hey, lady. You fancy an early night? I mean, if we're going to be woken up by Meton's broccoli it might be an idea to get some sleep in first. And I don't trust these nuts.'

'They look all right to me,' Perilla said. She paused. 'Of course, there was the time at your mother's that Phormio produced dates rolled in dyed mustard seeds . . .'

We stared at each other, then at the nuts. True, the poppy seeds did look grey rather than black. Carefully, I reached over, dipped a finger and tasted. Bastard!

'Let's skip dessert,' I said.

'Very wise, I think.'

Disgruntled slaves are bad enough, but a rogue chef definitely has the edge. The drunken rhino wouldn't even come close.

30

I gave breakfast a miss, left Perilla to have a quiet word in private with Meton – that fate I wouldn't wish on anyone, but for him I'd make an exception – and headed down to Public Pond. Despite the threat of the broccoli I'd had a good night's sleep, and it was a beautiful morning with the sun bathing the upper Caelian to my left in a golden sheen studded with poplars. Lippillus wasn't no Valgius: he'd've been at his desk practically by first light, but depending what his deputy on the night shift had left for him he might already be out and about. I picked up a couple of hot sesame bread rings from a bakery near the Temple of Honour and Virtue and munched on them as I walked.

Public Pond, taking in as it does the south-easterly Aventine rise and the Remuria, is a pretty rough district, although the eastern half between the high ground and Ardeatina Road on the outskirts of the city is a lot more open. The Watch-house itself is in the tenement area, near the Capenan Gate: close by the region's northern and western boundaries, in other words, which is good planning because that's where nine-tenths of the crimes are committed. Lippillus had

had the commander's job for four or five years now –
he'd been promoted when Perilla and I were living in
Athens – which just shows you that occasionally the
buggers who run the city manage to get things right,
because despite being a no-name and looking like a
disreputable dwarf the guy was shit-hot.

I'd just missed him: a B-and-E, the squaddie on the
desk told me, down the road at Mercury's Spring.

'Uh . . . B-and-E?' I said.

'Breaking and entering, sir. A wine store. The big
one by the tack and saddlery factory.'

'Right.' I bit a chunk out of my second bread ring
and set off again. Well, at least it wasn't far: Mercury's
Spring was only a few hundred yards the other side
of the gate, and I'd do better joining him there than
waiting for him to get back. That was another thing
about Lippillus. Most regional Watch commanders
saw the job as an opportunity to dump the actual
workload on their squaddies; he'd be out there himself
sniffing around. Delegation's necessary, sure, and so is
paperwork, but make too much of it and you can lose
the plot. Lippillus believed in keeping his hand in. Me,
I'd be the same, which was why we got on so well.

I found the place no bother, largely because of the
usual knot of gawpers: a cement blockhouse with bars
on the windows and a door hanging from its hinges
with the heavy iron crossbar pulled from the hasps
and lying in the roadway. Crude, and Jupiter knew
what the buggers had used to yank it free; maybe a
chain fastened to the yoke on a pair of oxen. Lippillus
was standing in the entrance talking to a little old

bald-headed tunic with literal tears in his eyes. Clearly, the bereft owner. He gave me a nod and a 'hang-on' wave, and I kicked my heels until he'd finished.

That took about two minutes. At the end of them he left the tunic to be sucked in to one of the commiserative groups of gawpers and came over.

'Hey, Corvinus,' he said. 'What brings you down to the Pond?'

I shrugged. That could wait: the guy was obviously busy. 'Problems?' I raised an eyebrow in the direction of the still-sobbing tunic.

Lippillus grinned his evil-goblin grin. When I'd first met him in the dim and distant past I'd taken him for a twelve-year-old. He'd picked up a good few creases, a touch of grey and a receding hairline since then, but he still looked like the first soft breath from Zephyrus's downy cheeks would send him bowling arse over tip. Not that the impression was borne out by the facts. I'd seen Lippillus sort out two squaddies almost literally twice his size and weight without even breaking stride, and they weren't putting it on, either.

'Nah,' he said. 'Just Coryphus and his brother from Butcher's Alley celebrating their mum's birthday. Happens every year, never varies. They break in, take two jars of Massic and one of whacky Falernian and spend the Megalensia pissed as newts. The mother too.' He nodded towards the wrinkled tunic, who seemed to have cheered up considerably and was chatting to his gawper pals. 'The gods know why old Thanno there doesn't just send the booze round a couple of days before and save us all a lot of trouble.'

'He seems pretty cut up about it anyway.'

The grin widened. 'Thanno? The old bugger enjoys the attention. Besides, the Butcher's Alley twins aren't bad lads. Once they've sobered up they'll be back round full of apologies and with the first instalment of the payment. It'll take them to the Winter Festival, sure, but Thanno'll get his money. And Coryphus is a blacksmith. This time ten days the door'll be good as new.'

'How did they bust the bar? Tame elephant?'

Lippillus chuckled. 'Uh-uh. They just pulled, one either side. They're big boys, that pair. Get it from their mother. That lady could lift a hippo in each hand. So, Corvinus. What can I do for you?'

'It may take a while. You got the time?'

'Sure. You can tell me over breakfast. I usually grab a roll in the baker's round the corner from the Watch-house, but I didn't have a chance this morning.'

'Suits me, pal.' We walked back the way I'd come, towards the Capenan Gate. 'How's Marcina?' Marcina was Lippillus's stepmother and de facto wife, a big beautiful African lady with vowels you wouldn't believe.

'Expecting.' That got me another grin. 'You wouldn't credit it after all this time, but there you are. She's due in another couple of months.'

'Congratulations. Perilla'll be pleased.'

'Looks like twins, from the size of her. Either that or the kid'll take after her side. Perilla well? How about that adopted daughter of yours?'

'She's still with Perilla's Aunt Marcia in the Alban

Hills. The old girl's hitting eighty, but she's fit as a flea and the kid loves it up there. Too much to bring her to Rome. We see her occasionally.' I fought down the smallest twinge of envy. 'Holidays. That sort of thing.'

'Yeah. Right.' We walked on in silence for a bit. 'So. What are you mixed up with this time?'

'You hear anything about the death of a Whites' driver?'

He stopped. 'Pegasus?'

'That's the lad.'

'Knifed in an alleyway in the Eighth District ten days or so back. Sure I heard. Story is that it was an open-and-shut case. Killed for his purse.'

'Wrong, pal. Whatever the motive was, it wasn't robbery. And if the purse was missing it was taken later as a blind. Trust me. I was there.'

He gave me a sharp glance and carried on walking. I'd thought he'd ask me more questions but he didn't. In fact, he clammed up completely. Interesting.

We reached the bakery. It was bigger than the holes in the wall you normally get, and the owner had put two folding tables in the spaces either side of the oven. I'd bet the place would be pretty popular in winter, and there was enough room on the pavement outside to shift them there when the temperature rose. At the moment, though, we had it to ourselves, except for the big guy with hairy, flour-dusted arms marking the sections on a trayful of flat round loaves.

'The usual, Quintus,' Lippillus said. He cocked an eye at me. 'You eaten yet?'

The sesame rings had filled a gap, but I could always manage a bit more, if only to be sociable. 'Make that two, Quintus,' I said. The big guy nodded, wiped the flour from his hands with a rag and reached down a wooden platter from a shelf. All done at the considered pace of an arthritic sloth. A man of few words and careful and deliberate habits, evidently.

'So.' Lippillus took one of the chairs and set his elbows on the table. 'You want to ask me about Titus Valgius, right?'

I said the guy was smart. I hadn't missed the tone, either: flat and level as a Paduan's back garden. 'Uh, yeah. Right. Among other things.'

'He's a colleague, Marcus.'

'He might also be a murderer. Or at least an accessory to murder.'

That got me another sharp look. 'Delicatus?'

So he knew the name, and the fact that he'd made the jump without any prompting was interesting again. 'Uh-huh. That's the theory I've been working on, anyway.'

'Shit.' He closed his eyes, and for a moment he looked grey and tired. I waited. Finally he opened them again. 'Okay. Let's have the gory details.'

I told him; not the whole thing, just the Natalis side. Halfway through Quintus the baker set the platter with a couple of rolls and a bowl of honey and curds in front of us, but Lippillus ignored them.

When I was finished, he said, 'You've told the city judge's office about this?'

I shook my head. 'No. I threatened to, but if push

came to shove I've no actual proof. Not even for the missing purse. Like I say, it's just a theory.'

'It squares.' The goblin face was grim. 'Look, we're not having this conversation, okay? If anything comes of it then fine, we talk to the city prefect, but I'm taking my commander's hat off now for the duration and as far as I'm concerned it doesn't go any further. Agreed?'

'Agreed.'

He broke off a piece of his roll, scooped up some of the honey and curds, chewed and swallowed. 'Valgius is a worm,' he said. 'And Delicatus is a snake. Everyone in the business knows the Eighth District Watch are rotten, but so long as no one important gets hurt no one cares.' His voice was matter-of-fact, and if I hadn't known him I would've thought he didn't care either. Which would've been about as far from the truth as you can get. 'The key word there, Marcus, in case you missed it, was "important". Up to now, the bastards have had their pal Sertorius Macro to sweep up their messes. Usually they don't even need him, the threat's enough to discourage any complaints. But if you're right then maybe this time they've overreached themselves.'

'Yeah. I had the impression Valgius knows that, and he's shit-scared.' I helped myself to the curds. 'You think he's capable of murder?'

'Not Valgius. Not personally. Delicatus, though, sure, no problem.' Lippillus kept his eyes on the food, and I noticed that when he wasn't speaking his mouth was a hard, sour line. Understandable;

these two bastards weren't ordinary crooks, they were Watch. And to make it worse, friend though I was, I was an outsider. 'There was an . . . incident two, three months ago. Small-time villain had his throat slit in an alley off Tuscus. Delicatus found the corpse himself, or that's what he claimed. Then it transpires that they'd been seen walking into the alley together, with Delicatus twisting the guy's arm behind his back. He didn't deny it, either, just made some private comment to the effect that it was the bugger's own fault for not checking his personal list against the Watch's.'

Yeah. Right: Crispus's protection racket. I said nothing.

'Result: no action to be taken. File and forget.' Lippillus was stabbing a chunk of roll viciously again and again into the curds and honey. 'That's only the most recent incident, mind. There've been four or five similar over the past three years. And probably a lot before them because it was only when Macro took over the Praetorians and backed Valgius for the Eighth District commander's job that Delicatus could risk crawling out from under his stone. Now he doesn't bother covering up for himself. He's no reason to, not when he has his immediate boss's approval and no one else dares say boo because of Valgius's connections. Plus he's doing a good job, no one would argue with that. The Eighth District is one of the quietest in the city. And when push comes to shove who's going to nail a fucking Watchman for ridding Rome permanently of a few fucking crooks?'

I shot him a sideways glance: Lippillus didn't swear,

or not often. And he didn't get so coldly angry, either. Maybe I should back off. 'Yeah,' I said quietly. 'Yeah, okay, pal. That's enough. Point taken.'

He looked up. The hard eyes didn't thaw any or his mouth lose its line, but he shrugged. 'Fine. I'm sorry. So in brief, Marcus, your answer's yes. Murdering charioteers isn't exactly in Titus Delicatus's line, but if my colleague Valgius put him up to killing your Whites' driver then he'd've done it neatly and professionally with no compunction whatsoever.' He tossed the mangled bit of roll out of the open doorway. 'Satisfied? Next question.'

'You sure you want to go on with this?' I said.

He was quiet for a long time, staring after the roll. 'You think we're proud of what the bastards are doing around Market Square, good track record or not?' he said finally. 'Any of us? Or maybe that we're proud of ourselves for ignoring them?' He turned back to face me. 'Corvinus, believe me, if Valgius and Delicatus do end up facing a murder charge then every honest Watchman in the city may feel that little bit dirtier by association but he'll want to shake your hand. And I'll be first in the queue. No, I don't want to go on with this, because talking about these two makes me sick and ashamed to my stomach, but that isn't relevant. Ask your next question.'

'For the theory to work, Valgius has to have a connection with Minicius Natalis and the Greens faction. Not necessarily a clandestine one. You any idea what that could be?'

'Sure. No problem there. They've been friends for

years. Valgius has always been a big Greens supporter – that's genuine, by the way, nothing to do with sucking up to Gaius – and he used to spend a lot of time at the stables when Natalis was top driver. In fact, that's how he got his job as Watch commander. When Prince Gaius and his mates – including Macro – took Natalis on as a protégé Valgius got sucked into the group as well. Or he crawled into it, rather.'

Well, that was pretty decisive. 'Incidentally, I heard the last Greens boss died under suspicious circumstances. Anything you can tell me about that?'

'Not a lot. He took a sudden belly-ache, it got worse and was dead inside a day. Sure, it could've been poison, and there were rumours to that effect, but there were no obvious signs.' He frowned. 'Not that you'd expect them. Minicius Natalis is no fool, Marcus. He may be crooked but he's careful. If he were mixed up in anything like that he'd cover his tracks.'

Something tugged at the back of my mind and was gone. 'Titus Valgius told me he'd reopen the case. Of Pegasus's murder, that is. You think that's likely?'

Another shrug. 'I told you, he's a worm. Delicatus is the one with the guts. If you put the frighteners on him and if like I say he thinks he's overreached himself then it's possible. Without backing from Macro he's nothing and he knows it. My guess is he'll go through the motions, run around asking questions like a blue-arsed fly and do nothing with the answers. That way he's covered. But it's an Eighth District matter, Corvinus. There I can't help you.'

Uh-huh. Well, I couldn't expect anything else. 'One more thing, pal. Not concerned with Valgius. You know anything about the junior consul? Lucius Vitellius?'

'How do you mean?'

'He's brother-in-law to the Blues faction master Sextilius Acceptus. And I understand he's also friendly with the cartel boss Eutacticus. I was just wondering about a triangle, that's all.'

He was staring at me. 'Corvinus, Eutacticus is not someone you want to mess with.'

'Yeah, I know,' I said drily. 'So everyone tells me, and personal experience bears them out. Even so.'

'If there was anything going on then I wouldn't know about it. Not specifically, certainly not officially. Eutacticus is one of the city's respectable crooks. He's worth ten million in his sandals, he's on first-name terms with half the Senate, he gets his dirty work done at third or fourth hand, and tracing a connection would be about as easy as carrying a handful of snow across Libya. Even then, the chances of getting a charge to stick aren't worth quoting. The consul sails pretty close to the wind. He's been mixed up in two or three property scams, but you show me the broad-striper who hasn't. Acceptus I haven't come across, not in that way. He's a hard nut by reputation where business is concerned, although no harder than most, and a bad loser. Sorry, that's all I can tell you.'

'Bad loser?'

'Not in the gambling way. Acceptus is no gambler. If he plays he has to win, and he usually does, somehow.'

I must've made some kind of movement, because he shook his head. 'No. Nothing illegal. I told you, Acceptus is clean. On the surface, at least, which might only show how clever he is. If the three of them are working together then you're dealing with a collection of very smart cookies.'

Yeah; put like that, I could see I might be: Eutacticus the wealthy organised crime boss, Vitellius with his political clout and Acceptus with his single-minded approach, united by a common racing interest. There might be mileage there right enough. I stood up and pulled out my purse. 'Okay. Thanks, pal.'

'Breakfast is on me. Just nail these buggers in the Eighth District if you can.'

'Right.'

'Oh, and Corvinus?'

'Yeah?'

'Be careful.'

But that advice I didn't need.

31

The next day was the start of the Megalensia. That's no time for sleuthing: the ten-day festival of the Great Mother may not be as important as the Winter Festival is, but it's still a major holiday, with the public side of city life just ticking over and the accent on private dinner parties and general loosening up. Although Perilla and I tended to play things quiet – we'd been away from Rome too long to build up the usual network of friends and acquaintances – it still meant we had to fulfil the family requirement of having Mother and Priscus round for dinner, and to that end I'd backed Meton into a corner and threatened personally to scrub his omelette pan with wire if I caught the bugger monkeying around with the menu by as much as one whackily stuffed olive. Not, to be fair, that Meton needed the warning: like I say, he and Mother's pet chef Phormio are at filleting knives drawn, and any chance he has to show off he grabs with both hands. Dinner – we'd arranged it for the first day, to get the ordeal over with – was to be a showpiece: sweet apricot hors-d'oeuvres, moray eels, a whole tunny in raisins and wine, braised pork in an aniseed marinade and a selection of cakes and candied fruit to finish. Also,

I'd arranged with our wine supplier to send us a jar of his best Caecuban: if I was to get through an evening with Mother and her dried-prune husband spouting respectively off-the-wall health and wholefood advice and little-known facts about the use of the Sabine dative then I wanted to be comfortably stoned.

In the morning, along with the rest of Rome, we went to see the procession. Cybele has her temple on the Palatine – I'd been there just a few months back to talk to the chief priest about that murdering bitch Myrrhine – and the festival starts with the goddess being taken to be washed in the Almo where it joins the Tiber, half a mile or so down the Ostian road. Bathyllus came as well, with Tyndaris in tow, although maybe it was the other way round because to tow that lady would've needed a set of heavy-duty hawsers, and I gave them a handful of coppers each for the guys with the collection baskets. We grabbed ourselves a prime stretch of pavement on Public Incline between Cattlemarket Square and the corner of the Circus, fought off the encroaching punters and settled down with our dried fruit and nuts to wait.

Me, I'm not one for processions; you spend an hour twiddling your thumbs, either frying or freezing depending on the season, and all you get for it is five minutes of stuffed mantles on their dignity, an elbow in the ribs and some short-arsed bugger using your feet as a ladder. Cybele's is special, though. The Lady Goddess may've been a naturalised Roman citizen for the last three hundred years, but she's no compromiser and no stuffed mantle; she and her devotees are pure Asia and always have been.

They don't let you forget it, either, especially at the Megalensia procession. The first thing that hits you from about a quarter of a mile off is the noise: the rattle and thump of the tambourines and the wailing of the flutes. At that range it's bearable, just; any closer and it's sheer murder, like having your brains beaten through your ears with a brass club and your guts hauled out and tied in knots, both at the same time. Then there's the priests. The home-grown Roman priestly colleges – barring these mad buggers of Salians at the Lupercal with their wolf pelts and rawhide whips – are a pretty staid, not to say po-faced bunch, and any normal procession of the pig-sheep-bull variety is about as full of life as a fishmonger's slab. The galli are different. Jupiter – or Cybele, rather – knows what they're on, but whatever it is it ain't Roman and it ain't ordinary wine, neither. Maybe it's just the noise – like I say, the flutes and tambourines grab you by the balls hard enough when you're in the crowd, and what it must be like to have it in your ears and head for a good solid hour I can't imagine, even if like these poor bastards you don't have any balls to be grabbed by – but my guess is the whole boiling are high as kites on that whacky *qef* stuff they smuggle in from Parthia. Whatever the reason, imagine fifty or so screaming, shaven-headed maniacs in yellow robes leaping up and down like demented apes and slashing themselves with flails and knives, add to that the racket from the tambourines and flutes previously adverted to and where Cybele's procession is concerned you'll have the general picture.

Family worship at the Altar of Peace it ain't.

They were still about fifty yards off, and communication was still a theoretical possibility. I leaned over to Bathyllus standing beside me.

'You ever think of taking up the priesthood, little guy?' I yelled.

He turned sideways. His mouth said: 'Pardon, sir?' but with that racket going on I couldn't hear a thing either. As the procession drew level the pavement began to vibrate under my sandals and the wall of sound became so dense you could've hammered nails into it. I shrugged, shook my head and made a 'doesn't matter' sign with my hand.

A temple slave with a collecting basket – there was a scattering of coppers in the bottom, but no more; the great Roman public don't like to pay for their shows – held it out to me, and I chucked in my contribution. That's another peculiarity about the Megalensia procession: Cybele's the only god or goddess who has the right to solicit from non-participating punters. The story goes that it's because her first temple in the city was paid for out of a mass of pennies collected from the common people. Me, I'd say taking the opportunity to swell the temple coffers was just standard canny Asian business practice. Mind you, that said, if the Great Goddess had had to wait for enough collecting baskets to fill before she had a place to call her own then she'd still be kicking her divine heels on Mount Ida.

I noticed that the slave carrying the basket had what looked like wool stuffed in his ears. Ah, well; we can't all be religious.

Tyndaris was certainly enjoying herself, which made sense because coming as she did from Ephesus this would be home from home. I was glad we'd brought her. Not only did it lend a sort of family outing feeling to things, but she only had to shift feet to clear a yard of pavement. At the beginning I'd worried that some poor inoffensive punter might be edged off the kerb into the path of a mad flailing gallus and cut to ribbons, but most of them were keeping well clear. Very wise.

Perilla was watching with a cool detachment I found almost eerie. Any moment I expected her to pull out a wax tablet and stylus and start taking notes.

The first instalment of the marching band was past us now. They were followed by my pal the archigallus, rolling along like an overloaded imperial barge in a fetching purple dress, necklace and diadem. I gave him a wave, but either he didn't notice, didn't recognise me or more probably wasn't letting on. Living gods have their dignity to maintain. Behind him, and ahead of Marching Band Part the Second, was the goddess herself in her chariot pulled by a dozen priests sweating costly saffron dust from every pore.

This wasn't the cult statue; that would've been too big, and, besides, what gets washed at the Megalensia isn't an image. The goddess is a shapeless lump of black stone, polished like glass but soaking up the light rather than reflecting it, and she looks older than Cronos. Someone, some time, had added a woman's head in silver with a towered crown like the one a soldier gets for being first over an enemy rampart, but that was just decoration: the stone itself is what matters. I'd heard, even through the rattle and crash of the tambourines, the low moan spreading towards us and seen a sort of ripple in the crowd. Now it caught us up, and people all around us were kneeling like they were part of a collapsing wave. Not everyone, sure, not even half the punters – most of the crowd were just there for a good time – but a fair percentage. The hairs rose on my neck.

Then she was past, and it was time for the brass clubs and gut-twisting again, backed by the long tail of celebrants chanting their Greek hymns. Most of them were women, and of these about nine-tenths were Asian-Greek tunics, but there was a scattering of mantles. I even saw one purple stripe. The rites of Cybele may be unRoman, but they're catching on. I'd hoped to see my flute-player pal Aegle blowing her cheeks out but she wasn't there. Maybe she had another engagement, or – more probably – the temple had enough flute girls of its own without hiring them in.

Suddenly the tail-enders were a hundred yards down the incline and people were rising to their feet. It felt like all the sound in the world had been used up and we were left with a gaping hole.

'Interesting,' Perilla said.

'Yeah.' The only reason I'd got the word was that I'd read her lips. My ears were still ringing and I pushed my palms against them, shook my head and swallowed. Hearing gradually returned. 'Just once a year, though.'

'What did you want to say to me, sir?' Bathyllus asked.

'Forget it, sunshine. You wouldn't want to pay the entrance fee.'

'I did enjoy that!' Tyndaris was beaming. 'Brought things right back!'

'Yeah.' I turned to go. 'It must've—'

I stopped. A dozen feet away two tunics were talking together. One of them had glanced at us, grinned and looked away to speak to his pal; obviously making some kind of comment. Now, my ears might not be working too well at present, but there was nothing wrong with my eyes.

The tunic who'd grinned had a missing incisor on the right side of his jaw, just where the kid Stephanus had pointed it out.

The pair turned their backs and ambled off in the direction of the Circus. I watched them go, frowning.

'Marcus? Are you all right?' Perilla was staring at me.

'Hmm? Yeah, yeah. Sure.' Shit; it was coincidence, it had to be. With the number of sweetmeat-sellers and careless bakers around, guys with missing teeth were two a penny in Rome. And Tyndaris was worth commenting on in anyone's book.

Even so, my scalp was definitely prickling.

We survived the dinner. Just. On the plus side, we were playing on home ground – Mother had had us round for the Winter Festival, and one of the good Roman traditions is reciprocation – so with Meton squared the meal itself was safe. Also the wine flowed free. Priscus is no drinker – the desiccated old bugger isn't all that much of anything, except academically – and although he has a fair palate and serves a decent vintage he reckons that any more than one jug among the four of us constitutes a bacchanalian orgy. On the minus side the conversation was just as riveting as I'd thought it would be, and as usual Priscus managed to splash sauce down Perilla's best mantle at a distance of three yards.

Duty done for another few months.

The second day we lazed around. The third, Perilla dragged me to a Greek-into-Latin comedy at Marcellus Theatre: plays are big at the Megalensia, and the third of the festival is Performance Day. Me, I can never see the point in these things because the plots are rubbish. The young hero always gets the girl, who may be a prostitute but turns out to be a wealthy heiress kidnapped at an early age by pirates and sold to a brothel, while the cheeky lynchpin-slave is a pain in the backside and the all-singing-all-dancing chorus set my teeth on edge. Still, Perilla enjoys them, and if I snore too loud she can always dig me in the ribs. This particular example had the smartass slave covering up for a wild party and the ongoing presence of the prostitute-heroine by convincing the young hero's father that his own house was haunted and therefore a no-go area. The plot would've insulted the intelligence of a five-year-old; and that went double for the jokes.

Perilla laughed all the way through. This, mark you, is the Perilla who eats Plato for breakfast with Hecateus for elevenses. I'll never understand that lady.

The fourth day we had Lippillus and Marcina round, plus Agron and his wife from Ostia. They stayed over, and on the fifth we all went to Sallust Gardens. The sixth, seventh and eighth passed. And the ninth.

The tenth – the last day of the festival, and the day of the chariot race when we'd got passes for the Whites' faction row – I had a message first thing from Lucius Cammius.

Someone had got to Polydoxus. The horse was dead.

32

'It was Typhon.'

We were in Cammius's office. The guy looked . . . *haggard* is an understatement. Cammius looked like one of these ogres from the kids' stories had been feeding on him all night and sucked not just the flesh but the soul out from under the skin.

'Typhon?' Oh, yeah, the weasely little placard man I'd talked to about Pegasus the first time I'd been here. 'You're sure?'

'Certain.' That was Hesper, standing by his boss's chair. He just looked angry. 'The bastard is – was – the faction gopher. A mascot, almost. He took the guards their supper last night, including the fucking drugged wine that put them out.'

My stomach felt cold. '"Was"? You mean he's dead?'

Hesper made a move like he was going to spit, but didn't. 'Nah, worse luck. Run off. His things're missing.'

I glanced at Cammius. The only other times I'd seen him he'd been perfectly in control: big, beefy, confident. Now like I say he looked like he'd been gutted. A sack of barley would've had more backbone.

'You want to tell me what happened, sir?' I said gently. 'Exactly?'

That got me a glazed stare. His hand rose from the desk and made a movement towards Hesper.

Hesper frowned and turned back to me. 'Standard procedure the night before a race. The stables're sealed; no one goes in or out, double guards on the gate, four men doing a circuit of the perimeter wall. Any horse that's racing plus the cars are kept under watch. Polydoxus had two of our best in the stall with him, under orders to stay awake all night. Typhon took them their supper and a half jug of wine. That's all they remember until I found them at dawn snoring their fucking heads off and the horse dead beside them.'

'That was the normal procedure?' I said. 'Typhon bringing the supper, I mean?'

'Nothing out of the ordinary. Like I say, he was the gopher. Been with the faction for years.' He scowled. 'I trusted that bastard. If I ever see him again I'll kill him with my bare hands.'

'What happened then?'

'The boys fingered Typhon. When we finally roused them, that is, because they were out like lights. I went and checked his mattress myself. No sign, and the bag with his stuff had gone. The gate guards hadn't seen nothing of him so he must've gone over the wall.' He shrugged. 'It's easy enough, there're plenty of places and you can't watch them all. Wall's designed for keeping people out, not keeping them in.'

I looked at Cammius. He hadn't moved, just sat

staring into nothing. 'Uh . . . you able to add anything to that, sir?'

His eyes didn't move, but he shook his head. I waited. Nothing else came. 'Where's Cario?' I asked Hesper.

'Getting things ready for the race. We'll just have to run a second-stringer as lead.' The guy's mouth closed and I could hear his teeth grind together. 'Bastard!'

Yeah, well; the show had to go on, I supposed. And from the look of Cammius the Whites' boss wasn't up to organising himself a shave and a haircut. 'You didn't notice anything? Typhon acting suspiciously over the last few days, nothing like that?'

'Nah. Not that that'd be anything strange. You met him yourself. He's always been a funny bugger, but I never thought he'd do this, never. He's gutted us right and proper.'

'What was it? Poison?'

'Yeah. We had our vet take a look, but it was pretty obvious. The poor beast had choked its lungs out. Blood and foam all over the straw.'

Cammius's eyes closed suddenly and he shivered. 'That's it, Corvinus,' he said, and I had to bend closer to hear him. 'First Pegasus, now Polydoxus. Finished, all finished.'

Shit. I looked at Hesper. 'Maybe someone should get him home,' I said quietly.

'We've tried. He won't go.'

I sighed. 'Typhon. Any idea where he might've run to? A relative? A friend maybe?'

Hesper grunted and made to spit again. 'If I did –

if any of the lads did – you think we'd've bothered
sending for you?'

Fair point. One thing was sure: if the faction ever did
catch up with the bugger there wouldn't be enough of
him left to burn. Wherever he was, if he was wise, it
would be far, far off. The main question, though, was
who had got to him. Natalis or Acceptus, sure, it had to
be one of them, but you paid your money and you took
your choice. And unless I could find Typhon himself
and sweat him, the chances of deciding between the
two were as close to zero as made no difference.

There wasn't anything more I could do. I left Hesper
to clear up the mess and went home to my unfinished
breakfast.

We watched the races, Perilla and I. Cario led the
White faction's part of the procession that opens the
games with a circuit of the track, and the placard
behind him and in front of Uranius with the lead
team read 'Dassus' instead of 'Polydoxus'. Where
you'd find a list of wins, it was blank. The Greens'
and Blues' sections of the bleachers – there aren't
any official faction areas in the Circus, but the fans
of each Colour naturally tend to gravitate together
anyway – whistled and jeered and stamped their feet;
the Whites' fans, what there were of them, were
totally silent. Cammius hadn't turned up, not even
to sit on the faction master's bench. That we had to
ourselves.

I looked across to the other faction rows; they were
all within a few yards of each other, close by the

finishing line. Acceptus was there with his wife and a couple of what must've been sons, plus a gaggle of hangers-on. He gave me a formal nod like a constipated camel's then turned to speak to the man next to him, and I recognised our jowly junior consul Vitellius. On the Greens' bench Natalis sat stiff as a ramrod with his daughter Galatea beside him, but he didn't even glance at me, and nor did she. There was no sign of Macro, although the bench had its full complement of the up-and-coming great-and-not-so-good. Pudens and Felicula were there to represent the Reds. The rest of their row, like ours, was empty.

The games started. The Blues and Greens had the day between them, with White and Red nowhere. Uranius was on last; the last race of the day is the plum, when the Colours field their best teams. I'd put a couple of silver pieces on White for conscience's sake, and the odds I'd got showed that the bookies weren't too worried they'd lose out in the end: with Pegasus and Polydoxus I'd've been lucky to get evens, but Uranius and Dassus were offered at thirty to one. Even the Reds with Laomedon did better.

'Do you think he has a chance, Marcus?' Perilla said as the eight teams were led into the starting-boxes.

I shrugged. 'He's an okay driver, lady. And no race is over until they cross the line.'

The President of Games dropped his napkin, the gates sprang open with a clang and the Circus roared.

If you ignore the noise of the fans, the first laps of a race after the initial scrimmage between the break-line when the drivers are allowed to leave their lanes and

the first turn are always pretty subdued affairs, with
the teams sorting themselves out and getting into their
stride. By the end of the fourth – halfway through –
the cars had bunched: a clutch of four leading, the two
Greens in front, the first Blue jockeying for position
and the second a dozen yards behind hanging point
to cut off a run by the White and Red leaders –
Uranius and Laomedon – who formed the second
knot. The Whites' and Reds' own back-ups were
nowhere, but that wasn't unusual: they'd be genuine
second-stringers, drivers and horses that had something going for them but needed the experience of a
first-league race. And there was always the possibility
that if they held back a multiple pile-up among the
leaders later on would give them the chance to slip
through the wreckage and win against the odds.

The fifth lap came, and as the cars came round the
starting-gates turn again I could see that Uranius was
doing well. He was hard on the Blues' heels at the
turn, two horses' lengths ahead of Laomedon and
going like a bird. The race was speeding up now; not
a hard gallop yet, but the drivers were almost flat over
their rails and as the teams passed us with a thunder of
hooves the horses were beginning to throw out flecks
of foam. The sprinklers were out on either side of the
track, ready with their buckets for the last two laps,
and the course rakers were smoothing over the sand
as soon as the last car was by them. The rumble of the
crowd had swelled to a steady, ear-hurting roar, but
there was a long way to go there as well: we were still,
so to speak, barely past the hors-d'oeuvres and into the

main course. By the end of the race – the seventh lap – when the metaphorical tables were cleared for the dessert a hundred and fifty thousand people would be screaming themselves hoarse and you wouldn't be able to hear yourself think.

They went into the sixth. The two Greens were still leading but the Blue had narrowed the gap until the noses of his front pair were almost level with the rear of the second Green's car, while his partner was coming up fast on the outside track, tempting the Green to swerve away from the central barrier to cut him off, which would've let the first Blue through. Laomedon had closed up, and he and Uranius were neck and neck a car's-length behind, with Uranius in the better position on the inside. The first of the sprinklers – a Green – ran out, threw his bucketful over the sweating horses and darted back to the safety of the barrier as the Blue team hurtled past a hair's-breadth from his shoulder. I couldn't see my lackwit Whites pal, but maybe he was stationed nearer the turning-posts, or on the other side of the track.

We waited as the White and Red tail-enders galloped by: barring accidents, they were out of it, but the last lap pays for all, and trailing a dozen lengths behind or not with a bit of luck one of them might still end up in the top three. The leaders vanished past the Eggs, round the far turn and on to the Palatine stretch in a spray of sand. The next time we saw them they'd be into lap seven: two turns to go, then the final dash to the white line.

From the spectators' point of view racing's a stop-go business, especially this close to the sand. We could see both turns – just – and the whole of the Aventine stretch between, but the clutter of buildings and statues on the barrier meant that we were practically blind to whatever was going on on the far side. Something was happening, sure: the solid mass of Greens' fans on the Palatine bleachers opposite Agrippa's dolphins at the starting-gate turn gave a sudden roar, and the punters settled down to a thudding chant of *Ni-ké-tus! Ni-ké-tus!* with the accent on the first two syllables. Nicetus was the Greens' lead driver, and *niké* is Greek for 'victory'; whatever it was, it didn't look good for the Blues.

There was a swirl of sand and the cars were coming towards us again: two Greens, a Blue, a White and a Red. No sign of the second Blue, or maybe it was the first.

'Shit! The Blues've lost one!' I said to Perilla. I glanced over at the Blue bench. Acceptus didn't look happy, not happy at all. I remembered what Lippillus had said about the guy liking to win, and his chances had clearly just been halved. The last lap, with one car down and two teams belonging to the one Colour in front is no place to be if you're a faction boss.

The cars were drawing level, with sprinklers running out every few yards. Jupiter knew how any of these kids survived at all, certainly not the ones from front-runner factions. I saw one catch a clip from a wheel that knocked him spinning, but he was thrown the right way off the track and over the lip of the flooded ditch that protects the bleachers when the Circus is used for beast fights. It was deep, sure, but if he could swim he'd be okay, and there were plenty of hands ready to pull him out. I looked back at the race.

The two Greens had pulled ahead: it must've been the first Blue that'd crashed at the turn, because there was a clear gap, which explained the chant and Acceptus's concern. They were running half-and-half, the leader hugging the barrier and his second's first pair of horses six feet out from his offside wheel. The Blue was a scant team's-length back in the middle. I could see what the Green guys were doing: the inside track's the key to a win, especially in the last lap, because the turns are tighter. To have any chance of passing, the Blue would have to get between the first Green and the barrier; but the moment he tried that the second Green would slacken off, swing in behind his partner and force the Blue to slow. By the time the Blue had pulled his horses round to pass on the outside – if he could pass after reining in – the first Green would be fifty yards off and going like the devil. Team strategy. No wonder Acceptus was looking sick. Also, the Blues guy had troubles of his own. Uranius and Laomedon were still neck and neck, Laomedon on the inside now, on either side of the guy's back rail and about a whisker behind, whips poised, both watching for the opening . . .

Which was when it happened. As they hit the white line the Blue leaned out over the rail until he was practically level with the backs of his second-row horses, lashing the two leaders with his whip. The horses screamed, threw up their heads and broke into a full gallop. The car pulled away towards the barrier, streaking for the space between it and the second Green. A heartbeat later, Uranius and Laomedon did the same; only Laomedon moved right, to pass the Blue on his off-side, while Uranius, three feet away, kept going straight. The two wheels – Laomedon's off-side, Uranius's near-side – met and shattered. The crowd roared.

Everything seemed to go slow. I remember seeing Perilla's hands move towards her mouth; the two cars lift into the air like they were suddenly light as eggshell; the two drivers, the reins still fastened round their waists, jerk forward like puppets behind the speeding horses; one of them smash to the sand by the barrier's edge and be dragged bouncing and rolling past the three columns with the statues on top as he sawed at the leather with his curved knife, the other spin sideways into the track's centre, hack himself free and scramble desperately towards the ditch a dozen yards off. Then the two tail-enders, following behind, hauling on their reins years too late and the scrambling figure vanishing under the hooves of the first car's team to reappear seconds later behind the car as a tumbling, broken doll. And I know I couldn't've seen this as well, but I swear I remember Galatea on the Greens bench jumping to her feet and screaming. Then there were people running out on to the track as the crowd howled and the five remaining cars sped for the Consus turn and disappeared in a cloud of sand.

Green won; first and second, with Blue taking third. I'd thought the dead man was Uranius, but it was Laomedon.

'He had it coming.' We were down near the pavilion by the processional gate, and Hesper was frowning at the rakers smoothing the sand in front of the turning-posts. The Circus was empty now, except for the gang of public slaves clearing the litter from the bleachers. The ones on the upper tiers far above us looked like ants. 'He didn't give Uranius no warning, just swung straight into him. You don't do that on the sand, Corvinus. The punters may think you do, but you don't. The other guy ignores the warning, fine, that's his risk and yours, but you always give it.'

'How is Uranius?' I said.

'He'll be okay. Broke his collar-bone, an arm and a couple of ribs. That's one of his nine lives gone. We've got our doctor with him now; Galatea as well.'

'Galatea?'

'Yeah. Natalis's daughter. She may not be much in the looks department, but she's one strong-minded female.' Hesper showed a flash of teeth. 'Bastard's been playing that one close to his chest, but the secret's out now. Natalis is fit to be tied.'

Yeah, that I'd believe. I hadn't known all the faces on the Greens' bench, but most of the ones I had could've bought and sold me twice over. Sitting a marriageable daughter down with a good cross-section of Rome's wealthiest young bloods constituted a pretty strong hint. I wished the pair well, but I wouldn't give even the odds I'd got on Uranius as a driver that he'd get that business past the white line without coming a cropper. Pity, but there you are; that's life. 'How's Cammius? Any better?'

Hesper looked away. 'Nah. Nor will be, either, if I'm any judge. The faction neither, because there isn't any difference between them. They may both be breathing but they're dead all the same.' He turned back to face me. 'It's not your fault, Corvinus, you tried. The whole racing business is rotten, you have to live with that. All you can do is try to stay one up on the buggers who're trying to pull you down, and if you don't manage that there's no use crying.'

'Yeah. Right.' I felt depressed as hell. All that chasing around and it had got me nowhere. Theories, sure, I had them by the bucketful, but I couldn't turn any of them into fact; not without hard proof, like getting my hands on that bastard Typhon, and I had as much chance of tracing him as I had of flying. If he was still even above ground to trace, which I doubted: one got you ten whichever of my prime beauties had been behind the poisoning – and presumably Pegasus's murder – had paid him off with a knife in the ribs, because letting him live would be just too damn dangerous. My personal bet was that Typhon was currently pushing up daisies in an unmarked grave or at the bottom of the river chained to a concrete block. In any case, like Hesper had said, it was all academic now. With both Pegasus and Polydoxus dead the Whites were gutted, and there was no use crying.

'Marcus? Have you finished? We should be getting back.' Perilla was coming towards us from the direction of the starting-gates, where she'd been examining the mechanism that sprang all the doors simultaneously. Gadgets are another of the lady's things, and she doesn't pass up an opportunity to pry.

'Yeah. I've finished, lady. Totally and completely.' The understatement of the year. I turned to Hesper. 'I'll see you around, pal. Give my best to Cammius, and to Uranius.'

'Right.' The Whites' master of stables hesitated, then held out his hand. 'Thanks for all you've done, in any case.'

We shook, and the action had a sort of finality which matched the way I was feeling. No accident, either: the case was effectively over, and we both knew it.

We'd brought the litter in honour of the games and to keep our mantles street-mud-free – technically, a race meet is a sacred event and so the guys on the doors have the right to refuse admission to anyone not looking their snappy best, although the gods help them if they ever tried to enforce the rule – and the littermen were parked round the corner on Circus Road. Perilla glanced at me once or twice as we walked back to it, but she didn't say anything. Me, I was feeling too sick to make conversation. We got in and our four lardballs took the strain. We'd gone as far as the Septimontium before either of us spoke.

'Does the fact that the Whites lost make that much of a difference, Marcus?' Perilla said quietly.

I sighed. 'No. Not in itself. But it puts the cap on things. Their best driver's gone, their best horse is gone. They're back to scratch. Like Hesper said, the faction may still be breathing but it's dead on its feet. For the foreseeable future, anyway. And you didn't see Cammius, lady. The team takes it spirit from its boss, and the guy's an empty shell. Even if we did find out who was responsible now – and the gods know how we'd go about it – it wouldn't matter a straw.'

'Of course it would. Not to the Whites, perhaps, but it would matter to you.'

I stared out through the curtains. We'd been among the last to leave, and away from the temporary she-beens around the Circus itself where the fans were still celebrating the streets were practically empty: race days make for an early dinner. 'Perilla, I'm stymied, okay?' I said. 'I may know who was behind things, or at least shortened the list to two, but I can't go any further, not without hard facts to use as proof. So long as all I have is theory, Natalis is sitting pretty. He's got Macro behind him and a Watch commander in his pocket, because that bastard Valgius isn't going to stir himself if he and his sidekick were involved. All I have on Acceptus is that he's friendly with Lucius Vitellius, and he's currently got political and judicial clout in spades. So where do I go from here? You tell me, because as Jupiter is my witness I don't have a fucking clue.'

'Polydoxus was poisoned. That's a criminal offence in itself.'

'Only if it's formally reported. Cammius isn't going

to do that; the guy's beat six ways from nothing. Cario might, but my guess is he won't bother. What's the point, lady? Like Hesper said again, racing's a dirty business, and if you get hurt there's no use crying. What's done is done and there's no mending it.'

'You could try finding this Typhon person. And I've arranged a meeting with Sextilia for tomorrow afternoon.'

'Typhon's dead or long gone.' I felt the anger bunching up inside me. 'And sure, I'll go through the motions but I doubt if Sextilia'll be much help, especially if she and Vitellius are estranged.'

'Corvinus, that's enough!' Perilla turned on me so fast the litter shook. 'If you're going to be negative about this then very well, you go ahead, drop the case. But when you come out of your damned sink of self-pity you'll regret it as much as I do.'

I grinned weakly: the lady had a point, even in my present state I could see that. And when she was in this mood you didn't argue. 'Okay, Tisiphone,' I said. 'I'm open to suggestions. You have the floor. Cushions, rather.'

She was still frowning. 'For a start, you don't *know* that Typhon is dead. Or for that matter that he's out of reach.'

'It's a logical assumption, Perilla. Unless the guy responsible is a total headbanger – which neither Acceptus nor Natalis is – he'd've made sure the loose ends were tied up firmly. And Typhon wouldn't've poisoned the horse on his own account. He had no reason to.'

'Granted. All of it. But you can still assume he's alive and make the effort to find him even if it's wasted.'

'And how do you suggest I go about doing that?' I tried not to make the question come out sarcastically, but it didn't quite come off. 'Hesper was no help. The guy was a permanent fixture in the stables – no family, no friends outside. Rome's a big place, lady, and Italy's even bigger. Not to mention the fact that he could've skipped anywhere in the empire on a boat from Ostia.'

'Ask Eutacticus.'

I sat back. 'What?'

'He must have connections. In the criminal world, I mean. He may even know something about the poisoning.'

I mulled that one over. Sure, it made sense in principle; more sense than Perilla knew, because about the last thing that bastard had said was that he owed me one. And someone with dodgy connections was just what we needed here. There was only one objection, and that was a clincher. 'Eutacticus is a pal of Vitellius's, lady. Which means, by extension, he's on Acceptus's side of the fence. If Acceptus is the one we want then Eutacticus is just about as likely to help as put his weight behind a clean-up-the-government bill.'

'It's worth a try,' she said calmly. 'He can only say no.'

'Perilla, the last time the guy's name came up in conversation you warned me off touching him with a bargepole. Quite rightly so. And if he is directly involved and I tell him to his face that I'm trying my best to rip the scabs off Polydoxus's death then he can do a hell of a lot more than just say no.'

'Desperate times call for desperate measures. And I'm not having you grizzling around and flagellating yourself like a priest of the Great Mother for the next six months because you gave up an investigation in a fit of pique.' Ouch. There again, she had a valid point: I was feeling bad enough now. 'Do you honestly think that he *is* involved? Because that's what it comes down to, doesn't it?'

I had my mouth open to answer, but I closed it. The question needed thinking about, because as the lady said it was crucial. Sure, if the answer was yes then heading up to the Pincian with a song on my lips and hope in my heart was about the stupidest thing I could do. On the other hand, crook or not, hard man or not, where Pegasus's murder was concerned, at least, Eutacticus hadn't struck me as anything but straight. Added to which, if he had had a hand in the poisoning, what would he gain? For himself, not Vitellius or Acceptus, I mean? A strong Whites team could only benefit the bookies in the long term, since the chances of any one faction winning would be split three ways instead of two. At worst, a live Polydoxus, even with a driver who wasn't quite top-shelf, would blur the betting, and if the odds were representative then again he could only come out ahead. Doping the horse before the race as a one-off I could see the value of, definitely: after the rumours that'd been going around, Polydoxus's name on the race-card would've been enough in itself to have attracted big money, especially if the touts had dangled the bait of favourable odds, and if the beast had been secretly got at without either the punters or the stable knowing then Eutacticus would've cleaned up. However, killing it was a different matter. Everyone would know – as they did – that the Whites' star horse was a second-rater and would bet accordingly. Trying to run a scam under these conditions would be like using your own dice in a dice game after filing off the top two numbers; it just didn't make sense. The benefits for Natalis or Acceptus were obvious, sure, but Eutacticus wouldn't be any the better off. Quite the reverse. Of course, he could still have been in on it for altruistic reasons, but the words 'altruism' and 'Eutacticus' just didn't go together, somehow.

And if Eutacticus *was* clean – in this case, anyway – then Perilla was right; having him on the team would be a definite plus. In fact, it'd be the only definite plus we had.

You make your bet, you take your chance. And really I didn't have any choice.

'Yeah, okay, lady,' I said. 'You win. I'll talk to him tomorrow.'

33

All the same, I wasn't feeling too confident as I climbed the Pincian. One bout with that saw-toothed bastard had been enough to last me a lifetime and I'd no wish to repeat the experience. The knowledge that at least on this occasion Perilla knew where I'd gone and could blow the whistle if I didn't come back wasn't much consolation. I'd thought of taking two or three of my largest slaves with me for insurance, but decided against it: that would only be provocation, and the last thing I wanted was for Eutacticus to feel provoked.

Like they had been the first time, the two gorillas – Laughing George and his pal – were lounging outside along with the gate-slave. Laughing George was chewing on a straw. When he saw me he straightened, took it out of his mouth scowling and gave me the hard eye all the way to the gate.

'What the fuck do you want?' he growled.

Well, I'd take it from the boss, but not from the hired help, however big he was. 'To borrow a cup of milk? Wrong. To collect for the Launderers' Guild Widows and Orphans fund? Wrong. You like to try for a third guess, pal, or should I just spoil the game and tell you?'

The scowl deepened. 'You taking the piss, Corvinus?'

'Yeah, that would be a pretty fair assumption. Eutacticus at home?'

'He's in.'

'Fine. Maybe you could sort of ask him if I could have a word. If that's not putting too much of a strain on your abilities.'

He glared at me while his mate did a good impression of a brick wall with attitude. Finally he turned to the gate-slave. 'Do it,' he said.

The guy scuttled inside. The two heavies watched me like I had nefarious designs on the gatepost tritons. Five minutes later he was back.

'The boss says okay,' he said.

Laughing George grunted; I had the distinct impression that the answer had disappointed him and he'd been hoping for permission to test how far I would bounce. 'Fair enough,' he said. 'But just remember, Corvinus, any funny business, any jokes, and when you're finished I'll break both your arms. Follow me.'

He went through the open gate and I followed. The garden in front of the house was immaculate: low box hedges with here and there topiary peacocks or nymphs, clumps of spring flowers edging red-chipped gravel paths raked within an inch of their lives, and more marble statues than you could shake a stick at. Not that contemplating the beauties of tamed nature made me any happier, knowing what I was headed for; given the choice of Eutacticus and a visit to a tooth-puller in Cattlemarket Square I'd've taken the guy with the pliers every time. Especially with Laughing George's sunny little quip putting the icing on the cake. As we climbed the steps towards the open door I crossed my fingers for luck.

This time we didn't go up to the study. Eutacticus was in his private gym, stripped to his undies and exercising with dumb-bells. When we came in he laid them down on a wooden rack with half a dozen others of different weights, reached for a towel and mopped his face, chest and neck. He was in good shape, I'd give him that; big as he was, there wasn't an ounce of flab on his gut, and he wasn't puffing, either.

'Well, Corvinus?' he said.

The tone was about as encouraging as an ice-bath, but then I hadn't expected to be treated as a long-awaited guest. 'Uh . . . you hear the news?' I said. 'About Polydoxus?'

That just got me a look of contempt. Yeah, well; I suppose it was a silly question to ask a racing mogul. He finished patting himself and threw the towel over a stool. 'What about it?' he said.

No point in beating about the bush. 'I need to find the guy who did it. I thought maybe you might help.' No mention of the promised favour; that wasn't the Roman way. He'd work that out for himself.

'Typhon?'

Shit; his contacts were good, right enough. The poisoner's identity would be common knowledge in the Whites' stables, sure, but outside that closed world was another matter. Unless, of course, he'd had the information already . . .

'Yeah,' I said. Then, carefully: 'You, uh, know anything about that, by the way? The, uh, actual poisoning?'

Bad move; *bad* move; I knew that as soon as I asked the question. The hard, cold eyes skewered me, time seemed to stop, and at my back I heard Laughing George grunt like someone had run a needle into him. An eternity later, the eyes shifted and I breathed again.

'No,' Eutacticus said. 'It was no doing of mine, if that's what you meant.' Sure I had, but I didn't comment; I'm not that stupid. Luckily, like there had been some prearranged signal, a slave had come in with a white woollen dressing-gown over his arm. Eutacticus took it from him and put it on, and by the time the guy had left my gaffe had been quietly pushed to one side. 'That's better. You take a regular work-out, Corvinus?'

'Uh . . . no.' Jupiter! Conversation, no less! Well, maybe this was some sort of 'human break' from the demands of an in-your-face aggressive job. 'Not as such.'

'You should. Fitness is important. I'd have every fat-bellied slob on the Senate benches out on Mars Field one day a month exercising like they used to do before the city went rotten.' He belted the dressing-gown; human break over, evidently. If, from the sound of that last squib, you could call it human. Not that I didn't sympathise with the thought of six hundred porkies with faces the colour of their mantle-stripes doing bunny-hops on Rome's traditional exercise ground, but the guy was clearly six steps to the right of Cornelius Scipio. Interesting insight, though: if Cornelius Scipio had still been in charge buggers like Eutacticus would be pulling an oar in the galleys. 'Now you listen and I'll tell you something. Killing a horse is crass. Just as crass as killing a driver, only it's more difficult to arrange, more dangerous and more expensive. I don't kill horses if I can avoid it, Corvinus, any more than I do drivers. Unless all else fails and there's an overriding need, of course, and in Polydoxus's case there wasn't. I'm levelling with you now, you understand. That's a professional opinion and I suggest you take it on trust. You with me?'

'Sure.' Not that I had all that much of an option. He'd put it politely enough, but his tone suggested that giving any other answer would be a very bad mistake indeed. 'Any idea who did do it?'

'Typhon.'

I bit back a comment; not wise, Corvinus, not wise. 'Off his own bat?'

Eutacticus shrugged. 'Maybe. Maybe not. How should I know?'

'Do you?'

I was sailing very close to the wind here, but the question had to be asked. It got me a definite growl from Laughing George, but Eutacticus waved him down. 'I thought I'd made that clear,' he said. 'No. I don't. Not for certain at present, but I will. I have my theories, as no doubt you have yourself, and like I told you before, no one kills in the racing business behind my back. That goes for horses as well as men. If it's the same person who took out the driver then

I'll add Polydoxus to his bill. And believe me, when I have firm proof then I will collect.'

'Even if it turns out to be the junior consul's brother-in-law?'

The room went very quiet. I could hear the squeak of Laughing George's sandals on the marble floor behind me as he shifted his weight.

'Now why should it be Acceptus?' Eutacticus said softly. His eyes had turned hard again.

'It makes sense. Him or Natalis. If you're looking for a simple *cui bono* then the Blues and the Greens are the obvious contenders.'

'Natalis I can understand. The Blues are allied to the Whites. I ask you again, why Sextilius Acceptus?'

'He likes to win; *really* likes to win. He sees the Whites as a back-up team, and that was changing, which he didn't like at all. He was jealous as hell of Pegasus and Polydoxus. These three'll do for motive. As far as opportunity's concerned, it would be a lot easier for him as a Blue to get at our friend Typhon than it would be for Minicius Natalis because Typhon was the White faction's gopher, and there's a lot of coming and going between the two stables.' I paused. 'Finally, like I say, he's a relative of Lucius Vitellius.'

I'd left that last one hanging, but Eutacticus was no fool.

'Who is also a friend of mine,' he said.

I didn't answer, which was an answer in itself. Now I could almost feel Laughing George's breath on my neck.

Eutacticus grinned suddenly; one flash of teeth

then nothing. 'You're a brave man, Marcus Valerius Corvinus,' he said. 'Or a fool. Perhaps both. I've told you I had no hand in Polydoxus's death, and you can believe me or not as you like. I also told you that when I do have firm proof of the killer's identity then I will settle the score myself and in my own way. That you can certainly believe. If it does turn out to be Sextilius Acceptus – with or without Lucius Vitellius's connivance – the same applies. Where business is concerned I don't play favourites. Now I've things to do. It was nice talking to you, but I think you'd better go.'

I felt Laughing George's hands grip my arms like iron clamps, but I didn't move. 'What about Typhon?'

'Oh, I'll find Typhon. If he's alive.' The matter-of-fact certainty of the tone sent a shiver down my spine. 'I have questions of my own to ask that gentleman. And I also pay my debts, Corvinus. I told you last time we met that I owed you a favour for drawing my attention to Pegasus's murder, and I haven't forgotten. If you want a word with Typhon then so be it; when I do run him to ground I'll arrange for you to borrow him for a short time. Only borrow, mind, because I'll need him back. You can leave the delivery arrangements to me. Also, it will, I hope, show you that I really am acting in good faith here.' He looked over my shoulder at Laughing George. 'Show him to the gate.' The grip tightened until I could almost feel bone crushing. I winced, and Eutacticus made a small movement with his hand. 'No. Gently. He's not to be damaged in any way.' The gorilla let me go and stepped back. 'He may be a fool, but he has more sense than to be an enemy. That's so, Corvinus, isn't it?'

I rubbed my arms.

'We'll take that as a yes, shall we?' Eutacticus turned away. 'A pleasure to have met you again. Go safe and stay healthy, you hear?'

Well, I couldn't argue with those sentiments. The latter two, anyway. All the same, I reckoned that my first stop once I'd got shot of the bastard would be the wine garden down the road. After that little interview what I needed was a drink.

It'd have to be a comparatively quick one, though, because Perilla had arranged a confab with Vitellius's wife Sextilia for late afternoon, and the lady insisted on me being bathed, groomed and sober, which was fair enough: you didn't call on the Great and Good smelling like a donkey and looking like an overindulged newt who's been dragged through a hedge backwards. I strolled down the hill with Laughing George's eyes boring into my back every foot of the way – the guy hadn't been happy about letting me off without tying my arms in a knot; it had showed – and into the Garden of Delights. Primrose – only he was Violet this morning because he'd changed his tunic – smiled at me like I was an old and valued customer; probably on the principle that anyone could wander in off the street once by accident and find themselves soaked, but a second visit argued moneyed eccentricity. Added to which, he'd seen me walk through Eutacticus's front gates twice now and come out again with all my bits attached, and obviously anyone who managed that merited careful handling.

'Good-day, sir,' he said. 'And what can I get you this fine morning?'

This time I was ready. 'You have any Caecuban from the thirteenth consulate of the Divine Augustus? That's the one where he had Lucius Cornelius Sulla as his second, not Marcus Plautius Silvanus, of course.'

He didn't bat an eyelid. 'Of course. With Lucius Vinicius taking the second term. The thirty-nine-year-old vintage. Yes, sir. Carafe or demi?'

Shit; I hate these clever-clever wine buffs. 'Uh . . . just make it the half,' I said. He'd have to: time aside, any more and I'd have to talk to my banker. 'Oh – and some bread and cheese.'

'What kind of cheese, sir? We have Gabalican, Docleatan, Vatusican . . .'

'The, uh, the second.' Jupiter! Cheese was cheese was cheese. Where was Agron when I needed him? I was beginning to sweat.

'Wheat bread? Barley and spelt? Or if you'd prefer something more unusual we have an interesting rye and buckwheat loaf baked with honey and caraway seeds, from a little German bakery near the Saepta.'

'Just bread, pal. Use your initiative, okay?'

'Thinly sliced, or . . . ?'

I gave him the eye, and he bowed and went off. Gods! I settled down at a table. The place was empty today; not that it would matter to the profits. It only needed one customer to pay the overheads for a month.

So; recap time. What had we got? First of all, a promise to deliver Typhon, provided the guy was still deliverable. That was a definite plus, and in itself it paid for the hike up the Pincian. Not that I'd care to be in the placard man's sandals when Eutacticus caught up with him: whatever that shark had planned in the way of a conversation I'd bet it didn't include cakes and honey wine for afters. Still, the bastard deserved all he got, and I doubted if the authorities would be any more kindly disposed.

Second was the disclaimer. I wasn't sure how to take that. Eutacticus had seemed straight, and I'd made the point about killing a horse to Perilla myself. All the same, the mention of Acceptus had struck a raw nerve somewhere, and Eutacticus had taken my arguments on board. Sure he had; enough to make the point that if the master of the Blues was responsible then he'd get short shrift. And he'd certainly had ideas of his own, which he wasn't sharing. I wondered if maybe Acceptus and his brother-in-law had had a scam cooking outwith Eutacticus's knowledge, and my theories had triggered a suspicion. That would make sense; like I'd said, with Typhon being the gopher, in and out of the Blues' stables regularly, opportunity wouldn't be a problem: Acceptus could've made his play for the guy's co-operation any time he liked with the Whites being none the wiser.

Whatever the explanation, Eutacticus hadn't been too pleased right from the start at the introduction of the guy's name into the proceedings. And that was interesting.

The wine came in its snow-cooled carafe, along with a jug of water for mixing. I was surprised the bugger hadn't offered me a choice there as well, but evidently even the Garden of Delights hadn't reached that peak of pseudo-sophistication. The cheese turned out to be the hard white variety, with a salty tang. Agron would've loved it. The bread was just bread. I mixed the first cup two-to-one and sipped. Beautiful. Absolutely beautiful. I'd have to watch my time, though.

None of this, of course, let Minicius Natalis off the hook, and from his track record he was the better contender. Certainly where putting the murder and the poisoning together were concerned, and if the two weren't linked I'd eat my mantle. With Pegasus, he was leading by a clear length: the business with Valgius and Delicatus checked out all the way down the line. How Acceptus could've engineered that side of things I hadn't worked out yet; it was possible, sure, but it left all the questions I had an answer to with Natalis still hanging. As the poisoner, too, Natalis was the more likely bet. I knew from my conversation with Cammius and the guy on the Whites' gate that he'd made two attempts already; more, that both attempts had had killing, not doping, as the objective, so he checked out on means as well as motive, at least where the final nature of the modus operandi was concerned. Opportunity, though . . .

Opportunity was the bugger. I sipped the Caecuban, feeling it slip past my tonsils like chilled silk. Acceptus,

sure, no problem: like I said, Typhon could've been
in and out of the Blues' gates and Acceptus's office
six times a day and no one would care; probably they
wouldn't even notice. But the Greens' stables were
another thing entirely, because Green wasn't even
a token ally, and that crucial first approach when
prospective seller weighs up prospective buyer – or
vice versa – to see if they'll play would be tricky as
hell to arrange in practice, if not impossible.

Unless . . .

Hang on. Hang on, now.

Carefully, like I was handling a cobweb, I laid out
the theory bit by tentative bit for mental inspection.
Typhon was a friend – or whatever – of Pegasus;
possibly the only friend he had in the Whites' stable.
Sure, the little weasel had said that he'd been pretty
close-mouthed, but mouths can slip. Especially if they
were drinking pals, which from what Hesper had said
they were. And in any case, I only had that bit of
information from Typhon himself.

I took a swallow of Caecuban. Okay. So far, so
good; at least the connection was there. Now let's
imagine that somewhere, somehow – maybe during
one of their drinking bouts – Typhon gets an inkling
of Pegasus's position as Natalis's agent-in-place. That
wasn't beyond the bounds of possibility: the guy might
be a weasel, but from what I'd seen of him he was
smart as a whip and on the look-out for the main
chance. So. Having weaselled out Pegasus's murky
secret Typhon does a Sopilys: instead of running
to Cammius or Hesper with the news, he comes

to a private arrangement. From Pegasus's point of view, Typhon's a good man to have on the team. He's been with the Whites for years, he's the faction dogsbody, no one pays him any attention. Better still, he's got the entrée to Polydoxus's stall, which Pegasus, being a new boy fresh from the other side of the tracks, probably doesn't, unsupervised anyway. Typhon, through Pegasus, sells out to Natalis. When the time comes, Natalis has his poisoner, and . . .

I stopped. Shit, it wouldn't work. Not the poisoning itself, sure, there was no problem there: Typhon would've managed it anyway, whoever he was working for. Did manage it. The problems came before the poisoning.

First of all, why wait? If Pegasus had recruited Typhon early on, then Polydoxus could've died at any time; certainly there was no point waiting until the night before the Megalenses when the horse would be especially closely guarded. And he had to have recruited him in good time, because fully half a month before the Megalenses Pegasus was already dead. Which was another problem. If Natalis knew – as presumably he did – that he had Typhon in his pocket then why should he kill Pegasus? At least – if he wanted both Pegasus and Polydoxus dead in any case – before he'd got rid of the horse, because killing Pegasus would surely have spooked Typhon. And that raised yet a third problem: if Natalis knew he already had two agents in place, one with good access to the horse, then why faff around with the two other attempts which didn't come off?

Then, finally, there was the problem of Cammius's evidence. He and Cario had caught Pegasus – Pegasus, not Typhon – trying to kill the horse. If Pegasus had Typhon on the team, and Typhon had the better access, what was he doing acting on his own account? You didn't keep a dog and bark yourself; that was axiomatic.

Shit. For all the drawbacks there was something there, I'd swear to it. I just wasn't seeing things from the right angle. I took another mouthful of wine.

Okay. Start again.

Let's say Pegasus didn't recruit Typhon at all: the guy was on his own, with a mandate from Natalis to kill the horse, as per the original theory. That got rid of all the problems at a stroke. The two attempts could easily have been blinds, to draw the Whites' attention away from Pegasus himself, the real potential killer in situ. Pegasus's own attempt was thwarted, which made him a liability and led to his murder. So far so good.

Enter Typhon. The guy knows, or knew rather, because Pegasus is dead by this time, that he was playing a double game; see above. More, he knows who for, and since Pegasus had to have arranged some sort of meeting schedule with Natalis he's had the wit to follow him and suss out the details, perhaps – again like Sopilys – with a view to blackmail. Maybe it was as simple as pinpointing Valgius and the Eighth District Watch-house. Then, suddenly, Pegasus is murdered. Typhon has no reason – then or later – to link the killing with Natalis: Pegasus is his agent, and why should Natalis have his own agent murdered? In any case, it clears the ground. Typhon knows that he's the only game in town, and he sets up a meeting of his own with the Greens' boss who – he presumes, rightly – is still interested in getting rid of Polydoxus. That would make sense. There was still the time lag, sure – the full half month plus between Pegasus's death and the poisoning – but any arrangement would take a while to conclude, and in any case for Typhon choosing the night before the Megalenses wouldn't pose a problem. Quite the reverse: his bringing the stall guards their wine was a standard thing, and all the faction's attention would be focused on strangers breaking in, not on purely internal security because the night before a race was the only time when they could be sure the stables were sealed. The aftermath was no problem either, because the guy wouldn't be sticking around, not when the whodunnit was obvious. And the interval would've given him a chance to plot his own escape in detail.

I sat back. It would work; sure it would. As a theory, anyway. The actual truth would have to wait until I – or Eutacticus, rather – laid hands on Typhon himself. The bottom line was that I could make a case against Natalis on the grounds of all three categories: motive, opportunity and means.

The problem was that the same went for Acceptus. As far as Polydoxus went, anyway. Bugger; sleuthing wasn't easy. Still, at least I was up and running again. Perilla had been right: if I'd chucked the case I would've been kicking myself.

I glanced up at the sun. Not all that far off noon. If we weren't to keep the Lady Sextilia waiting I'd have to get a move on. It was good brain stuff, though, that Caecuban. That had been a useful half-hour's work.

I took the rest of the carafe as slow as I dared, giving it the attention it deserved, which was a considerable amount. This close to lunch, the place was filling up a little: the Senate was in session again, but not all broad-stripers by any means were conscientious attenders and there was a fair scattering of the buggers at the other tables just getting into name-dropping gear. I winced as the voices carried over. Wine first-rate but pricey as hell, clientele the pits. Average it out and I'd rate the place six out of ten: worth the occasional visit, sure, if your bank balance could stand it, but give me Renatius's every time. I mixed the last cupful, drank it down, paid my score (ouch! But at least this time they hadn't asked for money up-front) and headed back to the Caelian for the bath and beauty treatment.

We'd have to see what Sextilia had to offer.

34

We took the litter. Perilla had on her best glad rags, and I'd had Bathyllus look out the snappy mantle the lady had given me for the Winter Festival that I hadn't got round to wearing yet. It felt uncomfortable and scratchy as hell.

Estranged in practice they might be, but Vitellius and Sextilia still lived together. The house was on the posh southern slope of the Esquiline, near the grove and shrine of Beech-tree Jupiter. It was expensive but not showy, yet again an indication that Vitellius was being careful to keep his head below the politically correct parapet, because the Wart, who was technically still in charge although he hadn't set foot inside the city boundaries for years, had a thing about ostentation. We drew up outside and I sent our chief lardball – carefully groomed – to knock at the door. Then we made our entrance.

While the slave went to check that the lady was all set to receive I gave the place the once-over. Nice; very nice. Decor pricey but subdued, good taste. It didn't have a very lived-in feel, though, and there was a coldness about it that had nothing to do with the weather.

The slave came back. 'If you'll follow me, sir and madam, the mistress is expecting you,' he said.

He took us into what turned out to be a sitting-room overlooking the garden. This had a lot more life to it: there were bowls of spring bulbs on the table, bronze and silver knick-knacks and one of those snooty pedigree Egyptian cats with the high pointed ears who stared at us from a cushioned stool with eyes like emerald ice then carried on with its interrupted ablutions. Fresh air blew in through the opening on to the portico and the garden beyond.

Sextilia was lying on the couch near the cat. 'Perilla, dear,' she said. 'Lovely to see you. And this must be your husband. *So* nice to meet you at last, Valerius Corvinus. Have a seat, please.'

She was a looker, or must've been when she was younger: small, prim, early forties maybe, impeccably got up. Nice voice, too.

'Did you have a good festival, Sextilia?' Perilla sat on a Gallic chair with red leather upholstery. I took the second couch.

'Very pleasant, thank you.' She smiled. 'I went to the production in Balbus Theatre with Silvia Gemina. The *Antigone*. You didn't see it? Oh, but you should have, dear, it was marvellous. Alciphron was *so* good as the princess, and the costumes you wouldn't believe!'

Uh-oh; here we went. I hate this social chit-chat stuff, and this bit I hadn't been looking forward to. I sighed mentally and switched off. We'd talked things over, Perilla and me, before we'd left and agreed that it was her show, which included handling the small talk.

Very wise. The lady hadn't, of course, let on to Sextilia about any ulterior purpose and officially we were here just for honey-wine-and-cake-klatsch reasons with me tagging along for decoration. Speaking of which, the refreshments turned up ten minutes into the dissection of Sophocles and the slave served me with a bumper cup. I set it down on the delicate little table next to me and forgot about it.

I was just nodding off nicely when Perilla said, 'We saw your husband and brother at the races, by the way. Marcus had passes for the Whites' row from Lucius Cammius. Such a pity for the poor man, first his lead driver dying and then that horse.' She turned to me. 'What was its name again, Marcus?'

'Polydoxus.' I sat up. Business at last. Mind you, I wasn't going to push things. Perilla could make the running.

'I don't really take much notice of racing.' Sextilia was holding her piece of cake delicately with the fingers of both hands. She reminded me of a very neat dormouse. 'It's very much a man's thing, isn't it? Father was a real aficionado, and of course Gaius has inherited his interest. Lucius, naturally—' She hesitated. 'Lucius enjoys it too. Rather too much, I'm afraid.'

Perilla sipped her wine. 'He's involved with the faction?' she said. 'On the business side, I mean?'

'Oh, yes. Since before we were married. Gaius has the acumen, but he doesn't have the money, and running a faction is so very expensive. Especially if one wants to build it up.'

'And Gaius does?'

'More than anything. He does so like to *win*; he has done since he was a child. It's all so silly.' She stretched over to the cake plate. 'More cake, dear? And your husband isn't eating. Such a quiet man, not at all as you described him. I wish Lucius was more quiet. You're very fortunate.'

Perilla shot me a glance. I picked up my slice and bit into it: sickly sweet, like the wine would be. 'It's, uh, very nice, Sextilia,' I said.

'Gaius must be rather relieved that the Whites have had so many setbacks recently.' Perilla sipped her honey wine. My teeth tingled in sympathy.

'Oh, he is.' Sextilia frowned. 'He wouldn't like to say so too publicly, of course, because they are supposed to be allies in a way, but it certainly hasn't done him any harm. Especially since his faction has been going through such a bad patch. One can hardly blame him, can one?'

'Of course not.' Perilla paused. 'Lucius would be pleased as well, I expect.'

'Lucius's feelings are not ones to which I am a party, dear.' Sextilia cut another slice of cake and held it out to Perilla's waiting plate. 'As you're no doubt aware.' Not so much the dormouse after all: there'd been an edge to that. I could sense Perilla backing off. 'But yes, he was pleased. Extremely so.'

There was silence while we ate our cake. Then Perilla said, 'I've always felt that the racing world was a' – she hesitated – 'well, not to put too fine a point on it, rather an *undesirable* one to become involved in.

Not that I'm implying that either your brother or your husband would have anything to do with that side of things, of course, but it must be very difficult at times to avoid it. Especially where business is concerned. Marcus was just telling me before we came out that he'd had a most unpleasant brush recently with one man in particular—' She turned to me. 'What was his name, Marcus?'

I swallowed my cake. 'Uh . . . Eutacticus?'

'That's right. A dreadful man, simply dreadful. You wouldn't know him or know of him, my dear, but—'

'The cartel owner.' Sextilia was nodding. 'Yes, I know Eutacticus. Lucius has him round to dinner quite often. Gaius, too, occasionally, as I understand, and they both visit him on the Pincian. You're perfectly right, he is a dreadful man.'

I tried to keep my face expressionless. Shit! Vitellius's friendship with Eutacticus I'd known about, of course, but Acceptus's was only theory. I had proof now that the three of them were an item, and that had very interesting connotations.

'You're . . . present yourself? When your husband invites him here?' Perilla asked delicately.

'Oh, Eutacticus is very strong on family values.' Sextilia didn't smile. 'Quite the old-fashioned conservative. I've never met his wife – he does have one, although he never brings her – but he insists that when he dines here I attend the dinner. Or so Lucius informs me. Until the dessert is cleared, at least, at which point I'm free to go. Which I always do, gladly, and come in here. I spend a lot of my time in here. Its one great advantage is that as a room Lucius hates it.'

I don't think I've ever heard so much quiet loathing in a voice. Not that Sextilia had put any sort of feeling into the words because she hadn't, quite the opposite, in fact: the tone was polite, well-modulated and, along with the rest of her, downright prim. Maybe that's what made it so chilling.

'So you never hear them talking business?' I said.

Perilla flashed me a glare, which was fair enough: I was in total breach of contract here and I knew it. All the same, it seemed a natural thing to say at the time.

Sextilia turned to me. If the question should've struck her as odd – especially since it was the first real contribution to the conversation I'd made since we sat down – she didn't show it. I had the impression, strangely, that she was somehow relieved. 'No, Valerius Corvinus,' she said. 'I don't. Unfortunately. I might find that quite interesting, if not exactly enjoyable; it would certainly be preferable to having constantly to deflect Eutacticus's questions concerning the doings of my children, both of whom take after their father. Given that the elder is currently being debauched on Capri and the younger trying his best to meet a similar fate in Rome you will understand the reasons for the preference.'

There was a painful silence while Perilla and I picked at our cake. I wondered if coming here had been such a hot idea after all. Sure, I'd got confirmation of Acceptus's involvement with Eutacticus, but that was all it was: confirmation. Hardly sufficient return for having to eat a lump of poisonous honey cake and sit through an episode of mid-life-crisis soul-searching.

Maybe Sextilia thought so too, because she set her plate down. 'I'm sorry, that was very boring of me. Treat it as a digression, if you will.' She paused. 'They do talk business, of course, and since you seem interested in the subject I have nothing particularly against indulging your curiosity. If it is simply curiosity which, forgive me, I very much doubt.' I didn't say anything. Smart lady. 'You see, I'm not quite stupid, nor am I blind, and Perilla has mentioned your . . . field of expertise to me before. It isn't so very long since Lucius Arruntius and the Chief Vestal asked you to look into the death of that young Cornelia at my husband's predecessor's house, is it? Three or four months at most?'

'Uh . . . four and a half. The Rites of the Good Goddess.' I didn't even glance at Perilla.

'Besides, I know my husband.' She reached over and picked up the cat, tucking it in against her mantle and cradling it. It gave a low yowl like a mewling baby and stretched its neck to be stroked. 'And my brother. Gaius may not be quite as bad as Lucius, but he is very single-minded, and scruples have never been a great obstacle to him once he's decided what he wants. If it is of any relevance, and as long as we're speaking truths, we have never got on well, especially since as head of the family after Father's death he sold me to Lucius. Now what do *you* want, Valerius

Corvinus? I assume this has something to do with the affair at the Whites' stables?'

'Uh, yeah. Yeah, that's right.' I was feeling a bit adrift here. The strange thing was, although the content of the conversation had taken a distinctly personal turn, Sextilia's tone hadn't changed from the Esquiline-genteel it had started out as. Unsettling, right?

She smoothed the cat's ears. 'You think that Gaius – and Lucius and that terrible man Eutacticus – might have been behind the poisoning of the horse.'

Now I did glance at Perilla. She had sat back in her chair. 'It's a possibility. No more.'

'Indeed.' Another hesitation; her eyes didn't leave the cat. 'They certainly discussed the new season and how to minimise the other two factions' chances. That I do know from the occasional remark made by Lucius in his cups, or when he thought he was talking over my head. Both Whites' and Greens'. I can give you no details, though.'

'Whites' *and* Greens'?'

'So I understood. Sit still, Nefertare,' she said to the cat, who was glaring at me and wriggling. Her eyes came up. 'I appreciate your earlier delicacy, Perilla dear, but I don't think that either my brother or my husband would hesitate for a moment to use underhand methods in furthering the faction's ends. Clandestinely, of course. Lucius especially has to be so very careful of his political image. A certain amount of . . . moral latitude is allowed, naturally, but there are boundaries. And although the Whites aren't too important, going against the Greens does have certain political ramifications.'

Yeah; I could see that for a political figure like Lucius Vitellius to be caught treading on the crown prince's toes might be a bad idea. Still, it made sense: the Whites might be up and coming but the Greens were the bigger problem long-term. If our unholy triumvirate were engaged in a scam to bring on the Blues then they'd have to have a plan to cover both. 'You really can't help with the details?'

'No. I do know, however, that Lucius regards Minicius Natalis as a prime obstacle because his name crops up frequently when Lucius and Gaius talk. Much of a faction's success depends on the quality of the leadership – you can see that from the terrible mess poor Rufrius Pudens is making of the Reds – and Natalis is an extremely good faction master. He has the contacts and the experience, of course, and also the ruthlessness to bring his faction on. If it were not for Natalis the Greens would be far less of a threat.'

I found myself grinning. 'I thought you said you didn't know much about racing, Sextilia.'

Her fingers reached under the cat's chin. It purred. 'That isn't racing, Valerius Corvinus, it's politics and the observance of human nature. I never denied either an interest in or an affinity for either of those things.'

True. And prim as the lady was, she had her head screwed on. Certainly she'd given me something to think about here.

'Now.' With a sudden movement she picked up

the protesting cat and laid it gently back down on its cushion. Her lips twitched in a smile. 'That is really all the help I can provide. Perhaps if you've fulfilled your purpose in coming you'll forgive me if I talk with your wife about more important things.' She turned to Perilla. 'Such as your late stepfather's own venture into playwriting, my dear. I came across a copy of his *Medea* in the Pollio Library yesterday and was very impressed with it, although I was puzzled by some of the allusions. If your husband has quite finished then perhaps you might help me with them.'

Oh, bugger. Well, I'd had my turn right enough, and it had to be paid for. Also by the looks of things discussing plays and poetry was about all the fun the lady was getting out of life, so I didn't grudge her her chance. A pity: there was a first-class brain there. I settled back and let Perilla take over.

We stayed for another half-hour or so until the conversation flagged. Finally, Perilla got up.

'We have to go, Sextilia,' she said. 'It really has been most enjoyable, hasn't it, Marcus?'

'Yeah.' I levered myself off the couch. My right leg had gone to sleep and the rest of me had nearly followed. 'Very.' The middle bit had been, anyway.

'I'm glad.' The lady had her well-bred party manners on again. She rose gracefully. 'Oh, and Valerius Corvinus?'

'Yeah?'

'I won't say, Good Luck with your investigation, for obvious reasons; however, I wish you well. If my husband and brother are involved, then they have only themselves to blame if any trouble results. You understand me, I hope.'

'Sure. I understand.' I did; Sextilia was getting as close as a gently brought-up, conventional, mild-mannered lady could to damning her nearest relatives' eyes and hoping they fried in hell. I had every sympathy.

'Good. Perilla, dear, I'll see you at our next meeting. I look forward to it.'

The slave showed us out. As we were getting into the litter, I noticed a couple of guys in tunics coming up the street from the direction of town, obviously headed for the house's servants' entrance. If they hadn't stopped for an instant and done an involuntary double-take when they saw me I wouldn't have given them a second glance; as it was, I did.

I knew them; sure I did. They were the pair of tunics who'd given us the eye at Cybele's procession. And the one with the missing incisor looked, when our glances met, guilty as hell.

Click.

I must've been beaming as we swung back down the road towards dinner, because Perilla said; 'Well, Marcus, are you satisfied?'

'Yeah. You could put it like that.'

She smiled. 'Glad you didn't give up after all?'

'Uh-huh.' I leaned over and kissed her. 'We're off and running again. Acceptus is a major contender for the poisoning, him and Lucius Vitellius, and if they did the poisoning then they did the murder as well.

One gets you ten it was a set-up; two birds with one stone. And now we've got solid proof.'

'How do you mean?'

'The thing was a Blue faction scam, lady. Our three beauties were out to hamstring the Whites and land Natalis in it at the same time. Or at least two of them were, because I'm still not sure about Eutacticus, not as far as the whole scenario's concerned, that is. My guess is they were playing an even dirtier game than he knew about.'

Perilla sighed. 'I'm sorry, dear, I'm not at my brightest at present. You'll have to explain.'

'Didn't you see the guy out there with the tooth? Or rather without the tooth? That's the clincher.'

'Marcus, what on *earth* are you talking about? Calm down and start at the beginning, please.'

Jupiter! I took a deep breath. 'All right. According to Cammius, Natalis had been targeting Polydoxus for months. There were two attempts, neither of which got past the gate. One was made by the kid Stephanus who'd been approached by a Green outside a wineshop, the other by a Greens' mucker-out masquerading as a hay delivery man. Yes?'

'Yes. Of course. But—'

'Wait a moment, Perilla. That's only the author-ised version. I assumed – Cammius assumed, we all assumed, because it was the natural assumption and that's the way the evidence pointed – that both attempts were Natalis's doing, but we were wrong. Oh, sure, Natalis wanted the horse dead and he wouldn't've scrupled to poison it on his own account, but he wasn't the guilty party. Not in this case, anyway. Like I say, he was set up.'

'Yes, but Marcus—'

'Sextilia made an interesting point. She said that her husband and brother were planning to scupper the Whites *and* the Greens. Okay, so how do they do that the most economical way possible? They poison the Whites' horse but arrange for the finger to point at Natalis.'

'Yes, but Marcus—'

'Obviously, Acceptus can't involve any of his own men in the scam, even as go-betweens, because the racing world's a small community and there's too big a chance of them being recognised, especially if the attempt doesn't come off and the guy with the knife or the poison is caught. In fact, if he *is* caught – preferably after he's done the business – it's all to the good because like I say the finger will point to Natalis. That's where Lucius Vitellius comes in.'

'Yes, but Marcus—'

'Hold on, lady. Let me finish. We don't know anything about the Greens' stable-hand because the poor bastard met with a terminal accident right after he was caught, but Stephanus told me the guy who recruited him had a tooth missing. One gets you ten that was the same tunic we saw at the Megalensia, because although I didn't know him he sure as hell knew me. I doubt if that was intentional – there was no reason for him to follow me around – but it was his bad luck we coincided; crooks like processions as much as anyone else, and Cattlemarket Square corner's a popular venue for rubbernecks. Seeing him up on the Esquiline headed for Vitellius's staff entrance is a different thing, and like I said it's the clincher. I'll bet a jar of thirty-nine-year-old Caecuban to a bad mussel he's our agent-provocateur, which means Acceptus and Vitellius are eyebrow-deep in effluvia and I can prove it because Stephanus will be able to identify him.' I sat back against the cushions. 'There, now. QED. You were about to say?'

'You're forgetting about Pegasus, dear. Not his murder, his attempt on Polydoxus. That had to be Natalis's doing, surely.'

That came out in her best put-down voice. I grinned. It wasn't often that I had a comeback to Perilla's objections; this time I did. 'Uh-uh. I'm not forgetting, lady. I never said Natalis was pure as the driven snow, just that he wasn't responsible for the two failed attempts. Sure it was his doing; maybe the actual poisoning was as well for all I know. What I do know now for absolute certain is that the Greens and the Blues were both after Polydoxus, with Acceptus and Vitellius running their double scam while Natalis was relying on his agent-in-place. And if both factions were targeting Polydoxus then ipso facto they both had a reason for targeting the driver. Right?'

Perilla was frowning. 'So who was responsible for actually killing the horse?'

I shrugged. 'Jupiter knows. That's the crucial question. If Eutacticus can locate Typhon then fine, but at the moment the two are neck and neck. I can make a case for either, especially now I've got Gap-Tooth in the bag.'

We were nearly home, which suited me perfectly: travelling by litter isn't my favourite form of locomotion, it had been a long day, Sextilia's cake hadn't exactly been filling and I was starving. Also, what with the only thing liquid on offer being honey wine, I'd've murdered for a drink. We pulled up outside the front door and got out. Bathyllus, as usual, was waiting with the tray.

I sank the first cup. Beautiful.

'Dinner nearly ready, sunshine?' I said.

'Yes, sir.' He poured again. 'Oh, and there was a message for you. From someone by the name of Sopilys.'

I paused, the cup halfway to my lips. 'Yeah?'

'He wants to meet you, sir. Tomorrow, in Ostia, at the same time and place as before. I got the impression it was quite urgent.'

I scowled. Shit; this didn't make sense. When I'd seen Sopilys I'd given him Agron's address in case he wanted to get in touch, but he'd said he'd told me all he knew. So why did the guy suddenly want to talk to me again? And urgently, what was more? 'The messenger say what it was about?'

'No, sir.' Bathyllus hesitated. 'Only that some information was involved. And that it would be expensive. He suggested that you bring with you the sum of twenty gold pieces.'

'He suggested *what*?' Luckily, I hadn't taken a mouthful of wine because I would've choked and sprayed it all over my nice new mantle. Sweet gods! For someone like the erstwhile Greens' groom and current barge-unloader twenty gold pieces was a fortune. Come to that, it wasn't chickenfeed to me, either.

'I was to add that the price was not negotiable.'

I glanced at Perilla, who'd come in behind me just in time to hear the monetary details. Her eyes were wide too. 'Anything else?'

'No, sir. That was all.'

Brain churning, I downed half the new cupful and reached for the jug. Sopilys might be a prime chancer, but he was no fool. Twenty gold pieces, non-negotiable, might be a hell of a lot of gravy, but on the other hand it argued that he had something really worthwhile to sell. Or thought he had, anyway. So what could it be?

I'd have to wait until the next day to find out.

35

I got to Ostia next day just shy of noon – perfect timing – and went straight down to the harbour. The wharf where I'd met Sopilys last time was straight-forward to find, only a couple of hundred yards from the main gates, so I parked the horse with a few others being looked after by the young entrepreneur near the port master's office on the corniche and did the rest on foot. I'd brought the money in a small leather pouch just in case, but whatever Sopilys had to sell it'd have to be pretty damn good for me to part with all twenty coins. Maybe last time I'd been too generous: he'd asked for five silver pieces and ended up with half a big one so perhaps he had an inflated idea of what he could screw out of me. That, at least, was one explanation, and it could well be the most likely. Still, I'd be seriously displeased if I'd come all this way for nothing.

The pile of hides was gone, of course, but its place had been taken by a mound of roof tiles; whether outward bound or inward, I didn't know. There was no sign of Sopilys. I glanced up at the sun: noon, more or less. I couldn't remember exactly when the meeting last time had been, but I doubted if noon was much out either way. I settled down to wait.

An hour later I was still waiting, and not too happy about it; we were definitely out of time here now with no possibility of error. I wondered if maybe for some reason I'd mistaken the place, but two or three yards off there was a bollard with a sizeable lump knocked out of it that I remembered noticing before. Shit. If the little rat had stood me up I'd kill him. Finally when a boat pulled up alongside me and a gang of stevedores moved in to load the tiles I decided I'd had enough. I picked one of the men at random as he hoisted a dozen or so of them on to his shoulder.

'Hey, pal.'

He paused in that sort of crick-neck stance you get when you're seriously weighed down between neck and shoulder-blade. 'Yeah?'

'You know a guy called Sopilys, by any chance? He was supposed to meet me here around noon.'

The guy chuckled. 'Sure I know him. Knew him, rather. If you're waiting to meet Sopilys, friend, you'll wait a hell of a long time.'

My guts went cold. Oh, no. Oh, bugger. 'He's . . . uh . . . Something's happened to him?'

'Little bastard got himself knifed last night in an alley round the side of Ma Glyce's place.' He shifted the tiles and spat. 'Good riddance. He was a lead-swinger if I ever saw one.'

'Ma Glyce's place?'

'It's a wineshop and knocking-shop opposite the gates. You can't miss it.' He turned ponderously and staggered off without another word across the boat's gangplank.

I just stood there feeling gutted. Shit. It couldn't be a coincidence; no way could it be a coincidence. Not the alley, sure: that was eerie in the context, but nine-tenths of the stabbings, bludgeonings and garrottings that happen in the less salubrious districts of Rome – and, presumably, in Ostia as well – happen in alleys, where the mugger drags or otherwise inveigles the muggee so the business can be conducted in private. Just the fact that, a few hours after he'd sent me a message saying he had important information to sell, Sopilys was conveniently dead. On the other hand, no coincidence or not, it didn't make sense. Ostia was sixteen miles from Rome, by his own account Sopilys had severed his ties with the stables and he was a spent coin. Except he wasn't, obviously, because either he'd remembered something that he realised was crucially important or he'd stumbled across some new information. But even so that didn't explain how chummie had known about it, let alone been so quick off the mark in shutting his mouth before he could talk to me.

Unless, of course, Sopilys had tried to blackmail chummie, been unsuccessful and turned to me instead on the rebound. That would be in character at least, and twenty gold pieces was an appreciable whack; certainly whatever information they represented would justify a special trip down to Ostia with a knife in your belt . . .

Ah, hell; I was trying to make bricks without mud

here. Before I could theorise I had to have facts to go on, and the only place I'd get them was this Ma Glyce's. I set off for the gates.

Halfway there a thought struck me. Practically the last thing Sopilys had said when we'd talked was that if word got out that he'd put me on to Eutacticus he was dead. Now he was. The cold gripped my gut again, but I shook the thought away. No, that couldn't be it, because I hadn't mentioned Sopilys, hadn't even hinted at him. Eutacticus was a well-informed bugger, but he wasn't omniscient, and in any case what did it matter? If he'd let me go with practically a nod, a smile and a cheery wave he wouldn't've bothered about the guy who'd put me on to him. At least, I didn't think so . . .

Jupiter! I could get paranoid here. Facts first, theories later. I went through the gates and crossed the road.

Ma Glyce's didn't have a sign outside, but it was obvious I'd found the right place, if only from the girl hanging around the door. With advertisements like that, you don't need signs.

'Special price between now and sunset,' she said. I'd heard livelier invitations to a burning.

'Uh . . . right. Yeah.' I grinned at her. 'That's pretty lucky, sister, because tonight's a full moon and after sunset things might get a little tricky.'

She gave me a nervous look and edged away. I flashed her another smile, took a detour round her prominent superstructure and went in.

Not the most upmarket wineshop – let alone knocking-shop – I'd ever seen. If the old Spartans had gone in for such things, which they didn't, not at home at any rate, they would've avoided the place because it was too basic. There wasn't even a counter, just a few benches scattered round the room that looked as if they were waiting to be chopped up and used as kindling. A greasy curtain across the door in the opposite wall no doubt hid the carnal side of the business from prying eyes. I was the only customer, which at that time of day was fair enough because I couldn't see the place catering for anything but bargees, and none too picky ones, at that, and they'd all be on the waterfront hefting roof tiles.

'You want wine?' The old woman on the trestle stool next to the curtain held up a ladle. As far as the grease-to-fibre ratio went, between her tunic and the curtain I'd've bet on the tunic.

'Uh . . . yeah.' I took out my purse – not the one with Sopilys's gold pieces in it, the everyday one – and opened it. 'What've you got, grandma?'

She wheezed to herself for two or three seconds, picked up a cup from a pile on the floor and dipped the ladle into what I'd thought might be an old stew-pot set there to catch the drips from the roof. 'That's a copper. And less of the "grandma".'

'Right. Right.' I handed over the coin and took the cup. Holy Bacchus! Eat your heart out, Garden of Delights! Still, it saved on eye-strain. 'I, uh, hear you had a stabbing last night. Guy called Sopilys.'

'You from the Watch?'

'No, I'm—'

'Only I can't stand these buggers.'

'I was due to meet him today. On business. You know what happened exactly?'

'The day I don't know what's going on in my own place you can lay me out on the timber and throw on the torch.'

'Fine. Fine.' I waited. Nothing.

'What's wrong with the wine?' she said.

'Uh . . . nothing.' I took a sip; no more, because I valued my tonsils. 'Delicious.'

She wheezed again. 'You're a bloody liar, son.'

I grinned and set the cup down on the nearest bench where it couldn't do any more harm. 'Yeah. So tell me what happened to Sopilys.'

'He was talking to . . .' She stopped. 'No, I'm wrong, that was the night before. He's in most nights – or used to be in, I suppose I'd better say now, the poor bastard – so I lose track. Last night he was with a couple of the lads from his gang, only he left early. One of the customers found him in the alley when he went for a piss.'

Almost Pegasus, but not quite. Close enough for the modus operandi to match, though, which was interesting in spite of everything. 'Any idea who did it?'

That got me another bout of wheezing: she was a cheerful old biddy, if nothing else. 'No. It happens, sometimes, round here but not as often as you'd think. Usually it's over a girl or something that's happened at work, and it's all up-front. Whoever killed him didn't do it for his money, anyway. The bugger was broke, which was why he left early. Not that that's surprising because he'd been splashing it around since before the Kalends.'

Well, I couldn't read much into that. He'd had my half gold piece, for a start, and I doubted if 'splashing it around' in old Ma Glyce's terms would amount to half a silver Wart in an evening. Certainly with wine at a copper a cup, horse piss or not, on half a gold piece he could've stayed drunk from now to the Winter Festival, and taken a large slice of his pals with him . . .

I stopped.

Yeah, right. Of course he could. So hang on, Corvinus. In that case why was he broke the day after the Megalensia? Sure, he could've spent the money elsewhere, but half a gold piece was half a gold piece and it was an interesting question that needed an answer, one way or the other.

I realised the old woman was staring at me.

'You all right, son?' she said.

'Uh . . . yeah. Yeah. You haven't seen any strangers around in the last couple of days, have you?'

That set her off wheezing again. 'In case you haven't noticed that's the harbour gates across the road. Strangers is something I see quite a bit of. Especially in my line of work.'

'I mean, uh, unusual strangers. Not bargees or nautical types.'

'None of these. I get the lads off the boats, mostly because of Chloe, and the stevedores like Sopilys, but that's all. The skippers, the mates and the travelling gentry go further along the corniche. You're the first purple-striper I've ever had in here.'

Well, that wasn't surprising. I couldn't see Gaius Sextilius Acceptus or Lucius Vitellius popping in for a cup of sedimenty vinegar and a chat. Mind you, if it had been them – or Minicius Natalis, for that matter – that were behind the stabbing I doubted if they'd've done it personally, and the actual killer would've been a nondescript tunic rather than a mantle. Which reminded me. 'You said Sopilys had been talking to someone when he was in two nights ago. That wasn't a stranger, was it?'

'No, son. Or not the way you mean. It was one of the hands on the *Phorcys*, name of Avillius. Quite matey, they got. And as I say Sopilys was splashing it around.'

'This Avillius a friend of Sopilys's?'

'No. He's not in here often enough to have regular friends. The *Phorcys* works the Sicily–Africa route as a rule, but now and again she'll go all the way along the Mauretanian coast and over to Baetica and Tarraco. Sometimes even through the Pillars and up to Lusitania.' I blinked, mentally: it wasn't often you got an old wineshop biddy with a working knowledge of geography, but then geography – the maritime sort, anyway – would be something you'd get to know pretty quickly in a dockside wineshop. Ostia, like any port, looks out, not in.

More to the point, the hairs on the back of my neck were prickling. Always a good sign. 'You have any idea what they talked about?' I said.

She shook her head. 'Sorry, son. Customers talk to me, I talk back, but I don't force myself into conversations and I don't listen in, neither. You do that and you end up hearing what you don't want to, and that only leads to trouble. They were thick enough, though. Heads together in the corner all evening, and Sopilys bought the drink.'

'He had plenty of money that night, then.' The prickle had moved up the scale to a full-blown itch. I was on to something here, sure I was.

'Oh, aye. It was last night he was broke.'

'You, uh, happen to know where I can find this Avillius?'

'He'll've slept on the boat. But I doubt you'll find the *Phorcys* still in harbour, not unless she hasn't managed to pick up a cargo.'

'Where would she be berthed?'

'The port master would know. But like I say, you're wasting your time.'

'Yeah. Yeah, maybe.' I took a silver piece out of my purse and gave it to her. 'Thanks a lot, mother. And thanks for the wine.'

She took to wheezing again. I turned to go. I'd reached the door when she said, 'Son?'

I looked round. 'Yeah?'

'If you go to Sicily then watch your back.'

I frowned. 'What?'

'If you go to Sicily then watch your back.'

The hairs rose on my scalp. 'Uh . . . why should I want to do that? Go to Sicily?'

She shrugged. 'I don't know. But if you do, be

careful. I've got the Sight, same as my mother had. Sometimes the words pop into my head and I have to say them, whether they make sense or not. You just remember, right?'

'Yeah. Yeah, I'll remember,' I said.

I walked along the corniche to the port master's office, stopping off to tell the entrepreneur with my horse that I'd be a while yet and giving the kid something on account. I got one of the pimply clerks.

'The *Phorcys*?' he said. 'That'll be master Maximus, out of Catana?'

Catana. Halfway down the east coast of Sicily, between the Straits and Syracuse. 'Yeah. Yeah, that's right.'

He consulted a wax tablet. 'I'm sorry, sir. She sailed this morning.'

Shit. 'You any idea when she'll be back?'

'No, sir. But I doubt it'll be much before next month, longer if she has a commission for western waters. What was your interest?'

'I was, uh, hoping to have a word with one of the crew. A man by the name of Avillius.'

'Ah.' The clerk frowned. 'If you wouldn't mind waiting just a moment, sir, I'll consult my colleague.' He got up and crossed over to another pimply guy at a desk in the corner piled high with wax tablets. There was a murmured conversation and the other pimple-face nodded once or twice.

What was going on here?

My pimple-face came back. 'I'm sorry, sir, I was just

checking on the name to make absolutely certain. I'm afraid Avillius was involved in a wharfside accident yesterday.'

I stared at him. Holy sweet gods! 'The guy's dead?'

Pimple-Face smiled. 'Coming off second-best in an argument with a marble column drum dropped from a crane does have that effect.' Then the look on my face must've registered, because the smile slipped. 'I'm sorry, sir, that was facetious. Was it a personal matter? There wouldn't be any next-of-kin I could refer you to, of course, and the ship has already gone, but—'

'No. No. I didn't know the man. It was just business.' My brain was still spinning. Oh, Jupiter alive! 'What happened exactly?'

The clerk shrugged. 'That I don't know, sir. We wouldn't have known about the incident at all – the docks are a big place, and accidents like this happen all the time – but one of my other colleagues was checking a manifest aboard another ship moored nearby shortly afterwards and he . . . saw the aftermath. It wasn't very pleasant.'

Yeah; I'd imagine it wouldn't've been. 'Look, pal,' I said, 'you wouldn't be able to put me on to anyone who actually witnessed the death, would you?'

He gave me a strange look. Well, I supposed you did get ghouls who were vicariously interested in things like that; I'd met some myself. 'That shouldn't be a problem. It happened on Wharf Fifteen while the ship was loading. The gang boss there is a man called Vultacilius. You could talk to him if you liked.'

'Where's Wharf Fifteen?'

'Go through the gates and turn right. It's about three hundred yards along.'

'Fine. Thanks.' I turned. 'Uh . . . the ship being loaded was the *Phorcys* itself, wasn't it?'

'Yes. That's right.'

I left.

Vultacilius was easy to spot; bosses usually are, because they're the ones who are standing with their arms folded while the other buggers work. Which was more or less the situation on Wharf Fifteen, where the loading gang was transferring big bales of cloth from an anchored merchantman to the wharfside while he watched them do it. I went over, identified myself and explained what I wanted.

'Sure. I was there at the time,' he said. 'It was pretty nasty.'

'You, uh, care to give me the details?' I said.

He stared at a big guy tottering down the angled gangplank with a bale twice as big as he was like the entertainment had been got up special. Finally he turned back to me. 'Happened yesterday morning. The *Phorcys* was loading marble drums bound for some rich bugger in Syracuse and we were using the crane.' He nodded over to the wood and rope construction on a turntable further along the wharf. 'Avillius was on deck, calling the drums down. One of them starts swinging when it clears the quay and Maximus – that's the ship's master – he yells at him to steady it.' I must've made some kind of a move because Vultacilius scowled. 'Yeah. Don't ask me what he thought the poor devil could do against that kind of weight, but that's Maximus for you all over. Anyhow, he's reaching up when the drum lurches towards him, the lock slips and the thing comes down on top of him like Vulcan's hammer.' He shrugged. 'Finish. Bastard didn't have a chance.'

'The lock?'

'Sure. I'll show you.' He walked over to the crane and I followed. The arrangement was pretty simple: a heavy windlass with three-man handles either side and a toothed wheel with a pivoted wooden lever that caught in the teeth and prevented it from moving backwards. 'That's the lock there. It must've kicked up and released the wheel. With half a ton of marble on the other end of the rope there ain't much you can do when that happens.'

'No one was holding the handles?'

'Uh-uh. The drum'd been raised and locked.' He pointed to the arm of the crane above our heads. It had two lateral ropes fastened to it with their slack ends coiled round a bollard either side. 'When that's done the boom's got to be swung through ninety degrees to bring the load over the deck, so the winders're busy managing the stays. Once it's in position they tie them off, take the handles again and lower away notch by notch. They were tying the stays when the lock slipped.'

I lifted the lever with my finger. It came up easy enough at the moment, sure, but then there was no load pulling the teeth the other way. If there had been, it would've been jammed tight. I was no mechanical buff, but the arrangement looked safe as houses. 'This ever happen before?' I said.

'Sometimes. A worn lock'll slip, if the load's heavy enough. Or the pivot'll shear.'

'That look like a worn lock to you?'

He examined it. 'Nah. Seems okay, and, besides, we check them regular. But then like I say the drum was swinging. It'd only take the teeth to shift back a shade and the pressure'd be gone.'

'Yeah. Right.' I flicked the lever up, clear of the teeth. Now I could see its underside. There was a small, rounded dip in the leading straight edge of the wood, like part of it had been forced in, and a matching mark on the framework of the crane. My stomach went cold. I pointed. 'Uh . . . you know what could've caused these?'

The gang boss inspected the marks critically. He sniffed. 'Could've got a bang some time. But it wouldn't've affected the strength of the lever any.'

'Fine.' I let the lever drop. 'Ah . . . who was operating the crane, by the way? One of your lads?'

'Nah.' Vultacilius spat over the side of the wharf. 'Maximus insisted his mate handle it. Didn't trust us not to drop half a ton of marble through his deck planking, he said. Cheeky bastard, but like I say that's Maximus all over. If one of my lads had been on the job the thing'd never have happened. As it is, he's down a deck-hand.'

The coldness in the pit of my stomach went up a notch. Right. Only the deck-hand had been the guy who'd talked to Sopilys the night before, and Sopilys was dead too. One coincidence I could swallow; a chain of them were a different thing entirely. And from Vultacilius's description of the accident the finger pointed pretty clearly in one direction, while the marks in the wood were a clincher. 'What can you tell me about this Maximus, pal?'

He shrugged. 'Not a lot. He's the owner as well as the master. Big, surly bugger, treats his crew like dirt. My lads as well. We see him three, maybe four times a year and that's three or four times too many.'

'He's Catanan, right?'

'Catana's where the *Phorcys* is based, so probably, but I've never asked him. Like I say, Maximus doesn't exactly encourage conversation and I've no mind to pry.'

'Avillius was a regular crew member?'

'I'd seen him a couple of times, sure, but he hadn't been with the *Phorcys* long. Maximus likes to hire Sicilians and Spaniards generally, and Avillius was from Puteoli.'

'You say the *Phorcys* was bound for Syracuse?'

'Yeah, but that's only one of her stops. She works the lower Sicilian coast route, down to Pachynum then along to Lilybaeum and over to Carthage. Spain and Lusitania, too, if she's got business there.'

Well, there wasn't a lot more I could learn here, and if I'd read the signs right the Sopilys trail stopped at the wharf's edge. The back of my neck was prickling like crazy: I hadn't forgotten Ma Glyce's last words, and suddenly they were beginning to seem horribly relevant. Shit; this was something I definitely was not going to enjoy.

Still, there was nothing else for it. I thanked Vultacilius and went back to the port master's office to make the necessary arrangements and collect my horse.

'You fancy a trip to Sicily, lady? Uh . . . leaving the day after tomorrow?'

Perilla set down her book and stared at me. '*What?*'

I topped up my cup from the jug and stretched out on the couch. 'Yeah. Right. It sort of came as a surprise to me, too. But when the port master told me there was a boat sailing in two days' time that calls in at Catana I had to jump at it.'

She was still staring. 'Marcus, have you gone completely mad? We can't just up and—'

'Sure we can. Anyway, I've booked our passage. The *Polyphemus*, bound for New Carthage. I slipped the captain half again over the odds to let us have the deckhouse. If I'm going to spew my guts out all the way, which I am, then I'll do it in private.'

'But why on earth would you want to go to Catana?'

'I don't. Believe me.' I didn't, either; me and boats are about as compatible as pigs and stepladders. Still, the sacrifice had to be made. 'I haven't got the option. Not if I want to find out what Sopilys thought was worth twenty gold pieces.'

'Didn't you talk to the man?'

'He was dead.' I told her the story. 'One gets you ten that this Avillius was the source, and I'd give you the same odds that *he* was killed for opening his mouth too wide. We have to follow the *Phorcys*. There's no alternative.'

'Hmm.' She was calming down now, anyway. Not that sea travel has any terrors for Perilla. Show that lady a grampus and she'll spit in its eye. And unlike me she's a natural traveller with a cast-iron stomach. 'You're sure the shipmaster – what was his name, Maximus – was responsible for the accident?'

'If he wasn't then I'll eat my sandals.' I took a swig of Setinian. 'Him and the *Phorcys*'s mate, maybe the rest of the crew as well, or the guys on the stays, anyway. The whole thing was a set-up from start to finish. Avillius was manoeuvred into position and squashed like a bug. The business with the lever proved it. Whoever was operating the crane must've shoved some sort of iron spike underneath and jerked it clear of the teeth when he was underneath the drum.'

'That's horrible!'

'Sure it is. But like I say it shows the whole boiling were in on it: Maximus to set the guy up in the first place, the hawser lads to make sure the load was swinging around and the mate to trip the lock. Organised murder.'

'You don't think that perhaps you're reading too much into this? Certainly to justify an on-spec sea voyage.'

'Uh-uh.' I shook my head. I'd been through this already in my own mind, and I had my arguments ready. 'First, whatever Sopilys had to tell me was major, the price says that, not to mention the fact that the guy was killed to keep him from telling me.

And whatever it was, it came from Avillius, probably in exchange for the rest of that half gold piece I paid Sopilys for services rendered. Second, as far as Rome's concerned I'm going round in circles. Sure, Eutacticus has given me his promise to find Typhon, but I'm not holding my breath. Even if I can trust the bastard and he's not spinning me a line to keep me quiet, we don't know that Typhon is still alive. I could wait to talk to him until the next Winter Festival and still not be certain it'd happen. Avillius opens up a whole new avenue. Third, the way he died points the finger pretty conclusively at the *Phorcys* itself. If this Maximus did kill him – which he did – then the chances are he knows what Avillius passed on to Sopilys; while if others of the crew are involved then we're looking at the ship, not just the master. It'd explain Sopilys's own death, too, and why it came so quickly on the heels of his message to me. We don't have to faff around with theories that he was blackmailing Pegasus's killer; all that'd need to happen would be for Maximus to find out that Avillius had split to him and both their cards would be marked.'

'Yes, but what could the information have been? As far as I can see this *Phorcys* of yours has no connection with the case at all.'

'Yeah.' I took a swallow of wine. I'd been puzzling over that myself.

'Except . . .' Perilla paused, then went on in a different voice: 'Marcus, didn't you say Minicius Natalis came from Sicily originally?'

A cold finger touched my spine. 'Yeah. Yeah, come

to think of it I did.' Cascellius had mentioned it, even named the town. Shit; where was it exactly? I went over places in my head: Syracuse, Panormus, Lilybaeum . . . 'Leontini. He's from Leontini.'

'Which isn't all that far from Catana, is it? Twenty, thirty miles?'

It could be coincidence, sure, but the lady could be on to something here. 'You think maybe there's a link between Natalis and Maximus?'

'It's a possibility. Although what bearing that could have on the murder I haven't the faintest idea.' Perilla got up. 'However, I'm afraid I have more urgent things to think of than sleuthing at present. You have, too.'

'Yeah? And what might they be?'

'Marcus, dear, you come home and inform me that you've booked us on a boat to Sicily leaving in less than forty-eight hours. I think perhaps that packing might be quite a priority, don't you? We have about an hour before dinner. I suggest you use it profitably.'

She disappeared in the direction of the stairs. Hell; I hadn't thought of that aspect. I'd better check the study strongbox, as well. The twenty gold pieces had made quite a dent, and although they hadn't gone into Sopilys's pocket after all I'd needed a largish slice to pay for our passage and the use of the deckhouse. Travelling isn't cheap, and travelling at no notice is even more expensive, because you have to rent rather than do the Roman thing and stay with friends of friends. Still, I could send Alexis down to my banker in Market Square tomorrow morning; Bathyllus would be coming with us, of course, and he'd have things to do . . .

That brought me up short. Bugger; I hadn't told Bathyllus. Or, for that matter, Meton, who'd also be coming with us unless we wanted to live on weevily biscuit during the voyage and risk the vagaries of local Sicilian cookery after we arrived.

Right. Best get it over with.

I went out to the lobby and yelled for Bathyllus.

36

We took the coach down to Ostia the following evening: me, Perilla, Bathyllus, Meton and Perilla's maid Phryne plus about ten tons of luggage stowed in the boot, on the roof, and in every other scrap of available space. The gods alone knew what we needed all that stuff for, but the lady seemed to think it was necessary so I didn't argue. I just hoped the *Polyphemus* was sailing light otherwise, because if not we'd never make it out of harbour.

I'd only had the chance to cast my eye briefly over the boat – that's always a good idea; the time to find out that your projected mode of transport's actually a worm-gnawed hulk crewed by morons is before you pay the fare – but she'd seemed okay: a seventy-five-tonner, slightly bigger than your usual jobbing merchantman but built on the same lines. Meaning she had the proportions of a lardball purple-striper and would probably move like one as well. The skipper-owner, on the other hand, was a cheerful little Neapolitan dumpling who'd struck me more as the type to sell sausages off a street-corner grid-dle than splice the marline-spike and close-haul the bilges. Which was absolutely fine by me. Grizzled old sea-dogs with eyes like the winter stars and salt in their beards may look the part, but they get right up my nose.

We boarded just after dawn. There were only three other passengers, travellers respectively in oil, walnuts and bath suite fitments who were dropping off before we were and who could all've modelled for a string bean in a pickle barrel. They weren't too friendly, either, although that was understandable: having the deckhouse is a perk that can really get you hated by the guys dossing down in the scuppers, and the prospect of a bedless night when you've spent the day as the sport of Neptune, his assorted tritons and half the winds in the mariner's card doesn't exactly encourage toleration and general bonhomie.

Not that the weather was bad. Maybe it had something to do with the breakfast bowl of sea-urchin soup with the spines boiled in – a recipe of Perilla's seafaring aunt – that she'd had Meton cook up, or maybe I was finally just getting used to this sailing lark, but when we'd got past the Ostia bar and were scudding down the Latian coast fast as a speeding sea-snail I was still miraculously on my feet with my guts unspilled, queasy but unbowed. Not so Bathyllus. At the first pitch – or maybe it was a yaw – the little guy turned an interesting pea-green and made for the side with a speed that must've popped his hernia. Still, it took his mind off Tyndaris. When we'd set out for the port he had been a sad and moping major-domo. Love is a many-splendour'd thing, and the bald-head had it in spades.

I was standing at the rail trying to ignore the consequent sounds and looking out for dolphins when Perilla came up.

'Are you feeling all right, Marcus?' she asked.

I kissed her. 'Sure,' I said. 'Not so much as a twinge.' A lie, but not a serious one. Besides, if the lady could look that good after a late-night trip in a coach, four hours' sleep in a hotel – we hadn't even considered Agron's place, not with five of us including one sulking chef, and Ostia, being a major port, has such rarities – and an early start, then there was a certain amount of pride at stake here.

'We're certainly fortunate in the weather.' She eyed the up-ended rump of our senior slave further along the thwarts. Bathyllus had already lost his breakfast and was starting on yesterday's dinner. Jupiter knew where Meton had got to, but that guy was too single-minded to be seasick. 'The captain was just telling me that it isn't usually this calm. On the other hand—'

'Hey!' I pointed. Fifty yards off our beam three streamlined shapes were cutting through the water like champion racehorses overhauling an ox-cart. As I watched, the leader rose in a glittering arc of spray and sliced back through the surface without breaking speed and with barely a ripple. The second followed, then the third. 'Look at that!'

Perilla smiled. 'Yes, dear. Beautiful.'

'Look at them go!' The dolphins had veered into a broad sweeping turn, disappearing round the bulk of the prow. 'The little buggers're running circles round us!' Laughing their beaks off while they did it, too.

Dolphins're great.

'You know they feed on their backs?' Perilla said. 'They can't eat the right way up.'

Like some senators of my acquaintance. That lady is a mine of useless information.

'Is that so, now?' I said. 'You think if I threw them a bit of bread they'd go for it?'

'I doubt it, Marcus, but you can try if you like.' She was still smiling. 'You know, this was a very good idea, the case aside, I mean. It's quite a holiday, and I've never been to Sicily.'

'Yeah. Me neither.' I was looking back towards the stern. A few seconds later the lead fish reappeared with the others at his tail, going like the clappers. Jupiter, these things were fast! 'Hey, Bathyllus!'

He raised his ravaged face from the rail.

'You're missing all this, little guy!'

His lips framed a word that I didn't know our major-domo used and he bent back down again. The holiday spirit seemed to have caught all of us, in its different ways. I grinned.

'It's a shame we're not going as far as Syracuse,' Perilla said. 'The historical sights are particularly interesting. The citadel especially.'

'Yeah. Yeah, right. *Holy gods!*' All three dolphins had lifted at once, and the one at the back had shaken itself in mid-air. How the lady could be interested in things like citadels when there were shows like this going on beat me completely.

'I don't suppose we could? Go on, I mean?'

I took my eyes off the dolphins. Warning bells had

started ringing. You have to watch Perilla; a lovely lady she is in many ways, but when she gets on a culture jag she ain't logical. 'Uh . . . maybe some other time, when we're not so pressed.' Or never, for preference.

'Hmm.'

'They say Catana's a nice place. Very hot on temples.'

She frowned. 'I don't *think* so, Marcus, apart from the one to Ceres, naturally. Perhaps you're confusing it with somewhere else. But then of course there is Etna.'

My blood chilled. I'd been trying to forget about Sicily's top tourist attraction, or rather not to put the idea into Perilla's head. Illogical, I know. Even in the unlikely event of a razor-sharp geographer like Perilla not knowing already that it was within spitting distance of the town, the chances of sailing right past the brute without her noticing the presence of a snow-clad ten-thousand-foot-high active volcano off our starboard beam were about on the scale of teaching a brick to whistle.

'Uh . . . yeah. Etna. Yeah, right,' I said.

'I wonder if it might be possible to visit the actual crater? There are guides, I know. When we arrive, dear, you must make enquiries. It would certainly be an experience, wouldn't it?'

I didn't answer. Oh, shit! I needn't've bothered with the pussyfooting because the lady had been ahead of me all the time. Experience would be right; possibly a terminal one. Temples were bad enough, but the only risk you ran with them was boredom; traipsing round the slopes of active volcanoes at the wrong time could get you seriously fried. Still, we'd cross that bridge when we came to it. At least I'd had my dolphins.

I wondered if Meton had seen them. Not that he'd've been impressed; the bugger would just've thought about sauces.

The calm didn't hold, or maybe the wind shifted. By sunset, when we were about level with Tarracina, we started plunging like a half-foundered carthorse and my stomach finally decided that being jerked up and down in a line between my knees and my throat wasn't on any more. Bathyllus was long gone from the rail – the poor devil had turned himself inside out hours before – but String Bean Number One had taken his place. Not that he noticed me. I joined him for ten very unpleasant minutes and then took the opportunity of an emptied stomach to stagger along to the deckhouse.

Perilla was in residence, with Phryne.

'Oh, hello, Marcus,' she said. 'I was just going to find Meton and have him set up the little portable brazier and make a start on dinner. You remember he brought that leftover tripe stew?' She stopped. 'Marcus?' Then: '*Marcus!*'

I lurched forward. Luckily, we were well provided with bowls for just such eventualities, because my stomach wasn't empty after all.

You don't want to know about the next two days. You really don't.

* * *

I came out the other end on the morning of the third day. We've done our share of travelling, Perilla and me, and I'm pretty fatalistic now about seasickness. So, fortunately, for different reasons, is the lady: it can't be any fun sleeping next to a groaning bundle of misery that tries to throw up every half-hour, and Perilla is definitely not your ideal nurse at the best of times. Forget the cool hand soothing the fevered brow, for a start. She'll sympathise, sure, but largely what you get is the brittle smile and the gritted teeth. Oh, and the cheerful commentary about where you are in relation to terra firma and what a lovely man the captain is.

Not that it was all that pleasant for me, either.

The third morning, I woke starving. We got Meton to make some porridge – that bastard hadn't so much as burped since we weighed anchor at Ostia, seemingly – I shovelled it down and went out on deck, feeling weak as a kitten.

Beautiful day. We were through the straits and past Messana – I'd missed all that – but we hadn't got out into the Siculan Sea proper yet, and the mountains behind Rhegium to our left made it seem we were sailing down a wide blue river rather than skirting the Sicilian coastline. Ahead of us the snow-capped peak of Etna glistened white against sky blue above the lower hills between. It didn't seem to be smoking at present – there was just the faintest haze – but when we got closer it might be a different matter. I didn't trust that bugger an inch, certainly not enough to go poking my nose down its crater. Maybe when we reached Catana a small sacrifice to Vulcan wouldn't go amiss.

Still, after being shut up in the *Polyphemus*'s deck-house for two days it felt good just to breathe. I leaned against the rail, filled my lungs and watched the rugged coastline slipping past.

'Feeling better, Valerius Corvinus?'

I turned. The captain.

'Yeah, not too bad.'

'Do your deep-breathing exercises while you can. Closer to the mountain with the wind in the wrong direction the air stinks of sulphur.'

'Oh, joy. That's something to look forward to, then.'

He chuckled and joined me at the rail. 'You'll get used to it. Anyway, it's not far now, and we're doing well. We should make Catana this time tomorrow if the wind holds.'

'Fine. Fine.'

'Your wife was telling me that you're chasing the *Phorcys*. She didn't go into details but it seems you have business with Publius Maximus.'

I felt a spark of interest kindle. 'You know him?'

The captain hesitated. 'We've met. The *Phorcys* works the same route and we overlap sometimes.' Something in his voice suggested that he didn't exactly look forward to it. 'Different cargo, mind, on the Sicily–Ostia stretch, so we're not in direct competition.'

'What's he like?'

'As a seaman? First-rate. Been sailing in western

waters for thirty years and knows every scrap of the coast from Tarraco to Tripoli like the back of his hand.'

'Not as a seaman. As a person.'

'Oh, now.' The Neapolitan dumpling rubbed a hand over the three-day stubble on his chin. No one cuts their hair or shaves at sea because it's supposed to be unlucky, which it damn well can be: one pitch at the wrong moment while you're holding a bronze razor and you're breathing through a hole in your throat. They're no fools, these sailors. 'I don't want to be speaking out of turn here, Valerius Corvinus. I hardly know the man.'

Yeah, I'd bet. I knew equivocation when I heard it. 'He's a bastard, right?'

That drew a slow grin. 'He's been so described several times in my hearing, yes. And judging from my personal experience I wouldn't disagree.'

'What kind of bastard?'

'Honest enough by his lights as far as business goes, if that's where your interest lies, and reading between the lines I think it does.' I said nothing: a smart lad, this Neapolitan dumpling. 'He'd have to be, mind; try fooling with the manifest and word soon gets around. Loyal, too. Make a friend of him and he's a friend for life so long as you don't cross him. There's your difficulty. He's a thrawn bugger, doesn't make friends easy, and he's hell in hobnails to most things on two legs. As an enemy' – he spat over the thwarts – 'well, let's just say he's one I'd rather not have myself.'

Fair enough. As assessments go, I'd guess that had been pretty objective. 'He have any particular contacts in Rome that you know of? Rome, not Ostia.'

'Sure. In his line that's natural.'

'His line?'

'Racehorses.'

I turned to stare at him. '*What?*'

'You didn't know? That's what the *Phorcys* ships. From Africa and Sicily inwards, anyway. The return journey she takes what she can get that's bound in the right direction. But she transports racehorses from the breeders to stables all the way up the Italian coast. Custom-built, stalls below decks, the lot.'

Shit! Holy Jupiter! 'He, uh, deal with any particular faction in Rome?'

'The Greens. They've got him under permanent contract, exclusivity clause. Sure, he ships horses for any stable in Capua or Paestum, say, that likes to hire him, but Rome's different. There he only deals with the Greens.'

Oh, sweet and immortal gods, I'd got my link! And with Natalis, too. I'd been right to come, sure I had. 'What about the other end? The breeders?'

'Oh, now that I can't tell you. There're any number of them, scattered all over. Maximus isn't involved in the buying, of course; the stables have their own reps who travel round looking at suitable colts and buying what they can afford. He just picks them up and delivers.'

'He been working for Natalis for long?'

'Natalis is the Greens' master?' I nodded. 'A fair

time. Nine or ten years, anyway, which is as long as I've known him. Maybe longer, I can't say.' He shot me a quick look along the line of his hunched shoulder. 'What would this be about? If it isn't a rude question.'

There wasn't any reason not to tell him. Besides, he seemed a chatty-enough guy and you never knew what information you might pick up. 'I'm, uh, looking into a murder. There's racing connections. And before he sailed one of Maximus's crew died under what you might call suspicious circumstances.'

The captain had raised his eyebrows; he was surprised, sure, but maybe not quite as much as he could have been. Which was interesting. 'Avillius,' he said. 'I heard about that, poor bugger. But I hadn't heard there was anything suspicious involved. Accident with a crane, wasn't it?'

'That's right. Only a couple of nights before he'd been talking to a guy who used to work at the Greens' stables in Rome. And the night after that the Greens' groom was knifed dead in an alley. Oh, and the man working the crane was the *Phorcys*'s mate.'

That got me another sharp look and a long, contemplative silence. Finally, the captain cleared his throat and spat again. 'Leon,' he said. 'Neptune's holy balls, Corvinus, you're mixing with a proper mess of stinking fish here right enough.'

'Leon's the mate's name?'

'Aye. He's Maximus's cousin, and if we're talking bastards you can add him to the list with gilt on. Ask any wetback this side of Tarraco and he'll tell you the same. And a fair slice of them have the knife scars to prove it, the ones who're still walking. Maximus is straight enough, but he's not a man to get on the wrong side of, is Leon.'

Uh-huh. 'Is that so, now?'

We watched the coastline slip past in silence. I thought of knives.

'You mentioned a racing connection,' the captain said at last. The man you want to talk to in Catana is Pythias. Runs a corn-chandler's business in Two Gods' Street behind the Roman market. Give him my name.' Yeah; that was Phrontis, I remembered. 'Oh, and Corvinus?'

'Yeah?'

'When we get to Catana, if you're asking questions about Maximus then watch your back. It's his home ground, and he has a lot of friends there.'

Something cold touched my spine. *If you go to Sicily then watch your back* . . . 'Yeah. Yeah, I'll do that,' I said. 'Thanks for the warning.'

He shrugged. 'No problem. And now if you'll excuse me I've got things to do. We're calling in at Tauromenium; not for long, only three or four hours, but it'll give you and your lady a chance to stretch your legs.'

'Fine.'

I watched the coast for a bit longer then went back to the deckhouse, my brain buzzing.

Maybe the captain had been ribbing me about the sulphur, or maybe we were just lucky with the wind, but the approach to Tauromenium wasn't all that bad, and the strange thing was that Etna directly to the south but screened by the rising ground wasn't too obvious either. Certainly what countryside we could see between the shore and the hills looked fertile: lush and rolling, with vineyards, orchards and bank upon bank of red flowers.

Tauromenium was a different matter entirely. From what the captain had said, I'd imagined a cosy little town with a market-place an easy stroll in from the harbour, with maybe – I'd been fantasising here, sure, but what the hell – a convenient wineshop that I could pass the time in while Perilla did her rounds of the local sites. What I actually got, when we rounded the headland and came in clear sight of the place, would've given an eagle migraine: a town on a mountain, seven hundred feet above its harbour, at the top of a zigzag track that gave me, in my weakened condition, palpitations at the thought of climbing. I may be a natural hoofer, but my idea of distance tends to favour the horizontal rather than the vertical. I gazed in horror.

'Oh, shit,' I murmured.

'Come on, Marcus, don't be silly.' Perilla was up on deck too, looking disgustingly windswept and healthy. 'A bit of a walk will do you good.'

'Walk, yes. Climb's different.'

'There is a road.'

'Yeah, I can see there is. Even so, I hope you packed the crampons.'

'Don't grouse, dear. We're on holiday.'

We pulled in at the quay, and I saw the mules. The captain caught my eye and grinned. Bastard! He'd known all along, of course, and so had Perilla. Me, I don't usually go a bundle for any four-footed method of transport, but given the alternatives of a trip to Tauromenium on two legs or on four I was all for the latter. Not that I was against an outing in principle, far from it: four hours wasn't much for a there-and-back stint, but if you've been tossing about on a boat for what seems like for ever you grab whatever chances are offered. And there might still be the wineshop.

We hired the mules and took the half-hour trip up (and up) into town.

I'm not going to describe Tauromenium, let alone give you the potted history Perilla gave me on the way. It was a nice enough place, not that it had all that much going for it, apart from some stupendous views of Etna at one end and the coast we'd just sailed along at the other. The lady and I did the sights, such as they were, on our own: Bathyllus, well provided before we left with holiday pocket-money, had wandered off somewhere with Phryne – the little guy had got over his seasickness faster than I had, but he was still moping – while Meton had headed straight for the market with a gleam in his eye and a song on his lips. Eventually, by way of a theatre and a couple of incidental but unexciting temples, I managed to steer Perilla in the direction of a tight little restaurant that I'd spotted right at the start, perched on the cliff edge and with a trellised courtyard overlooking the sea. We sat down and ordered grilled red mullet, fresh bread and olives in their oil, a salad and a jug of the local wine, while Perilla had a sort of diluted fruit juice cordial with herbs in it which the proprietor swore by; which didn't altogether surprise me, but then that was her business. Then I stretched out my legs and took my first sip of wine for two days. Not bad, not bad at all. Thin, sure, but made from good grapes and cellar-chilled to just the right temperature. Made even better by the scent of the grilling fish that had my mouth watering in anticipation. I sighed. The lady was right; case or not, a holiday was just what I needed.

'Feeling more human now?' Perilla said.

'Uh-huh.' I took a long swallow of the straw-coloured wine. Delicious. 'Maybe there's something to be said for travelling after all.'

She smiled. 'It's certainly a lovely spot, and it's so nice to get off the ship, isn't it? Not that we've far to go now.'

'Yeah. Now about this connection with Natalis—' I said.

The smile faded. 'Marcus, can't we leave that, please? At least until we get to Catana. Sleuthing's all very well, but it isn't everything in life. Why don't you forget about murders and poisonings and just enjoy yourself for once?'

Jupiter! Well, I supposed the lady had a point, and it was her trip too. And she was right: nothing of a town though it might be where tourism was concerned, once you'd actually managed to reach the place Tauromenium was a lovely spot, and a complete change from Rome. Quieter, for a start: I hadn't heard so much as a donkey cough.

We sat for a while in silence and watched the afternoon sun glinting on the sea. If you're going to look at large expanses of water then sitting under a vine trellis with a cool jug of wine beside you is the best place to do it, and it gets my vote every time. Watching it from the heaving deck of a boat is a complete mug's game.

'We should have brought Marilla,' Perilla said eventually. Marilla's our adopted daughter, squirrelled away in the Alban Hills with the lady's old Aunt Marcia. Her choice, not ours. Certainly not Perilla's.

'There wasn't time.'

'No. I suppose not. Still, she would've enjoyed it. We don't get away all that much. Not as a family, anyway.'

Uh-oh; the lady was in one of her pensive, maternal moods. She doesn't get them often, and they don't last long, but they always make me nervous. Luckily I was saved by the fish: a dozen beautifully grilled little mullet with a sprinkling of sea-salt, olive oil and mountain herbs that would've had Meton crying his eyes out, along with a loaf of crusty bread, the home-grown olives and a green vinegar and oil salad. We hadn't exactly been living on hard-tack and bilgewater for the past three days – or at least Perilla hadn't – because the *Polyphemus* had made regular stops, but a meal like this was special.

It cheered Perilla up, anyway. By the time she made a start on her third mullet the mood had vanished. We didn't have time for dessert, but the break had been long enough. I paid and we walked back down the steep mule-road to the harbour: downhill's different.

Two of the menials were there already: Phryne had persuaded Bathyllus to buy a straw sun-hat that made him look like a louche prune. Meton rolled up ten minutes late dragging one of the biggest barbels I'd ever seen; the gods knew where it'd come from – barbels're freshwater fish – or how he expected to cook it, especially when we were arriving in Catana the next day, but that's Meton for you, a professional to his fingertips. We all piled aboard, and half an hour later we'd left Tauromenium behind us.

37

You don't realise how big Etna is – I mean longways, as it were – until you sail past it. At Tauromenium we'd been more or less level with the northern slopes; Catana, at its southern end, is a good thirty miles as the crow flies further on. Sure, there're foothills either side and a lot of the distance is base, but that is one big mountain.

We got to Catana a couple of hours after dawn next day: there had just been enough light, when we drew level with them, for Perilla to point out the lumps of black rock sticking out of the water, that the ship's namesake had thrown at Ulysses when he came this way and did a runner from the big bastard's cave. Me, I'm no more credulous where these old stories go than the next guy, but it still gave me a shiver. Even if Perilla was right and what had done the throwing was the volcano a long time before Ulysses came on the scene it wasn't a comforting thought. The countryside between coast and mountains might be a farmer's dream now, but anything capable of beaning you with forty tons of rock at a distance of several miles deserves a bit of respect. I just hoped Etna had settled down in the last thousand years.

Catana's not like Tauromenium. It's a lot more prosperous, for a start, largely because the city fathers had the good sense to back Augustus (before he was Augustus) in the civil war and the place was raised to the status of a colony. Also, lying as it does at the northerly end of the plain that stretches from the foothills of Etna south towards Leontini, it's a lot more accessible: the harbour is part of the town, which is directly behind and around it.

We anchored at one of the quays – like the rest of the town, the harbour and its mole are built of irregular lumps of black basalt and tufa blocks from the old lava flows – and disembarked, plus luggage. I'd been worried about transport, especially after Tauromenium, but it was no problem: there were plenty of carts for hire, even a carriage, and no ban, like there is in Rome, on wheeled traffic within the city boundaries during daylight hours. I left the dickering to Perilla. Bathyllus, whose job it really was, may be an organisational genius, but he's no dickerer, especially when he's sporting a sun-hat that'd make a mule laugh, and Meton is worse than useless because if he doesn't get his way – completely, and immediately – he gives the whole thing up and wanders off in a sulk. Me, I just shrug and pay, which offends the bastards' professional sensibilities as well as turning out expensive as hell. As a dickerer, Perilla's perfect, if unorthodox: she just names her price, fixes the most likely looking candidate with her eye and doesn't let go until the bugger gives in. Simple but effective.

Phrontis the captain had recommended a place he

knew just beyond the town's north gate, the self-
contained half of a villa that one of the more enterprising Catanans had built to catch the upper side of the
tourist trade: like I say, Etna's the island's prime tourist
attraction and, after corn and sulphur, gawpers from
Rome are the city's biggest earner. It might be already
taken, of course, even this early in the season, but that
was the risk you ran when you travelled on spec, and
it sounded a hell of a lot better than putting up at an
inn. Meton could cook his barbel, for a start. Apropos
of which, I noticed that, while Perilla negotiated the
hire of the carriage and a cart, he was standing to
one side with his precious collection of knives and his
best omelette pan clutched in one massive hairy fist
and the barbel in the other, in a pose that would've
had an artist of the Realist school screaming with
joy and reaching for his brushes: Pensive Ape with
Kitchenware and Fish.

Perilla concluded arrangements, and the carriage-
driver and carter, both wearing that numb, what-the-
hell-hit-me look that showed they'd been well and
truly hired, loaded the ten tons of luggage on to the
cart. Then we said goodbye to Phrontis and trundled
up Harbour Road in the direction of the centre.

It felt funny being in a city again after seeing nothing
but water, sky and the same faces for four straight
days, and the fact that we were headed for the north
gate meant that we got the through tour. Nice place,
Catana, although the black lava used in most of the
buildings and for all of the paving slabs made it quite
samey. A lot of it was new, probably part of the civic

improvement scheme of the past fifty years, but some must've been forced by earthquake damage: living within striking distance of Etna has its drawbacks. There was the scent of money around, mind, which there hadn't been at Tauromenium; I noticed a pretty snazzy public hall over to the left of the market square, and the jutting curve of a theatre beyond it.

'Oh, look, Marcus!' Perilla said. 'There's the Temple of Ceres! Isn't it marvellous?'

'Uh . . . yeah. Yeah, very nice.' Bugger; why is there *always* a temple? This one was a whopper, too, dominating the main square, faced with marble and with a long altar in front decorated with statues either end. I could almost hear the lady making a tick on her things-we-had-to-see list. 'Let's just get settled in first, okay?'

We carried on up the main drag past a line of prosperous-looking shops and through a suburb of upmarket houses with walled gardens to the north gate. Just past it the coachman took a left on to a dirt track between two fields of beans, and with the turn I saw Etna again. We must've been heading straight towards it. Gods, that thing was *big*! Close, too: the town's agricultural hinterland, field upon field, stretched up towards the foothills, then merged with the tree cover that stretched most of the way up the slopes. Above it was the volcano itself: bare rock heaving into the sky, with broad patches of snow at the crown and half hidden by cloud. Maybe it was because we were beyond the city smells now, or the sight of the mountain had made it more noticeable, but the air seemed to have taken on a definite and sinister reek of sulphur. The hairs on the back of my neck stirred.

'Uh . . . maybe we'd be better off looking for something in town, lady,' I said.

She sniffed. 'Don't be silly, dear. It's quite safe.'

Yeah, right; I'd bet that was what they'd told Damocles when he asked about the sword. Even so, not the site I'd've chosen for a country house. Having an active volcano practically in your back garden isn't exactly conductive to calm, tranquillity and a good night's sleep. Still, it was too late to change plans now.

The track ended up at a big walled villa in an oleander grove. Home sweet home for the duration, or at least I hoped so. Barring little accidents like unexpected volcanic eruptions, that was.

We passed through the gates. A slave pruning the whatever-it-was plant that climbed up the villa's front gaped, then ran inside and came out with a short tubby guy clutching a bread roll. Obviously the enterprising owner, hauled from his breakfast. I got out, but let Perilla do the talking. Five minutes later, our accommodation was arranged and the coachman and carter, helped by the plant-pruning slave, were ferrying in the luggage.

'It's absolutely lovely, Marcus!' Perilla was beaming. 'And not expensive at all.'

'Yeah.' I looked round the sitting-room. The furniture was heavy and dark, with a lot of gilt – my bet was the guy had bought it wholesale from a cat-house somewhere; it even smelled of scent – but the room opened out into a small private garden that looked ideal for lounging of an evening with a jug of wine. 'Mind you, I think that side of it came as a bit of a surprise to our landlord.'

'Nonsense, dear, he was quite satisfied. I offered a very fair price. Especially since it's so early in the season.'

'Right. Right. I just thought, when he choked on the roll, that he might've been expecting a bit more, that's all.'

Meton loomed in from the direction of the kitchen. I felt a momentary qualm, but the guy was smiling. Or doing what passed with Meton for smiling, which was not scowling too hard.

'Uh . . . everything okay, Meton?' I said cautiously.

'Callias's chef doesn't have no asafoetida,' he rumbled – Callias was our tubby host – 'and I'm missing an eighteen-inch fretalis, but otherwise it's not bad. Not bad at all.'

I breathed a quiet sigh of relief. Callias's chef – he was stocking our kitchen with the basics on account – must be shit-hot. *Not bad* in Meton's terms was the culinary equivalent of a laurel wreath and a major ovation. 'Great,' I said. 'That's just great.' I paused. 'Uh . . . what's a fretalis, pal?'

He ignored the question. 'Only if it's all right with you I'll go back into town straight away and suss out the market.' His eyes beneath the beetling brows gleamed with an unholy light on the last word. With Perilla it's temples; Meton's bag is markets, especially the more outré variety. Obsessive isn't the word; set him down waterless in the middle of the Arabian desert and the first thing he'd look for would be truffles.

'Yeah. Yeah, go ahead.' I fumbled with my purse and handed him half a dozen silver pieces. 'Enjoy.' The first rule, when we arrive anywhere, is get rid of Meton. Easily done, but pricey. Still, when it came to dinner-time you got value for money.

Meton loomed out again. I wondered if the Catanan stallowners had an inkling as to what was about to hit them. Maybe they did: some of those doom-and-gloom soothsayers're pretty good.

Bathyllus was next. 'That's everything stowed, sir,' he said. 'Phryne is dealing with the mistress's wardrobe. And I've ordered the baths heated. We have access to the owner's suite, and I thought perhaps you and the mistress would like to bathe.'

I caught the faintest suggestion of a sniff; not the usual Bathyllus-type sarky-bastard sniff, but a genuine one. A not-so-subtle hint, probably. Yeah, well; the little bald-head had a point. Four days aboard a merchantman with very basic sanitary arrangements don't do wonders for your state of cleanliness, especially if you've spent a large part of them tossing your guts out. 'Yeah. Good idea,' I said. 'Oh, and Bathyllus?'

'Yes, sir?'

'Make enquiries next door about local wine suppliers, would you? Then arrange delivery of something suitable.'

'Yes, sir.' Now that *was* a sarky sniff. Still, the bastard ought to know the priorities by this time.

*　　*　　*

We had a leisurely bathe followed by lunch. I'd just chased down the last scrap of bread and sausage with a swallow of the wine we'd brought with us when Perilla suggested an investigative trip into town.

'I've made a list from Timaeus, dear,' she said. Timaeus of Tauromenium, if you're wondering at all; I'd met him, through his *History of Sicily*, ad nauseam at regular intervals over the past couple of days. 'The Temple of Ceres, of course, is an absolute must, but he mentions several other interesting shrines such as—'

Oh, gods. I held up a hand. 'Look, lady, let's knock this on the head right now, okay? Visit as many temples as you like, but don't drag me along.'

'But, Marcus—'

'Perilla, watch my lips: no temples. They bring me out in lumps. And that includes shrines, sacred groves, picture galleries, statues and other notable curiosities. You have your holiday and I'll have mine.'

'Sleuthing?'

'Come on, Perilla! We had a deal. I wouldn't mention the case until we were in Catana. Now we are.'

'And you expect me to help, I suppose.'

'Uh . . . yeah. With the thinking part, anyway.'

'Corvinus, sometimes you make me very annoyed indeed.'

Jupiter! Women! Well, she did sound quite peeved, at that. 'What have I done, lady? I told you, you're perfectly free to go round as many temples as you like, just don't expect—'

'We're on holiday. *We* are.'

'Yeah, in a sort of way, but—'

'*Not* in a sort of way! Marcus, I've never been to Sicily before. I don't mind missing out on Syracuse, but as you say here we are in Catana. Now although I do realise that our main reason for being here is to solve your damned murder problem, as *I* said there is more to life than murders and poisonings.'

Uh-oh. I caught a glimpse of Bathyllus out of the corner of my eye. The little guy had been coming over to clear, but he changed his mind and faded back into the woodwork. Very wise. I swallowed: warning bells were going off all over the place. I had a kind of feeling that to say 'Really?', although the word was on the tip of my tongue and it would've been an honest reaction, wasn't the most tactful reply I could make and in the lady's present mood might even get me a sock in the jaw. So instead I said, 'Uh . . . compromise?'

She was quiet for a long time. Then she said, 'Compromise.'

I breathed again. Spat over. Jupiter, that had been a bad one.

We compromised on Ceres's temple.

Another aspect of the compromise – details to be announced – was the visit to Etna. Sometimes, with Perilla, I get the impression that I've been outman-oeuvred.

Callias the owner had offered us the use of his litter-slaves – borrowing of the bought help, to a limited degree, was included in the price – but he wasn't too pressing, and after four days of being heaved up and down in a boat litter journeys have a sort of horrible *déjà vu* feel to them, so we went on foot. The town wasn't very far in any case, no more than half a mile, max, to the centre, and it was a lovely afternoon, warmer than Rome but still not too hot, and smelling – if you ignored the slight overtones of sulphur, which might've been my imagination – of herbs and flowers. We found the Greek-style market square again no bother. There was a tidy little wineshop in one corner with a few lucky Perillaless buggers out on benches watching the world go by, but I stuck to the compromise and ignored it.

Ceres's temple was where we'd left it, unfortunately.

'Impressive, isn't it?' Perilla said, looking up at the frieze (the Rape of Persephone, with attendant nymphs. File and forget).

'Yeah.' I supposed it was, if you liked friezes or rapes. However, I had to show willing.

'And so unusual to find an Ionic temple in a Sicilian city.'

'Right. Right.' I paused. Then, because she seemed to expect something more: 'So it's, uh, Ionic, is it?'

'Oh, Marcus, don't be ridiculous! You can see perfectly well for yourself that it's Ionic!'

Uh-huh. So much for the extent of my architectural knowledge. I know there is a difference between Doric and Ionic and that it's pretty fundamental, but apart from the fact it has something to do with the pillars that's as far as I go. A temple is a temple is a temple.

'According to Timaeus it was built as a thank-offering when the original Naxian inhabitants managed to expel Hieron of Syracuse's Dorian settlers. That's the Sicilian Naxos, of course, the Chalcidian colony, not the Greek island of the same name. The choice of the Ionian order was a political statement.'

'Is that so, now?'

'Corvinus, you are *not* co-operating!'

'Sure I am, lady. Hieron of Syracuse. That would be, what, three hundred years back, right?'

'Five hundred. And ten, if you want to be exact.'

I didn't, particularly, but with the lady in this mood I wasn't going to say so. While she went on to point out vital and significant details of height-to-width ratios and depth of relief in the carvings (don't ask; *don't* ask!) I leaned against a pillar and thought about more important things. Like Maximus. The *Phorcys* hadn't been in dock when we'd arrived, but then I hadn't really expected her to be. While Perilla had been dickering with the carriers, I'd asked one of the guys you always see hanging around harbours about her and he'd said she'd sailed the day before for Syracuse. No surprises there. It was like Achilles and the tortoise. Catching Maximus himself was out of the question; no ship we could take would overhaul him – that'd need a government trireme – so it'd be a case either of waiting until he came back or finding out what he might have cooking with Minicius Natalis from another source. Like, for example, this corn-chandler guy Pythias that

Phrontis had mentioned in Two Gods' Street over by the Roman market-place. Perhaps he could put me on to . . .

'*Marcus!*'

I blinked and jerked upright. 'Yeah? What?'

'Marcus, you're hopeless, you really are! I've just told you that the temple was built with the aid of three hundred performing elephants and that Hannibal's grandmother modelled for the cult statue and you nodded your head to both.'

Probably an instinctive reaction; I certainly wasn't conscious of having heard her. 'Did she?'

'Don't be silly!' She grinned suddenly. 'Oh, go and sit in a wineshop, for goodness' sake! Or do whatever you were going to do today before I dragged you along here.'

Hope sprang. 'Uh . . . you sure? I mean—'

She kissed me. 'I'll see you back at the villa. Dinner an hour before sunset. It'll be Meton's barbel, so don't be late.'

'Yeah. Yeah, right.' I kissed her back. Not a bad lady, Perilla, she just gets obsessed with things.

I stopped a guy in the street outside and asked for directions to the Roman market-place.

Two Gods' Street was no more than a back alley, with the shrine to the Dioscuri that gave it its name set in a little square in the centre. Pythias's place was easy to spot. I went in.

A slave was measuring corn into a gunny-sack. I asked for Pythias and he showed me into a small back office where an old guy that looked like a schoolmaster on a bad day was making out bills.

'Uh . . . you Pythias?' I said.

The guy looked up. His eyes were a washed-out blue. 'I am. What can I do for you?'

'The name's Marcus Valerius Corvinus. I've just made the crossing from Ostia with Phrontis on the *Polyphemus*. He suggested I come to see you.'

'Indeed?' He set his pen down. 'About what?'

'The name Maximus mean anything to you? Publius Maximus?'

'It does. He ships racehorses.'

'How about Titus Minicius Natalis?'

'Natalis is the master of the Roman Greens faction, I believe. Not that I know him personally, only by reputation.'

'Right. Right.' The washed-out eyes – I wondered if the guy was maybe half blind – were making me feel uncomfortable. His manner wasn't exactly encouraging either; I'd met less prickly hedgehogs. 'You, uh, happen to know whether there's a connection between the two?'

He frowned. 'But of course there is; a self-evident one, surely. Maximus transports Natalis's horses. You hardly needed to come all the way to Sicily to learn that, young man. Now what is this about, please?'

'Uh . . . I don't exactly know myself. But I've got an interest in Maximus. I'd appreciate anything you can tell me.'

'Such as what, for example?' I hesitated fractionally, and he tutted. Schoolmaster was right; I felt like I'd been caught trying to bluff my way through a home-work test. 'Valerius Corvinus, I'm perfectly ready to do everything in my power to answer whatever questions you may have – although I can't quite see what this "interest" of yours is – but I've just returned from an extended business trip myself and I have a great deal of work to catch up on. I must ask you to be more specific.'

Jupiter! 'I'm looking into a murder in Rome. Two murders, now, probably three, plus a poisoned race-horse. I think Maximus and his mate Leon are involved.'

He was staring at me. 'Is this official?'

'No. It's a long story, but I think there might be a Sicilian connection.'

'Indeed. And why with Catana in particular?'

I shrugged. 'It's as good a place as any. Maximus is based here, and Natalis came originally from Leontini which isn't all that far away. To tell you the truth, sir, I'm just looking for some sort of loose end I can get a hold of.'

'I still don't know how I can possibly help you.' Pythias was still frowning, but with the mention of the murders he'd softened up on the schoolmasterish tone. Or rather the metaphorical cane was back in the desk. 'I know of Maximus, naturally, and although he has a certain reputation as a hard man to deal with there is nothing to suggest that he might be involved in any outright criminal activities. Leon, of course, is another matter, but then the fellow's no more than a thug and never has been.'

Shit. I was getting a cold feeling in my stomach.

Maybe this whole trip had been a wild-goose chase after all. I tried again. 'What I'm looking for is some sort of common ground – local common ground – between Maximus and Natalis. What that might be I don't know. Family, friends in common, local business connections.' Hell, I was clutching at straws here and I knew it. The fact that the guy's face was still politely blank wasn't encouraging, either. 'Any sort of link at all, really.'

'Family.' He picked up the pen again and tapped his teeth. 'As you say, Natalis is from Leontini. He went to Rome as a driver many years ago as plain Titus Minicius, and I understand he drove for the Greens very successfully under the sobriquet of Olympius.' Yeah, I remembered Cascellius telling me that. And Phrontis had been right to recommend Pythias to me as a contact: the man obviously knew his racing. 'Not that that's unusual in itself, it quite often happens; Sicilians are a very horse-oriented people, Valerius Corvinus, and racing is in our blood. Natalis, as he is now, may well still have family on the island, but you'd have to make enquiries in Leontini itself.'

'How about Maximus?'

'That I don't know. I can tell you quite definitely that he's not Catanan by birth, although he is a resident of several years' standing, but where he originated I don't know him well enough to say. He could be from Leontini, in which case a connection is possible, but I'm afraid I can give you no definite information on the subject.'

Bugger; it looked like I was in for another trip.

Leontini wasn't far – only about twenty-odd miles – but that I didn't fancy, not without a better reason for it than I'd got. 'Is there anyone locally who'd know for sure?'

'Oh, yes, of course. I was going to suggest the man anyway on the business side. A breeder by the name of Quintus Florus, one of our best local breeders, in fact. He has a farm a little way out on the Leontini road. He's been a regular supplier of the Roman Greens for many years now, and naturally he knows Maximus well. I'm sure he'll be able to help you.'

That sounded more promising. 'Great,' I said.

'His farm is to the right of the road, midway between the third and fourth milestones and just past the Shrine to the Mothers.' He reached for the bill that he'd been working on when I came in. Obviously a dismissal.

'Right. Fine. Thanks very much for your time, sir,' I said, backing out. Pythias hadn't turned out to be such a bad old stick after all, but he still reminded me of the teacher I'd had before I put on my first mantle. 'You've been a great help.'

'My pleasure, Valerius Corvinus. I wish you luck.'

I got out before he could add: 'And by the way, what're three-fifths of two hundred and fifteen, you little bugger?' No point pushing your chances too far.

38

It was too late to think about looking Florus up, even if I hadn't had the added complication of finding my way to his farm. On the other hand, there was still a slice of the afternoon left before I headed back home for the barbel. Time enough for a wander around.

I made my way back to the Roman market-place, but only for passing-through purposes. Greek towns often have Roman-style market squares as well as their own *agorai*, and I've never really been comfortable with them. Oh, sure, the idea's straightforward enough: a forum always has a solid, businessy feel to it that an *agora* lacks, and providing one is a tug of the Greek forelock to Roman cultural and political supremacy. However, at the same time it serves the very practical purpose of providing somewhere for professional expat bores to get together and slag off the local system of government, climate, social mores, culinary peculiarities, standards of domestic service and any other aspects of the place that differ from those of Good Old Rome, at great length and in loud Latin voices; which means that the rest of the city centre's comparatively and blessedly free of the buggers. No coincidence, in my view. They're clever cookies, the Greeks.

I walked down the main drag to the harbour, which would be where the south-bound Leontini road would start. I still wasn't a hundred per cent recovered from the voyage, but the stopover in Tauromenium had helped, and just the feel of solid pavement beneath my sandals and the familiar crowds around me were doing wonders. Besides, it was a beautiful day, warmer than it would've been in Rome and with a sky like a freshly dyed blue silk mantle. Slow and easy does it. There was a big grain ship loading at the end of the deep-water jetty – it's no accident that Ceres is the city's patron; local farmers can manage five harvests in a good year – and I watched that for a while. Then I strolled along to one of the smaller quays at the southern end where a couple of the local fishermen were sorting through the day's catch. Catanan fishermen, evidently, didn't do so badly either, both in the way of bulk or variety. Not a bad place altogether, if it weren't for the mountain.

They looked up, nodded sociably and then ignored me. Finally when I'd had enough of the Spot the Type of Fish game I caught the nearer man's eye.

'Uh . . . you happen to know if there's a livery stable around here, pal?' I said.

'Sure.' He tossed a lobster on to a pile with its antennae-waving friends. 'Over there by the gate. Just keep walking and you can't miss it.'

I nodded my thanks and carried on. The Leontini Gate wasn't all that far, maybe three or four hundred yards down a corniche bordered by granaries and covered storage areas. I saw the livery stable straight off: a fair-sized concern with the stables themselves set back from the road and a cart-yard to one side. A big guy with a grizzled beard was sitting on a bench in the sun. That's one thing about Sicily: no one seems to be in too much of a hurry. Even the slaves loading the grain ships hadn't looked like they were pushing themselves.

I gave Grizzled Beard a wave – not that there was any point, because his eyes were closed – and went over. 'Afternoon, friend,' I said. 'You the owner?'

He opened one eye. 'Could be.'

Jupiter! Laid-back was right! 'Fine. You hire horses?'

'Yeah.' Well, at least I'd got his full binocular attention now, and he'd noticed the purple stripe, which always hooks a trader's monetary interest. 'How many? When for?'

'Just the one, for tomorrow. The morning'll be enough.'

The avaricious gleam faded: there ain't much profit margin in a one-horse half-day hire. 'Well, I think we can manage that.' He stood up. 'You want to look the beast over first?'

'Sure.'

He led me to one of the stalls and a long equine nose shoved itself over the gate to meet us. He scratched it. 'This is Dapple. Five silver pieces. Eight for the whole day.'

'Fine.' Actually, it was pretty reasonable. And the horse wasn't bad either. Hire a hack in Rome and that's more or less what you get: knock-knees, feet like soup-plates, ribs you can count just by looking and a back with more curve to it than the Bay of Naples. This one wasn't exactly a thoroughbred, but she had a lot more going for her than most of the nags for rent I'd had dealings with in the past. It was easy seen we were in real horse country here and customers expected quality. I reached for my purse. 'Three on account?'

'Fine.'

I paid him and he shoved the coins under his belt. Maybe the financial transaction had loosened his jaw muscles up a bit because as we walked back to the bench and I was about to leave him to his interrupted siesta he said; 'You arrived this morning on the *Polyphemus*, right? With the lady who hired the carriage?'

'Uh . . . yeah.' I was cautious: I could've been imagining it, but there seemed to be a sour note in the second half of the question. If so it was understandable, as was my associate status: drivers who've been Perilla'd tend not to keep the experience to themselves, and word soon gets around. 'That was yours?'

'Sure. Only one for rent in Catana. The cart was mine, too.' Ouch; now that sounded *definitely* sour. Suspicions confirmed. Still, he didn't seem to hold all that much of a grudge.

'Is that right?' I said.

'Yeah.' He stared at the carts for a while. I thought his jaw had seized up again and I was just turning to go when he added; 'You here on business or pleasure?'

'A bit of both.'

'What kind of business? If you don't mind me asking?'

'I have to talk to a guy called Florus. He has a farm down the road there.'

'Quintus Florus? The breeder?'

'Yeah. That's him.'

He grunted. 'You're in the horse trade yourself?'

'Uh . . . not really. This is more of a holiday.'

That got a definite reaction, which, now I was getting the measure of the guy, wasn't surprising: use certain key words in the hearing of any entrepreneur who has dealings with foreigners – words like 'holiday', 'tourist' or 'sightseeing' – and you can guarantee you'll hear the merry click of abacus beads. Which was what happened. His interest sharpened.

'You'll be headed up the mountain then?' he said.

Oh, Jupiter! 'My wife did mention it as a possibility, yeah.'

He nodded and sucked a tooth. The avaricious gleam was back with a vengeance. 'Made your arrangements yet?'

'No.' I hadn't exactly promised Perilla that I'd ask about tours. I wasn't rushing into things, either.

'You don't want to go all the way up to the top, not at this time of year.'

He was telling me something I didn't know? 'Friend, I don't want to do that *any* time of year.'

He gave an amused snort. Maybe he was waking

up a bit, or he just scented a business opportunity. It turned out to be the latter, because he said; 'I can do you a deal if you're interested.'

Uh-oh. Still, he seemed a sensible type. I'd liked that bit about not going all the way to the top, for a start. 'Yeah? Like what?'

'Like I say, it's too early in the season for the summit. In three months' time, sure, no problem, but not now. Down here at sea level you get the wrong impression. Up above the tree line it's a different story; to get to the top and back in a day you'd have to overnight on the mountain, and believe me you can freeze to death up there. Not to mention being choked by the gases. Me, I wouldn't advise it. Not with a woman along.'

Oh, Vulcan! I'd picked a right cheery bugger here. He certainly sounded like he knew what he was talking about, though. And with Perilla dead set on a trip of some kind I was open to suggestions. 'So?'

He sucked on the tooth again. 'There's a place on the east side up beyond Crocinium, name of Ox Valley. It's high, sure, but it's a lot lower down than the actual crater and easier to get to, and believe me it's impressive as hell. If you think the lady would settle for that then I'll do you a package. One gold piece and I'll throw the hire of Dapple in for free.'

'Sounds good. What kind of package?'

'Carriage up as far as Crocinium – that's as far as the road goes, about an eight-hour drive from here and it'd take you to just under the tree line. Sleeping carriage, not the usual kind. We'd overnight there, then go the rest of the way by mule. Say another three hours. I'll take you myself.'

'You know the mountain?'

'Sure. I'm Catanan born and bred. Summer months I take tourists up the cone proper, but like I say I wouldn't recommend it for now. You won't do better, trust me.'

Yeah, I'd go for that. It would certainly keep Perilla happy, and one gold piece sounded pretty reasonable. I held out my hand. 'You have a deal, friend.'

'Fine.' We shook. 'When would you want to go?'

Best to get it over with. 'How does the day after tomorrow suit?'

'No problem. Weather permitting. And I'll have Dapple saddled and waiting tomorrow morning.' He took out the silver pieces I'd given him and held them out. 'Pleasure to do business with you, uh . . .'

'Corvinus. Valerius Corvinus. And keep the silver, friend, you've just lifted a load from my mind.'

He grinned. 'The name's Histrio. Have a good day, Corvinus.'

I left him and went back to my barbel.

I had a quick breakfast next morning and set out for town feeling pretty pleased with myself. Perilla had been delighted with the arrangement for the outing; she'd heard of Ox Valley, seemingly, and my new pal the horse-renter had been right when he'd said it was impressive.

'It's the old crater, Marcus,' Perilla had said. 'I was going to suggest it anyway, because as the man said this isn't really the time of year to climb the mountain. And a gold piece with everything in is very good value.'

I picked up Dapple and headed out the Leontini road. Fertile was right; sure, there were patches of cactus and prickly pear by the immediate roadside and filling the occasional hollow, but most of the landscape both sides and as far in front of me as I could see was cheek-by-jowl fields. Stacked fields, too, not the scrubby apologies you have in some farming districts. You name it, the Catanans've got it, and got it in spades: corn, grapes, olives, vegetables, fruit. It beats me how sterile volcanic ash can produce soil that rich, but there you are.

With the number of farms around I was being pretty careful to keep Pythias's directions in mind, but I needn't've worried. A couple of hundred yards past the third milestone the cornfields and vineyards on the right gave way to grassland, and I saw the colts. There were a dozen of them, all legs and silky manes, ranging from pure white to jet black. Me, I'm no horseman and never have been; I can sit one of the beasts okay, well enough not to fall off at a gallop, and I can tell a decent proposition from a wind-shot nag, but that's about it. Even I, though, could see that these youngsters – none of them could've been older than two – were the cream: high necks, small heads, tight, short bellies and muscles that showed as clear as if they'd been pressed out of bronze sheeting. They were grazing when I came up to them, but as I got closer the one nearest the wicker fence tossed its head, wheeled and shot away from me across the grass, moving like the racehorse it would probably be when it grew up and taking the others with it.

As Pythias had said, the farm track led off to the right after the little shrine to the Mothers. I turned Dapple's head into it – she was fidgeting herself by now – and urged her into a trot. The ruckle of colts, who'd been heading in the same direction, took a right-angled turn away from us but stopped at a safe distance and stood watching.

It was a big concern, obviously. On a fine spring morning like this, the horses were all outside, and the grassland either side of the track, divided up into paddocks, was thick with them; mostly youngsters but with the occasional more sedate stallion cropping the grass in splendid isolation. These'd be the studs, no doubt. I was sorry we hadn't brought Lysias, our coach driver; I hadn't seen so much prime horseflesh gathered in one place in my life, and Lysias would've been professionally gobsmacked.

The track ended at a sprawl of stable buildings with a covered exercise yard to one side. You see these things sometimes as optional extras in swanky Janiculan villas, but here it'd be an essential: horses have to be exercised, whatever the weather or time of year, and with prime stock you don't take risks with chills and broken bones. There was the usual gang of stablehands with shovels and pitchforks mucking out – that was another thing I'd noticed since I'd turned down the track, the rich smell from the middens – and I asked one of them for the boss.

'He's in the ring, sir,' the guy said, laying down his fork.

I dismounted. 'The where?'

He took a grip of Dapple's bridle. 'Behind the hay barn there. Just go on, sir. I'll look after the horse.'

'Right, fine. Thanks, pal.'

I followed the line his eyes had pointed and rounded the side of the barn. Like he'd said, behind it was a fenced-off circle of sand maybe fifty yards wide. In it were a man and a horse, or a colt, rather. They were standing facing each other, about ten feet apart, the man perfectly still, the colt fidgeting, ducking its head and blowing down its nostrils. I was on the point of going over, but the guy – Florus, presumably – must've glimpsed me out of the corner of his eye because without turning away from the horse he stretched his hand out in my direction and made a sort of patting motion. I stayed where I was in the barn's shadow and watched.

There was a tangle of leather and metal in Florus's other hand. I hadn't seen it – it had been screened by his body – but the colt evidently had, and it explained the beast's nervousness. He lifted it, holding it out in front of him.

'Nothing to worry about, see?' he was saying quietly. 'It won't bite you, it's just a piece of tack, ordinary leather tack, nothing to be frightened of, nothing to be frightened of at all. What we call a bridle. This metal bar here' – he took it between thumb and forefinger like he was demonstrating – 'well, that's called a bit, right? Made of metal so's you can chew on it, slips in smooth as cream above your tongue and behind your teeth, you'll hardly notice it in time, a big strong lad like you, eh?' The colt pawed the sand, but he ignored it. The way he was talking to it – chatting'd be a better word – the beast could've been a real person capable of holding up its own end of a conversation. 'You see these loops? They take the reins, one either side. Have to have reins so's you know when to turn, when to turn just right past the posts. Nothing to worry about there either, is there? Just an ordinary bridle, nothing special, nothing special at all.' He took a pace forward and stopped. The colt snorted but didn't move. 'You have a look at it. Take all the time you want, there's no hurry, none at all, it's only a bridle, big strong lad like you, well, you're not frightened of a little thing like a bridle, are you? Not a big strong lad like you . . .'

I blinked and shook my head, and the voice went on: same conversational tone like the two of them were chatting over a cup of wine. Nonsense, sure, but the youngster was listening with both ears pricked; and although every so often it snorted and turned its neck it stayed where it was, while Florus moved closer.

Finally, when the horse and the man were standing together, the horse sniffing and nibbling at the bridle, Florus slipped the leather straps gently over its head. The colt snorted and threw up its nose, then quietened, shivering, as he scratched it between the ears and whispered to it.

I'd thought that he'd fasten the buckles, but he didn't; just talked to the shivering horse for a few more minutes before slipping the bridle off again.

Then he patted its neck and walked over to me, leaving the freed colt staring at his back.

'Very impressive,' I said.

He shrugged. 'It's enough for today. You can't hurry things, not if you want quality. And that boy's a beauty. One of my best.'

'Yeah.' I held out my hand. 'Marcus Valerius Corvinus.'

'Quintus Florus.' We shook. He smelled of horse. 'What can I do for you?'

'You have dealings with a guy called Maximus?'

'Yes. The owner of the *Phorcys*. He transports for me.'

'To Minicius Natalis? Master of the City Greens?'

'Among other people, yes.'

'There, uh, somewhere we can talk?'

He gave me a sharp look. 'We're talking here,' he said. 'What's this about?'

'I've just got in from Rome. I'm looking into a murder. Three murders. A driver by the name of Pegasus, an ex-groom called Sopilys and one of Maximus's deck-hands. Guy called Avillius. Also the poisoning of one of the Whites' racehorses, name of Polydoxus.'

I'd used the names carefully, watching each time for a reaction. He was frowning. 'I've heard of Pegasus, of course,' he said. 'And that he was dead, the gods rest him.' There was something in his voice, an inflexion that I couldn't quite place. 'Polydoxus as well, although not the poisoning. The other two men, no. I'll ask you again. What's this about?'

Shit; it was Pythias all over again. 'Maybe nothing.

The guy I really want to talk to is Maximus, but he's off on the *Phorcys*. I was given your name as someone who might be able to tell me something about him.'

'Like what?' He was beginning to sound none too friendly. 'I told you. He transports for me and has done for several years, but he's a business acquaintance, no more. And if you know anything at all about him already you'll know that's nothing unusual where Maximus is concerned.'

'You could vouch for his honesty?'

'I wouldn't trust him with my horses if I couldn't.'

'So you wouldn't be able to hazard a guess why he should arrange for one of his crew to have a fatal accident while the *Phorcys* was loading at Ostia?'

Florus was staring at me. 'Why the hell should he do that?'

'Because the guy concerned – the Avillius I mentioned – opened his mouth too wide to the ex-groom over a jug of wine.'

'About what?'

I shrugged. 'That's what I need to find out.'

'You think Maximus was responsible? *Maximus?*'

'I'd give good odds, pal. The whys and wherefores are another matter, but Maximus was behind it all right.'

'But . . .' Florus paused and ran a hand over his chin. 'You mentioned three murders. And the poisoning. You believe that they were all connected?'

'It's logical, yeah. Though what the connection is I don't know.'

'Aulus's—' He stopped. 'Pegasus's too? But Pegasus

was killed for his purse. Knifed in an alley at the back of a wineshop.'

'Yeah.' It was my turn to frown; there was something definitely screwy here. 'So he was. Barring the purse part, anyway. You're well-informed, friend, and Catana's a long way from Rome. You mind telling me how you knew that little detail?'

'We're a port, Corvinus, and sailors keep up with the racing news. Besides, I made it my business to find out all I could. We may not've liked each other, but family's still family.' His lips twisted. 'Maybe we'd better talk in private after all. You see, Pegasus was my brother.'

39

We went through a gate into the garden of the villa itself. I'd been expecting the usual arrangement of flower beds and formal walks, but it looked as if it'd been laid out before Sicily was even a gleam in Rome's eye: a rich, rambling chaos of flowering shrubs, trellised vines and espaliered plum and fig trees. In one corner there was a natural spring that came bubbling out of the ground and flowed down a channel of rocks and greenery into a wide concrete basin with a statue of Pan in the centre and a flagstoned patio with a marble table and wooden benches at the edge.

'Sit down, Corvinus,' Florus said.

I took the nearest bench. 'Nice place.'

'I like it.' He sat down opposite. 'I've lived here all my life. Father, grandfather too, right back. You want some wine?'

'Sure.'

There was a slave hovering. Florus made pouring motions and the guy nodded and disappeared through the pillars of the portico. 'Now. Tell me what this is about. In detail.'

'You first, pal. Pegasus is your brother?'

'Younger brother, six years younger. His real name's

Aulus. We haven't seen each other for five years. Or maybe I should say *hadn't seen* now.'

His tone was carefully expressionless. 'Uh . . . just because he was in Rome?' I said delicately. 'Or was there another reason?'

'We didn't get on.'

'You care to tell me why not?'

That got me another hard look. 'No, I wouldn't. Because I'd say that it was none of your business.'

Hell. Pussyfooting around at this stage I could do without. Still, he was within his rights, and he didn't owe me any favours. 'True,' I said. 'Even so, it might help me to find out why he died.'

He raised an eyebrow and frowned. I thought he wasn't going to say any more, but finally his shoulders lifted. 'All right. Not that it was anything out of the usual. These things happen in any family. We never did get on, even when we were children.' His eyes moved to the Pan statue. 'Partly it was the age difference, but only partly. Me, I've never looked past the family business, but Aulus wanted more. He always wanted more than he'd already got.'

Yeah, well; that fitted what I already knew about the guy, but I didn't say anything, just waited. Florus's eyes were still fixed on the statue.

'We weren't always this big,' he said. 'In my grandfather's day this was just a small farm, corn mostly. We bred racers, but only for the local market. My father built the place up piecemeal over the years, phased out the corn, bought in a dozen brood mares and a couple of prime stallions from Africa, started selling the colts as far afield as Capua. There were only the three of us, father, me and Aulus, and we were working like crazy just to keep our heads above water. Then one day – it'd be twelve, thirteen years back – Aulus comes to Dad and tells him he wants out. He's had a try-out with one of the factions in Syracuse and they're willing to take him on as a driver. Only thing was, the terms of the deal meant he had to sub himself: no salary, just prize money, and he'd have to work his way up to lead before he had a sniff of that. Sure, he was good and likely to get better – the faction master wouldn't've taken him otherwise – but we needed all the spare cash we could get to plough back into the business. To cut a long story short, Aulus kept on at Dad until he agreed to put up the money. What with the hard cash and the loss of labour it set us back five years.'

The slave came over with a tray. Florus waited while he set out jug, cups and a plateful of cheese and olives, then sent the guy away and poured for both of us. I sipped: a local wine, probably the villa's own, but not bad, not bad at all.

'In Syracuse, Aulus cleaned up. Three years after he started he was driving lead for the top team and winning most of his races. We expected the return of the loan but it never came. We never saw hide nor hair of Aulus, either. Then we sold our first colt to the Roman Greens.'

My interest sharpened. 'Natalis was the faction master?'

Florus shook his head. 'No. Natalis was still driving himself then as lead. I forget the man's name. In any case, the next thing that happened was a letter came from Aulus saying he was moving to Rome to drive for the Greens as their third. Nothing else, just that. That was the last I heard of him until Dad died, five years back. We were doing pretty well by then. Not as well as I am now, but we'd built up the stable and we were selling regularly at premium prices to the top factions. Especially to the Greens.'

I sipped my wine. 'Yeah. I've heard about that. They run an exclusive contract system, right?'

'Not exactly. But since Natalis took over they have first refusal on all the colts. Top rates, though, and no quibbling, so I'm not complaining. Once they've had their pick then we can sell the rest as we like.'

'What sort of numbers are we talking about? Where the Greens are concerned?'

'It varies. Run-of-the-mill horses, maybe three or four a year. That's run-of-the-mill in racing terms, mind, which means colts that can hold their own in a professional field but don't quite have the polish of a winner. They go for the back-up teams, third-stringers and under, or to the two-horse cars for the less experienced drivers. Real champions, like the one you saw me working with, we're lucky if we get one in every three to four seasons. That's enough, though. A champion'll go for a round million against say two hundred thousand for an ordinary horse.'

I whistled. Gods! Big business was right! 'There's that much difference between the two?'

Florus smiled. 'Yes and no. As I say, we're talking top of the range. The colts the Roman Greens buy for their seconds would be prime contenders on any of the provincial tracks, but set them against a real champion and the difference is obvious. At that level if a horse gives away just three, four lengths – less than a dozen yards – over the course of a five-mile race, consistent, then it's always going to be an also-ran, however good the driver. If you're a faction master with your eye on the races-to-wins statistics it's those dozen extra yards you pay for.'

'So how do you spot your champion?'

'Oh, now that's tricky. Telling a racer from a good riding horse is easy enough, but you can't judge a champion from an also-ran just by looks. You're a racing man yourself?'

'Uh-uh.'

'Then if I tried to explain you wouldn't understand anyway. All I can tell you is that once you've been in the business as long as I have then you *know*. From the look in the eye, the way the colt holds his head, the way he moves, even at the walk. How he sees you, how he sees himself. It all adds up. And surface appearance isn't everything, either. I've had colts who look like they should be winners but would never make third place even on a local track. On the other hand, the best I ever bred looked a classic second-stringer.'

'You ever make a mistake?'

'Corvinus, in this business you can't afford to make mistakes. Reputation is everything. Sell just one underperformer above his value and you don't last long enough to sell a second.'

I took another mouthful of wine. 'Okay. You were

saying. The last time you saw your brother was five years back.'

'Five years or thereabouts. Dad caught a summer fever and died. Aulus must've heard somehow because three months after we burned the old man he turns up wanting his half of the stable or the cash in lieu.' Florus's face was expressionless. 'I told him to clear off. He'd had his share and more when he needed it and he'd put nothing into the business since. The family didn't owe him anything, quite the reverse. Besides, all the spare cash was going on the horses. To raise the amount he was asking for I'd've had to sell up or borrow, and either would've finished me. I wasn't prepared to do that, certainly not under the circumstances.'

'How did he take it?'

'He wasn't pleased.' The lips twisted. 'He took the case to court, but the judge and jury were local men, they knew the situation, and they found against him. Aulus went back to Rome and I never saw him again.'

'You had no contact? None at all?'

'I heard about his career through the Greens' rep and from other sources, but not directly, no, not after that one visit.'

'Did Natalis know who he was? That he and you were brothers, I mean?'

'Of course. As I said, he was driving lead for the Greens when Aulus joined them. How much he knew about the estrangement, though, I don't know. Nothing from Dad or me, that's certain, because as far as we were concerned it was private family business. From Aulus – well, I'd guess not from him either. Aulus always was tight-mouthed, and he didn't make friends easily.' He reached for the wine jug and filled my cup. 'All right, Corvinus. It's your turn. All I know is that Aulus transferred to the Whites six months ago and was killed for his purse outside a wineshop. Or at least that was what I thought I knew half an hour back. Now I may not have liked him, but he was the only brother I had, so I'd appreciate anything you can give me.'

I told him the whole story, or the salient details, at least. I expected him to jib a little when I roughed out the scams with Eutacticus and Natalis, but he just shrugged.

'That was Aulus all over,' he said. 'He liked money, he didn't have a moral bone in his body even when he was a child, and if he came out ahead at the end he wouldn't much care about the means. Natalis is the same. I've done business with the man for years but it's always been at a distance, and I prefer to keep it that way. Racing's a dirty game, Corvinus, and always has been. You need a certain kind of mind to get ahead and stay there, and Natalis has got it. Good luck to him, he'll go far, but I can't say I envy him. Me, I wouldn't fancy the price.' He took a sip of his wine. 'Poisoning a horse, though, that's something I can't understand, not under any circumstances. Especially if it's a champion like this Polydoxus. You happen to know who the breeder was?'

'Uh-uh. Cammius, the Whites' boss, said he'd brought it over from Spain.'

Florus grunted. 'Makes sense. The Spanish studs've come on a lot these past ten years. Give them another ten, twenty at most, and we'll have a proper fight on our hands. As it is, the only real edge we've got at present is distance, and the big horse-transporters they're building now are chipping that away.'

'Yeah?'

'Fact. Horses and boats don't go together, but you have to use them. The big purpose-built boats are more stable, the horses scarcely know they're not on dry land, and that's important healthwise. They don't even have to put in to shore to exercise them any more because the decks are big enough to use as walkways.'

'You're talking about boats like the *Phorcys*?'

'No. Oh, yes, the *Phorcys* was built to take horses, and she's as good as they come, but she isn't a tenth of the size of these new ones. They're the real future. And as I say, they're far better for the animals. Horses are sensitive, especially thoroughbreds. Even with a vet on board and making the trip in short stages with breaks on land between they can sicken very easily on a pitching boat. An actual death isn't all that common, but it does happen now and again and the factions have to accept the risk.'

'You can't insure them?'

'Yes, of course you can. The bigger factions have a standing arrangement with their local bankers, but the premiums're crippling.' He frowned into his wine cup. 'Even so, money can never replace a good horse. That's why a reliable shipper's so important.'

'And Maximus is reliable?'

'I've already told you. I wouldn't trust my horses to him if he wasn't. Nor would Titus Natalis. In the fifteen years I've used him I've only ever lost one animal, and believe me where shippers are concerned that's nothing short of a miracle.'

Bugger; this Maximus might be an odd cookie and I'd lay good money he had some sort of scam going, but he was turning out much too lily-white for my liking. 'You've used him for fifteen years?'

'Ever since he moved to Catana from New Carthage. At first we only sold to the smaller factions south of Naples, and they used him as a regular contractor. When we began selling to the Roman Greens Dad recommended him and they took him on. As I said, in this business reputation is everything. If a breeder has a long-term connection with a shipper and has found him reliable then they're happy to let the arrangement stand.'

'So you came first, Natalis second, right?'

'Certainly. By a long way.'

'And Maximus's relationship with him is strictly business?'

'As far as I know. In fact, I'd be very surprised if they'd ever even met one another.'

Hell; so much for establishing a link. Sure, there might still be one at the Roman end, but I had the distinct feeling that getting any sort of grip on Maximus was as difficult as mud-wrestling eels. Even so, my gut told me that he was the key to the whole boiling.

Florus had been watching me over the top of his wine cup. Now he set it down and cleared his throat. 'Corvinus,' he said, 'there's one question I've been careful not to ask. I meant to let you go without asking it, but when push comes to shove I find I can't. You think Maximus and Natalis killed my brother, don't you?' He held up his hand. 'No, I don't mean that you think one of them physically held the knife, nothing so crude. But that they were collectively responsible for his death.'

I took a long time to answer; not because I didn't have an answer ready, but because I knew how important the question was to him: estranged or not, Pegasus had been the guy's brother, and for a Sicilian especially family ties override everything. A casual stabbing by some nameless thug in an alleyway was one thing; that he could shrug off. A planned murder by people he knew, and long-term business acquaintances at that, was something else again. 'Not Maximus,' I said finally. 'He's involved, sure, somewhere along the line – the how and why I don't know, but I'd take my oath on it – but not directly because at the time of the murder he wasn't even in Rome. Natalis . . . honestly, I don't know. He had a vested interest in your brother's death, certainly, and if he was responsible I could make a case for how it was managed, but that's as far as I go. I'm sorry. I can't be any clearer than that.'

'I see.' He frowned. 'Well, I thank you for your

honesty at least. And if at any point you are sure –
or if I can help at all, in any way – then you'll get in
touch, won't you?'

'Yeah. I'll do that.' I stood up. 'Thanks for your
time.'

He held out a hand. 'Enjoy your stay, Corvinus. It
was nice meeting you.'

We shook, and I went to collect my horse.

On the way back, I thought things over. As far as the
actual case went I wasn't all that much further forward, certainly not as far as Maximus was concerned.
On the other hand, coming to Catana had been a
good move. Me, I don't go much for coincidences, and
the fact that Pegasus had been the brother of one
of Natalis's suppliers fitted in too neatly for accident.
How it fitted in was another matter; that I couldn't
even begin to fathom. Still, it was another piece in
the puzzle. Even if it did leave me with the feeling
that I was wading through glue up to the neck

The little nugget of information that Natalis had
known about the relationship was interesting, too. It
helped to explain, for a start, why – independent of the
agent-in-place scam – he'd acted so out of character
in not giving Pegasus the boot when he'd discovered
that the guy was two-timing him: given that he knew
nothing about the estrangement – and my guess, like
Florus's, was that he hadn't – he'd've thought twice
before publicly humiliating the brother of a long-term
business associate, especially one with Florus's track
record as a successful breeder. Like I say, family's

important in Sicily: touch one, you touch them all, and they don't either forgive or forget. No doubt Natalis could've picked up colts just as good as Florus's elsewhere, but there'd be no sense in alienating a prime supplier if he could avoid it, and with the Blues poised to exploit any likely new loophole in the market he couldn't afford the risk.

Which was about as far as I went. Maximus was still the bugbear. *Where* the guy fitted, and *how* I just didn't know, and I needed to before I could take the next step; needed so bad I could taste it. Whatever information Sopilys had had, it'd been important enough to shut his mouth permanently before he could pass it on, and important enough to justify a follow-up murder. Maximus was no natural killer, that I was sure of. Oh, yeah, by all accounts he was a thrawn, morose bugger who wouldn't give you the time of day if his life depended on it, but that's not the same thing, not the same thing at all. So why should a man like that kill, not once but twice?

Horses. Maximus transported horses; that was his life. There had to be a connection with horses . . .

Something Florus had said – said twice, in fact – came back to me.

In this business reputation is everything.

Something tugged at the edges of my mind, but at that point Dapple put her foot in a pothole and I almost lost my balance. By the time we'd sorted the problem out whatever it was had gone.

40

We were up bright and early the next day for our trip to Ox Valley. Me, I wasn't looking forward to it – I'm strictly a city man, and the thought of all that savage scenery without a wineshop in sight brought me out in boils – but Perilla was definitely chirpy.

'Callias was telling me we should have lovely weather for it, Marcus,' she said as she packed our overnight stuff up for loading. Callias, if you've forgotten, was our genial host, the guy with the roll.

'Yeah?' I was filling our biggest travelling flask with the first of the wine Bathyllus had bought in town. Not Setinian standard, or even close, but it'd keep me going through the dark and difficult times ahead. 'Is that so, now?'

'Apparently if the sky above the mountain is clear of clouds in the evening it's a good sign for the next twenty-four hours. Last night it was.'

'Oh, great. There wouldn't happen to be a sign that says we aren't liable to get caught in a major eruption as soon as we set foot on the bugger, would there?'

'Don't be silly, dear. It's perfectly safe.' She rolled up Timaeus of Tauromenium and slipped him into his leather tube. Light reading for the coach, no doubt. 'Besides, we aren't going anywhere near the cone.'

'Just make sure you wear your thickest hat, lady. And I notice that neither Bathyllus nor Meton are favouring us with their company.'

'You know Bathyllus can't sit a mule for two consecutive minutes without falling off. And do you *really* want to spend the best part of three days in Meton's company?'

Put like that, I had to admit she had a point. Etna was bad enough without a surly chef to contend with. And at least he'd given us a good breakfast and a packed lunch, plus enough cold goodies including the remains of the barbel in an almond and wine dressing to last us a month. 'Uh . . . maybe not,' I said.

'Fine.' She frowned at the bag. 'It's sure to be freezing above the treeline, especially if we're on mules. Do you think we've got enough woollens?'

'Perilla, if we just wear all the stuff you've got in there already we'll need a couple of elephants. That's if we can sit down at all. Now pull the drawstring, will you?'

'All right. Only don't complain that you're cold when we get there and it's too late.' She closed the bag and nodded to the hovering slave. He was a big guy, but I saw him stagger as he shouldered it and carried it off to the waiting coach. 'This is all rather exciting, isn't it?'

Yeah, if the prospect of eight hours in a coach and an overnight stop in some god-forsaken village a stone's throw from an active volcano followed by three hours of having your backside rubbed raw on top of a mule excited you. Still, if the lady was happy that was what mattered. I kept a judicious silence.

'One thing, Marcus.' She picked up Timaeus: no bag for that lad, he was evidently travelling up front with us. 'We're on holiday. You mention Pegasus, Natalis, Maximus or murder just once and I pitch you into the nearest fumarole. Preferably an active one, if I can find it. This is a warning. Do you understand?'

'Yeah, fair enough.' I kissed her. 'My lips are sealed.'

'Just don't forget, then.' She took a last look round the room. It was pretty empty, except for the larger bits of furniture which wouldn't fit into the magic bag. 'Well, we'd best be off. Has Meton loaded the food?'

'All done.'

'Walking-sticks?'

'Jupiter, Perilla! Histrio'll take care of all that. He's probably got bloody crampons for the mules.'

She sniffed. 'Don't be facetious, dear. Off we go, then.'

Histrio was waiting outside with the carriage. That at least looked promising. Sleeping carriages are cumbrous and slow as hell, but you can stretch out in them and they're a lot more comfortable than the usual kind.

'All set, Corvinus?' He opened the door and pulled down the steps.

'More or less.' I looked round. 'Where're the mules?'

'They'll be waiting for us at Crocinium. I've got an arrangement with one of the farmers up there.'

'Fine.'

'You've chosen a good day. The mountain was clear last night. That means—'

'That the next twenty-four hours'll be fair. Yeah, I know.'

He grinned. 'We'll make a Catanan of you yet.'

'I'll settle for not being fried, gassed or flattened, pal.'

'No fear of that.' He nodded towards Etna. 'She's been quiet enough these last few years.'

'When was the last eruption, incidentally?' Perilla asked.

'We had a small one about twenty-odd years back, ma'am. Scarcely more than a spill, and there was plenty of warning. Like I told your husband, the main danger's the gases, and you only get them in the last two thousand feet before the top. Ox Valley's quite safe.'

She turned to me. 'There you are, Marcus. Now stop overdramatising.'

I shrugged and held the door while she climbed the steps, then got in beside her. Histrio mounted the box and whipped up the horses – no thoroughbreds, these, just big lunks with shoulders like oxen – and we were away.

The road up to Crocinium took us through some nice countryside, prime agricultural land like the stretch I'd ridden through the day before. I didn't see any more horse studs, but there were plenty of flocks and herds, plus acres and acres of cornfields and vineyards, with clusters of farm buildings what must've been every half-mile or so at most; in good repair, too, so the locals couldn't've been short of a copper piece. The only indications that we were in volcano country were the occasional black, lichen-covered rocks that stuck up like lumps of clinker from some huge furnace and the great bowls of dark rubble filled with scrub and prickly pear where part of a field had collapsed, or maybe been blown out from underneath. They all looked reassuringly old, though. Maybe I had been overdramatising after all.

Perilla had Timaeus open on her lap. 'According to this, Marcus,' she said, 'there was a major eruption some four hundred years ago which stopped the Carthaginian army under Himilco from reaching Catana.'

'Is that right, lady?' I took a swallow of wine; one good thing about moving at a pace that makes outstripping snails a problem, you can hold a wine cup without half of the stuff going over your wrist. 'Fascinating.'

She sniffed. 'Don't be sarcastic, dear. Considering how seldom a large eruption happens it was quite fortuitous for the locals.'

'Tough luck on Himilco, mind. You do your careful planning, then suddenly you find you have to wade through boiling lava before you can get down to the rape and pillage. You think he'd taken out travel insurance before he left?'

'Marcus, you're impossible. I don't believe you have a cultured bone in your body.'

'True. You want a game of Robbers?'

'No, thank you. I'm reading.'

'How about Odd-and-Even?'

'*No!*'

'There's no need to shout.' Bugger; hardly more than an hour into the journey and I was bored stiff already. Sitting outside a wineshop in a city street watching the world go by is one thing; doing it through a carriage window when the world consists of a slowly changing panorama of olives, vines, cabbages and flatulent livestock is something else. There was nothing for it but sleep. I drained the cup, settled back and closed my eyes.

We reached Crocinium eventually; not that you'd've noticed necessarily, because there wasn't all that much more to the place than some of the bigger farmhouse complexes we'd passed: a cluster of huts built out of the usual black volcanic rock with the road petering out into a cart-track beyond. The reason for the name, though, was obvious: the low hills on every side were a mass of yellow flowers.

'Marcus, it's beautiful!' Perilla said.

Well, I wouldn't quite go that far, but it was pretty impressive all the same. We pulled up in what must've been the village square. Histrio got down from the box and opened the carriage door.

Eight solid hours in a coach, barring stops for the necessary calls of nature, don't do a lot for your powers of mobility. I came down the steps like an arthritic tortoise and looked around. The current visible population numbered two donkeys, an evil-looking goat tethered to a fig tree, several chickens and a nose-picking kid; plus three senior citizens who scowled at us from a bench over the tops of their quaintly carved ethnic walking-sticks like we were the advance party of Himilco's army. Call me city slicker if you like, but Crocinium looked like it had as much going for it as a used boil plaster.

Except . . .

The bench with the oldies had a table beside it, and on the table was a jug of wine and three cups. I was reminded of that philosopher guy shipwrecked on the coast of Greece somewhere who gave himself up for lost until he caught sight of a set of geometrical figures drawn in the sand. A wineshop. Civilisation.

'Afternoon, granddad,' I said to the nearest Tithonus lookalike.

The Tithonus grunted. I'd met friendlier basilisks. Still, at least I'd shown willing.

Perilla had come out behind me. 'Well, this is nice, Marcus,' she said. 'And so pleasant to be out of the coach.'

'Yeah.' The snotty-nosed kid had run inside and come out with a larger version of himself. The landlord, obviously. I brightened and turned to Histrio. 'You fancy a jug of wine, pal?'

'Sure.' He nodded to the landlord. 'This is Septimus, by the way.'

The guy grinned revealing a set of teeth like an abandoned graveyard. 'Snow-cooled?' he said.

I blinked in surprise; civilisation was right: back in Rome, snow-cooled wine was definitely a luxury item.

Maybe I'd been too hasty in my judgment. 'If you can manage it.'

'No problem.' Septimus disappeared inside.

There was another pair of benches and table to one side in the shade of a trellised vine. Histrio waited until Perilla and I had sat down, then eased himself on to the bench opposite: the only thing worse than eight hours in a coach is eight hours on top of one. 'You're on the mountain now, Corvinus,' he said. 'Snow's there for the picking up, eight months of the year anyway. All year round if you're willing to go high enough. In the winter the locals cut it out in blocks and store it underground or pack it in straw to transport to the coast.'

'Is that so?' I said.

'It's one of the local industries. That and saffron from the crocuses. I know you've brought food with you, but Septimus's wife does a saffron chicken with mountain-herb stuffing that your Roman gourmets would die for.'

Things were definitely looking up. 'Sound good to you, Perilla?'

'Marvellous.' The lady was smiling.

'You'll be from Rome?' That was my pal Tithonus One, in an accent you could've cut with a knife. So; the natives were friendly after all, or curious at least.

I turned to him. 'Yeah, that's right.'

'Thought so,' he said smugly. 'I was there a few years back, in the Divine Augustus's time.'

A few years back. Jupiter!

'Big place. I've a son makes carts in the Subura. He

showed me around. Nice place, fine for a holiday, but you wouldn't want to live there.'

Ah, well; to each his own, and I wasn't going to argue. I stretched out my legs. There was a breeze off the mountain; I expected it to smell of sulphur, but it didn't, just of greenery with a faint scent of thyme. *Definitely* too hasty in my judgment. A wineshop makes a big difference to a place.

The wine came, with a lump of snow in it as big as my fist, plus a plate of black olives and diced cheese in oil and thyme. 'I brought a jug of iced water too for the lady,' Septimus said. 'No fruit juice, I'm afraid, but I've put a sprig or two of mint in it.'

'Lovely,' Perilla said. I winced.

I ordered the saffron chicken with some bread and a green salad. Then I settled back against the vine-stock. Yeah; I could definitely get to like Crocinium after all.

Histrio poured the wine. It was thin and straw-coloured, but it had a herby tang to it that I hadn't met before, and the melting snow made it ice-cold. Nice. 'We'll have an early night, if you're agreeable,' he said. 'The mules'll be here just after dawn. It's a three-hour trek to the valley, and if you want time to see around and get back before the sun goes behind the mountain then we'd best make an early start.'

'Sounds good to me,' I said, reaching for an olive. Today's sun had gone in now, but even with the breeze it wasn't cold. One of the donkeys brayed, and off in the distance back the way we'd come another one answered him. Apart from that the only sound was the growing chirping of the evening grass-hoppers.

Maybe holidays weren't so bad after all. The chicken was good, too, when it came.

I was awake at first light next morning, largely because of a big bugger of a cockerel that had decided to perch on the carriage roof. Probably a relative of the saffron chicken on a revenge jag; like I say, family's big in Sicily. Getting out of the coach, I could see what Histrio had meant about this being the wrong time of year to spend a night on the mountain; we'd been snug enough with the extra blankets Perilla had packed for bedding, but even here on the lower slopes it was chilly as hell and everything was covered with a glistening sheen of frost. The joys of country living; there probably wasn't a hypocaust within thirty miles, and as for bath-houses, forget them. I stretched until my joints cracked, took a few deep breaths – at least the air was good up here, if you ignored the donkeys' contribution – then shoved my head back inside.

'Hey, lady.'

The mound of covers shifted. 'Wrstfgzzt?'

Me, I enjoy early mornings, at least if there hasn't been a serious night-before, but Perilla's one of nature's dedicated sleepers, and it needs more than a cockerel going off a yard above her head to bring her round. I poked the nearest prominent bulge until it squirmed out of reach. 'Come on. Rise and shine. It's a beautiful day.'

'Go away, Marcus.'

I grinned; well, at least that had been intelligible. 'The mules're here. We're leaving in five minutes.'

The heap of blankets erupted and she came out tousled and blinking. '*What?*'

'Joke.'

'Corvinus, I will kill you.' She yawned. 'What time is it?'

'Just after dawn.' I glanced up at the feathers of smoke that curled to the left of the main roof: like a lot of places in these mountain villages, the wineshop's cooking arrangements consisted of an open wood fire in a separate kitchen at one end of the building. I'd noticed quite a few plumes from the nearby houses, too; the village was waking up, and there was a distinct smell of piney woodsmoke. Lovely. 'If you hurry we might be able to cadge a wash and some hot porridge.'

'Marcus, it is *freezing* out there!'

'Yeah. I know.' I looked over towards Etna. The morning sun was shining full on the cone where it rose high and grey above a horizontal line of silver mist that veiled the trees stretching halfway up the slope. Patches of snow glittered in the higher dips. 'Come on, you're missing this.'

'You're not supposed to be this cheerful. You hate the countryside.'

'Oh. Right.'

The wineshop door opened and Histrio came out stretching. 'Good morning, Corvinus,' he said. 'You sleep well?'

'Not bad.'

'We've time for breakfast, if you and the lady would

like some. Bread and omelette. Catia's making it now.'

'Great. Any sign of the mules?'

'They should be arriving shortly. The farmer who owns them lives just down the hill.'

'Fine.' I ran a hand over my chin. Shaving would have to wait for the duration: in this cold weather a scrape with even a freshly honed razor wouldn't be too pleasant. 'What about a wash?'

'There's a kettle of water on the boil. I'll bring it out to you.' He went round to the lean-to kitchen.

Perilla joined me. We'd slept in our warmest tunics, and she'd slipped on a thick mantle with a cloak over it. 'All set?' I said.

She shivered. 'It certainly does get cold up here, doesn't it?'

'You're the one who wanted to see Etna.'

'Stop acting so smug, Marcus. It's too early in the day.'

I grinned. 'You'll feel better once you've had a wash and a hot breakfast. And I have to admit I'm impressed so far.'

'It is impressive, isn't it?' She was looking over at the cone. The sun had risen a notch or so higher, and the sky above the mountain was beginning to turn a deep blue. No clouds, either, and the bank of mist was beginning to thin. 'Glad we came?'

'Ask me that when we get back, lady.'

She gave me a quick kiss. Histrio reappeared with the steaming kettle and a basin. We took turns washing – just face and hands, but it warmed us up and we felt fresher – then went in for breakfast.

There ain't nothing better than new bread and omelettes made from eggs straight out of the hens.

Half an hour later the guy turned up with the mules: one for each of us plus a fourth with saddlebags for the food and extra cloaks. Their breath steamed in the morning air. The village was getting busier now: the local farmers were heading off to the outlying fields where there were weeds to be cleared and late vines to be pruned, and the women were out grinding the day's corn into meal. The air smelled of wood-smoke and pine resin. Old Tithonus from the evening before went past with a mattock over his shoulder and gave us a cheery wave. Horace would've been in ecstasies.

We mounted the mules and set off. Muleback isn't exactly the most dignified way to travel, but it's marginally faster than walking. Also, the beasts seemed to know which among the branching paths to choose without all that much guidance. It's always good to feel that you're in the hands – hooves – of professionals, and these little buggers evidently knew their business.

'You come up here often?' I asked Histrio. He half turned: although we were less than a quarter-mile beyond the village the path had narrowed too much to ride abreast so we were nose to tail in a short line.

'Maybe about five, six times a year, spring to autumn' he said. 'Like I told you, Ox Valley's a popular alternative to the cone, but you sometimes get the occasional tourist who wants to do both. In which case we take the southern route and come back down this way.'

'It's certainly beautiful countryside,' Perilla said.

It was. We were still passing through fields and vineyards, but as we got further from Crocinium I noticed more orchards and fruit trees. Chestnuts, too. There seemed to be a lot of chestnuts.

'You won't notice a lot of difference until we get higher up, ma'am,' Histrio said. 'We've still a while before the main lava fields. Enjoy it while you can.'

We rode in silence for a couple of miles. The sun was fully up now, sucking the moisture from the ground, and it was warmer, but sure enough the landscape was beginning to change, becoming more broken with the orchards giving way to clumps of oak, beech and pine. Still the chestnuts, though, and the local farmers – there had to be some, at least – had cleared patches of undergrowth away to grow catch-crops of corn and vegetables. We'd just passed one of these when Histrio pulled up and pointed.

'That's the first of the lava,' he said. 'Just a small section, but there'll be a lot more of it from here on.'

I looked. The gradual slope to our left – towards the mountain – was thickly overgrown with ferns and broom, but on the other side of the path where the ground rose sharply was a long stretch of blackish, dis-coloured stone like the edge of a wave that had broken against the hillside and frozen where it had settled. The path was different, too: stonier, with patches of black sand and gravel with only the occasional blade of grass pushing through the surface.

'How old would that be?' I said.

Histrio shrugged. 'Who knows? The lower stretches

on the southern route are a lot more noticeable because the undergrowth has had less of a chance to re-establish itself. This is old stuff. Mind you, like I say, we'll see a lot more of it shortly.'

We did. As the path rose and we edged closer to the mountain the trees thinned further until we were passing through mostly scrub, broken by long stretches of scree either side that got wider and wider the further we went until they were more like black rivers of stone flowing left to right across our direction of travel. Etna was much closer now, taking up most of the skyline. There were clouds – or maybe it was smoke – gathering above the summit. I noticed, too, that most of the birds had disappeared.

The ground began to rise more sharply. There wasn't much greenery now, let alone trees, just the occasional clump of bracken or cactus clinging to the surrounding rocks or filling the hollows. No birds, no insects, hardly any signs of life at all. The mules slowed their pace to a steady plod, their hooves crunching on dark gravel, and that was the only sound. We still had the sun – the sky was an almost perfect cloudless blue – but I felt myself begin to shiver, and the hairs were rising on the back of my neck. I looked back at Perilla. She obviously felt the same. This was a terrible place, made even more terrible by the thought of what lay just below us: a dead, dreary landscape littered with smashed and jagged boulders and ugly lumps of black rock streaked and stained with red and orange and yellow – every colour but green. If the actual cone itself was worse – and by all accounts it was – then I was glad we hadn't gone that way.

'This is the scenic route, pal?' I said to Histrio.

He grinned and reined in his mule. 'It's not too pleasant, is it?' he said. 'We've done well, in fact we're nearly there. The valley's just round the next bend.'

Thank Jupiter for that. It'd been an experience, sure, but not one I'd want to repeat. I turned to Perilla. 'You okay, lady?'

She was looking as grim as I felt. Histrio might be cheerful enough, and the mules didn't seem all that concerned, but then they were locals and used to it. A gold piece to come up here suddenly seemed dear at the price; me, I'd pay good money to be back where the world wasn't one great slag heap. 'Yes, thank you, Marcus,' she said. 'It's . . . quite striking, isn't it?'

'Like hell's antechamber,' I said. 'And I'm not kidding, either.' I wasn't: surroundings like those take all the bounce out of you.

She managed a smile. 'Fair description.'

'Ready for the last bit?'

'Of course.'

We rounded the bend . . .

If we'd been in hell's antechamber, we'd come within sight of hell itself. I had to admit Ox Valley was impressive, but it made me almost physically sick. Ahead of us was a huge amphitheatre which stretched ahead and to the right as far as I could see, ringed with cloud and bounded by sheer cliffs of black rock. I stared.

'Sweet holy gods!'

Histrio had dismounted. 'We go on foot from here,' he said.

I swallowed. 'Uh . . . where to, pal?'

'The best view's up ahead.' He stooped and picked up two or three fair-sized stones. 'Don't worry, it's perfectly safe.'

Yeah, right. He led the way, and Perilla and I followed. The path – what was left of it – took us over the brow and on to a wide shelf of rock. I stopped, but Histrio went on until he was standing almost on the very lip.

'That's Ox Valley,' he said.

'Amphitheatre' didn't do it justice: forget the Games, you could've held a full-scale battle there and still had room for two or three more besides. We were halfway up a cliff that could've come straight out of a nightmare: I swear there were clouds below us as well as above and on either side, and they swirled past curtains of sheer black rock stained top to bottom with long rivers of multicoloured lava and patches of dirty snow. Without the sun (and I doubted if this place ever did see the sun) it was bitterly cold, and if stone could rot then the wind that blew directly into my face without pause or variation smelled of the stench it would give off: a dusty, dark, sulphurous stink that caught the back of my nose and throat and almost made me gag. As far as the eye could reach, the valley floor – what you could see of it through the clouds, and Jupiter knew how far down it was – was a smashed chaos of stone and blocks of lava heaved up in waves like a petrified sea, with here and there huge misshapen boulders and columns of rock standing out from its surface like islands. There was no sound, not even the drip or run of water, and no life or movement. The whole place, mile upon mile of it, was dead; worse, it had never been alive.

Hell was right. The hairs on my scalp bristled.

Perilla must've felt the same, because she murmured: 'Avernus. *Aornos*, the birdless place.' I glanced back at her and saw her shudder. Yeah; not even vultures could live here. There wouldn't be nothing for them to live on. 'Horrible.'

'It's the old crater,' Histrio said. 'Three miles wide, almost a mile deep.' He walked to the edge of the platform. 'Come and see this.'

'Uh . . . no, I think I'll pass on that, pal,' I said. 'Whatever it is.'

'Come on, Corvinus. I told you, it's perfectly safe. And it's part of the tour.'

I glanced back at Perilla – she hadn't come any closer than the top of the brow – and edged forward. I've got a better head for heights than most, and it wasn't just fear of falling; the place itself had me by the scrotum and I could feel my balls shrink. They say everywhere has a *numen*, a sort of inbuilt personifying spirit. If so, then Ox Valley's was so alien it wasn't even close to human.

When we were standing together I stopped.

'Watch,' Histrio said. He hefted one of the stones he'd picked up and threw it into space. It curved in an arc and dropped through the swirling clouds. I caught myself trying to follow it with my eye and waiting for the *toc!* as it hit the valley floor. Nothing. A mile's a long way down.

Histrio held out a second stone. 'Your turn,' he said.

I took it and he moved away. I turned to face the drop – the edge was only a scant yard in front of me – and threw . . .

'*Marcus!*'

Why I did it I don't know, but when Perilla screamed I dropped to my knees and froze to the rock. Something hit me hard on the back, then it was over me and gone. I heard Histrio yell, just once, but in that yell was all the terror in the world.

Then there was silence; a long, empty silence.

Shit.

I picked myself up, brain numb. Somewhere someone was sobbing. Then Perilla had a hold of me and was pulling me away.

There was no sign of Histrio. But then, the guy would be long gone.

I shook my head to clear it. I was beginning to shake. 'What the fuck happened?' I said.

'He rushed at you.' Perilla's face was pressed against my neck. 'He just rushed at you.'

Sweet gods! I glanced back at the cliff edge. A mile. The guy would still be falling . . .

'Marcus, I thought he'd pushed you over!'

Yeah. He would've done, too, if it hadn't been for the lady's scream. She has a good pair of lungs, Perilla. I closed my eyes. A mile . . .

If you go to Sicily, then watch your back.

Why the hell had he done it?

41

We were lucky that the mules seemed to know their way home. Although the path back was downhill and pretty straightforward, there were a couple of places where it forked and I couldn't remember which way we'd come. In the end I just left the beasts to it, and once we were down as far as the cultivated area there were plenty of people to ask. Even so, the sun was only just above the bulk of the mountain when we reached Crocinium.

Septimus the wineshop owner was sitting at the table under the trellised vine with his wife and kid, in the middle of their evening meal. He frowned when he saw the two riderless mules.

'Where's Histrio?' he said.

I dismounted, helped Perilla down, and told him while the woman and the kid watched and listened with round eyes.

'He tried to kill you? *Histrio?*'

I remembered Florus's reaction when I'd told him about Maximus being responsible for the death of his deck-hand Avillius. The two were identical: total disbelief. Maybe coincidence, but interesting all the same.

'There wasn't any doubt,' Perilla said. 'He got Marcus standing with his back to him on the edge of the drop and then tried to push him over. I saw the whole thing and I wasn't mistaken. It was quite deliberate.'

'Not Histrio.' The guy was shaking his head numbly. 'He wouldn't've done that. It doesn't make sense. Histrio wouldn't hurt a fly.'

'Look, pal,' I said; I wasn't about to waste any tears on that bastard, or shed any crocodile ones either: flies might've been safe, but it had been open season on Roman purple-stripers, and if he'd got me then Perilla would've been next. 'We've had a trying day. Any chance of a jug of wine and whatever's left in the pot there?' I glanced at Perilla. 'How about you, lady?'

'Wine would be much appreciated. Under the circumstances.'

Septimus blinked and got up. 'Yes. Yes, of course. I'll get it now.' He moved a few steps, then turned. 'Holy Vulcan, I've known the man for years! He's up here with clients half a dozen times every summer, he's practically one of the family! What reason could he have had?'

'Your guess is as good as mine. In fact, I was rather hoping that you could tell me.' I eased myself down on to the bench that the three Tithonuses had been occupying the evening before. 'Let's have the wine first, though.'

The woman, after she'd sent the kid to deal with the mules, disappeared inside after her husband with the half-full plates. I was sorry I'd disturbed the family meal, but no doubt they'd have plenty to talk about.

Sure enough, it was a good five minutes before Septimus came back out with the wine and two cups. Maybe he'd had a belt himself in the interim, because he looked a lot more with it and he looked serious as hell. 'My wife's reheating the stew,' he said. He sat down on the bench opposite. 'Now. I'm sorry, sir, but you'd better tell me exactly what happened. The village is too small to have a judge's representative, but presumably you'll report this to the authorities in Catana and they'll send someone up to ask questions.'

Shit; I'd forgotten about that aspect of things. Still, it was fair enough. There wasn't much more I could do other than repeat what I'd already told him, but I did it anyway.

'There wasn't any sort of quarrel?' he said. 'Disagreement, even?'

'Uh-uh. He just suddenly went for me. I ducked and he tripped. That was it.'

'And you hadn't had any dealings with him before?'

'No.' I took a swallow of the wine. 'I'd never so much as met the guy. I'm in Sicily to look into a murder back in Rome. One of the people who might be involved is a ship's captain called Maximus.' Not a flicker. 'He's a Catanan himself, or he's based there at least. Transports racehorses.'

Septimus frowned; the guy was obviously thinking. 'Histrio has – had – a stable in Catana,' he said.

'Yeah, I know. That's where we met up. I rented a horse from him.'

'That's not what I meant. He breeds himself, in a

small way, just as a sideline. He has a stud farm outside the town on the Hybla road.'

The back of my neck prickled. 'Is that so, now?'

'It's nothing major. Most of the colts go for riding horses, but he's sold a couple of winners to the Blue faction in Leontini.'

Quite an entrepreneur, this Histrio: livery stable, tourist business, now horse breeding. Mind you, they were all connected, and these small-town types tend to have several irons in the fire at once. And things were beginning to gel. 'He run it on his own?' I said. 'The stud farm, I mean?'

'More or less. Like I say, it's only a small business. Technically his brother's co-owner, but he's away a lot.'

'Brother?'

'I don't know anything about him other than the name. Man called Leon.'

Everything went very still. I noticed that Perilla was staring at me wide-eyed. 'Uh . . . you sure about that, pal?' I said carefully. 'No mistake?'

'Could be Leontes. He's mentioned him once or twice, no more.' He looked up; his wife was coming from the direction of the kitchen outhouse carrying a loaded tray. 'Catia, what was Histrio's brother's name?'

'Leon.' She set the tray down on the table. 'He's some sort of sailor, isn't he? Off on one of the boats.'

Oh, sweet and holy Jupiter! The *Phorcys*'s mate, it had to be! There was a connection after all!

Septimus was watching me. 'The sailor bit I'd forgotten,' he said. 'That make sense to you?'

'Yeah. Some, anyway.' It still didn't explain why Histrio had tried to kill me, mind – even if he and his brother had happened to talk when the *Phorcys* had called in at Catana neither Maximus nor Leon could've known that I was following them – but it couldn't be coincidence; no way could it be coincidence. Which meant that Histrio, for some reason or other, had decided on murder off his own bat.

Horses. It all came down to horses. Pegasus drove them, his brother bred them, Maximus and Leon transported them and now I found that Leon had a brother of his own who dealt in them and had done his best to push me down the crater of an ex-volcano. Planned it, too: I'd bet the whole trip had been a set-up from the start.

So what the hell was going on?

We hired one of the locals the next day to drive us in the coach back to Catana. The murder attempt had effectively lifted Perilla's ban, so we spent the first bit of the journey chewing it over.

'They weren't natural killers,' I said. 'Neither of them. That's what bugs me. Maximus is an antisocial bastard, but no one I've talked to has suggested that he was capable of murder; even Florus wouldn't't've accepted the idea if I hadn't presented it as a fact. And Histrio was just a wheeler-dealer. So what pushed them over the edge?'

'Not a very happy phrase, Marcus, in Histrio's case.'

I tried a grin that didn't work. 'Black humour's not like you, lady.'

She turned away to look out of the carriage window: we were back with the pastoral scenery again, and I for one wasn't sorry; you don't appreciate fields and vineyards until they're gone. 'Let's be clear about this, dear,' she said quietly. 'I don't feel any regret or pity for that man. None at all. He deserved all he got. And I don't agree with you about their comparative innocence, either. The only difference between Histrio and Maximus, or indeed between him and the murderer of Pegasus, is that the latter two's murder attempts succeeded.'

'Yeah. Right.' Nevertheless, I tried to blank out the thought that had been with me ever since Ox Valley: a mile; a whole *mile*! And knowing, all the way, what lay at the bottom of it. She could be hard, Perilla. 'But they weren't movers. Or not prime movers. The guy responsible for all this – ultimately responsible – has to be someone who benefits both from Pegasus's death and the poisoning. That means Natalis or Acceptus.'

She was facing me again. 'So which one?'

'Before we came to Sicily my money would've been on Acceptus, but now I'm not so sure. Natalis is the only one of the pair with links to all three. Plus to Pegasus himself, of course, through his brother. And one gets you ten that the key to the whole shooting match is horses.'

'Hmm.' Perilla rested her chin on her hand. 'You don't suppose it could have something to do with revenge, do you?'

'How do you mean, lady?'

'You told me that Florus and Pegasus were at daggers drawn five years ago over their father's will, and that Florus was responsible for cutting his brother off without a penny. Florus has built up a very successful stud farm, and a lot of the success has come from his supplying of horses to the Roman Greens.'

'Yeah, that's right. So?'

'It's just that Histrio was a breeder too, and his brother is the mate on the *Phorcys* which transports for the Greens. I was just wondering what would happen if Pegasus managed somehow to persuade the two to exchange one of the colts supplied by Florus for one of their own.'

A cold finger touched my spine. 'Go on.'

'That's all, really. But the result would be that Natalis would get a second-rate horse when he'd paid for a champion racer. Where would that leave him vis-à-vis Florus?'

I felt a prickle of interest. What had Florus said? *In this business you can't afford to make mistakes. Reputation is everything.* It would work; sure it would. 'Florus's reputation with the Greens would go right down the tube.'

'There you are, then. Pegasus's brother has refused to give him – in his eyes, at least – his proper share of the joint inheritance. In revenge Pegasus ruins – or tries to ruin – Florus's market with the Greens.'

'Yeah, but lady, it didn't happen like that. Florus is still trading with Natalis. And if Natalis had thought he'd been sold a ringer then the first thing he'd do is scream to Florus and the game would be up.'

'Unless he wasn't taken in. I did say "tries to ruin", Marcus. Remember, he did know that Pegasus was Florus's brother and the two men had and have a long-standing business relationship. Or at least Florus had one by that time with the Greens as a whole. Natalis might have decided to absorb the loss and bide his time to take a revenge of his own.'

I shook my head. 'Perilla, it wouldn't work. There are too many holes. First of all, if this happened as much as five years back then why hasn't there been any sign of it? Pegasus was still driving for the Greens up to six months ago and Natalis is still using Maximus as a transporter. If he knew both of them had tried to screw him he'd've settled the score long since. Also there's the problem of Maximus himself. The guy's a businessman, he relies on his reputation for honesty. You think he'd be ready to throw that away in exchange for a few gold pieces from Pegasus? Third, it doesn't explain either of the other two murders or the poisoned horse. The dead deck-hand wasn't aboard the *Phorcys* five years ago. Whatever beans he had to spill must've had a connection with something a lot more recent than—'

I stopped. Oh, shit. Oh, holy, immortal Jupiter!

Perilla frowned. 'Marcus? Marcus, what's wrong?'

I waved her down. I had to think. I remembered the guy with the thimbles and the pea in Cattlemarket Square: around and around and around . . .

Five years. Pegasus had been at his brother's stud

farm five years ago. Maximus might be a surly bugger, but businessman or not what friends he had he stuck to. Histrio didn't know me from a cold in the head and couldn't've known I would be in Sicily, but he knew I had to die all the same. Sopilys, with a secret that was worth twenty gold pieces and earned him a knife in an alley. Pegasus, with his penchant for blackmail . . .

They don't even have to put into shore any more.

It fitted. It all fitted sweet as a nut, everything bar none. Around and around and around. I might not have all the answers yet, not by a long chalk – there was the question of the vet, for a start, and the markings, and above all Typhon – but it was only a matter of time because I knew now which thimble the pea was under.

I had to have another word with Florus. And after that catch the first ship back to Rome.

42

It took us twelve days in total to find a suitable merchantman and make the trip to Ostia, and even so the
captain had already let the deckhouse to a rich Sicilian
and we had to bed down al fresco, so I arrived like a
half-wrung-out dishrag. Still, I was happy enough: I'd
got what I wanted, and the information from Florus
checked out all the way down the line. We spent the
first day back recuperating, and I sent Alexis round to
the three sets of stables – Greens, Blues and Whites
– to arrange a meeting. Sure, I could've talked to the
principal protagonists individually but if I was right,
and I'd bet a month's income to a button that I was,
the solution to the case was so tangled that I'd need
them all together.

They agreed to meet at the Greens' stables the next
day, with Cario representing the Whites: Cammius, it
seemed, was out of it completely now and had been
since Polydoxus's death. When the gate troll steered
me into Natalis's office they were already there. Not
that the atmosphere was exactly convivial. The faces
that turned towards me could've been carved from
marble.

'Uh . . . hi,' I said.

'Sit down, Corvinus,' Natalis snapped. He didn't look much more prepossessing than the last time I'd seen him. 'Socrates, wait outside.'

The gate troll gave me a parting scowl and left, closing the door behind him with exaggerated care. There was an empty chair to the right of the desk opposite Acceptus and Cario. I pulled it up and sat.

It wasn't just me. Put three faction bosses – and it seemed I'd have to include Cario in that category now – in the same room together and it's like hosting a wolverine's convention. They'll get on well enough in public, sure, but egos that size need space, and if you listened hard enough you could hear the elbows flexing. Acceptus, especially, was looking like a mule had shat in his porridge.

Natalis leaned back. If the charioteer statuette on his desk had still been there he'd've disappeared behind it altogether, but it'd been taken away. Probably to leave a clear line of fire. 'All right,' he said. 'What's this all about?'

Well, I appreciated the guy's directness, anyway. 'The case is solved,' I said. 'I know who murdered Pegasus and why. Also who poisoned Polydoxus.'

I had a good view of Acceptus and Cario. The youngster was looking pale but his jaw was set. Acceptus crossed his legs. Neither of them said anything.

'Is that right, now?' Natalis said. You could've used the glare I got to lance boils.

I turned to him. 'You lost a colt about a year back. From a Sicilian breeder called Florus.'

He shifted. 'Right. So?'

'You care to recount the details?'

'That's private faction business, Corvinus.'

Shit; we had to get this out of the way now, or we'd never get anywhere. 'Look, pal,' I said evenly. 'One of the main problems in this whole boiling has been that where racing and horses are concerned everyone has closed up like a fucking clam. Now we can play this from two sides. One, you can all take your communal fingers out for the duration or, two, I leave right now and have a long talk with the city judge. Your choice. Me, I don't particularly care any more.'

There was a long silence. Acceptus cleared his throat, uncrossed his legs and then crossed them again. Cario scowled. Natalis glanced at both of them and turned back to me.

'Okay,' he said. 'The colt's name was Aster. I bought him from Florus last March. He died on the way to Rome. These things happen; not often, but they happen. The horse was insured so I didn't lose out. End of story.'

'The transporter was a guy named Maximus?'

'Yeah. That's right. Maximus transports all of Florus's horses.'

'You happen to know how the colt died?'

'No. I don't know the medical details, but my vet on board signed the certificate.'

'This vet. He still on your staff?'

Natalis shrugged. 'Sure. In fact, he should be on the compound now.'

'You mind if I talk to him?'

That got me a long look. Finally Natalis stood up, crossed to the door and opened it. The eyes of both Acceptus and Cario followed him. 'Socrates?'

The troll appeared. 'Yeah, boss?'

'Fetch Harmodius. He'll be down at the sick bay.' He closed the door. 'Now. This had better be relevant, Corvinus, because if it isn't then you're in deep trouble.'

'It's relevant,' I said.

Natalis grunted and sat back down behind the desk. 'Florus tell you about Aster?'

'Yeah. He said Maximus had only ever lost one of his animals in the fifteen years he'd been shipping. Aster was the one. He was a good horse, right?'

'The best. Young for racing – he was only a five-year-old at the time – but I've come to rely on Florus's judgment. He's a top-notch breeder. If he said the colt was a champion in the making that was enough for me.'

'"Aster",' I said. 'That means "Star" in Greek. There any particular reason for the name?'

'Sure. He had a white patch on his forehead.' Natalis's finger sketched the place. 'Five points, perfect. So?'

'What happened to the body?'

'It was buried at the next landfall, just south of Messana.'

'That's usual?'

Natalis shrugged. 'Corpses make horses nervous, and horses on a boat are twitchy enough already, especially thoroughbreds. We've got a good relation-ship with our insurers' – he glanced at Acceptus – 'unlike some of the other factions. The vet's certificate was good enough for them. Besides, it's standard procedure. Animals're inspected for health and fitness before they're loaded, sure, but if one dies en route we don't keep it. Even vets make mistakes, and if the real cause of death happens to have been something catching then we want the body off the ship as soon as it can be managed.'

'Uh-huh.' I paused. 'This, uh, vet, by the way. Harmodius. He reliable?'

That netted me the long stare again. 'All my staff are reliable. I told you that before. If I find they aren't for any reason then they're out.'

'Okay.' I shifted ground. 'He been with you long?'

'Not all that long. He's a good man, though, one of the best in the business.' His mouth set. 'I'm no fool, Corvinus. Are you saying that the death was a fake and Harmodius was in on the scam? Because if so—'

'No. The horse died, all right. That's the whole point.'

'Then why the hell is it relevant?'

'Maybe we'd better talk to Harmodius first.' I glanced over at Acceptus and Cario. They hadn't said a word so far, which was fine with me, but I was getting looks from them that should've made my hair curl. 'While we're waiting you can tell me about Pegasus.'

'What about him?'

'You knew he was Florus's brother, right?'

Out of the corner of my eye I saw Cario shift in his seat. Interesting.

'Sure I did.'

'You didn't think to tell me?'

'Why should I? That was private faction—'

'Business. Yeah. It would've cleared up a lot of things before they got sticky, though. Did you know the two didn't get on?'

Silence. Natalis frowned; I had him at a disadvantage, and he didn't like it. 'No,' he said at last. 'No, I didn't know that. Neither of them told me.'

'When you caught him throwing races for Eutacticus you didn't chop the guy, because – or so you thought – Florus might be upset.' I waited, but there was no response. 'Instead you and he came to an arrangement. He'd join the Whites but he'd still be working for you. Especially where nailing their new wonder-horse was concerned.'

I'd been looking at Natalis, but I had half an eye on Cario. Even so, I wasn't prepared for the reaction. The guy's nerves must've been wound tighter than a catapult winch, because he was out of his seat and two steps from Natalis's throat before Acceptus could grab him. Me, I didn't move; let the bastards settle this one between them. Cario didn't say a word, but as Acceptus forced him down into his chair he was glaring blue murder.

Natalis hadn't moved either. He was cool, I'd give the bugger that. 'Yes,' he said. 'If we're speaking truths.' He shrugged and glanced at Acceptus and Cario. 'That's the racing business. You do what you

can how you can. Besides, it didn't come to anything.'

'Maybe you were just lucky, pal,' I said.

He turned to me and frowned. 'Why?'

There was a knock on the door and Socrates came
in with a thin, weedy, buck-toothed guy in a stained
tunic. When the gate troll had knuckled his way out
again he stood shifting from foot to foot like an
apology for existence.

Cario had settled down again, although he was still
glaring at Natalis. The little episode seemed to have
cheered Acceptus up because he'd sat back in his chair
with his arms folded and a smile on his lips like he was
watching a comedy.

'You're Harmodius?' I said.

The thin guy nodded. He looked worried, but then
I suspected that might just be his natural expression.

'You want to pull up a stool?'

He dithered. 'Oh, sit down!' Natalis snapped.

We waited while he sorted out his own seating
arrangements. I had the impression that dealing with
the world was not something Harmodius did well.
Maybe he was happier with his arm up a horse's
rectum.

Natalis turned to me. 'Go ahead, Corvinus. But
remember what I told you about relevance.'

I ignored him. I might not know the exact details,
but I knew the general story. This was just for confirmation, and for Natalis's sake. When we came to
the nub, I'd need all the supporting clout I could
get. 'You were on the *Phorcys* fourteen months back

transporting horses for the faction between Catana and Ostia, right, pal?' I said.

He cleared his throat. 'Agrigentum to Ostia, actually. Three from Agrigentum, two from Gela. Five, if I remember correctly, from Syracuse—'

Jupiter, we had a right one here, I could tell that now. I held up my hand and he stopped like his mouth had been stitched. 'Fine. All I'm interested in is one particular horse, name of Aster, taken on at Catana from the breeder Quintus Florus. You like to tell us about that?'

'It died.'

I caught a snigger from Acceptus. 'Just tell the story from the beginning, friend. You took it on at Catana. Who made the delivery?'

'Florus himself, sir. He always completes the handover personally and insists on a receipt.' His eyes flicked to Natalis. 'That's the standard practice, as I understand.'

'Yeah, right. You examined the horse before it went on board?'

He drew himself up like I'd stepped on his professional corns. 'Of course. Standard practice again. The colt was perfectly well.'

'So why did it die?'

'You wish the full medical details?'

I shook my head. 'No, I'm no vet. Just the bottom line.'

'It fell ill during the night between Tauromenium and Messana. By the time I'd been notified it was dead. I diagnosed a sudden rush of black bile to the brain causing a severe imbalance and consequent haemorrhage blocking the throat and nostrils leading to asphyxiation.'

Well, that was concise enough. 'There wasn't any warning?'

'No, sir. The horses are carefully monitored twenty-four hours a day, naturally, but in this instance there was nothing to be done. Certainly no blame could be attached to the watchman. As to the cause, some authorities hold that there are things called "bad seeds" which may lie dormant for—'

I held up my hand again. 'That'll do me, friend. This happened during the night, you say?'

'Yes, sir. We'd called in at Tauromenium so the colts could be exercised. Standard practice again. Aster fell ill in the small hours of the following night. The man on duty summoned me immediately but as I say the horse was already dead when I arrived.'

I had to go careful here. 'This was below decks, right?'

'Of course. The colts are happier in a familiar environment, and the below-decks area is divided into stalls with a ramp leading from the stern.'

'You want to tell me what happened? *Exactly* what happened? From when the watchman called you?'

Harmodius closed his eyes. Now we'd got on to professional ground the guy was gaining in confidence. I noticed that Natalis had leaned forwards; maybe he'd seen where this was leading. Cario was still glowering. 'I went down into the stalls area. The horse was lying on its side, obviously dead, with large amounts of fresh blood soaking the straw around the nose and mouth—'

'Hang on, pal,' I said. 'How could you see this?'

He blinked. 'The watchman had a lamp, of course.'

'Just one?'

'It was all I needed. As I say, the animal was already past help.'

Natalis grunted. Yeah, he'd caught on now, I was sure he had.

'Fine,' I said. 'You, uh, happen to notice the head marking at all?'

He looked at me. 'Pardon?'

'The white blaze on the forehead.'

'Yes, of course.' He paused; a stickler for the truth, Harmodius, for all his faults. 'At least, so I seem to remember. The light, as you say, was not all that good, and that wasn't my concern at the time.'

'Right. Right.' I glanced round. Acceptus was looking interested too, now, and he'd uncrossed his legs. 'How about the brand?'

'There was no reason to examine the horse's rear quarters, sir. The trauma was confined to the head area.'

'Fair enough.' I hesitated. 'You say the colts were exercised at Tauromenium. Were you around when they came back on board?'

'No, sir. The captain – Quintus Maximus – took a sudden stomach-ache. I'm no human doctor, naturally, but I do possess considerable medical knowledge. He had asked me for a consultation and I was with him in the deckhouse.'

I nodded. 'Great. Thanks a lot, pal. You've been a great help.'

'I'm delighted to have been of service.' He looked at Natalis. 'If you're quite finished with me, sir, I have a case of colic to attend to.'

Natalis was glaring back like the guy had just pissed in his ear. 'Go away, Harmodius,' he said.

Harmodius swallowed, and left. There was a long silence when the door closed. Acceptus was whistling softly through his teeth and examining his finger-nails. Cario looked grey as death. Natalis just looked furious.

'I'll have that fucking idiot nailed to the poxy gate,' he growled.

I shrugged. 'He's not the smartest intellect in the world, sure. But it wasn't completely his fault. As scams go it was a beaut: the colts were switched when they were ashore at Tauromenium, Aster was taken away and hidden somewhere for later and what was brought back on board was a doctored ringer supplied by Maximus's mate's brother Histrio. Then smother the ringer with a blanket, spill a pint or so of chicken blood around its head and you're up one pricey racehorse.'

'Very ingenious,' Acceptus said. He hadn't raised his eyes. 'If that's what really happened.'

I turned to him; that bugger's patrician drawl really got up my nose. 'You like to give me odds, friend?' I said evenly.

He smiled. 'Don't misunderstand me, Corvinus. I'm impressed. But you heard the man yourself; he'd inspected the colt at Catana. He'd've known it was a different animal.'

'Below-decks in a ship in the middle of the night? With only one lamp? And I bet the bastard holding that wasn't too conscientious. Besides, Harmodius was expecting to see Aster. That's what he saw.'

'He saw the blaze as well.'

'White lead's cheap enough, pal. And it would only be for five minutes. Also, you see something as distinctive as a star-shaped forehead blaze, even subconsciously, and other details tend to get lost. Especially if what you're dealing with's just a corpse.'

Cario had been fidgeting. Now he blurted out: 'What about the br—'

He stopped suddenly, like his mouth had seized up on him; he was no fool, Cario, even if he did make mistakes. I finished the question for him. 'The brand,' I said. 'Yeah. Harmodius might have noticed that, even if in the event he didn't. Only if the horse wasn't Aster then why should the brand be a problem, pal? If Histrio had supplied it then he could've put whatever one on it he liked. There's only one reason a brand's important, and that's when it's on a living horse.' You could've cut the silence with a knife. Acceptus's head came up, and he was staring at me. 'We haven't mentioned Polydoxus yet. Maybe now's the time.'

Out of the corner of my eye I saw Natalis stir, but he kept his peace. 'So,' I went on conversationally, 'Maximus and his pals made the switch. "Aster"'s dead and buried, Natalis here has lost a colt but like he says these things happen and thanks to the insurance guys at least he isn't out of pocket. No one's really hurt, except the bankers, and who cries for them? End of story. Or that part of it, anyway. Just out of interest, Cario, and by the way. You care to tell me who Polydoxus's breeder was?' Silence. 'Come on, pal! It'll be on record anyway. You want me to go to the bother of checking?'

'A man called Velocius.'

'Is that so, now?' It'd been an outside bet, sure, but it'd have to have paid off, and it had. I turned to Natalis. 'You heard of him?'

Natalis shook his head. He was staring at Cario. If looks could kill the guy would've been a grease spot.

'That's not surprising.' Cario's tone was aggressive. 'He's a Spaniard. Small-time breeder. He has a stud near Tarraco.'

'Yeah? So his brand would be – let's see – VEL or VELO, right? And Florus's, well, that'd be—?'

'FL,' Natalis growled, his eyes still on Cario. 'Bastard!'

'An initial V and a third bar to the F,' I said. 'Simple enough to change, right?' Cario said nothing. 'And if Velocius didn't exist anyway then choosing a name to fit without the need for falsifying the existing brand would've been easy-peasie. There's still the problem of the blaze, of course, but we'll come to that later.'

'What about Maximus?' Natalis said. 'I trusted that bugger. You're saying he was behind the whole thing?'

I shook my head. 'Uh-uh. He was only the middleman. He worked the scam as a favour to a friend. An old friend, someone in the shipping line that he'd known in Spain.' I looked at Cario. 'Before your father retired and took over the Whites he had a merchant shipping business in New Carthage. Which was where Maximus was based before he moved to Catana, right?' Cario was glaring at me. He shrugged but didn't answer. 'Cammius was desperate to build up the team. My bet is that when he found out that his old shipping pal was transporting prime horse-flesh for the Greens the temptation was too much for him. He approached Maximus and they cooked the scam up between them; strictly as a one-off, low risk. Once they had the horse it was all plain sailing, or should've been: Aster's dead and forgotten, a month or so later Cammius takes delivery of a Spanish colt named Polydoxus. Faction horses – especially the star performers – are guarded closer than a Parthian's daughter, so there's no chance of anyone outside the faction itself getting close enough to check out their finer points. In Polydoxus's case, the only problem would be the white blaze, and keeping that covered with a spot of dye'd be easy.' Cario was still glaring, but he didn't open his mouth. 'Okay. The Whites race Polydoxus, and he's a winner. No problem, only then things begin to screw up.' I paused; all three of them were watching me now like hawks. 'We'll leave that for a moment and finish with Maximus. Unlike Cammius he still has his livelihood to think of. He can be sure of most of his crew, but when one of the deck-hands spills the secret about Polydoxus to our pal Sopilys he's caught. Both of them have to go or he'll never work again.'

'So he kills them,' Acceptus said. 'Or has them killed. Corvinus, you have been a busy little bee.'

I ignored him. 'Fine,' I said. 'Now we come to Pegasus.' I didn't think the tension could wind itself any tighter but now it did. I glanced at Cario: the guy was the colour of a dishrag. 'Pegasus was the fly in the ointment. From the Whites' side he was a real catch: a top-notch driver to go with their top-notch horse. What they didn't know' – and I glanced at Cario – 'was that they'd taken on the only guy in Rome who would recognise Polydoxus for what he was. I checked that out with Florus. Aster was born when Pegasus came back to the farm to talk over his father's will, and he helped at the birth. He'd know that Natalis had bought the colt for the Greens, naturally, because he was driving lead for them at the time; also that it'd died en route. I can't be sure exactly what happened at the Whites' stables, but my guess is that he noticed the dye on the horse's forehead, got suspicious and put two and two together. Then, Pegasus being Pegasus, he worked up a private scam of his own.' I left the sentence hanging; the conclusion was obvious, and I let them reach it. The two pairs of eyes turned towards Cario.

'If you're saying that either I or my father murdered Pegasus, Corvinus,' he said quietly, 'then you're wrong. The business with the horse, sure, there's no point in denying that now. But not murder. We're not murderers, my father and I.'

'Pegasus was blackmailing the Whites. He could've blown the whistle any time.'

'That's nonsense. If he had been I'd've known, and I didn't; I swear that.'

I sighed. Yeah, well, maybe he hadn't; he sounded convincing enough. And in a way it made things a lot simpler.

'Let's go and talk to your father,' I said gently.

43

We didn't have far to go – the house was just up the road past Triumphal Arch near Tiber Field – but even so we took one of the Greens' coaches. It was a silent journey, and I noticed that both Natalis and Acceptus avoided eye contact with Cario like the guy was some kind of leper. Which I suppose was fair enough under the circumstances; like I say, anything goes in the racing world where dirty tricks are concerned, but once you're caught it's a whole new ball-game.

The door-slave opened up smiling, but when he saw our faces – especially Cario's – the smile vanished. 'The master's in the garden,' he said. 'But he already has visitors.'

I looked at him sharply. 'Who would that be, now?'

'They didn't give names, sir. I'll have some more chairs brought out.'

Cario led the way through. It was a small garden, but everything was neat and well tended. Yeah, I'd've expected that from Cammius: whatever he was involved in he'd see that it was run in a proper, businesslike fashion. He was sitting on a bench under the spreading quince in the centre, talking to two men with a third standing beside them, and as we came through the portico he looked up. I wouldn't've known him. When I'd seen the guy last he hadn't been at his best, sure, but now he looked less than two steps from an urn.

The two men turned, and I recognised Eutacticus and Typhon. The guy standing was my old pal Laughing George, and he was obviously on duty. My stomach went cold.

'Ah, Corvinus.' Eutacticus smiled. 'I did call round at your house earlier but they told me you were out. Never mind, we seem to have an errand in common after all.' He nodded to the others. 'Gentlemen.'

I glanced at Typhon. The little runt's face was grey and his mouth and hands were twitching like he had a fever. Not a happy man. I'd guess that his presence here wasn't of his own choosing and if it hadn't been for Laughing George a foot from his elbow he'd be several miles off and still running.

'How are you, Eutacticus?' Natalis was stiffly polite. Acceptus was staring at Typhon. If the guy could've looked any sicker he'd've been for the urn himself.

'Oh, quite bonny. Quite bonny.' Eutacticus's smile widened. He stood up. 'I see you have business with Lucius Cammius here. We've just this moment arrived ourselves, but my own business with him can wait. I'll withdraw inside and allow you some privacy, shall I? No, Typhon, not you' – the runt had got up as well – 'I promised Valerius Corvinus an opportunity of talking with you at the end, and I suspect this is as good a time as any. I don't, though, advise attempting to leave.' He turned to

Laughing George. 'Watch him. From a distance, but watch him.'

He went back in the direction of the house, passing a couple of slaves carrying folding stools. Laughing George ignored me. There was a stone bench a dozen yards off between two espaliered peach trees. He crossed to it and sat down.

Cammius hadn't moved. I looked at his eyes, and then wished I hadn't. What stared back at me was a trapped animal. Cario was looking at him too. I saw his mouth open, then close as he darted a glance between his father and Eutacticus's retreating back.

The slaves set the stools down and waited, but they weren't going to get anything from either Cammius or Cario so I said quietly, 'That's all, lads. Off you go.' They gawped at me and left.

We sat, all except Typhon. The guy was still shaking, and his eyes were as wild as Cammius's. The gods knew what was going on inside his head, but for my part they were welcome to the knowledge.

There wasn't any point in going round the houses, not at this stage. 'You killed Pegasus, didn't you?' I said softly to Cammius.

'Yes.'

The word came out as a whisper, and it was almost lost behind Cario's shout of: '*No!*' How the other two reacted I don't know, because I wasn't watching them, but I had the impression that Natalis had grabbed Cario's arm and forced him down.

I hesitated. I had the admission, but I owed the guy more than that. 'You want to explain?' I said.

'He'd found out about Polydoxus. You know about Polydoxus?' I nodded. 'He was threatening to tell the Greens.'

'So you followed him to Renatius's wineshop where he was meeting your son, waited your chance and stabbed him.'

Cammius smiled: on that face, with these eyes, the effect was horrible. I felt my scalp crawl. 'There was nothing else to be done,' he said. 'I'd willingly have paid, or paid more, rather, but that kind of man is never satisfied. Worse, as part of the price he wanted control of my faction. *My* faction. However great his loss as a driver, that I couldn't have. He had to die. Of course he did. You see that, Corvinus, don't you?'

I shivered; we could've been discussing the price of fish. 'Yeah. Yeah, I see that.'

'So as you say I followed him to the wineshop. Not, of course, that I knew where he was going, or why, but he was leaving the stables and killing him there would have been too much of a risk. I was lucky. There was an empty tenement just opposite that was being renovated.' He looked down at his tunic: he wasn't wearing a mantle. 'I got wet plaster all over my clothes. Ruined, quite ruined. You remember remarking on that, Cario, when I got back.'

I glanced at Cario and saw for the first time the horror of realisation dawn. I felt sorry for the guy, bitterly sorry. No, he hadn't known about the blackmailing, or the murder. He hadn't known about the significance of the plaster, either, because I hadn't mentioned it to him. If I had, the realisation would've come sooner.

'The Eighth District Watch,' I said. 'How did you square them?'

'I didn't.' The smile disappeared and he frowned. 'You mean the business of the purse.' I nodded. 'Taking it to ascribe the motive for the killing to simple theft must have been the Watch commander's own idea.' His eyes flicked towards Natalis. 'I understand he's a keen Greens supporter. Pegasus wasn't too popular in that quarter either. If I'd thought to remove the purse I would have done so, Corvinus, but it didn't occur to me. Unlucky, of course, since it got you involved, but that's fate. I thought I'd got away with it until you forced Valgius into a proper enquiry and he came round to the stables asking questions.'

Uh-huh; so that was what had triggered the rest of it. I'd been wondering about that myself. Valgius must've taken my threat to go to the city judge's office seriously after all; seriously enough to get up off his backside and go through the motions, anyway. And the effect on the Whites' boss of the threat of an official investigation on top of my private one must've been like a basin of ice-water in the face. 'So you had to dispose of the last piece of evidence,' I said. 'You had to poison Polydoxus.'

I'd been concentrating on Cammius, naturally, but the indrawn breath behind me pulled me round. Typhon was staring at the old guy like he'd sprouted horns. Two seconds later he'd shouldered past me and had his hands locked round Cammius's throat.

I moved fast, but Cario was faster. I'd hardly got a grip on the runt's tunic before he'd pulled him away and tossed him down like a doll, his fist bunched and raised to smash the guy's face in.

'*Cario! Wait!*' I snapped.

I didn't think he'd obey, let alone that he'd heard me, but his arm stopped and the fist unclenched. He straightened slowly, then stood over Typhon glaring down at him.

Typhon struggled to his knees, eyes fixed on Cammius, and shot out a finger.

'You bastard!' he screamed. 'You bastard! You fucking set me up!'

I glanced over at Laughing George, but he hadn't moved. *Watch him*, Eutacticus had said. Well, Laughing George was watching. It must be nice to be so uncomplicated. I looked back at Typhon. He was on his feet again; Acceptus too, his face the colour of parchment. They were both staring at Cammius slumped against the arm of his bench.

The last piece of the puzzle slipped into place. Yeah; that had to be how it had happened. It'd been a possibility, but I hadn't been sure until now.

'Tell them,' I said to Typhon.

The dull, desperate look was gone. The little guy was pure, hundred per cent undiluted venom. His eyes never left Cammius's face. 'I'm going to be fucking killed,' he said to him softly. 'And you knew all the time. All the fucking time.'

'*Tell them!*'

Typhon took a deep breath. 'I'd agreed.' He jerked his thumb at Acceptus. 'With him there. For fifty gold pieces, paid in advance.'

Acceptus had sat down again. His face was set, and he was still staring at Cammius, but he didn't speak.

'Tell it from the beginning, Typhon,' I said.

'Three days before the race *he*' – another stab of the finger at Cammius – 'sends me round to the Blues stable with a message. Private, to Acceptus himself.'

'That was unusual?'

Typhon frowned. 'Sure it was. I was the gopher and I delivered plenty of messages to the Blues' place, but not to the boss. Not ever. Standard rules, you give them to the gate guard and he passes them on in. Cammius tells me he wants this one handed over personal, face to face in private.'

I looked at Acceptus. He'd recovered his poise enough to control his expression, but he was still pale. 'Ordinary race arrangements,' he said bitterly. 'I wondered about that at the time, but it wasn't important.'

'So you took the opportunity to try a little bribery?' I said.

He shrugged. 'Who wouldn't, given the opportunity? The man could only have refused. Besides, I didn't want to kill the horse, only incapacitate it for the next day's race.'

Yeah; that I'd believe the day I saw a squadron of pigs flying above the Palatine. It might be what he'd told Typhon, and what he was saying now to get himself off the hook, but I'd bet different. Fifty gold pieces was fifty gold pieces, and a hell of a lot of gravy. Also, it explained the guy's initial reaction: the news that someone else had been responsible for

Polydoxus's death had left him gobsmacked. I turned to Cammius. 'Typhon's right, isn't he? You set him up. You set both of them up.'

The old guy was massaging his windpipe; I could see the livid red welts made by Typhon's thumbs clearly on either side of the Adam's-apple. Cario had moved to stand beside him. 'Yes,' he whispered.

'What would've happened if neither had taken the bait?'

Cammius swallowed painfully and cleared his throat. 'It was a risk,' he said. 'Not a big risk. Typhon is a greedy man, and Acceptus a jealous one. I was certain that one of them would make the offer, and if he did the other would accept. But if it didn't happen then I'd've arranged things myself and made sure Typhon was blamed anyway.' He coughed and swallowed again.

Typhon lunged, but this time I was ready and got a grip on him. Cammius watched dispassionately without even an attempt at defence.

'I'm not proud of myself,' he said quietly when Typhon had calmed down, and whether he was speaking to me or to him I didn't know. 'Not proud at all. Don't think that. It was an evil thing to do. Telling you this is a relief, not a penance.'

I gave him a sharp look; yeah, I'd believe him. Unrepentant murderers didn't have that grey expression of self-loathing. For the first time I began to feel a little sorry for Cammius. Still, I had a job to do.

'Okay,' I said. 'Carry on, Typhon.'

The guy was still glaring at Cammius. 'I had a

sleeping powder for the stable guards and a bolus for the horse. I slipped the powder into the lads' wine, waited half an hour and went back with the bolus.' He paused. 'After I'd given it to the horse I had it away over the wall before someone turned up and grabbed me.'

Leaving Gaius Acceptus believing he'd done the dirty successfully. As of course he had, although the plan hadn't been his at all. Clever. 'Where did you go?' I asked Typhon. 'Just as a matter of interest?'

'I was with a friend in Ostia. Not a racing friend. Her cousin captains a ship on the Alexandria route and he'd've given me passage no questions asked. Only thing was, the guy wouldn't be back for a month so I was stuck. I didn't know until yesterday when Eutacticus's men turned up that the horse was dead.' He shot Acceptus a look of pure venom.

Acceptus stared back frozen-faced. 'The dose must have been too strong,' he said. 'Or the horse had a weakness. In any case it was an accident.'

I noticed that no one, not even Cammius, was looking at him or paying him any attention at all. The guy was nailed, and they knew it. Acceptus knew it, too: his face might be devoid of expression, but his eyes were panic-stricken. I remembered what Eutacticus had said about not having favourites where business was concerned. The guy could wriggle and bluster all he liked, now and later, but in my considered opinion Gaius Sextilius Acceptus was up shit creek without a paddle.

Typhon's hand was clutching at my mantle. 'Corvinus, you know the truth now, right?' he said. 'These bastards set me up, both of them. Doping, sure, I'll admit to that, but I didn't know the horse would die. You heard Acceptus here; the plan was just to put it out of the Megalenses. As far as I knew, at least. Tell Eutacticus that, will you? Soon as we leave that fucker's going to kill me. Straight up, no kidding.'

Yeah, he just might, at that. Not that I could muster a great deal of sympathy, because if Typhon had thought for one second that Acceptus would pay him fifty gold pieces up-front just for nobbling a horse for a single race then he wasn't the streetwise guy I took him for. I didn't believe him any more than I believed Acceptus.

'Oh, I think Eutacticus knows the truth already, pal,' I said. 'He wouldn't be here if he didn't.' How he'd gone about it I didn't know – certainly not by the route I'd taken – but that I'd bet my last copper on. And, in the light of our last conversation, Eutacticus's knowledge was relevant to what happened next. Our arrival had certainly interrupted something, and it didn't take much imagination to guess what. Typhon wasn't the only guy currently with one foot in the urn.

Apropos of which, it was time to consider our next move, practically speaking. I glanced over towards Laughing George. The guy was sitting with his arms folded, glowering. I reckoned the five of us – including Typhon and Acceptus, who'd both have a vested interest, but counting out Cammius – could take him, and daily workouts or not Eutacticus himself wouldn't be a problem. We could worry about the repercussions when the time came, but at least we'd've got the old man to the comparative safety of the city judges' offices . . .

Maybe Cammius had caught the edge of my thought, or, more likely, he'd made the obvious link from what I'd just said. Or, there again, maybe he'd just said all he wanted to say himself and made his mind up. Whichever it was, he got to his feet suddenly.

'Have we finished?' he said. 'If so if you'll excuse me I have a little business to take care of in my study.'

My guts went cold. Oh, shit. One thing about having a purple stripe to your mantle and six hundred years of tight-arsed, poker-backed aristocratic forebears is that you recognise a good old Roman euphemism when you hear one. Throwaway lines like *I have a little business to take care of in my study* tend to have a significance over and above their surface meaning.

Cario had got it too. He stiffened, but didn't move.

'Uh . . . there's no need for that, sir,' I said quietly. 'Pegasus was blackmailing you after all. Extenuating circumstances. And you weren't the one who actually poisoned the horse. The city judge'll—'

He turned on me. I wouldn't've believed that the human skeleton that Cammius had become would have that much energy left to spend, but his eyes blazed. 'You think I feel guilty about Pegasus?' he said. '*Pegasus?* And, Corvinus, I did poison Polydoxus. You accused me of that originally, and you were right: Acceptus and Typhon here were just my agents. I had to do it, yes, but that fact remains. I killed him, and I killed a faction. My faction. I can do the judging myself. Now let me go to my study, please.'

I remembered my conversation with Florus. There were a lot of similarities between the two men. Yeah; maybe the murder of Polydoxus and the death of the faction were the real crimes after all. At least in the mind of a racing man. I swallowed; it was his decision, and his right. And the end result might be the same in any case. 'Okay,' I said. 'Go ahead, friend. We'll give you half an hour.'

He smiled. 'That should be ample. My thanks to you. Natalis, my apologies.' He turned to Cario. 'Cario—'

He didn't finish the sentence, just stopped after the name. As he walked away towards the house itself Laughing George uncrossed his arms and half rose. I waved him down, and for a wonder he nodded.

I expected Eutacticus to come out, but he didn't; we found later that, in the event, he'd gone. Maybe Cammius had had a word with him on his way upstairs. For half an hour we sat. We didn't talk, we just sat. Then we went up to the study.

Cammius was lying on the reading couch. It wasn't a pretty death: he must've taken the stuff that he would've used on Polydoxus if Acceptus hadn't done the job for him, and it obviously worked as well on people as it would on horses. He'd laid a cloak on the back of a chair, probably on purpose: the guy was neat and businesslike to the end. I draped it over the body, covering the face, and left him to his son and his slaves. I didn't speak to Natalis, or to Acceptus. Typhon was gone, too, and Laughing George was just a memory. They may have left separately or together, I didn't know, and I didn't want to know, either.

I went home.

44

I called in at Renatius's on the way to the Caelian to tell the guy the news. Also to get quietly smashed, because although Cammius's death hadn't been any of my doing it had still left me depressed as hell. Charax and his pals, I noticed, had finished renovating the tenement opposite. Or at least the scaffolding and other signs of building work had gone. The place still looked pretty scruffy, though, and I wondered if the old pennypincher who owned it had finally realised what a pack of skivers he'd landed himself with and cancelled out on the contract.

Whatever the reason, Charax and Co. were in residence at their usual table. The god of building sites and odd-job plasterers knew where they got the money from, but it must've been in some sort of regular supply because even the placid Renatius wouldn't've put up with his wineshop being used as a headquarters by the trade's biggest cowboys rent-free, and whatever shining points of character were writ large on Charax's roll of fate pleasantness of personality wasn't exactly prominent.

They gave me the big wave. 'Afternoon, consul,'

Charax said. 'Haven't seen you around for a while. How's it going?'

'Okay.' I moved over to the counter where Renatius himself was tucking into a plate of sausage and a cup of wine. 'Jug of Spoletian, Renatius. A full one.'

He raised his eyebrows, got up and reached for the jug shelf without a word. I pulled up a stool and sat down. 'You finished with the tenement, Charax?'

'In a manner of speaking,' Charax said. One of the acolytes sniggered. 'The job sort of came to a natural halt.'

'Yeah? Old what's-his-name – Atellius, wasn't it? – given you the boot?'

'Nah. He's dead. Had a bit of an accident.'

Renatius was decanting the wine. 'Fell through the floorboards on the second floor while he was inspecting the building and broke his neck,' he said neutrally.

'Well, we hadn't started up there, had we?' Charax lifted his wine cup and sipped. 'The floor was riddled with dry rot. Silly bugger went up without telling us. If he'd said where he was going we'd've warned him.'

'You weren't around to ask,' Renatius grunted. 'You were all in here.'

'Yeah, true, but we couldn't be on the job all the time, could we? 'S not reasonable to expect that.'

I sighed and poured myself a cup.

'So the old guy's heir dispensed with their services.' Renatius went back to his sausage. 'They were lucky not to be prosecuted.'

'Oh, I reckon the heir thought we'd done him a

favour.' Charax beamed. 'Atellius might've been in his seventies but he was a wiry old stick. Could've gone on for years.'

'Didn't get the chance, did he?' Renatius turned to me. 'So. How's the Pegasus business doing?'

'It's over.' I drank. 'The murderer was the Whites' boss Cammius. He killed himself a couple of hours ago.'

That got a respectful silence, even from Charax: faction leaders are big figures in Rome, even the two minor ones. Consuls, city judges and the like don't even come close.

'You want to tell us the details?' Renatius said eventually.

'No,' I said. 'I think maybe I'll keep these private.' The guy had a right to know who'd knifed his customer, but the ins and outs of the Polydoxus scam were another matter. That was between Natalis and Cario; how they would settle it I didn't know and I didn't much care, but it wasn't for wineshop consumption. 'You ever notice something interesting, Renatius? Villains – real villains – never seem to get really hurt. It's the half villains that end up nailed, or nailing themselves.' I took a long swallow of wine. 'Makes you wonder, doesn't it?'

'"Justice with her even steps has passed from out the world",' Charax said.

I turned, frowning. 'What?'

'It's poetry, consul. Means the lady with the scales isn't here any more. She's long gone.' He raised his cup to his lips. 'Well-known mythological fact, is that.'

'Yeah. Right.' Jupiter! I turned back to Renatius. 'He wasn't a bad man, Cammius, not compared with some of the other bastards in the case, like your Watch pals Valgius and his sidekick Delicatus' – let alone Pegasus himself, only I couldn't say that – 'yet he's the one who ends up chopped.'

Renatius shrugged. 'You said it yourself, Corvinus. He was a murderer. He deserved all he got.'

I grunted and topped up my cup. Sure, that was a fair way of looking at it, especially if you didn't know the background, but I had the nagging suspicion that Cammius would've finished by killing himself anyway, even if I hadn't interfered. That was the point: he'd judged himself, and no mistake, without my help, and when I'd covered the guy's face with his cloak I'd felt just a little bit guilty on my own account. Maybe our homespun plasterer-poet was right: there wasn't any justice any more, she was long gone. Look at Eutacticus; that bastard must've been responsible for dozens of deaths. And Acceptus. He'd pay in some way, I was sure, but I was willing to bet the price would be no more than he could afford.

The trouble with rooting around in dirty linen is that whether you like it or not your hands pick up the smell.

'*Panta rhei*, consul.' That was Charax again. 'Everything flows. The old giveth place to the new. Bit like plaster, really.'

Oh, shit. I had to grin, though. I turned round again, holding my wine cup. 'Is that so, now, pal?' I said.

'Sure. Take Atellius. Arriving on site while we were

having lunch, going upstairs and falling through the
sodding floor was what you might call a fortuitous
concatenation of circumstances. For the heir, anyway.
The old bugger might've been close enough to skin
a flint but he was a cheery soul and I'd nothing
against him personal. It was a complete accident,
right? Nothing anyone could do about it.' He beamed.
'We may not have justice any longer, consul, but we've
still got luck. Me, I'm one for the vagaries of fate,
myself. The cosmic googlies. Like that millionaire up
your way who's hitching up with his housekeeper, for
instance.'

'Yeah?' I set down the wine cup. 'Who's that,
now?'

'Guy called Petillius. Owns half the mantle-dyeing
businesses in Rome.'

I stared at him. '*What?*'

'Truth. You hadn't heard? The story was all round
the city this morning.'

My guts went cold. Holy Jupiter! This was no
time for soul-searching and maudlin wine-binges. If
Charax was right – and the guy had an ear for gossip
that would've put Midas's donkey version to shame –
then all hell would currently be breaking out on the
Caelian.

I paid for the undrunk wine and made a bolt for
the door.

It was true, all right: I knew that as soon as I
saw Bathyllus's face. I'd been wrong about the hell,
though, because he had on his noble self-sacrificing

look. An expression somewhere between that of a boiled trout and of a high priest with piles.

'Uh . . . Tyndaris is marrying Titus Petillius, right?' I said as I peeled off my mantle.

'Yes, sir. She told me this morning. I understand they had agreed to keep it quiet until she had been officially freed and the engagement could be announced legally.' He folded the mantle carefully. 'Which was yesterday.'

'You, uh, were round there yesterday evening, weren't you?'

'Yes, sir.'

'And she didn't mention it?'

'No, sir.'

I took the cup of wine from the tray he'd set on the hall table. 'This would be . . . ah . . . a sudden decision, would it? Or reasonably sudden, anyway?'

He put his lips together. You could've used the line to cut marble. 'On the gentleman's side, sir, yes. I have the impression that his own proposal – made while we were in Sicily – came as rather a surprise to himself.'

I winced. 'I'm, uh, sorry about this, little guy.'

'Sympathy isn't necessary, sir.' He gave a distinctly Bathyllus-type sniff that had nothing to do with tear-duct activity. 'I have been tricked and deluded throughout. My only role by that woman's design, right from the first, was to rouse jealousy in her intended suitor and precipitate an avowal of an equal devotion on his part. I am well rid of her.'

I paused, the cup halfway to my lips. *Jealousy?* Jupiter, the mind boggled! Certainly no dramatist worth his salt would've touched that kind of love-triangle with a bargepole. Still, Petillius was marrying the lady, you couldn't get round that. Unlikely as it sounded, Bathyllus was probably right. 'Even so, you have my condolences,' I said. 'It's a pity things haven't worked out.'

'Yes, sir. Thank you, sir.'

I picked up the jug and went through to the living-room. Perilla was on the couch. I kissed her.

'You've heard, then,' she said.

'Yeah. Seemingly the news is all over town.' I settled on my own couch. 'The guy seems quite philosophical about it.'

'I think it's simply dreadful. The woman used him.'

I shrugged. 'He'll get over it. Me, I think he had a lucky escape. She would've eaten him alive. You can't trust those culture-vultures as far as you can throw them.'

'You don't think so?' She was grinning.

'Present company excepted. Mind you, for that lady you'd've needed a legion-strength ballista.'

'How did your business at the stables go?'

'Okay.' I kept my voice neutral. 'We went on to Cammius's place afterwards. He's dead. Suicide.'

The grin vanished. 'Oh, Marcus, no!'

'There wasn't anything I could do. He wanted to go.' I took a swallow of wine. 'Maybe it's for the best. That's what my pal Charax would say, anyway.'

'Charax?'

'A pain-in-the-backside plasterer. Thank your stars you don't know him, lady.' Bathyllus oozed in. Taking things philosophically or not, the poor bugger still looked like Socrates after he'd downed the hemlock. 'Oh, hi, sunshine.'

'A message from the kitchen, sir. Dinner will be late. Meton has had a major crisis with the sauce.'

Well, to do a Charax, as someone said somewhere: '*You can pitch Nature out with a fork, but the lady always comes back.*' It was nice to think life still had some certainties, and domestic crises came high on the list. The googlies just provided the ups and downs that made things interesting. I sank another mouthful of Setinian and refilled the cup.

'That's okay, little guy,' I said. 'We're happy here with the wine.'

Author's Note

A fair modern-day parallel for the position of chariot-racing in AD 34 Rome would be a combination of horse racing and football: the first, obviously, for the general background of racing stables, betting and doping scams etc., all of which were present at the time, and the second for the sport's popularity: the Latin tag *panem et circenses* – 'bread and Games' – as a summing-up of the primary interests of the Roman lower classes being well merited (the 'bread' part of it refers to the government-issued corn dole to low-income earners). Not that interest in the Games was confined to that group only, of course: as I've indicated in the book, many of the upper classes, including the imperials themselves, were keen if not fanatical racegoers, the most notable being the later emperor Gaius (Caligula) who was an ardent Green. Besides supplying us with the most widely known racing-related story about Gaius, that he planned to make the horse Incitatus ('Speedy') consul, his biographer Suetonius also reports that he regularly had the neighbourhood of the stables picketed overnight by troops so that Incitatus could sleep undisturbed by the noise of passing carts, that he gave the driver

Eutychus ('Lucky') presents worth twenty thousand gold pieces, and that his most famous (or infamous) vitriolic quote ('If only the Roman mob had just one neck!') derived from an occasion in the Circus when the crowd cheered for the wrong team. The prospective consul, incidentally, was provided with a marble stable, an ivory manger, purple blankets, furniture and a full set of household slaves, all at Gaius's expense.

As to the factions themselves, first-century Rome was only the beginning of their influence. By the sixth century in Byzantium – which had become after the split into eastern and western empires and the decline of the west Rome's de facto successor – the Blue and Green factions had developed into political parties of immense consequence within the state; the most notable instance of their power being the so-called 'Nika Revolt' in 532 (*Nika!* means 'Win!' in Greek, and was the battle-cry of the rioters).

A brief word on names in racing. Chariot-drivers, like the golden-age Hollywood film stars, chose for themselves – or were given by their faction masters – 'performing names' which would attract the interest (and so the bets) of the punters, and I have used this as a central detail of the plot. Similarly, the names of the horses (cf Incitatus above) were carefully chosen to appeal: Polydoxus simply means 'Famous'. Which last raises another point, because the word is Greek, not Latin, and there was an actual horse of that name, although not at the time I have set the story. The fact that both drivers and horses often had Greek, rather than Latin, names at Rome may seem odd at first sight considering that chariot-racing was a mass-appeal sport. There are three (at least!) explanatory reasons: first, that the Circus (as opposed to the gladiatorial games) was as much a Greek tradition as a Roman one; second, that many of the horses and drivers came from the 'Greek' parts of Italy such as Campania and Sicily; and third, going back to golden-age Hollywood, that a Greek name had a certain *cachet* for the Roman crowd; compare the box-office pull of 'Lamour' or 'Valentino' as opposed to 'Kaumeyer' and 'd'Antonguolla'.

I have invented Crocinium on the slopes of Etna, or rather I've adopted a real village/small town which may not for all I know have existed in Roman times but occupies the same position, Zafferana: my name is simply the Latin form of the Italian, and it means 'Crocus-' or 'Saffron-place'. Similarly, my 'Ox Valley' is the Val del Bove. I haven't been there – I hope it doesn't show in the writing, and readers who have will, I hope, be indulgent towards any topographical gaffes – but I did find two marvellous period books written by travellers in Sicily in the very early years of last century, which I recommend (if they can track them down) to anyone interested. Both books are simply entitled *Sicily*; one is by a Hamilton Jackson and the other by the splendidly named pair Augustus J.C. Hare and St Clair Baddeley, and they provide a fascinating account of the difficulties and dangers involved in an ascent of Etna in days when tourists had to fend for themselves and take the rough with the rough. The mountain, by the way, exerted just as much of a touristic pull on ancient Romans as it does today (remember that, for pre-AD 79 Romans, Vesuvius was not an active volcano); and although the real fillip to the Etna tourist industry came later than my period when the scholarly Emperor Hadrian made the ascent – and had built, probably, the still-extant Torre del Filosofo (named for the philosopher Empedocles, who threw himself into the crater) as a memorial to his visit – I don't think I'm stretching things too much by giving it an established status. Perilla, certainly, wouldn't've passed up the chance of a closer look.

My thanks, as ever, to my wife Rona; to Carnoustie library; to Roy Pinkerton of the Department of Classics at Edinburgh University; to his research colleague Sinclair Bell for his information on the Circus side of things; to Alan and Angela Dunlop; to Sam Duff of the Provost Veterinary Group in Ceres, Fife (no connection with the Roman corn-goddess; I've checked); to Mark Jarvis of the Horse Doping Forensic Lab in Fordham, Cambridgeshire; and particularly to Jenny Paterson of just-round-the-corner who put me on to cassia senna. Any mistakes – especially in connection with horses – are mine. I hope they don't spoil the story.